A SHATTERED
CALM

BRUCE F.B. HALL

 FriesenPress

One Printers Way
Altona, MB R0G 0B0
Canada

www.friesenpress.com

ISBN
978-1-03-913483-6 (Hardcover)
978-1-03-913482-9 (Paperback)
978-1-03-913484-3 (eBook)

1. FICTION, THRILLERS, CRIME

Distributed to the trade by The Ingram Book Company

A SHATTERED

CALM

PART ONE

CHAPTER ONE

NATE VICKERS PULLED INTO THE parking lot and exited his rental car. His eyes focused on a neon sign on the side of a nearby building, flashing erratically. Its neglect added to a sense of dread that had been festering all day, as he awaited the rendezvous that would change the course of his life.

He spotted Jess Reed leaning against the driver door of her late-model Ford Mustang and approached her as she searched the area for unwanted company. She wore black jeans and a matching black sweater, a stark contrast to her usual flamboyant and colourful attire. He wore black jeans as well, and a light black coat over a black t-shirt, as she had requested. The irony of how good they looked together, should someone see them, was not totally lost on him.

Nate smiled nervously at Jess. The wind had picked up, and it was noticeably cooler than earlier in the day. He thought that was a good sign, as they wouldn't stand out wearing the clothes they had on. Nate was also glad it was Sunday. The warehouse district was quiet, and few, if any, people would notice them.

"Hi," he said to her.

She looked tense, and her dark brown eyes darted this way and that, before briefly locking on his, acknowledging his presence. Her curly blonde hair blew in the wind.

Sensing her agitation, he said, "Jess, are you sure you want to do this?" It was the third time he had asked the question.

"Would you give it a rest," she rasped. "I told you, I promised Digger I'd make a change to my life, and I will, but not before I take what is in that warehouse."

Digger was Jess' brother. Nate never knew if he had a given name as she simply called him Digger. So, Digger it was. He was a quiet and distant guy who was hard to get to know. He didn't like Nate, that was obvious, but Nate felt sure it had to do with the reduced attention he received from his sister. But to his credit, he was devoted and only wanted the best for her. He did not approve of her lifestyle and made repeated requests for her to make a permanent change. Nate had stayed silent during those exchanges but was surprised when she agreed to do just that. So, here they were. Now he wondered if she had discussed her plan with her brother. He felt sure, he wouldn't approve.

"I get it. It's just that I look at you, see how tense you are, and I ask myself — why take this risk? Hell, you don't even know how much is in there."

"I know that it will be sizeable. They always collect the money on a Friday, and I look after moving it to our connections the following week." Jess studied his angular boyish face with an uncomfortable intensity, finally settling in on his dark blue eyes. "Look, Nate, I told you, they won't have a clue who hit them. They have a lot of enemies. I'm doing this with or without you. It will be a game changer for both of us, but if you are not up to it, then now is the time to take off."

Nate looked at her, pain showing on his face. "Why are you always so harsh?"

He had met her and her brother a month earlier. He had just finished a shift at the annual ski show, for his employer. He had ordered a drink from a bartender in the lounge of Calgary's most iconic downtown hotel when introductions were made. Initially, he wasn't impressed, but after her brother had left them, he fell hard for her. Her "bad girl" persona thrilled him, as she was unlike any woman he had ever known. She proved to be all in when they were intimate and at other times distant and self-absorbed. She could be kind and considerate when she needed something, or brutally frank, crude, and crass, as she was being now. He was never sure how she would act. In short, she was interesting.

"I didn't say I wasn't in. It's a big risk and I want to make sure you get that. Besides, I don't think you can do this by yourself, and you know it."

"I'd figure it out." Jess drew her hand through her hair, checking out the early evening sky.

Nate ignored the taunt. "Maybe, but then your risk skyrockets. Look, let's just get on with it."

"We need to wait for the sun to set. Should be another half hour," she said, as she pivoted and reached into her car. "In the meantime, here is your balaclava. Did you bring the tools and the knapsacks?"

"Yes, they're in the back of the rental." Nate moved to get the bag out of the car. "How far away is the building?" he asked, when he returned.

"It's just around the corner." Jess said, flicking her head in its direction. Nate looked where she indicated and saw an old warehouse made of brick. He questioned why he hadn't scouted it out beforehand, despite her insisting he didn't need to.

"The red brick one?" he asked.

"Yeah," She took the bag from him and looked inside. "Hope I have anticipated everything," she mumbled. "You paid cash for all this? Right?" she asked.

The uneasiness in Nate's stomach grew. He nodded. "Yes, and I bought everything from different stores, as instructed. Thanks for the money." Nate tried for humour but failed. "Listen, since we have a few minutes, let's go over the plan again."

Jess looked at him, sneered and sighed. "Again, really?" Nate allowed silence to be his answer. "Whatever. At least it will pass the time."

Thirty minutes later, reacquainted with every detail, they locked their cars and headed for the warehouse, confident they had everything they would need within their knapsacks.

***

Twilight had set in. Streetlamps cast pockets of light in the gloom, and thunderheads rolled above without dropping their load of rain or hail on them. Arcs of lightning flashed in the sky north of them. *Good,* Nate thought to himself. He didn't want to get rained on while they were breaking in.

They turned the corner, moving south from the parking lot of the warehouse, each of them pulling on their balaclavas and matching black latex gloves. Designed for cleaning, they would work equally well preventing any fingerprints being left behind. Nate glanced at Jess and would have smiled at how they looked if he wasn't so nervous. Dressed all in black, with their balaclavas over their faces and black knapsacks on their backs, Nate thought back to his childhood, remembering the youthful games he had played with his uncle. But this was no childish antic.

They picked up the pace, moving swiftly across the parking lot, disappearing around the corner of the building, heading for the compound fence. Nate felt his anxiety grow, as they marched silently to it. His mouth felt as dry as a desert, and he had an overwhelming urge to ask Jess if she had brought water. He pushed the thought from his mind.

He pulled his knapsack off his back and dropped it at the base of the fence. Unzipping it, he pulled out a large wire-cutter and began cutting through the chain links of the fence that abutted the corner of the building. In a few moments, he had clipped enough of the wires to allow Jess to pull the fence material back, giving them access to the poorly lit yard.

They ran to the rear door of the building. Nate dropped his knapsack and pulled out a can of black paint and handed it to Jess. Bending down, he cupped his hands. Jess stepped into them, and he hoisted her up so she could spray-paint the lens of a security camera. Now they were committed. There would be a record of their entry into the yard, but no one would know which way they had gone from there. Jess had determined they'd have no more than twenty minutes to get what they had come for. Her task completed, she jumped down, grabbed the bag, and moved it closer to Nate. He extracted what he needed from it to work the door lock. While he was busy, she reached into his knapsack, grabbing a pair of small wire cutters and a cordless drill and placed them on the ground beside him. She waited beside the door, readying herself to cut the security system line once they entered the building. Her employers had not gone to a wireless system. After this day, that would change. There was a chance they might still trigger the alarm, but at least there would be no noise.

Nate battled with the door lock, a hammer and punch in his hand. He aimed a centre punch at a point directly above the keyhole and hit it with the hammer. A small depression on the lock was the result, allowing a guidance point for the drill that he picked up from the ground. He could feel resistance as the bit punched through each pin in the lock. He pulled the drill out and repeated the process with a larger drill bit until he felt the pin snap. The sound of the drill was unnerving to him in the quiet of the night. He tossed the drill back into his knapsack and pulled out a small flathead screwdriver, which he then inserted into the lock. Turning it to the right, he felt the knob turn and he was ready to open the door. He was pleased — it had taken fewer than four minutes to disable the lock. He tossed the last of his tools into his knapsack, zipping it closed, then slung it onto his back. *Amazing what you can learn on the web,* he thought, grateful that it had worked.

"Ready?" he asked, knowing he would get no answer, and opened the door. Jess stepped inside and quickly snipped the line to the alarm. Other than the usual beeping, there had been no other sound. The lack of an internal alarm meant there was no back up battery for the system. Good.

Jess ran to several large storage barrels, located in one corner of the warehouse. She reached for the lid of the first barrel and yanked it free, then a second one, and a third. Soon there were six barrels with the lids removed. Meanwhile, Nate was knocking over various other stacked containers, spilling out the contents of each all over the floor, as Jess had instructed, in the hopes it would make what they were doing look like a random theft. Jess then pulled old clothes from the top of each of the barrels she opened and threw them on the floor. They were used to pack the containers full, while camouflaging their true intent. Swinging the large knapsack from her back, she dropped it to the floor, pulling out three large light-weight duffel bags from inside. She threw two over to Nate, who had run back to her to help load the bags. She kept one of the bags, plus her now-empty knapsack. Pulling her balaclava to the top of her forehead, she glanced at her watch and said to Nate, "Eight minutes, Nate...go fast."

Within the allotted time, they stuffed their bags to overflowing with wads of cash that had been stored in the barrels. As each was emptied, Jess kicked it sideways and out of the way. "Let's go," she yelled.

Nate hoisted on his pack and then slung a heavy bag over each shoulder. The weight of the money and the knapsack full of tools strained his muscles to the limit, despite the twice weekly weight training he did. He watched as Jess pulled her backpack on and stooped to pick up her duffel bag. She saw him straining with it, reached down and grabbed it herself. He followed her to the door, conscious of the moments ticking by. Nate looked above the door header and for the first time noticed a crest, with the colours of the *Devil's Raiders* hanging above it. He stopped. Jess carried on. Nate turned and glanced back inside and noticed two spotless choppers parked in the far corner of the warehouse. They had been hidden from his view, by the stacked barrels, when they had entered.

Nate reeled at the enormity of what they had done. He felt a bead of cold sweat run down his spine. He did not move.

"Come on Nate," Jess yelled, returning to him through the door. She pulled her balaclava over her face again. "We are out of time." She stepped back into the rear yard.

Recognizing the logo of the city's most feared biker gang forced all his anxieties to crash upon him. His eyes scanned the rest of the warehouse quickly and came to rest on a small red light blinking from a camera, in the corner of the warehouse, pointed directly at them. He hadn't noticed it when they entered. *Shit.* Nate bolted for the door. The weight on his shoulders felt overwhelming, crushing down on him from the added weight of his fear.

"Jesus...Jess!" Nate screamed at her as they ran for their cars. Nate could hear sirens in the distance. He tore his balaclava off when he saw she had pulled hers off.

"You didn't tell me you worked for the *Raiders!*" he screamed at her. She had told him that she was a mule, running money for a group of locals, not for a gang like the Raiders.

"What difference does it make?"

They rounded the corner of an adjoining building and saw their cars.

"Difference? The difference is they are nasty people. The difference is they had an internal camera on us that we didn't know about." They slid up in front of their cars. "You told me they were a group of businessmen. This is way different, Jess."

Jess's face went white. "What?" she said, panting to catch her breath.

"You told me they were businessmen."

"What fucking camera?" she interrupted.

He could see the strain on her face. He told her what he had seen.

Her eyes darted about the area. "Here…you take my bags too." She shrugged her duffel bag and knapsack off her shoulders and dropped them at Nate's feet.

Nate looked confused. Having him take everything was a deviation from their plan.

"We will meet as planned tomorrow at six p.m." She opened her car door.

Nate started loading the money into his car, confusion etched on his face.

"This'll change everything. We are going to have to run. They may have seen my face. Shit. Why did I take my mask off?" She climbed behind the wheel of her car and shot an angry look at him. "And don't even think about not coming."

Nate considered all that had just happened and thought the threat was a little on the lame side. She obviously didn't trust him, despite knowing how he felt about her. His shoulders slumped. He closed the trunk of his rented Car2Go.

She rolled down the window and threw her balaclava and gloves at him. "Get rid of these too, Nate." She stomped on the gas pedal and her car lurched out of the parking lot.

Picking up the mask and gloves from the ground, Nate tossed them into the rear of his car with the money. The sirens grew louder. It was not lost on him that he now bore all the risk of their caper.

Jumping into his car, he gunned the engine and headed into the street, turning in the same direction as Jess. He was now on a main thoroughfare, heading for a connector road that would lead him out of the district. Trying to calm his racing heart, he forced himself to proceed slowly, driving the speed limit and trying not to attract attention.

A police cruiser, lights flashing, roared past Nate as he headed south. He watched, in his rear-view mirror, as it turned down the road he had vacated, obviously intent on reaching the location of the alarm. His fingers hurt from clenching the steering wheel so tightly. Once the cops were out of sight, he stepped on the gas, wishing he had a more powerful car. They would have noticed his rental and he'd likely be the subject of a search, once they determined there had been a robbery. His eyes darted back and forth between the road and his rear-view mirror. He stomped on the accelerator twice. *Can't this thing go any faster?*

He was approaching a bend in the road when he noticed lights flashing in front of him. His heart stopped for a moment, and he slowed down. Was it over? As he approached the police car, he saw that Jess had been pulled over. A cruiser was stopped behind her, lights ablaze in their distinctive blue, yellow, and red colours. He saw an officer walking to Jess' door.

Nate glanced at her as he passed by. She ignored him, focusing instead on her side mirror. He could only wonder what was going through her mind as she watched the constable approaching. He half expected to be waved over as well. Once he passed them and knew he was in the clear, he sped up a bit. He could feel his heart assaulting his ribcage.

He had to ditch the rental car as soon as possible. He wasn't sure how much time he'd have. For now, he was free. He felt his panic diminish the further down the road he went. He hoped he was in the clear. His mind turned to Jess. He was glad the evidence wasn't with her. She would be all right. They had nothing on her.

The video link in the *Raiders* warehouse would not be available yet. All the risk was with him, for now. Her move to give him everything had been fortuitous, albeit self-serving.

The consequences of what would happen, if he were caught, played out in multiple scenarios as he sped down the road. None of the results gave him any comfort. His eyes dropped to the speedometer, and he slowed the car. It would serve neither of them if he was pulled over for speeding now.

Light rain began to fall. Nate could see that the clouds had dropped lower, looking cold and sullen, the city lights emphasizing their intent. He switched the windshield wipers on and felt a renewed sense of dread grow as the rain began. His hands trembled and he shuddered from within.

"Were we out of our freaking minds?" he yelled into the night, slamming his hand against the steering wheel. "Jess...Jesus, Jess, please be okay. I can't do this without you."

CHAPTER TWO

NATE TOOK SEVERAL LARGE BREATHS, exhaling slowly, willing himself to calm down. The ache in his stomach wouldn't ease up. He thought he might have to pull over and throw up, but the fear of a cop pulling over to help, pushed those thoughts away. Repeatedly he played out the events of the night in his mind, wishing they had done things differently, or not at all. He punched the radio's button, and cranked up the volume, trying to silence the voices in his head.

He turned west onto Glenmore Trail, leaving the warehouse district behind. His headlights cut the darkness of the night, illuminating the road ahead of him. His wipers pushed rain drops from the window. For a moment, the eerie darkness, accentuated by the rain, gave him a sense of security. He knew it to be false. With the radio blaring, his thoughts returned to Jess and the cop. In a matter of seconds, he imagined her driving away from the police, then in a flash, saw her being taken away in handcuffs. *Thinking in the abstract is not helpful,* he lamented. She had nothing in the car to implicate her, so reason dictated that she'd be fine.

A love song on the radio cut through Nate's thoughts. For a moment, he listened to the words, then he stabbed the off button. That wasn't helpful either.

He needed focus.

He felt sure she wouldn't give him up, no matter what happened. Not while he had the money and not given her personality. Besides, she had feelings for him.

"Right?" he said out loud, as if she were in the car with him.

Her distrust of him created doubt. The more he thought about it the more anger and disappointment resonated. He shook his head, trying to free negative thoughts about her.

There was little traffic this late on a Sunday night, but enough that Nate felt that he'd remain undetected. Three lights appeared ahead of him, travelling at high speed. Nate knew from experience that the lights belonged to motorcycles and given their speed despite the rain, he had no doubt where they were headed. Even though he was on the opposite side of the meridian, Nate turned his head away, as they passed. Cold sweat ran down his back, for the second time that night. It was something he expected he would experience frequently now.

Nate signalled his entry to Deerfoot Trail and stepped on the gas to merge into the highway traffic. He was glad for the anonymity of the additional vehicles. He instinctively monitored his mirror to look for the motorcycles. Why had she not told him it was the *Raiders*? Would it have made a difference? Of course, it would. Stealing from a white-collar group was far different than stealing from a crime ring. *Really, Nate? Stealing from one group is better than another?* He shook his head again, wishing one more time that he could turn back the clock.

Driving down the freeway, his thoughts returned to Jess and the past month with her.

She'd talked a lot about herself, telling him about her likes, her dislikes, how lousy her parents had been, and the physical or verbal abuse her father had laid on her and her brother whenever he drank. She'd spoken admiringly of her brother, Digger, and told Nate how she had raised him since he was fourteen, after she had found the means to get out of their abusive home. He'd soaked up her story.

She would listen quietly as he told his tale, although at times he could tell she wasn't really listening. He'd described how his mother had died in a car crash when he was a boy and that his father was also dead. He'd told her about his relationship with his Uncle Frank who had raised him. He deliberately didn't mention anything about his uncle's connection with organized crime in the city. Nor did he mention how much he longed to get away from the parade of constant and less than savoury individuals who paraded through his uncle's home, even though he knew she would be fully attentive at that disclosure. Some things were just better left unsaid.

He'd learned about her unusual job. At first, he was shocked, but he had slowly grown to accept it when she explained that her risk was limited. Then she explained about the promise to her brother, who she said worried about her, and laid out her retirement plan for Nate, which he'd slowly warmed up to. He ignored how much he was slipping into the shadow world he had wanted to escape. He saw it as a method to escape the drudgery of his own life and allow his dreams to flourish. Dreams with her.

He strayed into an adjoining lane and forced the car to correct. *Pay attention.* His mind snapped back to the present.

She had not told him they were hitting the *Raiders*. Mistakes had also been made. He could feel his dreams fading before his eyes. Could they be saved?

He headed down the freeway, mindful of his speed. Things had not turned out the way Jess had planned. Despite everything they had gone over, every detail discussed ad nauseam, she missed the internal stand-alone camera. How had she known where the money was hidden and not known about the camera? Maybe it was new. Maybe she just hadn't seen it, but that made little sense.

Now what? Run? Even if the camera didn't confirm it was her, The *Raiders* would suspect her. They needed a new plan. Where could they go? What did they have to do to escape the reach of these guys? *Do I love her enough to run with her?* He was shocked at himself then. *How the hell did the word "love" pop into my head?* Nate groaned.

He knew she would be scrambling to put together a new escape plan. He had to think of his own, make her believe in its merits. She had proven how rash she could be, but together they would figure it out. That is, if she trusted his judgement. Bile rose in his throat as he recalled how often she dismissed his point of view.

He reached a cross street and pulled off the freeway. Ten minutes later he was on a bridge crossing the Bow River, into the downtown area. He used a circuitous route, avoiding main roads. Within minutes, he parallel parked the Car2Go and got out, opening the hatchback with a key fob. He reached into his pocket and pulled out another fob, pressing it to open the hatchback of his own car, previously parked in a location away from the view of street cameras and residents. He considered that might not have been the best plan, now that he saw how dark it was.

Nate quickly transferred the contents of the rental to his black Ford Edge, checking frequently to see he was not watched. He noted a couple of street people down the block, heading his way. Satisfied that he had nothing left in the rental, he locked his car and got back into the Car2Go. He drove it to a designated parking spot down the street. He pulled out a wet wipe, he had brought with him and wiped down the car handle, steering wheel and door handle in the hopes it would remove any fingerprints he'd left behind. Moving quickly to the rear of the car he did the same on the trunk handle, then stuffed the wipe in his pocket.

He left the rental and walked two blocks back to his car. He broke into a run when he saw that the street people were now peering in the windows of his car, determining if there was something worth stealing. He yelled out and charged towards them. They panicked and ran off in separate directions, leaving their grocery carts filled with their life's contents, unattended. Anger at how close they had come to stealing from him engulfed him, and with the accumulated stress he was feeling, he kicked over one of their carts, spewing its contents on the ground. He opened his car door and slipped behind the wheel. He saw they had stopped running and joined back up, as one. They turned to look at him, no doubt worried that their prey might, in fact, steal from them. He stared back.

Clenching his teeth until his jaw hurt, he reached down, put the car in gear and slowly pulled away from the curb. He pulled onto Fourth Avenue and headed west through Calgary's downtown core. Nate usually liked driving through the office towers at night, resplendent with their coloured lights and unique architecture, but not tonight. He felt exposed by the brightness of their lights. He was sure that the driver in each car that passed was looking at him with suspicion. He longed for the dark again.

Leaving downtown, he crossed another bridge over the Bow River and headed west on Memorial Drive. A few minutes later, he pulled into a quiet parking lot and got out of the car. Assuring himself he was alone he opened his trunk. The rain eased off, transforming to more of a cold wet mist. Reaching into his knapsack, he pulled out the tools they had brought to the warehouse and walked along the river throwing each tool into a different part of the water. He knew they'd sink into the mud at the bottom and be hard to find. By the time he returned to his car, he was soaking wet but glad he had disposed of the incriminating evidence. All that was left to do now was get rid of the gloves and masks which were soon disposed of in four separate garbage cans, as he headed north.

Questions filled his mind. He wondered if he should call Jess, on his cell, to make sure she was all right, but knew that would be a very bad idea. They had agreed that he would not use their phones after the heist. She wanted to ensure there was nothing to connect them after the robbery. *I wish they still had public phone booths,* he thought, determining to get a burner phone in the morning.

The gnawing in Nate's stomach became more insistent and he decided to pull into a drive-through for some junk food, reasoning the food would satisfy the problem. It didn't. The feeling in his stomach returned with a vengeance, as he headed home.

He pulled into his designated parking spot and stared at the entry to the duplex he rented. He laid his head back against the headrest, exhaustion taking hold. It would be so easy to go in and just lay down, pretending nothing was different from the previous night, but everything was different. He leaned forward, laying his head on the wheel, and closed his eyes. With a burst of insight, he sat back up, put his gearshift into reverse and backed his car out. He couldn't stay here. He drove down the street wondering if he would ever go back to his meagre home again.

Twenty minutes later, he, two knapsacks and three duffel bags full of cash were in a small seedy motel room in the city's "Motel Village." He sat on the bed and stared at the bags he had propped against the door to prevent an unwanted entry. He pulled out his phone and looked to see if she had phoned him, knowing she hadn't. They had their plan, and he would see her tomorrow.

He peeled off his wet clothes, hanging them on the bathroom shower rod to dry. He noticed a bug crawling along the tile adjoining the stained tub but made no effort to kill it. Too tired. Walking back into the room, he put the night lock on the door, pulled the sheets back on the bed and crawled in. He hoped there was nothing he would catch beneath the sheets. His mind went numb as he stared at the bags propped against the door. His eyelids dropped. The last thing he wondered, as he drifted into sleep, was if the bags were speaking to him. "What have you done? What have you done, Nate?"

CHAPTER THREE

JESSICA REED PULLED HER MUSTANG to the side of the road and waited. She stared into the darkness. She felt herself hyperventilating and willed her breathing to be steady.

"Be calm," she whispered, aloud.

The police officer stepped out of his car and walked toward her.

She had foreseen a possible exchange with the police as part of her planning and had her story worked out, in advance. She watched a second cruiser roar past her, obviously heading to the alarm and hoped Nate had gotten away. The last thing she wanted was for all of this to be for nothing. Out of the corner of her eye she saw Nate's car pass. She breathed a sigh of relief.

She knew she had to keep this exchange brief, if she were to escape more serious questioning, after the police put two and two together. She pressed down on her window control and waited for him to take the last few steps to her.

"Good evening, ma'am," he said.

"Hello, officer," Jess replied sweetly. "Did I do something wrong?"

"You were going pretty fast," he responded. "We're investigating an incident in the area, and when I saw your car speeding down this road, I was wondering why the hurry."

Jess was about to answer when he interrupted. "Why are you even here, at all, this late at night?"

Jess smiled in a nonconfrontational way. She was glad that her tattoos were covered by her sweater and that she looked a little less the rebel than she was. There was something to be said for looking average. She doubled down on trying to be obliging.

"I know I was going a little too fast," she said, deliberately sounding urgent. "I'm on the way to my brother's house. He's headed to the hospital, and his wife asked me to get over and be at the house before their daughter gets home from her friend's."

"What's wrong with your brother?"

"They think it's a heart attack," she said.

"The ambulance picked him up?" he asked.

"No, his wife was driving him."

"What hospital?"

"South Campus."

"Where were you coming from?"

"Marlborough."

"Through here?" His expression declared his doubt. Jess could feel her heartbeat rising.

Just then the radio on the officer's shoulder blared "Charlie?"

Officer Charlie then stepped back from the car window and Jess could no longer ascertain what was being said. Charlie returned to the car, a few moments later, hand on the handle of his firearm. "Ma'am, please open the trunk of your car."

Jess felt things unwinding and stressed. "I have to get to my brother's house."

"Now," he demanded.

Jess reached down and popped the trunk lid. The officer stepped backwards to the side of the trunk, never taking his eyes from hers, as she studied him in her side mirror. He reached down, fully opening the lid and stepped behind the car. Jess could hear him lift the cargo lid in her empty trunk and felt the back of the car depress as he pushed it closed. He then shut the trunk and retraced his steps to her window.

"All right," he said. "Let me have your driver's licence." Jess reached down and pulled it from her wallet, which she'd removed from the glove box of her car. She handed it to him.

"Wait here," he said, returning to his cruiser. Minutes passed like an eternity before he returned, licence in hand.

"This your current home address, Ms. Reed? I thought you said you lived in Marlborough?"

"Yes, it is. I'm sorry for the confusion. I don't live in Marlborough; I was visiting a friend." Jess started to scramble.

A light rain started to fall, droplets hitting her arm through the open window. Charlie's radio squawked again, and he stepped back once more.

Returning, Charlie handed back her driver's licence.

"Off you go then, but slow down. Sounds like your brother's daughter needs you to get there in one piece."

"Will do," she responded, taking her licence back from him. "Thank you." She feigned a smile.

He nodded. "We may have to come by your place to discuss what, if anything, you might have seen as you came through the area. Seems there has been a break-in nearby."

Jess was about to respond, but Officer Charlie had already turned, heading for his cruiser. He ran the last few steps, as the rain started to come down harder. She watched as his car pulled a U-turn and accelerated down the road in the direction she had come, lights flashing.

Jess let out a long breath. She was happy to see the back of his car, but she was not thrilled that she may see him again. She had not contemplated that. She would have to make sure that she was long gone before that call came. Pity she would have to leave her things behind, but she'd have plenty of money to replace them.

With that, she stepped on the car's accelerator and headed down the road. *Where are you, Nate?* She thought about whether she should phone him right away, but she knew that would create a trail, especially if he was caught. She had reacted well to put all initial suspicion on him. It bought her time. Now that she was almost home free though, she wanted to be back in control.

They had a plan, she knew that. They would meet up tomorrow. That seemed so far away now. She had to get control of the money and get it out of town.

She thought about how Nate was momentarily in charge. She grimaced. It wasn't that she didn't trust Nate specifically. She didn't trust anybody. She had made him take everything to take the risk off her, but now felt exposed to a possible double-cross. Would he show up? Would he cut her out? There was a lot of money in those bags. She told herself to settle down, but one thing was certain — she wanted the money away from Nate, as soon as possible. She would find a way to move their timetable forward.

As she drove, she thought more about Nate. He was a nice guy, no doubting that, and she enjoyed being around him. She smiled at the memory of how they had jumped into a taxi, the night they met, and made their way to her downtown apartment, where one thing had led to another. She wouldn't call it an explosion exactly but sparks certainly flew as their bodies came together.

Her smile faded. Was that a reason to split the money, her money, with him? It was her plan and she bore far more of the risk. Sure, he had helped, but that wasn't worth half of her money. Maybe she'd leave him a hundred thousand or so, but it was time to find a way to cut him out. She could always find another guy to spend time with. First though, she had to get the money. She resolved to call his phone, in the morning, if he hadn't called her.

Her thoughts jumped to the warehouse camera. That was a problem. *How the hell did I miss that? They must have added that after my last visit. Why would they do that?* She figured she had a day, at most, to disappear. She lamented lifting her mask. That was stupid.

She really didn't want to run, but she didn't know how much the camera would reveal. Besides, that damn cop was coming, and she didn't think her story would hold up to further scrutiny. She knew by running that she would implicate herself, but there was no choice. She also understood what the *Raiders* would do, if they found her. She had witnessed their brand of justice on a few occasions. Jess shuddered at the thought.

She was under no illusions that she would ever be truly free. She would have to constantly be aware of her surroundings as she built a new life — somewhere. Jess started to smile again. A new life...why not? She figured she had gotten enough money to start over in a big way.

It would be too bad about Nate. That was the way life worked sometimes. What do they call that? Collateral damage? It might be a bit of a reach, but the same thing.

"Sorry, baby — just the way it is," she said aggressively, finalizing her decision. She knew he wouldn't come after her; he was too nice a guy for that. Besides, he really didn't like conflict. She had learned that about him. It was his weakness.

She pulled her car into her underground parking spot and quickly headed to her apartment. *Best to not stay here tonight,* she thought as she opened the door with her key. She turned on the hallway light, opened the coat closet and pulled out two pre-packed travel bags. She headed for her bedroom and punched the light-switch. She quickly undressed, throwing her black jeans and sweater on the floor beside her bags. She was glad she had already packed them in anticipation of escaping with Nate. It meant she'd be out of her apartment quickly. She headed into her bathroom and turned on her shower.

She wanted to wash away the sweat and bother from the night before she left. She was pretty sure the police would tie up the "boys" for a while. That gave her time. Jess closed her eyes, letting the warm water caress her. Climbing out, she towelled off and reached for her robe.

There was a knock at the door. Fear engulfed her. She moved to the kitchen and drew a knife from her knife block. A further knock followed.

Maybe it was Nate. That wasn't their plan, but then botched plans called for revised plans. *This might work out well,* she decided.

Jess walked to the door, cinching the belt of her robe around her. She pushed her hair from her face and looked through the peephole. She jerked back from the door, trying to figure out how she would handle things, when, with a loud bang, her door flew inwards, wood splinters showering over her.

CHAPTER FOUR

NATE VICKERS WOKE WITH A start. The sun streamed through the edges of the drawn drapes. He listened to the call of a magpie through the closed window. The clarity of the previous day's events penetrated the morning fog in his brain.

"Shit," he said to himself. He flopped back onto his pillow and groaned.

Nate reached for his phone to check on the time. It was nine in the morning. Wow, had he slept. The screen indicated he had messages. He opened them and saw that he had four pending. He hadn't heard them, silenced by the "do not disturb" night instructions he had programmed on his phone.

"Nate, it's me," the first message announced. "Call me."

"Nate, why aren't you answering? Give me a call, please."

"Nate, call now — *please*."

The final message was a silent click.

Nate longed to respond but he needed a burner phone. He wasn't sure he had ever remembered her saying "please" before. Maybe he should take control of the money more often. He smiled at the thought, even as a sense of foreboding formed in his mind. He climbed out of bed and pulled on his dirty jeans.

Why had she called him on his phone? They had decided against that. Nate stared at his phone, listened to the messages one more time. He removed his sim card and walked into the bathroom, tossing it into the toilet which he flushed. He didn't know if this really did anything, but he'd seen it done in the movies, so it gave him a sense of comfort. He then turned the phone off and pocketed it. He was sure the *Raiders* would not work with the police, but he wasn't going to take any chances.

He wondered what they'd said to them when they arrived at the break in. What would the answer be when they were asked if anything was missing? No — they wouldn't work with the police but that didn't mean they didn't have the means to track him and his phone. Best to get a new one, he needed the burner.

Nate walked back to the door and moved the bags onto the bed. He knew what was in them but opened them and stared at all the cash for a few minutes. Grabbing Jess's knapsack, he dumped all the money from it on the bed. Picking up a bundle of cash, he thumbed through it. All one-hundred-dollar bills. He grabbed another bundle...the same. Before long Nate realized that every bundle from her bag contained only one- hundred-dollar bills. He reached into one of the duffel bags and removed another bundle from the top. This one had fifty-dollar bills. There was a lot of money here. How much money did these guys rack up in every week? *There's going to be some really pissed off bikers wandering around town, looking for this money,* he thought. *Why did we have to rip off these guys?* Jess's lie flared up. A familiar sense of fear rose within him.

He knew, then and there, he would never be going back to his previous life. No doubt that was why Jess was calling. She knew they'd have to make their escape. They were not going to meet until later in the day, but she had phoned for a reason. He had to get a phone, call her and work out a plan. First, he had priorities of his own. He wasn't throwing caution to the wind, despite how urgent her calls sounded.

Nate replaced the money in the bags, keeping out a one-hundred- dollar bundle for himself. He needed some ready cash to buy some clothes and essentials. He decided to have a quick shower and headed into the bathroom. The same bug was in the same place, but this time Nate killed it.

After cleaning up as best he could without a morning kit, Nate checked out online and transferred the bags of cash to the trunk of his car. He left the key in the room and closed the door.

He felt reasonably fresh and sat staring through the window of his car, determining what he should do first. With an imperceptible nod, he put the car in gear and headed for the Calgary International Airport. The storm that had dumped rain and hail on parts of the city had passed. It was a beautiful sunny morning.

Before long, he pulled into a short-term parking lot. He left the car, making sure it was securely locked. It was a busy day at the airport, making him all but invisible, which Nate liked. He found the shopping directory and was soon at the entrance to a luggage store where he purchased two large suitcases and a pair of locks. After paying the surprised store clerk, with hundred-dollar bills, he left the airport's main building. He felt that passing travellers were suspiciously eyeing him, as he pulled the suitcases behind him. He was relieved to place the bags in the back seat of his car. Nate thought about making the money transfer right there, but decided he was too exposed.

He pulled out of the parkade and headed for the outskirts of the city. Minutes later he found a remote farming road and looked for a pull out, which he found, near a stand of trees. He backed into the space and got out of the car. Nate surveyed the area to ensure he was alone and then, after moving the suitcases to the rear of the car, opened the trunk. He removed the bags of cash and placed them on the gravel behind his car. He then opened one of the large suitcases and began stuffing it full of the cash from the duffel bag. He repeated the process with the second bag, then from the third. Nate was annoyed that all the cash didn't fit into the two cases, as he had hoped. Jess's knapsack remained full. Still, he was down to three bags instead of four.

"Man, that's a lot of cash," Nate murmured.

He saw movement and looked up to see a truck barrelling toward him, dust signalling its impending arrival. A cold chill shuddered through him.

He hurriedly zipped the suitcases closed and attached the locks. He pocketed the keys. He flung the suitcases into the trunk, then threw the knapsack in on top of them. The truck was nearly on him. He tossed the empty duffel bags and his empty knapsack into the tree stand behind him, satisfied that they were all but concealed by the undergrowth. He could see the end of one bag partially protruding from the brush, but it would have to do.

Nate climbed back into his car, as the truck sped past, dust flying from the rear tires, all but obliterating the Chevrolet emblem on its tailgate. He felt unnerved when the man's head turned to inspect him, as he drove past. Nate stared after the truck, edgily. He had to get his anxiety in check.

He got out of his car, once the truck had carried on down the road, and properly hid the bags within the brush. The dust trail from the truck was far down the road. No threat there.

Heading back to the city, he turned north onto the Queen Elizabeth highway. Soon, he pulled into the parking lot of a large mall, parking the car in a busy part of the lot, reasoning it was less likely to be broken into.

He headed into the mall looking for a menswear store and purchased a couple of shirts, a light sweater, and a spring coat, along with socks and underwear, then stopped at a drugstore and purchased what he needed for incidentals. Finally, he headed to the mall bathroom to change. Nate heard a door open, and a man walk to the handicap stall he occupied. He tried the door. Nate held his breath. The man moved to the adjoining stall and entered it. With a snap. the bolt slid closed.

Nate cinched his belt, grabbed his new light coat off the door hook, stuffed his old clothes in his bag, and left the stall. He was sure the adjoining door would fly open at any moment, and tensed for a fight, readying himself to drop the bag and pivot. But nothing happened.

He exited the bathroom and retraced his steps back to the mall entrance. On his way, Nate visited the information directory again and shortly thereafter, came out of another store with a burner phone in hand. He went over to a waiting area where no one was around and removed the phone from its packaging and readied it for use.

Why did she call me? he mused again, as he thumbed in her number. *We are supposed to meet at the agreed spot at six tonight.* He sat down in a comfortable mall chair. The phone rang six times before it was answered.

"Jess?" Nate asked. Silence.

"Jess...you there? Are we still good to meet?"

Nate heard the click of the phone as it went dead. A spasm of distrust engulfed him.

Were the police on the other line...or worse? Why wouldn't she answer? Maybe she couldn't talk right then.

There is no way she wouldn't have cleared out of her apartment last night. She knew it was too big of a risk. But something wasn't right. He was sure she wasn't on the other end of that line. Her line. *Who had that phone?*

He resolved that he would cautiously show up at the meeting place at six and find out what was going on. He hoped she was being as prudent as he was.

Nate rose and headed for the exit. Climbing back into his car, relieved that it was still there and not broken into, he started the engine. He had seen on the airport directory that there were storage lockers there. It would be best to store the money until they sorted this mess out. She wouldn't like that he had left the money, but too bad. They were in reactive mode now.

He put his car in gear and headed for the mall exit. He stopped the car at a stop sign, then cursed inwardly. He remembered from a trip the previous year, that you couldn't store luggage at the airport without giving your identification and a flight itinerary, to the staff managing the storage area. *Damn 9/11.* A car behind him blew its horn, forcing him onto the freeway ramp. He stepped on the accelerator. The bus station would have to do.

A short time later, Nate walked out of the terminal having committed the electronic lock to memory. He was glad to have secured the cash. He would've preferred leaving the money at the airport, but at least the bus terminal didn't have the same rules.

After checking his watch, Nate decided to walk over to a pathway along the Bow River, leaving his car in the bus station parking lot. The sun shone unhindered with rays dancing on the river rapids. Nate zipped up his new jacket to fend off the cool early afternoon breeze. He knew that in a couple of weeks the river would be swollen with the spring Rocky Mountain run-off, but for now it was calm. He enjoyed a brief respite from his thoughts, as he watched a boy tossing rocks into the river, monitored closely by his mother. He walked on. He could feel his fears easing and hoped it would stimulate clarity on what they had to do to get away from the *Raiders*.

He walked by a cafe in a downtown park and felt a pang of hunger, realizing that he had not eaten all day. He glanced at his watch; it was three-thirty. As he had a couple of hours before he would head out to meet Jess, he decided to loop the park before heading into the cafe. He was famished, but the walk was doing him good.

Taking a seat at a table, with his back to a window, he motioned to a server. He was glad there were few people in the restaurant and that he was there before the after-work crowd arrived. It allowed a good view of whoever came into the restaurant. Sensing something behind him, he turned to look out the window and saw a large man avert his eyes.

"Would you like a menu?" asked a young lady with a nose ring and a welcoming smile.

Nate accepted the menu, with a return smile, and turned back to the window. The man was gone. Nate monitored the door to see if he would enter. Seeing nothing, he peered out again and saw the man walking over a hill further down the park. Nate stretched the tension free from his neck, hoping the action would stop it from building within him again.

He watched a flock of Canada geese land gracefully on the lawn and closed his eyes for a moment, allowing the familiar honking to calm his jitters. He wanted the next two hours to fly by, so he could reunite with Jess. A new feeling engulfed him. Isolation. Aloneness grasped at him. Nate gazed out the window thinking about her. He missed her, his anger at her all but forgotten. He yearned to be back together. Trepidation had replaced his eagerness for a new life together, but he wanted to be with her again. Together, they'd figure out a way to put Calgary and all this mess behind them. They would get back on track.

The food arrived and Nate devoured it. He allowed himself to be lost in the flavours for a moment.

It wouldn't be long now.

CHAPTER FIVE

JESSICA REED WAS TIED TO a chair, slumped to one side. Blood poured into her eyes from the cuts on her forehead. The blood saturated the piece of her shirt that was stuffed into her mouth, leaving a salty iron taste. She was having difficulty breathing. She suspected her nose was broken and was having trouble drawing in a breath. She was sure the end would be soon.

They'd grabbed her from her apartment. There were four of them, at least that's how it had started. She had left her knife in the throat of one of the men. Two of the remaining men — one large muscular man and the other more diminutive — had marched her out between them. One had stayed behind and begun tearing things apart as they'd dragged her out through the door. She should have screamed as loud as she could, but she hadn't. Perhaps someone would have saved her. She remembered wondering why no one came to see what was going on.

Jess was watched closely by the smaller man after she was tossed into the back of a cargo van. The other drove them to whatever place she was now in.

Fist after fist had driven into her, and knives had sliced her, each one creating an agony she had never thought possible. She had withstood the pounding, but with each cut she had capitulated, telling them what they wanted, doing what they demanded. She'd wanted to hold back. It was impossible.

Until the knife had started its journey across her face, she'd had hope that she would somehow escape her predicament and retrieve her money. Now she understood her reality, and a calm had taken hold.

She stared at the floor, blinking the blood from her eyes. She wanted to close them, but her left eye was too swollen to do so without creating more pain. So, she stared, her one good eye darting to the boot of the man who stood a short distance away. She tried to see where the other man was. He was out of sight. The bloodied rag fell from her mouth.

Just get it over with, her minded screamed in silence.

A snarl formed on her lips, causing a flash of pain. She wanted to belittle the man who had harmed her. She said nothing. Blood dribbled from her lips. Her body began to shake. It was going into shock. At least the pain was subsiding.

She thought of Nate. She was glad he was spared this — at least for now. She had wanted all the money for herself, but now that her time was coming to an end, she hoped Nate was smart enough and tough enough to escape. Doubts quickly formed. He was too innocent for these guys and just too nice. *Poor Nate.*

Jess's head fell to her chest. She was very tired. When she heard movement, she forced herself to glance up.

The larger of the two men cleaned his knife on a towel. Returning to her slumped form, he reached down and grabbed a handful of hair, pulling her face to his.

"How could you have been such a stupid bitch? Nobody takes from us."

He let her head drop, turning to his accomplice. "You know what to do?"

"Of course."

"Do it after dark and take care of the mess."

The accomplice just smiled. "Got it."

"I will see you back at the club later."

"Where are you going?"

"I'm going to meet the boyfriend," the man said, nodding at Jess.

He pulled out his phone and made a quick call. Jess could hear him arranging for others to join him. "No," he said. "Two of you are fine. This guy will be easy to corral."

It had all been for naught. She blinked rapidly to clear the blood from her good eye. She watched her tormentor leave.

She heard the door slam, then turned her view on the remaining man. He pulled a chair in front of her and sat down. He was looking at her strangely. She had seen that kind of look before and knew what was coming. He reached out and grabbed a handful of her hair. Her suffering wasn't over.

Death would have to wait.

＊

Nate arrived at Calgary's premier downtown shopping mall at five-forty and headed for the first-floor escalator. All the best shops in the city were here, including Holt Renfrew, Hugo Boss, Harry Rosen, and many others. It was the kind of place that was perfect for a meet. High end, lots of people. Nate looked up at the block-long skylight. The sun had passed behind the downtown towers and was no longer bathing the shoppers in bright sunshine. Instead, it took on a more subdued hue, as if the space were mirroring his anxieties. The release provided by his brief walk and time in the restaurant had vanished.

He wanted to reunite with Jess and flee. He hated the thought of being tracked down by the *Raiders*. He was under no illusions what the outcome would be, if that occurred. Nate arrived at the top of the first-floor escalator, walked across a bridge to the second-floor escalator, and stepped on it. He looked down on the mall as he rose. Built to entice office workers from the adjoining office towers, to leave some of their hard-earned dollars in its stores, Nate realized it also allowed dangerous people to be hidden in the throngs of eager shoppers. Absorbing that meeting here may not have been the best idea, he wished they had chosen an alternate place.

The escalator deposited Nate at the entrance to the food court. Multiple aromas of fast food lingered in the air, adding to the confusion in his mind. His stomach churned. Something felt off. It wasn't anything he could put his finger on, just a feeling. He decided to listen to the little voice in his head.

He surveyed the area and spotted a table by the window. After sitting down on an uncomfortable stained seat, he looked down at the public walk below, watching people leaving the office towers, scurrying against the late-afternoon cool winds, in their efforts to get home. He turned and eyed the entrance to the third-story mall park, adjoining the court, where they had agreed to meet. As far as Nate could tell, there were few people in it. He could see an old man staring at a koi pond, but little else. He couldn't see the far end of the park.

He studied people around him. Two young girls were laughing at an inside joke. A businessman dressed up in a banker's suit was eating a noodle dish with chopsticks. He spotted a young guy sitting by himself. He wore faded blue jeans, a blue hoodie, and a New York Yankees ball cap that had seen better days. He looked a little down and out and was focused on a disintegrating hamburger. Nate rose and walked to him and sat down. A look of fear shot into the eyes of the young man.

"What do you want, dude?"

"Would you like to make a hundred bucks?"

Nate wondered if his offer registered as the young man stared at him. "Fifty now and fifty when you tell me what I want to know." Nate proffered a fifty-dollar bill to him.

"I'm not gonna do nothin' illegal," he announced, his eyes darting around. "I have enough problems."

"Nah, I'm just asking for information."

After telling him what he needed, Nate watched the young man stuff the last of his burger in his mouth, snatch the fifty from his hand and rise to stroll into the park. He was glad he had gotten change, when he'd bought his clothes at the airport and had a fifty to give to the kid. He didn't have another fifty so the kid would get a nice bonus when he came back with the information he needed.

Nate walked back to his previous table and sat down. Keeping his back to the window, he stared at the park entrance, waiting for the young man to return. He glanced at his watch. Nearly six. Jess should be here by now.

Nate caught a security guard looking at him, probably wondering why he wasn't eating anything. To prevent unwanted intrusion, he nodded at the guard and smiled. The guard smiled back and walked down the hall.

Minutes later, the kid returned and sauntered up to Nate.

"Sorry, dude, no woman of that description. In fact, there was only one woman in there and she was playing with her kid at the kiddie park. Don't think it was her, but you can check it out. A few other people, but no women."

Nate knew there wouldn't be a lot of people in the park. That's why they had picked this place. After work, it was always quiet, as the office towers cleared out for the day.

"You're sure?" Nate glanced over the kids' shoulder into the park again.

"I walked the whole thing, man. Nobody there like who you're looking for. You gonna pay me now?"

Nate reached into his pocket for another bill, deciding he had to go have a look for himself. He was about to hand it over to the kid, when his eyes caught movement of a man coming out of the park. He was large, with long greasy hair. His eyes darted about. He was muscular, but it was the tattoo on his neck that caught Nate's eyes. He did not belong here. Nate scoured the area, spotting another smaller man on the other side of the mall, studying people as he moved towards him.

"I will give you another fifty for your ball cap." Nate grabbed the cap from his head and put in on before could react. Nate dropped a hundred on the table.

"Come on, man." The kid ran a hand though his dishevelled locks.

Nate glanced at the park entrance again. The large man was staring straight at him now.

"Shit," Nate responded, throwing the cap back at the kid. It was useless now. He watched the kid's head swivel in the direction Nate was looking, quickly pocketing the money as he did so. He then rose swiftly from the table, his cap back on his head and headed away from Nate as if he were a plague.

Nate shot up, striding quickly to the down escalator. He looked back, saw the tattooed man running for him, yelling at his partner as he did. Nate leapt down the escalator, two treads at a time. The second guy was closing the distance. He focused on clearing the escalator. Nate nudged past a woman holding two bags. She let out a frightened squeal as he flew by. A guy with a ponytail was making for the bottom of the escalator. One of the men shouted something to him. Nate couldn't make it out. Ponytail was almost at the mouth of the escalator, planning to block his escape. He knew he had but a few seconds to act. With only a few treads left, Nate grabbed hold of the moving handrail and launched a sideways jump off the escalator with his feet aimed at the head of Ponytail. He heard a sickening crunch as he hit him squarely in the face. He suspected he broke the guy's nose.

The woman behind him screamed, catching the attention of the security guard Nate had smiled at. He wasn't smiling now.

Nate and Ponytail fell to the ground hard. A pain shot through his shoulder and arm as he tucked and rolled to his feet. He grabbed his damaged arm. Nate glanced back to see his pursuers reaching the top of the escalator. The guy on the floor was starting to rise. Nate turned back to him, still clutching his arm, and kicked at his face as hard as he could. Blood splattered from his mouth. He pivoted then, running for the plus fifteen walkway leading into "Bankers Hall." The security guard bellowed behind him. A scream caused him to swivel back. Bystanders, coming to the assistance of the bloodied man on the ground, were knocked to the side by his followers. They turned in his direction and bolted towards him.

Nate reached the end of the walkway and the stairs leading to the main floor of one of the two banks that the mall was named after. He glanced back, before tearing down the stairs, as quickly as he could. His adversaries were in close pursuit, sprinting across the walkway. Ponytail was nowhere to be seen.

He reached the bottom of the stairs and glanced up as the two men reached the top. They glared down at him, hatred in their eyes, and started down the stairs.

Nate flew through two outside doors, turning right, wincing in pain from his injury. Being on the outdoor pedestrian mall was a bad idea, nowhere to run. Taking three more strides, he turned into the entrance of a local bar, bumping into a woman waiting for a table.

"Sorry," he said, brushing past her.

The bar was packed with office workers, quaffing down beers, replaying their day with their friends. Nate bolted for a side entrance of the bar, grabbing a leather coat from the back of the chair of an undiscerning patron. He doubled back through another entrance into the east section of Bankers Hall. He had confused his followers with the quick turn into the bar but could see them at the entrance as he exited. Nate was sure the tattooed man had spotted him. He yanked off his light coat, stuffing it into a waste bin and pulled the slightly too small leather coat on. The pain in his shoulder screamed. He took a quick left and headed for the east exit of the building. It was crowded with people, who twisted their heads at him. Few people ran through here at any time of day. A large group came through the doors of one of the banks, making their way for the entrance. Nate eased into the group. They walked through the door. Nate glanced back to see his two pursuers looking wildly for him.

He stepped out into the evening air and noted a yellow taxi, barrelling down the street. Knowing how difficult it was to get a taxi in this town, Nate stepped into the street and flagged it down. The car pulled over at once, he jumped in, slouching down in the seat to be less visible.

"Head down Sixth Ave, I'll direct you," Nate barked at the cab driver, who stared at him with suspicion.

"Where do you want to go, exactly?" He hadn't moved the car.

Nate looked at him with exasperation. "The bus terminal. Quickly please. I'm going to miss my bus."

The cabbie nodded as he stepped on the gas.

Nate slouched down further in the seat.

The two men burst through the exterior doors.

The cabbie looked at him through the rear-view mirror. "Everything alright?" he asked in broken English.

Nate looked at the dark eyes in the mirror.

"I just learned somebody close to me died." He closed his eyes and rubbed his shoulder, ignoring the cabbie's condolences. His body trembled.

CHAPTER SIX

NATE STARED OUT THE WINDOW of his car at the twinkling lights on the houses across the river. He was deep in thought, rubbing his shoulder absentmindedly. A light rain fell, and he turned on his windshield wipers for an unimpeded view. He had retrieved the suitcases and knapsack and locked them in the trunk of his car after the cab had dropped him off at the bus terminal. He had driven east, checking repeatedly to ensure he hadn't been followed. After making a series of turns down several one-way streets and running a couple of lights, to be sure he was safe, he pulled into the small parking lot on the edge of Chinatown, where he now sat.

He had no doubt that the *Raiders* would have mobilized their contacts in their search for him. He knew he should be running as far away as he could, but he sat there, engulfed in a false sense of security from the darkness and early evening lights.

Nate sighed. They had gotten to her. Otherwise, they would never have known where to look for him. Was she alive or dead? He suspected she was dead, but would they kill her before they got their money back? Maybe they'd keep her alive. Was there a way to help her then?

Nate closed his eyes. Despair washed over him. He had to know her fate. How could he make decisions if he didn't know?

Exhaustion overcame him. The sound of the wipers swishing back and forth acted like a metronome. He rubbed his shoulder, in sync with the wipers, as he drifted off to a deep sleep, ravaged by dreams.

A storm was gathering, the likes of which he had never seen before. Birds circled overhead, floating on the afternoon winds, unaware of what was coming. Then the crows flew in circles in front of him, cawing at him through his car window, condemning him for the storm that he had created. The wind started to howl, gulls crying out a mournful song, as if they were warning him. "Beware the crows. Beware the crows." The crows increased their frantic cawing, pecking at the glass to break it, needing to get to his face. The pecking on the glass intensified, becoming louder and louder. Nate was sure the glass would break at any moment. The banging on the window continued unabated...

Nate awoke with a start. He groggily checked his watch. He had been asleep for about an hour. Another knock on the window brought him into full consciousness. Nate's head whipped around. His heart raced. He slowly lowered the window and stared into the eyes of a Calgary cop.

The constable nodded at him, rain dripping from the brim of his hat. "Good evening, sir," he said authoritatively.

Nate acknowledged the greeting with a nod of his head, looking puzzled.

"Are you alright?"

"I'm fine." Nate forced a smile.

"Your car has been running for some time and a concerned passerby thought there might be something wrong."

"Uh...no, no," he said, shaking his head in denial. "I just got off a long shift and found I was too tired to drive, so I pulled in here to catch a few, before heading home. Sorry I created a concern."

"Where was the shift?" the officer asked, studying Nate.

"Ski Shack," Nate responded naturally, falling back on his job that he had quit just before agreeing to go along with Jess's plan. He could feel a bead of sweat building on his brow, despite the cool air flowing into the car.

"Kind of out of the way, isn't it?"

"Yeah, I should've headed straight home, but I agreed to drop off a co-worker at his apartment downtown."

The officer looked at Nate for a couple of minutes and smiled.

"Okay, I think you better head home now then. That is, if you are all right."

"I'm fine." Nate smiled at him again.

"You have a good night, then."

Nate watched as the officer turned and headed back to his car.

He powered up his window. He let out a long breath and put his car in reverse and pulled out of the parking lot. Too close.

Nate turned to cross the bridge; the decision made. He had to know if Jess was alive, no matter the risk.

***

Nate saw lights flashing as he turned the corner to Jess's apartment. He pulled to the curb and sat there for a moment. He put the car in park, turned off the engine, and opened the door. The rain had stopped, but left a chill in the air, announcing that spring had not quite released its grip on Calgary. Nate headed into a throng of people standing outside the entrance to the building. Several police were milling about, talking to one another. Lights flashed from a pair of cruisers. A group of firefighters were standing by one engine, while others were up on a ladder attached to a second

43

engine, with hoses at the ready beside a window of the building. A small amount of smoke billowed from the now broken window. An attendant stood at the door of an ambulance, looking bored.

"What's going on?" Nate asked, approaching what appeared to be a young resident from the building.

"We've been evac'd," he replied, turning to look at Nate. Just then a CTV news truck arrived, and a young woman and camera-man jumped out.

"It's pretty bad," he continued. "Someone lit up a woman's apartment. Super says someone's dead too. Crazy. We're lucky the building didn't burn down, but they've got it mostly under control now. Jesus," the kid added, with a shake of his head.

Nate didn't respond, moving away from the kid. The CTV news crew were now set up and Nate could see the red light of the camera pointed to the reporter, as she announced her story. Nate stepped away, not wanting to be caught on camera.

Just then the building's front door opened, and paramedics wheeled a gurney towards the ambulance. There was a black body bag attached to the top of it. It all felt surreal to him. She was dead. Now what? Just a few days ago, they had been on top of the world, planning for a new future. How had it all come to this?

He felt his emotions collide. *This is all my fault, I should have said no to her or got her to see how stupid her idea was. Then she'd still be alive.* Nate convulsed.

He watched the gurney being lifted into the ambulance. The cameraman turned to pan the bystanders, pointing the camera directly at a group Nate was standing in. He shifted, hiding his face. Two tough looking men stood in another throng of people, scanning the faces of the bystanders. Not good.

Nate turned and lumbered back to his car. He knew what had become of Jess and felt sick about it. What could he have done differently? Halfway there he turned back, one of the men had broken away to follow him. Nate heard the deep-throated sound of a Harley firing to life. He broke into a run. In full flight, he pulled his key from his coat pocket and hit the button for the door locks. He grabbed the door handle, swung it open and jumped in behind the wheel. The man was almost on him. Nate reached for the door and slammed it closed. He inserted his key into the ignition, looked up and saw the man had pulled a gun. Nate fired his engine to life, slamming his hand on the door lock. The pain in his shoulder roared. He pulled his gear into reverse, as his side window exploded into a thousand pieces, smashed by the butt of the gun. Glass flew everywhere showering Nate's face and hands. Stunned, Nate was vaguely aware of the man reaching inside the window for the door handle. Nate gunned the accelerator. The man's arm remained lodged inside the car and Nate heard his body slam into the side panel, before his arm pulled free. He disappeared, falling to the ground. Nate smashed into a car behind him. He surveyed the crowd. The noise had caught the attention of some who were pointing in his direction. He threw the car back into drive as the man rose from the pavement. He was still clutching his gun. Nate drove the car at him and redirected at the last moment, to avoid hitting him. The man jumped out of its path. Nate sped away, two shots ringing behind him. The back window burst apart, shards of glass raining down on the rear seat. At the end of the block, Nate turned the corner too fast, jumped the curb, and careened off a lamp post, before forcing the car back onto the roadway. He accelerated; thankful it was late at night. He'd escape into darkness. In the rear-view mirror, he watched a cop car mobilize and head in his direction.

He heard the bike before he saw it. It was accelerating, heading directly for him. Nate shifted the car into the centre of the road, blocking him from coming along side. The biker pulled up behind him, reaching inside his coat pocket. He wasn't sure what he was doing, but he wasn't about to let another guy start shooting at him. He hammered his foot onto the brake pedal, locking them up. The biker had no time to react, lost control and leaned to the side to lay the bike down. Nate saw a gun launch from his hand as he fought against the fall. Nate hit the gas, the car bucked forward, as the bike narrowly missed its rear. The biker hit the ground, sliding along the pavement, one foot extended. Nate hit the brake again watching the rider slide pass him. Throwing his gear shift into reverse, Nate swerved the car at the riderless bike and felt it crumple.

The rider was rising, and Nate slammed the gearshift into drive again, this time aiming the car at the rider, who scrambled to the side of the road. Nate roared past him, pointing the car down the street. Glancing into the rear-view mirror, he saw the rider standing in the street, staring at the back of his damaged car as it pulled away. The last thing Nate saw, as he turned the corner of an adjoining street, was the police cruiser skidding to a stop behind the biker.

Nate knew he didn't have much time. First, his car was a sight likely to attract a lot of attention. Secondly, he had just committed a hit and run on the streets of Calgary, as the police watched.

The cops at the scene would have their hands full with the bikers, trying to sort out what happened and whether there was a connection to the abduction or fire that happened a half block away. Surely a call had gone out to mobilize other police in the area, to track him down. He would be a person of interest and they'd be motivated to find him.

What a mess, he thought, pulling his car onto Memorial Drive, heading back to the river. His freedom wouldn't last. The plates were in his name, as was the registration.

Nate pulled into a dark parking lot adjoining the river, beside a small power substation. He was a block from the main road on a quiet street. He felt sure he would be reasonably safe until the morning, when the car would be found and reported to the police, given its condition. Nate got out and went to the rear of his car. He heard the lock pop as he pressed his key fob. The lid didn't lift of its own accord, and he had to pull it open. It had been damaged during all the action.

He headed one block north to Memorial Drive, pulling his two large suitcases behind him, Jess's knapsack securely over his shoulders. No doubt he was a sight. Within minutes he was on a bus heading back into the city centre. The driver had looked him over, as he manhandled his two large cases and knapsack onto the bus. Nate had not seen him make any calls, which would've alerted him to a further problem. The driver could figure out who he was if he heard what had happened in the area, but by then he hoped to be long gone.

He pulled out his burner phone and arranged accommodation for the night. Once they found the car and put out a bulletin with his name on it, he'd have nowhere to hide. Nate got off the bus in front of the Palliser Hotel, with the driver smiling at him, as he laboured his bags down the steps and stood next to the entrance to the hotel. As far as the driver would know, he had entered the hotel. Further queries would likely resolve, that in fact, the driver did not actually see him enter the building.

Watching the bus drive away, Nate swivelled to look up at the hotel entrance. A sense of sadness overwhelmed him. It had all started here.

He drew a hand through his hair, turned back to the street, flagged a taxi down, and climbed into the backseat, after the driver placed his luggage in the trunk. He was eager to disappear.

***

After checking into another less than sterling motel, Nate sat on the edge of the bed, closed his eyes and allowed the events of the day to flood into his brain. *Jess.*

Shaking off a conjured image manifesting her fate, Nate walked over to his coat and pulled out his phone. He tapped in a memorized number and waited as the phone rang.

"Frank, it's Nate."

"Nate, what's going on? Pretty late for a call. Whose number is this, anyway?"

"Frank...I'm in big trouble and have very little time." Things were spiralling out of his control.

"Where are you, lad?"

After telling him, Nate called a local restaurant and arranged for some food to be brought to his room. He had no appetite but figured it would be some time before he'd eat anything substantial. Everything was now a matter of survival.

CHAPTER SEVEN

NATE STUFFED THE LAST BITE of what could only be described as tasteless food into his mouth. He waited for his uncle to arrive at the motel. He opened the suitcases and knapsack and dumped all the cash on the bed. He stacked the bundles, counted them, and slowly sat down in the room's only chair. Two million, three hundred thousand and change. He stared at the money; it was more than he had ever seen. Conflicting thoughts coursed through his mind. On the one hand, he felt guilty having the money Jess had given her life for. On the other, new possibilities for his life seeped into his view. Despite himself, a small smile formed on his lips, which disappeared instantly at the sound of a double knock on his motel room door. He rose from his chair and stepped to the window beside the bed. Seeing his uncle standing there, alone, Nate opened the door and stepped back.

Frank Ricci was in his late fifties with greying hair and a thick neck. One look at his six-foot, two-inch frame said this was a man who had once been very fit. Years of good wine and pasta had taken a modest toll, but Frank Ricci could still hold his own if pushed too hard.

A man with a rough past who had toiled as a mid-level thug for the mob, he earned his release through a major favour for the head of the Calgary organization, one don Antonio Belletti. Nate knew all this, as he and his uncle were quite open, but had never learned of the favour that earned his uncle the unusual release. Of this, Nate was told, there'd be no discussion.

Frank Ricci had, from that day forward, maintained a low profile, running a furniture store in the neighbourhood known as *Little Italy*. He had stayed in touch with the don, doing small, and for the most part, legitimate favours. Every Christmas he was invited to the home of Antonio Belletti for his swanky Christmas celebration, which he and his wife threw in the hopes of impressing the elite of Calgary.

Frank thought he had seen it all, but when he saw the stack of money sitting on the bed, his eyes went wide, his mouth gaped, and for a moment he was speechless. His eyes shifted from the money. He stared hard at Nate, who stood on the opposite side of the bed, as if he were a child again, waiting to be punished.

"You look like shit, Nate."

"Chasing the dream, Frank," Nate said, an attempt at humour that fell flat. He rubbed his shoulder.

"For years, I tried to get you into the business, only to be told you wanted a normal life. This doesn't look fucking normal."

Tears welled up in Nate's eyes. "I need some help, Frank." Nate had always called his uncle by his first name. Frank had insisted on it.

"Could this have to do with a certain theft from a certain biker community?" Frank asked.

A tear fell from Nate's left eye as he nodded his head. He forcibly swiped it away.

"My past employer won't be too happy about all this, Nate. A lot of people are going to be looking for you. Who was the girl, by the way?"

Another tear escaped his eye. "What's the family got to do with this, Frank?"

"Seems your newfound wealth might be owned by them. At least, that's the word."

"We took it from the *Raiders*," Nate said.

Frank looked sternly at him. Nate's shoulders visibly sagged, all the pieces falling into place, weighing him down.

"Who is 'we,' Nate?"

"Can you give it back to them?"

"Sure, and then I can plan to attend your funeral, assuming I'm alive to do so. You've created a real problem here."

Nate returned to the rooms' only chair and sat down, his head now in his hands. Nate felt guilt rain down on him.

His uncle had always been there for him. Always in his camp. Nate remembered when Frank took him in. It had taken days for his mother to go, after the car crash, but his uncle had stayed by his sister's side, day and night, unlike Nate's deadbeat of a father. She knew she was dying and had impressed upon Frank the need, no, more like the moral duty to look after the only good thing that had come out of her abusive marriage to Randy Vickers. Since then, Frank Ricci had raised Nate as his own and treated him as a son. He had held him in his arms when she died and again when Frank had told Nate his father had died too. Nate never learned how he died but was sure his uncle had a hand in ensuring Nate would never suffer his abuse again.

Now here he was, repaying the man for all his efforts. His thoughts clouded. How could he have put his uncle in this position?

Frank let out a long stream of air from his mouth, deep in thought.

"I'll ask again — who is 'we,' Nate?"

"Her name was Jess, but it doesn't matter now. She's dead."

Frank's face showed little surprise. In fact, it showed little of anything. No anger, no consternation, no empathy. Nate couldn't remember his uncle being this inanimate.

Frank exhaled, deep in thought. "Anybody see you doing what you were doing?"

"There was a chase, a couple guys might have gotten a look at me."

Frank nodded. "Perhaps you better tell me all about it." He sat on the edge of the bed, staring at the bundles of cash. "And don't leave out any details."

A half hour later, Nate waited for Frank to say something. He had listened intently to Nate's story and asked few questions. He allowed several minutes to pass before his eyes met Nate's.

"Pack it up...we need to get you somewhere safe," he said.

***

In another room, twenty-five kilometres away, a different conversation was underway.

"How'd you let that little *idioto* get away?" Pablo Cortez asked. He was a powerfully built man, born and raised in Mexico City. His parents had immigrated to Canada in the late seventies, hoping to spare their only child from a life of ever-increasing violence in Mexico. Pablo was proof that fate had a way of balancing all ledgers. He scratched at an old knife wound on his chin.

The large, tattooed man staring back at him said quietly, "He was resourceful, but we'll find him."

"Will you? Do you know who he is?" he said. The man shook his head.

"I thought not." Pablo glared at the man. "The trail is going cold, *amigo*. Not only that, but now we must lose a valued member of our team to a fucking lock-up. I trust you have impressed upon him the lifesaving need to stay silent."

"Of course, Pablo."

"I don't have to tell you that my employer is not happy with the way this has turned out, nor how much attention we are receiving from the press and *la policia*." The fact that Pablo had not yet talked to his employer was irrelevant. He knew what the outcome would be.

The man opened his mouth to speak.

"Shut the fuck up," Pablo cursed through gritted teeth. "Put the word on the street, quietly, and I mean quietly, I want this *idioto's* head in a bag at my feet. I don't care how long it takes. Do you understand me?"

The man nodded but said nothing.

"Now *vamos*, get out of here and hope that I can prevent my employer from shooting you while you're asleep."

He watched as his soldier left, then Pablo snatched up his phone. He paused for a moment to consider his approach, then punched in a number.

"*Senor* Belletti," Pablo said into the mouthpiece, "a moment of your time, *por favor*."

***

Antonio Belletti pressed the end button on his phone and set it down on his desk. He had been reading the morning edition of the *Herald*, coffee in hand, as he did every morning. It allowed him time to collect his thoughts, before his day began. The call had been an unwelcome intrusion.

Swivelling in his chair, he stared out the window that overlooked a large ravine full of fir and aspen trees. His reflection in the glass caused him to soften the angry image portrayed. He was a small man, five foot six, with hooded dark brown eyes and a full head of grey hair neatly combed to the side. What had once been a muscular frame when he started in the business had softened over time. His ever-extending belly proved how much he loved his life.

Those who knew him casually would call him a generous man, supporting his neighbourhood community, funding almost every request that came his way. He was famous for the weekly Italian feasts that he and his wife Sofia put on for the community after Sunday Mass. Those that knew him more intimately would say that Antonio Belletti also had a dark side. When displayed, it struck fear into most men and usually resulted in violence in one form or another, carried out by one of the two identical twin henchmen, often at his side. That's not to say that Antonio Belletti shied away from meting out justice personally. His attention was saved for those he suspected of disloyalty to himself or the family.

Antonio's mood soured quickly. He did not like losing money. Ever. To lose it to a pair of thieves, out of one of his own ware-houses, supposedly protected by a gang working for him — well, that was unforgivable. He was not looking forward to advising his Montreal masters either, as they would see this as his failure, and it would be equally unforgivable. Adding insult to injury, the aftermath was sloppy and would likely create a more difficult climate for Antonio and his associates to conduct their business, for a time. Local police did not like to look bad in the public's eye. With all the press this was going to get, Antonio knew, this would make them look bad. Montreal would not be happy with that either.

He opened the *Herald* and reread a pair of articles, in a new light. Antonio picked up his phone.

"Luigi?" Antonio paused for effect. "Did you hear about last night's events?" Luigi looked after the day to day "administrative needs" for Antonio.

"Just finished reading 'bout it. One of ours, I assume, from your call." Luigi's voice resonated the Bronx of New York.

"It was," said don Belletti." I want you to reach out to our friends on the force. Call in favours if you must. Our Associates told Pablo that they trashed the guy's car. It will be around. I want you to find it. See what you can learn from it. Also, see if there are any clear shots of our friends face on any of the city cameras."

"Done."

"And Luigi, do this quietly. There is going to be a lot of heat. I'd prefer it doesn't come my way."

Antonio ended the call and hit one of his frequently phoned numbers.

"Mario, I want you and Angelo to come and see me. We have a mess to clean up." He didn't wait for their response. He knew he could count on the twin henchmen to take care of all manner of unpleasant tasks that he required.

Antonio took a moment to compose himself. He was going to have to be convincing. He picked up the phone and punched in a number and listened to the phone ring. He tried to wave off the feeling in his stomach. Montreal would want assurances that Antonio was looking after their business interests and that he would make this right. And that was exactly what he would do.

A short while later, after Antonio had shaken off the effects of the stressful call, and having determined he had things in motion, he turned to some personal tasks. He looked at his calendar. Time to work out the details of the spring philanthropic dinner that he and Sofia sponsored each year. There was nothing that Antonio loved more than seeing his beloved wife being given the accolades for all the hard work that their organization produced for the community. After all, life was all about community.

As if on cue, his phone rang. He recognized the number and forced away his criminal personality. It was time to be charming.

CHAPTER EIGHT

FRANK RICCI SAT IN HIS office, reflecting on the past few days. The discussions started with an acceptance that Nate would have to disappear. Nate had wanted to keep in touch, but Frank made him understand that for the safety of all concerned, they'd have to stay away from each other, for a very long time. As they worked through the details of what would have to be done, they quietly finished the better part of an eighteen-year-old bottle of single malt Scotch, which Frank had been saving for some unknown reason. Promises were made, thank-you's were tossed about, and a warm hug between family occurred.

The next morning, Frank had gone off to set things in motion. Things would have to move fast. His biggest challenge was to use contacts he'd developed from years gone by, avoiding a trail of complicity that could lead back to him. It cost Frank dearly. The favours he now owed to a less than savoury man were something Frank wished he could've avoided. If this had been for anyone else, he knew he could have gone to the family to assist him. This wasn't anyone else though, and Frank had gone to "Fats" Domino to get a fake but strong identity for Nate.

Fats, nicknamed for his large mass and love of 50s music, had listened intently without asking a question. Once Frank had finished explaining what he needed, Fats sat his large backside on a rather small stool and contemplated the request. Frank stared at the rolls of his double chin, waiting for him to respond. After a couple of minutes, Fats nodded once, agreeing to help Frank, provided he pay his standard fee and assist with the laundering of a certain sum of money through Frank's furniture business, as a quid pro quo. Fats knew too well how he ran his business, which irked Frank. He had taken great pains to create, for the most part, a legitimate enterprise and here was this guy, trying to wedge himself into his day-to-day affairs. Fats made it quite clear that this part of his request was non-negotiable. When Frank wanted to know the source of the cash to be laundered, Fats had narrowed his hooded eyes, and in no uncertain terms, advised Frank that this was an unimportant detail. Dealing with Fats would be a risky exercise, especially due to Frank's existing relationship with the family, but the risk had to be borne, for the sake of Nate. Whether Fats had clued into the reason Frank wanted a new identity for his nephew or not, he never said.

That night, Frank heard a knock at the door of his tastefully decorated townhome. It was an older townhome, beside the Bow River, that Frank had spent a fair sum on to improve. Anxiety spiked when he opened the door to see a pair of police officers standing there, asking about Nate's whereabouts. He felt certain they didn't believe his "haven't seen him" response and he expected a further visit.

After they left, Frank made a quick call, then headed down to the basement. He walked to a bookcase, removed a book and flicked a switch. The door to a safe room popped opened, revealing Nate, laying on a cot, looking very bored. The safe room was built to provide shelter for Frank in times of need, although since his retirement he seldom entered the room and had considered dismantling it. Though it was hidden behind a false wall, Frank knew it would not survive a detailed search by local authorities.

"We need to move the plan up," Frank said.

"I'm for that." Nate sat up on the bed. "I'm bored out of my mind."

Frank did not respond.

Sheepishly, Nate added. "Sorry, Frank. I have no right to complain. What's happened?"

"Did you hear the doorbell?"

"No."

"That was the police, looking for you. I held them at bay, but I'm betting we have a day, maybe two, and they'll be back, warrant in hand. You need to be gone by then."

The press had kept the story alive, keeping the police engaged in their hunt for Nate. It was a story of intrigue, that helped sell papers, and as each day passed, the danger for Nate grew.

"How about my new I.D?" Nate appealed.

"My contact will have it mostly ready tomorrow morning. All it'll need is a photo. Then you move."

Nate nodded. Frank smiled, trying to reassure Nate, but he could see the stress behind Nate's eyes. He closed the door quietly and retreated upstairs.

The next day when Frank brought a disguised Nate in for the required photo, Fats took Frank aside, demanding additional funds to finish the job. The so called "risk parameters" had increased, naturally necessitating a risk premium. And of course, the amount of laundered cash would also increase, as an increment of that premium. Fats smirked at Frank, as he waited for his expected acknowledgment.

Frank knew he had little choice and conceded to Fat's demands, making a mental note to himself, that the "Fats" ledger would have to be dealt with in the future.

Four hours later, Frank was behind his desk at the store, fuming at how Fat's had gotten the better of him. Shaking his head, as if to clear it, he forced his thoughts back to the present. He poured himself a third cup of coffee, eyeing the payables in front of him. He was having a hard time concentrating.

The front door of his store opened; he heard Elena Romano, his store manager, ask someone if she could be of assistance.

"I want to see Franco." The voice was laden in a heavily accented Italian dialect. Frank closed his eyes.

"He's busy at the moment," he heard Elena respond, and watched as she stepped in front of the advancing man, who side stepped around her, his eyes locking on Frank's, who had now risen from his desk. Elena tossed her hands up as she looked directly at Frank with apologetic eyes.

Frank emerged from his office, smiling his best salesman smile at the advancing man. He wiped his sleeve across his brow to hide a bead of sweat that suddenly emerged. Mario de Luca, or was it Angelo de Luca, he never could get the two of them straight, was stomping towards him. To Frank's knowledge, neither of the two men had ever been in his shop, but the man knew exactly where he was going. It was always Luigi, or on occasion the don himself, that would come by, but never one of the don's henchmen.

"It's okay El, thank you" Frank said with a nod towards her. She held his gaze for a second until he smiled warmly at her. "I'll look after him."

She returned his smile, then turned back to dusting the furniture on the floor.

Frank gestured for the man to follow and walked back into his office. He closed the door and turned into a cold stare. He returned to his desk chair and sat down, immediately wishing he hadn't, as he looked up at the man glaring at him.

"Boss wants to see you, Franco."

"Sure, what's up?"

"Now, Franco," he said, ignoring the question.

Frank knew the arrival of this man meant things had taken a turn for the worse. He needed time to prepare.

"Kind of busy wrapping a few thinks up. How 'bout I come by this afternoon?"

"Now, Franco." The response came across as a low growl. He took a step closer to Frank to emphasize his point.

Frank fought the urge to close his eyes in surrender. "Okay, okay. Let's go." He stood and retrieved his jacket off the back of the door and slipping it on, opened the door. He headed to the front of the store with the henchman following close behind.

"Back in a while, El," he said. Seeing the concern in her eyes he added, "It's alright."

A short while later, Frank was standing at the open door to don Belletti's office. The don was on the phone but waved for Frank to take a seat in one of two overstuffed leather chairs, opposite his desk. Frank was grateful for the chatter, after the unnerving silent ride over in the de Luca car. The door closed quietly behind him as he sat down. Frank glanced back and could see de Luca had stayed in the room. He looked at Frank with dead eyes but said nothing.

The don laughed at something the person on the other end of his phone said, all the while watching Frank, with a chilly stare. "Listen, I have to go. I will look forward to hearing more about the funds raised, when we talk next." He laughed again, his gaze never wavering from Frank. "Perfect. Until then." Belletti laid his phone on his desk.

He leaned forward, clasped his hands in front of him, then got right to the point.

"Where's Nathaniel, Franco?"

"Nate?" Frank brushed the question off.

"That's what I said." Frank sensed the edge in don Belletti's voice.

"I have no idea, Antonio," Frank said, using the don's given name to personalize the discussion. "What's going on?"

Antonio Belletti stroked his chin, his blue eyes never moving from Frank's face. He wore a striped, black suit, that complimented his open collared white shirt. As usual, the don was dressed impeccably. In any other setting, Antonio Belletti could easily be mistaken for a banker, but this was don Belletti. Frank knew better than to underestimate him.

Belletti moved his hand to toy with a cufflink on the right arm of his shirt. "We have a long and valued history, you and I, Franco. For the sake of that history, and because I've always liked you, I am going to ask you the question once more. I hope you will do me the honour of answering in a more truthful manner. Where is Nathaniel?"

Frank forced himself to stare straight into Antonio Belletti's eyes. To look away could mean the difference between life and death.

"I haven't heard from Nate for about ten days," he said. "Antonio, what is going on?"

Don Belletti raised his hands to his face and bridged his fingers across his nose. He studied the face of Frank Ricci. A full two minutes went by. He did not say a word, nor did he look away from Frank's face. Frank held his gaze. He wanted to swallow. His throat was parched. He knew it would make him look nervous, so he waited.

"A week ago, one of my warehouses was broken into and the contents were removed by two people. One of the two people, I have come to learn, was Nathanial."

"What?" Frank feigned confusion. "Nate is a good boy, Antonio. Your information must be wrong."

"My information is never wrong, Franco," Belletti said, his voice rising an octave.

"Forgive me, Antonio. This doesn't make sense to me. What information?"

Antonio Belletti let second's pass. "There was a chase, Nathaniel got into a fight with some of our associates before escaping. A car was demolished. Some friends of ours confirmed the car was owned by Nathaniel."

"Perhaps his car was stolen. Nate isn't a violent guy. You've known him since he was a boy."

"No!" shouted the don, not allowing Frank to deflect his resolve. "Our associates confirmed his identity through a photo that I had Sofia provide." Sofia was the don's wife, who constantly took pictures of all who attended her functions.

Frank slumped in his chair. He went quiet.

"Now, Franco, where is he?"

Frank pulled out his phone. "May I?" he asked. Belletti nodded his approval.

Frank punched in Nate's number, knowing it wouldn't work.

The number you have dialed is not in service, the message announced across the room. Antonio Belletti continued to study him. Frank could almost feel his mind entering his; probing, searching, determining the truth. He had to be smart.

"I honestly don't know," he said, looking squarely at the don, hitting the cancel button on his phone.

"This is a very serious situation, Franco. He has stolen a lot of money from me. And... I want it back."

"What about the other person, perhaps you could find him. Maybe he could shed some light on all this. You know him to be a good boy, Antonio. There must be an explanation."

"He was a good boy," don Belletti corrected. "The other person is no longer able to provide us an explanation, Franco, but she gave up Nathaniel as well. I didn't wish to believe it, myself. How could the nephew of a trusted friend be involved in this? But our associates and friends have proven to me that loyalty, like all things, can be betrayed. Franco, you must give him to me. Wrongs must be righted."

"Antonio, please..."

"Enough." Belletti stood and walked around the side of his desk. "Find him, Franco, you have one week. Prove your loyalty to me. While I cannot forgive Nathaniel's indiscretions, I can make sure his punishment is just and as painless as possible, but only if you help right this wrong." Belletti laid a hand on Frank's shoulder and squeezed gently.

"Antonio..." Frank could feel the hand squeeze harder before Belletti spoke again.

"Mario will take you back now. You have one week." The don nodded to Mario who stepped to the door, opening it. Frank rose facing Antonio Belletti.

"I don't know where he is, Antonio."

Belletti turned his back on Frank to stare out the rear window. He did not turn around.

"One week, Franco...not a day more will be given."

Frank stared at Belletti's back. Mario quietly said. "This way, Franco."

CHAPTER NINE

NATE WAS IN A HURRY to leave Calgary. His new identity was convincing, giving him hope that he might get out of the mess he had stepped into. He liked the new name — Nate Beckett. It was the type of name that sounded like you were in control. The type of name that rolled easily off the tongue when telling someone your name for the first time. And he wouldn't slip up remembering a new first name. He had always liked the name Nate, and though his uncle had thought he should change both names, he was glad he'd stood his ground.

It took all his willpower to follow the strategy they had devised. He wanted to put as much real estate as possible between himself and Calgary, as fast he could, but he knew the plan was solid and he would stick to it. He wished he and Frank had tried to figure out everything together, but Frank thought it too dangerous for Nate. So, they had devised only the escape. The rest was up to Nate.

He expected the bikers to be searching for him but the revelation that he had crossed the family added another dimension entirely. The added pressure by the police wasn't helping either.

Nate felt his stomach convulse as he contemplated all manner of ways the plan could unravel.

He headed east in the direction of Medicine Hat, making sure that he didn't exceed the one hundred ten-kilometre speed limit, that was posted for Highway 1. He drove a sixteen-year-old Nissan that he purchased for six thousand in cash from a guy his uncle knew. It wasn't pretty, but he had been assured that it was of sound mechanical ability. With its age, it was unlikely to attract unwanted attention. It'd be discarded once he reached his destination. An acceptable expense for him to get him out of the city, quietly.

In the wee hours of the morning, he stuffed the cash in the side panels of all four of the Nissan's doors, leaving Jess's knapsack – that was never far from him – to deal with any unforeseen expenses on his journey. His efforts had gone unnoticed to the best of his knowledge, but he had not slept well. He felt it necessary to check on the car every hour, on the hour. His emptied suitcases now had enough new clothes for him to last a week or so. They lay in the trunk above the wheel well, where the spare tire used to be, also stuffed with cash. Having discarded the tire to free up another hiding space, Nate hoped he didn't have a flat.

He was sure that his picture was being circulated to a lot of people, some by the police who desperately wanted to talk to him about the events at Jess's apartment, others by the *Raiders* to an entirely different but much more dangerous group.

He looked at himself in his car mirror. Though he had used the last four days to grow a stubble on his face and had changed the colour of his hair to a dark brown, he knew his transformation was not yet complete. He would grow a full bushy beard; confident it would match his heavy eyebrows. There was nothing he could do about his bright blue eyes, but he knew that in time they would look better than they did now. He would cut and style his hair much shorter and look far less a rebel. In time, only those that knew him well would recognize him.

The image returning his gaze was tired. Tired from his broken sleep the night before. Tired from emotional drain. As he studied his face, he was convinced that he could see lines that had not been there before. Lines he attributed to stress. If only he had never met Jess. Why did she control him so easily? Was he chasing love? He would never know. The weight of her death smothered him. He should have said no. Now he was on the run. Would he ever be in love again? He doubted it. Hell, he wouldn't even be able to tell another woman his real name.

With a final look at himself, Nate brought his gaze back to the road. He had been nervous leaving the relative safety of his uncle's room, but nothing had happened. As far as he could tell, he wasn't being followed. He had deliberately stopped for gas just outside of Calgary, allowing himself to be caught on camera. He wanted anyone, who was able to track him, to think he was headed for Ontario.

An hour east of Calgary, after checking that there was no tail, Nate turned onto a dirt range road and headed south. He had never been happier to see the skyline of Calgary fade away. The dust plume behind him blocked out any chance to see if he was followed. Ten minutes later, he turned west onto another range road and glancing back, was glad he could see across the spring crops. No other dust plumes followed him. Nate made another turn, this time onto pavement and headed south again.

One by one, the Alberta farm towns of Vulcan, Champion, and Barons flew by. Nate wanted to pull over and satisfy his growling hunger, but he needed to blend in with a lot of people. No reason to take any chances now that he had a tail wind behind him. He thought about turning east into Lethbridge, but the sooner he made his way to the border the better. He drank from the bottle of water that he had purchased when he gassed up, hoping it would sate his hunger, and he let his mind wander again as he sped down the secondary highway.

He would probably be dead now, if it wasn't for his uncle. He reflected on how he'd always been there for him, with just the right amount of discipline and love, a kick in the pants here, a pat on the head there. His uncle was as good a father figure as anyone could ask for, even though he really had no idea what a good father should be like. He knew his uncle was probably disappointed in him, though it had never been voiced. Though he had asked Nate if he wanted in the business, Nate always thought he was secretly proud of him for wanting to extricate himself from the world that was his. One thing was certain, he now owed his uncle a debt he wasn't sure he could ever repay.

The guilt of his situation rolled over him. How could he have put his uncle in such a precarious position? He thought about pulling over to compose himself, but decided that was too risky, especially if a cruising Mountie should happen upon him. So, he drove on, allowing his thoughts to consume him.

He had to stop thinking about "what if." This penchant for guilt wasn't helping; guilt about his uncle, what had happened to Jess, and what he had done to his own life. It had to end. It was counterproductive. He was headed for a new life with a lot of money to get started. Nate Vickers was a mess, but he was dead. Nate Beckett had to think differently.

Nate nodded, as if that would make his mind as clear as the road ahead. He turned on his radio and allowed the music to act as a balm for his troubles.

At the junction to Highway 3, he considered heading into Lethbridge driven by the urge to satisfy his hunger, but with a steely resolve, he turned right and headed west to the mountains. Food would have to wait.

Nate had passed Pincher Creek, when he spotted lights in his rear-view mirror. They were moving fast. There had to be six of them, not cars. Bikes. Their scattered lights filled his mirror. He had come so far. The pangs of hunger he felt disappeared.

Damn you, Jess, he thought, not for the last time. *Why did I let you talk me into this?* Nate braced as the lights filled his vision.

***

Three hundred kilometres to the north, Mario was dropping Frank Ricci back at his storefront. Usually silent, Mario looked at Frank and repeated what had been playing over and over in Frank's mind. "One week," he said.

Frank got out of the car without responding, closed the door quietly and walked through the front door of his store. He did not look back.

Elena rushed over to him. "Are you alright?" She saw, in an instant, that he was not.

"I'm fine. Come with me."

Frank walked into his office and dialed the combination on his floor safe. Elena watched as he did, fidgeting, her nerves on edge. Frank withdrew four tall stacks of bills and handed them to her.

"There is forty thousand dollars here," he said. "It's for you."

"Frank?"

"Please don't interrupt, El. I am going away for a while. Maybe a long while. I want you to be looked after."

Elena's dark brown eyes teared up, in her slightly chubby face. Frank watched her emotions coming to the surface.

Elena Romano lived an ordinary life. Born to second generation Italian parents, she had grown up in Calgary, gone to a Roman Catholic school where she had been graded middle of her class, and went to work right after graduation. She had drifted through administrative jobs, never finding anything that challenged her, then she happened upon Frank Ricci at a local eatery. She had learned he was looking for help and had applied for the job. She had been with him ever since and they had grown very fond of each other. She was an average-looking woman, but what she lacked in looks she made up for in personality. A personality that Frank Ricci had grown to appreciate. One he would miss.

"Where are you going, Frank, and for how long?" she asked, her brows etched in consternation.

"I don't know El. I have to try and find Nate."

"What's going on, Frank?" Elena looked down at the money in her hands, then looked back at him. "Is he missing?" Her face changed to one of determination, then she went on, "Who was that guy you left with, Frank? I didn't like the looks of him at all. Does this have anything to do with your other life?"

Frank closed his eyes for a moment. If she understood his relationship with the family, she had never given an indication of her knowledge. She had seen him with many of the don's people over the years. Perhaps she had put it all together.

He looked at her, compassion in his eyes, then sighed. "It's complicated."

"There is no one here and I have all morning."

"El, I can't do this." Frank's heart lurched at the hurt in her eyes. He watched her blink rapidly, holding back tears that now threatened to flow.

Elena placed the money on the top of Frank's desk. "How long are you gone for?" she asked quietly.

"I really don't know." Frank took a deep breath. "Nate has gotten himself into some serious trouble. I helped him, but that help is unravelling. I need to find him, be there for him, and hope we can figure out what to do. I can't do that from here."

Elena looked at him and shook her head. "I want to come with you."

"El..." Frank said, gritting his teeth. "It's too dangerous." Frank understood her feelings for him, perhaps he had even encouraged it, but this was no game.

"I need you to stay. Lock up the store tonight, and don't come back."

"But Frank...the store, you can't mean that?"

"The bank can have it...this is serious, El. I have to find him."

"Do you know where to start?"

"No, but I know how he thinks, and I know the direction he has gone. I have some ideas."

Just then, the front bell signalled someone coming into the store. "I want to talk about this some more, Frank," Elena said, heading out to greet the customer.

Frank watched her go, then he rose from his desk, and picked up the money she had left behind. He stuffed it in her large purse, hanging on a hook on the back of his office door. He reached into the safe and withdrew five more stacks of money and a small 9mm handgun, along with a box of ammunition, and slid it into a knapsack he stored in his filing cabinet. Thinking twice, he reached down and withdrew the remaining one hundred thousand dollars he had in the safe, put two more bundles of cash in Elena's purse – which was now overflowing – and put the rest into his knapsack. Then, he closed the door and spun the combination lock and walked to the door.

Looking out, he saw Elena animatedly explaining the benefits of a dual controlled bed, and with sadness, turned and walked out the store's rear door, heading for his parked BMW. He knew his departure would be announced when he exited the door, so he hurriedly started his car and pulled out of the parking lot. He looked in his mirror and saw her standing in the doorframe, staring after him. His heart sank. He stopped the car, staring at her through the mirror for what seemed an eternity. She headed for his stopped car. He stepped on the gas and disappeared down the street.

He had never known love before and figured he never would. Now he understood that he had. He wondered if he would ever see her again. He suspected probably not. His heart ached to bring her. No, she deserved better.

Frank saw movement in his rear-view mirror, a black Mercedes pulled away from a curb and started to follow him.

He made no pretence of where he was going, pulling into the driveway of his townhome and waiting for the garage door to fully open. He drove ahead closing the door behind him. Once secured, he entered his home and tossed the knapsack onto his couch and strode over to the front window, peering out. As expected, the black Mercedes was parked down the street, under a tree, facing directly towards his home. Frank searched the opposite direction. A newer white Ford Taurus was parked alongside the curb. Near as Frank could tell, no one was in it. This was a quiet street. Frank knew most of the cars that were on it and that Ford was not one of the usuals.

A visitor or maybe not, Frank pondered.

He tramped into the kitchen, opened the refrigerator door and pulled out a beer. Twisting off the cap, he moved into the living room and sat in his favourite over-stuffed chair. It faced the street. He kept his eyes on the Mercedes.

Taking a long swig from the Mexican beer, he sucked the contents through his teeth and contemplated his next move.

CHAPTER TEN

THE HARLEYS CLOSED THE DISTANCE to the back of Nate's car in a flash. Nate's eyes darted between the road ahead and the bikes in his mirror. The first three pulled out and passed, just as a car rounded the corner on the two-lane highway heading for them. Throttling their engines, they went by, with a roar, then laid off the throttles, slowing down in front of him. The other three held back. Nate knew about bikes. He recognized two of the models; one was a Fat Boy soft tail, the other a Sportster model. The third he couldn't make out. These were not the bikes of a biker gang. The rear bikes pulled out to pass and rocketed by him, joining their friends waiting for them. Nate heard the thunder as they throttled up in unison and pulled away. He let out a mouthful of air as if he were a blowfish. He hadn't realized, until then, he had been holding his breath. The fear had been very real and palpable and was becoming far too familiar.

Nate pulled into a quiet back road, beside the meandering Elk River. He put the car in park and surveyed the area, hoping he was alone. Other than a lone fly fisherman standing in the water, lazily casting his line down river, he was safe, for the moment. He checked his door locks. The trees reflected light from new spring leaves, and the sky shone a bright blue on this cloudless day. Nate's eyes rested on the beautiful snow-capped mountains and thought how this would have been a perfect day, if he and Jess had come here to ponder their future, rather than taking the steps that found them in a dusty old warehouse, stealing from one of the most feared groups in Calgary.

The vision of the body bag conjured up thoughts of the gruesome death Jess must have endured. A profound sadness overwhelmed him, as he stared out of the window, watching the fly rod snapping its hook out into the river in search of its prey. It was not lost on him that many people were casting their lines in search of him, as well. How incredibly selfish he had been. He had bought into Jess's dreams because he wanted to be with her. Now he was alone. He had placed his uncle in extreme danger. He lost a chance at a normal life because of greed. Sadness grew, a tear slipped from his right eye. Before long, tears formed one upon another and his shoulders heaved. So much for leaving the guilt with Nate Vickers.

***

Nate awoke with a start, unsure when he had fallen asleep. The sun was setting, the fisherman long gone. Nate scanned the area for others. Feeling confident that he was now alone, he got out of his beat-up old car, and meandered to the river. His body ached from sitting too long. He stretched to ease his discomfort. He bent down and cupped a handful of the glacial water, using it to rinse his face and neck. He dried his face with his shirt. He took a deep breath and stared out over the river, marvelling at the late day shadows. Climbing back into his car, he fired up the engine.

The United States border crossing at Roosville was a short drive away. That would throw a curve at any potential followers. But as he sat there, his mind fresh from sleep, he understood how bad the idea was. If his car was searched, he'd never be able to explain the money. Besides, they probably had his photo, courtesy of the police. No, it was probably best to just get to where he wanted to go, via a circuitous Canadian route.

Nate peered out over the river again and with a sigh, put the car in reverse, and backed onto the road leading back to the highway. As he turned west, heading towards the setting sun, Nate resolved one thing. No matter where he ended up or what he ended up doing, his life was going to change. He would try, in small ways, to pay it forward with others. His days of living life on the edge were over. He owed that to his uncle and to the memory of Jess, even though he was quite certain she would have disapproved.

Damn you, Jess. He squared his shoulders and stepped on the accelerator, leaving the twinkling lights of Fernie behind him. He welcomed the coming darkness. It made him feel hidden and safe. He rubbed his shoulder. Still sore, but healing. He didn't think he had dislocated it, but he suspected he might have torn something. *Hopefully nothing too serious*, he thought. *I sure can't get it checked out anywhere.*

***

Frank Ricci rose from his chair. He analyzed every possibility and was as ready as he could be. He knew what he had to do. A shot of adrenaline coursed through his veins reminding him of his earlier years, when he'd acted as an enforcer for the very people he would now flee. He checked out the window again to see if the Ford had moved. It hadn't. Dusk was around the corner. He had effectively squandered one day of the seven that Antonio had given him, but that was the way it was.

Frank went into the kitchen, deciding he had better eat something. It could be some time before he was able to eat again. Once finished, he headed for his den and opened a cabinet door beside his desk. Pressing a hidden switch, a false door in the back of the cabinet popped open, revealing another stash of laundered money he had put away, courtesy of the fees he'd charged the family over the years. Frank removed it all, along with a small leather pouch that contained a new identity for him, if he needed it, and the details of his sizeable holdings that he had amassed over the years. He was glad he'd had the foresight to build his nest egg offshore.

He looked at the hidden compartment and left it open. His eyes cast about the room as if he was saying goodbye. Retracing his steps, he added the acquired money and pouch to his knapsack and tossed it over his shoulder. In the bedroom, he pulled out two changes of clothing from his closet and added it to the backpack. He tested the weight, deciding that was all he could take. He then changed out of his clothes into a dark pair of jeans and a navy sweater. He picked up his gun, double checked the safety switch was on, and tucked it into the top of his knapsack.

Frank closed the front blinds, then turned on several lights so that his watchers could see him settling in for the night. Doubling back to the kitchen, he turned off the lights, then moved to his patio door, which was now in semi darkness. Standing by the side of the door, he peeked out, allowing his eyes to adjust. There he was, they were so predictable. He didn't know who it was sitting on a bench beside the river, eyes trained on the back door of his home, but it made little difference.

Frank strode to a spare bedroom, closed the door and slid the window open as far as it would go, grateful he owned an end unit. He quietly removed the screen and slipped out the opening after dropping his knapsack to the ground. Moves like that were much easier when he was younger, he thought. He reached up and closed the window. No need for a neighbour to think something was askew.

Standing for a few minutes to make sure his friend in the park hadn't heard him, he crouched down and made his way below a hedge to a gate at the far end of the property. He had been quiet and no one, not even a dog, had set off any alarms. He slipped into the river park, backpack on his back, and hiked west, away from his townhome. He was going to miss that place and had no idea how he would deal with it now that he was leaving, probably for good. He had a thirty-minute walk ahead to get to a large central park with multiple ways to slip away. He was almost there when a remote snap of a broken branch alerted him. He glanced back. Two figures ran in his direction.

How in hell did they figure it out so fast? Frank ran, the weight of his pack slowing him down.

He rounded a corner on the path knowing the park opened to multiple sections. He had little time. He darted for a large grove of overgrown dogwoods while slipping his pack from his shoulders. He removed his 9mm gun and thumbed off the safety. He squatted behind the dense brush, slipping his pack into it and waited. The overhead path lights did not reach here, darkness became his ally.

Frank heard the men approaching cautiously. He was glad there was no moon tonight; it was difficult to see. He glimpsed a man's face reflected off the light of a cell phone he'd taken out to light the path forward. Bad idea.

The man's eyes searched the park. He nodded at his accomplice signaling he saw no sign of their target, then spoke.

"We need to assume Franco has gotten to the other side of this park. Head back and get the car. I'll search here and meet you at the park entrance across from here, hopefully with Marco. And Luigi...be careful. He's on the run. He may be older, but he's skilled."

"Angelo, you really think we should split up?"

"I'll handle that old man, if I find him."

With a grunt of acceptance, Luigi turned and ran back the way he had come.

Frank winced. Older? He gripped his 9mm tighter.

Reaching out, he quietly moved a branch. He watched as Angelo moved from bush to bush, tree stand to tree stand, looking for him, his phone lighting the way. Frank silently moved to the far side of the bush to stay hidden. He wished it was anyone other than Angelo looking for him. He knew him to be very capable. He stayed low and totally silent. The light approached. Frank crouched lower. The bushes rustled. Frank could hear a hand reach into them.

"What do we have here?" Angelo whispered.

Frank heard his bag being pulled from the dogwoods. He could tell the phone had been set down on the grass so that the bags zipper could be pulled back. Frank lunged from behind the stand, gun pointed directly at his target.

"I'll take that, Angelo."

Angelo spun in Frank's direction. From the light emanating from the phone, he saw the gun pointed directly at him.

Angelo moved toward Frank.

"Uh-uh...toss it at my feet. Don't make me kill you, Angelo."

Angelo stopped, recognizing his disadvantage. He tossed the bag to Frank's feet. Frank knelt slowly, retrieved the knapsack, his eyes and gun fixed on Angelo. He slipped the bag over his shoulder. "Toss me your gun too. Slowly."

"Why are you running, Franco?" Angelo bellowed.

"Keep your voice down. He's long gone. Toss me your gun. Now, Angelo...and the phone on the ground."

Angelo grunted. "This is bullshit, Franco. You can't cross Antonio."

He dropped to a knee, retrieved the phone from the ground, and flung it at Frank. Frank side-stepped it easily and watched it fall to the ground. The light went dim as it shone into the grass. Frank knelt slowly and picked it up, his gun never wavering from its target.

"I didn't cross anybody." he muttered, then added, "now, your gun, and don't be stupid."

Angelo unholstered his gun, while holding his jacket open and with two fingers on the handle, tossed the pistol to the ground.

"Knife too," Frank said as soon as the pistol was discarded. It joined the gun. Frank kicked the knife into a bush, leaving the gun lay where it had been tossed.

"Now move, we're going back to my place."

"What?"

"You heard me...I'll say it again, I don't want to kill you, Angelo, but I will, if you don't do as I say. Now move."

Angelo started back the way he had come. As he moved, Frank reached down and picked up Angelo's pistol.

"We just want the kid."

"I know what you want. Walk."

"Franco..."

"Shut up Angelo."

The rest of the walk back was in silence. Frank turned the phone light off when they reached the lit pathway. As they neared the river, Frank tossed Angelo's pistol into it. Angelo's head whipped around at the splash.

"It was just me. Keep going."

Frank expected Angelo would try something. He knew it wasn't in Angelo's nature to capitulate and the longer they were together the less Angelo would feel out of control. They were about halfway to the townhome when Angelo spun on Frank, leaping with his fist coiled to strike. Frank sidestepped Angelo and swung the pistol at his head, opening a gash below Angelo's eye. Angelo stutter-stepped backwards and stopped dead in his tracks when he saw the pistol levelled at his face. Angelo's face darkened as he wiped the blood from his cheek with the back of his hand.

"You will pay for this, Franco."

"Perhaps, but if you try that again, you won't get the chance. Am I clear?"

Angelo nodded, eyes boring into Frank's.

"Move."

He started walking again, Frank a few steps behind. They had just reached the back of Franco's townhome, when Angelo's phone rang in Frank's hand, startling both men. Frank hit the end button and tossed the phone into the darkness. Angelo said nothing. He turned to the rear door of Franks home.

"Change of plan. We're going to your car." Frank could see the Mercedes was still sitting there. If the call had been from Luigi and he suspected it had, it was only a matter of time before he backtracked, looking for Angelo.

Frank levelled the gun at Angelo from his waist so as not to be too obvious on a city street. They came alongside Angelo's car.

"Unlock the doors, then toss your keys onto the roof."

Angelo remained silent but did as he was told.

"Get in." Frank nodded to the driver's door.

Angelo didn't move.

"Last chance, Angelo, before I put a bullet in your head." Frank nodded at the car door again and raised the pistol up and pointed it at Angelo's head. He had to hope no one was watching.

Angelo got in and closed the car door, sitting behind the wheel. Frank retrieved the keys, walked around the front of the car, still pointing the gun at Angelo through the window. He opened the passenger door and got in.

Frank tossed the keys into Angelo's lap, with his left hand. The gun remained in his right hand, pointed at Angelo.

"Drive."

"Where?"

"Nose Hill Park, off Edgemont Drive. Take Crowchild Trail, we don't want to run into Luigi, do we?"

Angelo started the car but didn't put the car into gear. He stared ahead.

Frank sighed. "Now, Angelo. It's almost over, you may live if you do as you're told. Now move."

"I'm going to enjoy killing you, Franco."

Frank said nothing and Angelo made no move to drive the car.

"I am out of fucking patience." Frank growled. He raised the gun to Angelo's face, anger manifesting in his face.

Angelo sneered, put the car in gear and turned right, heading for Crowchild Trail, as instructed.

"You can tell Antonio that I didn't start this, and I don't want the fight. But there is not a chance in hell, that I will kill my own blood. Not for Antonio, the family, or anyone," Frank snarled as they pulled into the isolated parking lot at Nose Hill. "You got that?"

"I got it. It won't mean a thing when he finds you."

"Then I guess a lot of people will die. Now get out and leave the keys in the ignition." Frank reasoned it would take Angelo thirty minutes to trek out and find somewhere to make a call. That was long enough. They had no idea where he was headed.

Angelo opened the door and stepped out, leaving the car door ajar.

"Step back, Angelo." Frank aimed the gun at him. Angelo stepped two paces back.

Frank got out of the car and walked around to the driver's side. "Further."

Angelo stepped back two more paces. Frank slid behind the wheel, slammed the door shut, stomped on the gas until the wheels spun on the gravel, and sped away, to a chorus of Italian curses trailing behind.

CHAPTER ELEVEN

FATS DOMINO ARRIVED TO FIND the door to his warehouse kicked in. It was early in the morning and his staff would not arrive for two more hours. He went back to his car, opened the trunk, and withdrew a tire iron, which he kept there for this type of situation. He scanned the parking lot for a sign of who might have done this. Nothing. His eyes panned the dark corners of the building for threats. There was no movement. He made his way to the door, pushed it wide open, and peered around the corner, listening for activity. All was quiet. Stepping into the building, he reached to the side wall, flipped a switch, and waited for the lights to illuminate the contents of his building. He stood perfectly still and let his eyes wander. Everything appeared to be normal and untouched. He focused on the back of the warehouse, where his office remained in darkness. Advancing past the presses, ink stands, paper rolls, and other paraphernalia used in his profession, he could feel his heart pounding in his oversized chest. He gripped the tire iron tighter.

Fats inched closer to the office door and squinted inside. He cautiously reached around the corner and flicked on the light switch.

"Shit," he murmured.

Papers were strewn across the floor. Two filing cabinets were tipped over, their contents tossed haphazardly about the room.

What were they looking for? Fats wiped his brow that was now covered in sweat. He looked over his shoulder to validate he was still alone, then moved to his desk. Placing the tire iron on top of it, he removed his phone and gazed around the room again. Time for the police. First though, he had to determine what was missing. He placed his phone beside the tire iron and began working through the mess.

A door clicked and his head snapped up. He studied the warehouse through his office window. A shadowy figure moved towards him. Fats stood up and walked to the front of his desk, reaching instinctively for the tire iron. Why had he left that door open? He stood quietly and waited for the man to show his face.

"You responsible for this?" he asked, as the man came into his sight, fingers curling around the tire iron.

The man looked around at the disorder and smiled.

"You had something I wanted."

"I gave you what you wanted."

"Too may demands I'm afraid. You have forgotten my past."

Fats nodded his understanding. He thought he had but one chance. He slammed his fat leg into the ground and pivoted towards the man, the tire iron raised for a strike. The man ducked inside the swing and Fats felt a sharp pain in his abdomen. He looked down and watched his shirt changing to a reddish-brown color. Fats dropped to a knee, the tire iron clattering on the concrete floor. He slouched against one of the fallen cabinets and looked down. Blood was now seeping through his fingers.

He watched as the man shrugged his knapsack off his shoulders and place it on Fats' desk. He removed a rag and wiped his knife clean. Pulling off his gloves, he unzipped another pocket in his bag and pulled out a folder. He walked over and showed it to him. It was entitled "Beckett."

"This all there is?"

Fats stared at the man, wondering what he had to do to stay alive. The eyes told him everything he needed to know.

"Fuck you, Frank."

Frank Ricci smiled. He walked back to the desk, put the folder back in his knapsack along with his knife.

"I'll take that as a yes." He zipped up his bag. "You shouldn't have gotten greedy, Fats." Frank looked down at the obese man as he laboured for breath.

Fats could feel his life ebbing away. He coughed up some blood and didn't have the energy to wipe it from his mouth. He watched as Frank let out a long breath of air. He reached over for a box of Kleenex laying on the floor and removed a tissue. He then pulled over a chair, sat down and wiped the blood away gently. Fats made no move to stop him as he took his hand in his.

"Let's talk about more pleasant things," he heard Frank say. For some unknown reason, Fats found his voice comforting.

PART TWO

CHAPTER TWELVE

NATE BECKETT SAT IN A recently painted red Adirondack chair, gazing over the Gibsons marina to the Olympic Mountains beyond. It had been nearly a year since his run from Calgary. Cumulous clouds covered the mountain tops, sea haze all but obliterating the rest of their mass. The rain had stopped, and sunbeams were reaching through the broken clouds, lighting up stands of trees on neighbouring islands. It was a typical late spring day. Nate was glad to see the greyness of winter losing its grip. A sailboat rounded the point and headed towards the harbour, its sail luffing before it fell to its boom.

He'd chosen Gibsons for its isolation. Two hours from Vancouver, it was a sleepy town accessible only by ferry, known for its quiet beaches, hiking trails and amazing artists. Nate couldn't necessarily relate to the artsy types, but he wasn't likely to ever come across the type of people he left behind in Calgary, and that was just fine with him.

He studied the sailboat, docked below him, that he had purchased with the stolen money. It was beautiful. He enjoyed every moment he was aboard her. Nate was thinking of an evening sail, when his thoughts were interrupted.

"I'm glad you've been around to help from time to time, Nate. It's been a busier year than usual and I'm not sure Beka and I could've kept up with it all by ourselves. She never complains, but it's a lot for just the two of us to handle."

Nate shifted his gaze to the man that sat beside him in an identical chair. He was the owner of the marina Nate had chosen to call home. Milo Sinclair was an ocean man, born in Gibsons to a caring mother and father who ventured to the West Coast from England. His father was a fisherman, his mother a seamstress, and together they created a good life in their new home. Milo was an only child, and was devoted to his father, who taught him everything he needed to know about fishing and life on the ocean. When they weren't on the sea, he was being taught about guns, hunting, and how to fend for himself. Although rare, Milo's father was, in fact, Milo's best friend.

One day, when he was but seventeen, and home sick with a nasty cold, his father had headed out to sea as he did every day. The fishing boat was found empty, later that night, when the fishermen of Gibsons searched for their missing friend. No one could explain how such an experienced fisherman came up missing from his boat, but such was the way sometimes. With his mother's blessing, Milo had inherited the boat, along with a small amount of money and a lot of memories. But the love of fishing had died with his father, and Milo soon sold the boat, using the proceeds, along with a sizeable bank loan, to purchase the Gibsons Marina. His mother never recovered from the loss, moving to Vancouver to be near her sister, and away from the water. Milo seldom saw her now, despite her advancing age and her proximity.

Nate took a sip of his coffee. A couple of months after discovering the marina a year ago, he had made it a practice to join Milo for a cup of java in the morning. He seldom missed the opportunity to do so. He knew Milo enjoyed the quietness before his hectic day began and Nate enjoyed listening to his tales of life on the coast of British Columbia.

"I'm happy to help, Milo. You know that." Nate responded with a smile.

He would often see Milo doing small projects around the marina such as repairing a dock or washing a yacht that an absentee owner had hired him to do. Nate would go out of his way to wander over and offer a helping hand. He felt at ease in Milo's company.

"Besides, it's the least I can do. Not many guys would let long term moorage eat up a transient space."

"Still, I should pay you more for your time, Nate." Milo said. He still had a touch of a British accent, from childhood; it fit so well with the aging face smiling at him.

Nate laughed and held up his hand to stop the conversation. In truth, Milo never paid Nate anything, but that wasn't an issue for Nate. He had plenty of available cash and was happy to fill his days, even with menial tasks. He had little in the way of a daily routine, since coming to the marina, other than his weekly sailing instruction for a small group of Gibsons boys.

"I don't want your money, Milo."

Milo nodded, then went silent for a moment as he sipped his coffee. "I do have a favour to ask though," Milo said, setting his cup down on the worn table between them.

"What's that?"

"I need a pickup done in North Vancouver at *Coastal Supplies*. *Coastal* provides most of the product we need for our store. With the good weather, we missed our inventory projections for the coming weekend. I don't want to buy at the inflated prices at our local grocery store and I can't wait for next week's delivery."

Nate laughed but felt the usual angst when he thought about going to the big city. Nate was accustomed to running errands into town for Milo, or occasionally his rather attractive daughter, Beka, which he readily agreed to. But this was the first entreaty to venture to Vancouver, and Nate was uncomfortable with the request.

"Isn't that Beka's domain?"

"It is, but if I have learned anything about this business, it's that if I run out of the provisions we need, the natives get restless and go elsewhere. Given how busy it is right now, Beka needs to be around to deal with the weekenders and I need to be out in the marina making sure it is ship shape. I need those sales, Nate. It would be a big help. I hate to ask."

Nate watched a large black raven calling out its mournful call from the lower branch of a fir that had seen better days. "Tell you what, I will pay you a bonus," Milo added.

Nate laughed again. The last bonus Milo paid him consisted of some of his homegrown stash that he grew on a small piece of property he had in the mountains, north of Gibsons. Milo lived in town, but, after a particularly good year, he had purchased a ten-acre piece of wooded land with a rustic cabin and a dilapidated barn. He had been fixing it up, year after year, and hoped one day to retire there. In the meantime, he had found a way for it to provide for his daily pot consumption, a fact that was not lost on Nate, when he heard Beka chastise her father constantly about his usage.

"That's very considerate, Milo, but you know I don't partake. I would have to regift it and I don't want to experience the "look" from Beka a second time." She had scowled at a sheepish Nate when she spotted him handing his first "bonus" to a regular visitor.

"I was actually thinking of fifty dollars, Nate," Milo chuckled.

"Keep your cash, Milo," Nate said, reluctantly deciding he would help. He was confident that it would be safe. He couldn't imagine anyone recognizing him. Hell, he hardly recognized himself. His beard was now fully grown, a year on the water had firmed up his body and his blond hair was dyed a mousy brown. His bright blue eyes were usually covered with shades and his west coast garb was nothing like the prairie clothes he used to wear. He had to get past the paranoia plaguing him when leaving the Marina. After all, the one-year anniversary of his arrival was coming and there had never been any evidence he was still on anyone's radar.

"When do you want me to go?"

"This morning would be good. You know where *Coastal* is?"

"I think so. In fact, I think it is next door to where I bought my boat. I remember having a great lunch in their attached deli. Is that the one?"

"It is, great food," Milo mused. "Almost makes me want to go myself, but I can't. Take the van. They're expecting us to come by about noon. Let's go inside, I'll give you a cheque to cover our order."

With that Milo raised his short but muscular body from his chair and stared down at Nate.

"I wish I could figure you out, Nate. You come out of nowhere and quickly become a model citizen in our town, helping everybody you can in the process, including me. You have no job that I can tell, I don't see you as being gay, but you must be the only guy in town not hitting on my daughter, and you're not looking to leave. You ever going to tell me your story?"

"Pretty boring stuff, Milo." Nate sidestepped the question. "I like it here and I love living on my boat. I have no plans on going elsewhere right now. There's not much else to say."

Nate raised himself out of his chair, wanting to change the subject. "Let's go. It will take me a while to get to Vancouver."

"Yeah, yeah." Milo responded, labouring as he stood.

"Your leg bothering you?"

Milo had earned a permanent disfigurement to his leg from a block and tackle accident, several years back.

"Just when it rains. When are you teaching your next lesson to the kids?"

"Couple of days. Hey, Beka," Nate said as he walked through the door, catching sight of her stocking shelves.

Beka turned and smiled at him.

Beka was Milo's pride and joy, and he protected her fiercely from the lesser sorts who frequented Gibsons. Milo had met his fiancée, Molly, late in his eighteenth year. After a whirlwind courtship, he'd married her, believing he didn't deserve the love of such a remarkable woman. Within a year, Beka had been conceived, and Milo had thought his world to be fully recovered from the death of his father – until Molly's passing. A bizarre turn of events during labour had taken her from him. Beka had survived, but Milo struggled with his latest loss. At first, he'd been bitter, seeing Beka as the reason for his wife's death, but as she grew to be a toddler, and time dulled the grief, he was won over to the joys of fatherhood. She became the centre of his universe. Milo ensured that Beka was raised to be self-sufficient and that she answered to no one other than herself, and those that mattered to her most. She, in turn, adored her father.

"Our Nate is going to run into town and pick up those extra supplies for you," Milo said to Beka.

Nate was conscious of Milo's mild effort of matchmaking.

She turned her head to Nate. "Thank you."

As usual, her smile captivated him. He grinned back and turned to Milo, watching him limp into his small office in the back.

Milo returned with a cheque in an envelope addressed to *Coastal* and handed it to Nate.

"Beka, can you give Nate the keys to the van?"

Nate walked over to her as she reached beneath the counter and removed a set of keys from a hook. She handed them to him, allowing her fingers to rest a moment too long on his.

Nate blushed, turning quickly for the door.

"Later, Milo," he said and stepped out the door into the warmth of the sun. It matched the feeling radiating within him.

***

Nate arrived at the Langdale ferry terminal and eased Milo's van into the designated spot advised by the ferry attendant. A short time later, he was on the top deck of the ferry for the forty-minute ride to Horseshoe Bay terminal, north of Vancouver. He had ridden the ferry a few times and loved the short ride as it cruised between Gambier and Bowen Islands. He watched a bald eagle soaring on the thermals overhead, looking for its late morning feed, when his thoughts turned to Beka.

She was interested in him. He was only too aware of how great she looked. Those dark blue eyes, framed by her blonde hair, which she often wore in a long braid, captured him every time he saw her. Not to mention her toned legs. He longed for female companionship, but whenever he thought about asking her out for coffee, his mind flew back to those final days in Calgary and the devastating end of his last relationship.

The thought of Jess didn't consume his every thought any longer, and he was grateful for that. He shouldn't carry the guilt of her death anymore, or regret ending up with all that money, but he did. He played those days over and over in his mind and it all came down to the same conclusion — he should have said no to her hare-brained idea. Then she would be alive. He would still be poor, but the damn guilt wouldn't be smothering him like a wet blanket.

Still, things were improving. Gibsons had been home for almost a year and his life was evolving into something he'd hoped for during his escape from Calgary. He had his boat, he was developing a good friendship with Milo, and he had found a way to give back to his community by teaching sailing lessons to troubled boys sent to him from the local chapter of the Boys club. And now he was gaining favour with a very nice lady.

Nate let his thoughts pour over endless possibilities of what his future might look like. He let out a large sigh when he heard the announcement blaring out of the ships speakers, asking the passengers to return to their cars. He rose from his seat and headed back to the van, but not before appreciating the beautiful scenery surrounding the Horseshoe Bay terminal.

Nate arrived at *Coastal* just before noon and went in to see the order desk clerk for instructions on where to pick up his load. He pulled the van to the rear loading dock, as instructed. He was then told there would be a thirty-minute delay. Nate left the van, promising to return in a half hour.

He sauntered across the parking lot to the adjoining Marina, where he had bought his boat, *Serendipity*. He walked down to the docks to see the new boats moored there. The large "for sale" signs attached to their bow railings promised adventure to anyone flush enough to buy one.

He stood, admiring the lines of a Dufour 560 sailboat. There was always something better out there and he was wondering if one day he might be able to upgrade his boat, when he heard the presence of someone behind him. Why had he not heard him coming? Nate spun around, heartbeat accelerating, expecting a problem. Instead, his mouth fell open without a sound. All he could do was stare.

CHAPTER THIRTEEN

THE MAN SLUMPED IN HIS chair, the cords cutting into his wrists. He fought to move his feet but the restraints on his ankles held him tight. He was cold from the water dumped over him to shock him awake. He shivered, more from anger than the cold. The lump on the back of his head throbbed. He had a splitting headache. The blindfold across his eyes made it impossible to see who his captor was, but he kept moving his head, hoping the cloth would shift, allowing him a peek. He listened hard, needing to hear something that would identify the guy. He would make sure, at some point, that he would pay for what he was doing here today.

"Where's the money?" the voice asked with a quiet intensity.

"What money?"

The voice paused. "The money that was stolen from you a year ago."

"How do you know about that?"

The voice ignored him. "Where's the money?"

"I have no idea."

"Wrong answer." the man's head snapped back in response to a blow to his chin. The assault was done with a glove-covered hand, yet it felt as if it had been a bare-knuckled punch.

"Where's the money?" the voice repeated, this time more forcefully.

"Fuck off." The man's head was yanked harshly by his hair. He let out a growl of pain.

"I said, where's the money?" he heard whispered into his ear, the assailant's face inches away. The man yanked on his bonds as if they might snap and let him take this guy by the throat.

"Last chance."

"We don't have it."

"Who is we?"

"Do you know who I am?!" the man screamed. That question garnered another punch in his face. This time directly impacting his nose. Blood ran down onto his lips; it tasted sour.

The man felt panic welling up within him. No one did this to him. He was the enforcer, the man others called on to inflict pain. No one touched him. They knew the consequences. Who is this guy? For the first time in a long while he felt fear creep into his mind.

He needed a new tactic. "Do you know what we will do to you for this, you moron?" Another punch to his face was the answer.

He heard the assailant walk away. The man felt relief. Was it over? He heard his assailant whisper something. The man strained to hear what was being said. *There is another person in the room. What the...*

"Was it you who cut the girl?" his assailant said loudly. He could hear the assailant shuffling back to him.

He raised his head toward the voice and spit blood-soaked phlegm at where he thought he might be standing. He had no idea if it had landed. Three successive blows rained down on him with increased intensity. His left eye suffered a direct hit, blood was running freely from his nose to his lips. He tried to open his eyes beneath the blindfold, but the swelling in his left eye caused too much pain. He closed it, leaving his right eye open. He couldn't see anything anyway.

The beating stopped. He sensed his captor moving. Water running into a bucket filtered into his brain. He focused on a smell of wet straw that permeated the air. A barn. He couldn't remember how he got there. The last thing he remembered was leaving the bar and walking to his chopper. He remembered hearing footsteps behind him, starting to turn, then a blinding pain searing his brain. It was like someone had hit him with a board. Then nothing.

Cold water hit him in the face, washing some of the blood away. His head was pulled back, his mouth forced open in another gasp of pain. More water flooded his throat. A series of sputtering coughs followed, then gasps for air.

The questions were asked repeatedly. "Where's the money? Did you cut the girl?" Sometimes the questions were asked quietly; sometimes harshly. Most were followed by a punch to the head for a non-answer. Some with another gagging mouth full of dirty water. Little by little, the man's resolve withered. His left eye was fully swollen now, and he was pretty sure his nose was broken. He could taste a mixture of fresh and dried blood in his mouth. He thought he would lose a tooth as well, but the numbness across his face acted as a painkiller, so it was hard to tell for sure.

"Where's the money?"

The man involuntarily winced, expecting another hit for his non-answer. He felt his head being wrenched by the hair. "Bitch's friend has it," he gasped, not wanting to be hit again. The assailant went quiet.

"Who?"

The man contemplated his answer. He was sure he heard the swish of air, before the next fist landed on his jaw. It was the most forceful strike yet. His head careened to the side. This time the blindfold adjusted ever so slightly. He glimpsed his captor out of his functioning eye. *I see you. You will pay for this, you bastard.*

"Who is the friend?"

"The guy who was with the bitch."

"He's alive?"

"Yeah, he got away from us."

"Who is he?"

"Nate Vickers. I can help you find him if you cut me loose."

"How much did he get?"

"A lot." He felt his hair being grabbed again. "Wait...Wait... Wait... A million, I mean two million thereabouts... we hadn't done a full count."

Silence engulfed the space between them.

"Was it you who cut the girl?"

The man lapsed into silence. He was growing very tired. He made a hissing sound as he sucked air through his teeth.

"I will ask only one more time," the voice said quietly.

The hushed appeal coerced his return to the moment. "She fucking stole from us. Of course, we cut her up. We cut her up and we will cut him up too when we get him."

Despite the broken nose and his bloodied lips, the view of his captor spurred him to scream a response. "I told you. Let me go and I will help you get him."

He could see his assailant form a twisted smile. His captor could see his exposed eye. The man glared back at him and watched as the blindfold was yanked free and thrown to the ground.

"And how will you do that?"

"We have eyes everywhere." He turned his head, looking for the other person in the building. His assailant stepped in front of his vision.

"Who is "we," and you had better not make me wait for an answer."

The man felt fingers in his hair again. This time he did not cry out. "Don Belletti," he gasped. "He says we have to be patient; he's working on a way to get to him."

"What way is that?"

"How do I know? He doesn't share with me. But we will get him, like we got the girl, and I will pass it on to you as soon as I know. Now cut me loose."

His assailant retreated a step, allowing the man to see an approaching figure. He stared in disbelief and closed his good eye. He said nothing more. There was nothing more to say.

He heard the swoosh of air, expecting another punch to the face, then the taste of his blood flooded his mouth. His good eye flew open and locked on his assailants. He couldn't get air to his lungs. Gasping, he tried to reach for his throat, as if the cords were no longer there. He felt nothing. Gasps turned to a gurgling. A greyness muddied his mind. He saw his captor standing silently with a large bone handled knife, in his hand. He felt the blade being wiped on his pant leg.

The assailant slid it back into a sheath, attached to his belt. "Coming?" he said, "We need to be out of here before the farmer wakes up." His companion looked down at the man.

"Yes."

It was the last thing the man heard before blackness took hold.

CHAPTER FOURTEEN

"FRANK?" NATE GASPED, EYES DARTING this way and that, ensuring they were alone.

"Nate." A smile cracked Frank's face. "Good to see you. You've been a little hard to find and now that I have...I almost didn't recognize you."

"Well, that's good to know, but...what the hell? How?"

"Why don't we go to *Coastal*, have some lunch and I'll explain." Frank starting walking back up the gangway towards the brokerage office. Nate stood, staring at his uncle, attempting to put the pieces together. Frank walked on. At the top of the gangway, he glanced back at Nate. He was inching forward slowly, confusion written on his face.

"You coming or what? We have a lot to catch up on." Frank beamed at him.

Nate picked up his pace. He caught up to Frank as he reached the door to the marina's brokerage office. Frank yanked it open and yelled, "Tom, back in an hour or two."

Nate could hear Tom protesting as the door shut.

"Let's go," Frank declared.

They started across the parking lot, when they heard the brokerage office door slamming against its door stop.

"Frank, you can't just leave when you want. What the heck, man."

Frank stopped and turned to look at Tom. "Then I quit. Thanks for everything, Tom."

Nate almost burst out laughing at the expression on Tom's face. He turned and trotted after his uncle's now departing back. Frank was near the entrance to *Coastal* when Nate advised he had to talk to the shipping department.

"Don't get lost, Nate. I've expended a lot of effort finding you."

Nate laughed and headed off, his mind whirling. After meeting with the shipping department to adjust his departure time, he returned, slipping into a booth at the back of the restaurant. Nate was glad Frank decided to look at the wall, as it allowed him an easy view of anyone coming in the front door. His eyes scanned the tired restaurant as he sat down opposite his uncle.

"I know that look," said Frank. "Been hunted most of my life, in one form or another."

Nate gaped at him. He had an amused expression on his face and a twinkle in his eye. Nate wasn't as amused. He'd just been tracked down. If his uncle could do it, so could others.

"What are you doing here, Frank? And, how the hell did you find me?" Nate said.

Frank opened his mouth and was about to answer when Nate added, "I thought we agreed to break off contact."

Frank nodded. "One question at a time, Nate, one question at time. How much time do you have?

"An hour or so."

"Where do you have to be?"

Nate hesitated.

"Hold that answer. I'm going to answer your questions first, then you can decide if you want to tell me."

A waitress with a large ring in her nose and a mop of pink uncombed hair approached and took their order. Frank watched her leave, then began. He told Nate everything, from the discussions with don Belletti, to his misadventure with his henchmen, and finally about his departure from Calgary almost a year earlier.

Nate noticed a wave of sadness wash over his uncle as he paused. He had never known Frank to be overly emotional. What was that all about?

A bell above the restaurant door rang and in walked a man, dressed in a brown suit. He scanned the restaurant, his eyes crossing over Nate's face, before noticing and acknowledging the person he had come to meet at a different table. Nate's eyes didn't leave the man, as he sauntered over and sat down across from a woman, a couple of tables away.

"How did you find me, Frank?" he said quietly, not taking his eyes off the couple. Any sense that he was hidden from his past vanished on that dock when his uncle arrived. This was exactly why he had misgivings when Milo had asked him to come to Vancouver.

Frank deferred answering the question.

"You look good, Nate. I can see that. Something has changed though. More cautious, more reserved. I'm not here to hurt you, quite the opposite."

"The Calgary experience would change anybody, Frank. Funny what death and mayhem can do to a person's perspective." He shot another look at the couple as they laughed at something, turning his gaze back to Frank a moment later.

Frank held back, searching Nate's eyes, then continued. "I've known you all your life. Always believed that one day you would end up on the West Coast. Of course, I knew you were heading out this way, it was my plan. I wasn't sure if you had changed the plan though, after all, stress may make people do funny things. Regardless, I made a calculated decision to come find you, once I understood the risks don Belletti now created for you. He knows you were in on the heist and has vowed to make you pay.

"Since you had money and I had no idea how to find you specifically, I decided to see if you had bought that sailboat, you always dreamed about. One thing led to another, and I eventually found the marina where you purchased it. I reckoned one day, you would return for parts or something, so I settled in and have been biding my time. I'd almost given up, when who should I see but my favourite nephew walking onto our dock."

"I'm your only nephew, Frank," Nate said. "Still doesn't really answer how you found me. There are a lot of boat dealers in these parts."

"I came out here and started asking questions of every boat dealer I could locate. You're right, a lot of dealers in Vancouver. I took my time, getting to know a person from each of the brokerages."

The waitress returned. Nate's eyes swivelled to her, his eyes resting on her name tag.

"Food should be out shortly, fellas," she said, keeping her eyes solely on Nate. She topped up their water glasses.

"Thank you, Angie," Nate replied, smiling at her. He watched her walk away as she coyly looked back at him.

Nate ignored the flirt and turned back to Frank who grinned at him.

"Yeah, yeah — carry on."

"Right. People love to talk. All you need to do is know how to ask the appropriate questions and ply them with the occasional drink. When I got to this one, which took some time to find, they told me about a young guy who purchased a new sailboat recently. Which didn't mean a whole lot, until the guy said it was unusual to get a yacht paid for in cash. That caught my attention. I found it interesting that any dealer would sell a boat for cash these days, but I let that slide. I suppose they had their reasons. Of course, they didn't know where you were, that would have been too easy. So, I introduced myself and found out the owner was a guy named Tom, you kind of met him a few minutes back. I worked him and before long he offered me employment. That allowed me the ability to look over registration papers for your boat and confirm it was you who bought it. It was just a matter of patience, after that.

Nate didn't answer. He worked the math out in his head. His uncle had been searching for him for just under a year. His respect grew. What this man had given him, his whole life, was unfathomable.

"Go on," Nate said.

Frank paused as another waitress covered in tattoos, dropped off the food they ordered. They both stared at the inked skull on her back, as she walked back to the kitchen.

"Why do they do that to their bodies?" Frank mused.

"What?"

"The nose rings and bad tattoos. They're pretty enough girls, but all you look at is the stuff they do to their bodies, and you don't even notice them."

"I know," Nate stared at the girl who picked up more food which she delivered to another table near them. "Maybe that's the point...why are you here?"

Frank ignored him.

"Where's the rest of the cash, Nate? I hope it's safe and not sitting under a mattress somewhere."

Nate wondered about the question and why his uncle would even ask it. Did he have a hidden agenda? He waved the thought aside. This man had given up his world for him. He had no business doubting him or his motivations. "It's invested, for the most part. It is paying me a reasonable amount to live on. I keep life simple."

"What kind of investments?"

"Stocks, bonds, financial investments. Very safe, very liquid."

Frank smiled. "You've changed."

Nate laughed. "You mean that I am now actually using the commerce degree you paid for?" Nate flashed back to a heated discussion he and his uncle had undertaken years ago when he graduated from the U of C and decided he needed to find himself.

"How are you getting around the tax issues?" Frank asked quizzically.

"Believe it or not, it's easy to get your social insurance number reissued. I claimed it lost, produced my new I.D. And there you have it."

"That's why Fats always used dead people for his fakes. There is still a risk, you know."

"I know. I move the cash around to various banks to keep things very confusing. Best I can do."

"How'd you get the cash into a bank? There is no easy way to do that. Banks ask a lot of questions.

Nate stared at him for a minute, before answering.

"Banks," he said. "Many banks, lots of deposits under the threshold of government scrutiny. It was a lot of work." Nate smiled. "It cost me a couple of months of my life, but now it's set up and reasonably secure. Once money is in a bank, it's not hard to move it around."

Nate stopped there, not wanting to divulge anything further, even though his trust of Frank was absolute. He didn't feel an obligation to explain where the money was nor that he parlayed a good gain in the markets over the past number of months. Some things were better left unsaid.

Nate watched as the man in the brown suit and his lady friend rose and left the restaurant. He was happy to see them leave as they might have been able to hear their discussion, if they intended to. A small amount of his paranoia eased with their departure. He took a bite of his food, relaxed enough to swallow.

"I'm kind of confused, Frank. If Belletti is looking for you too, why chance getting a job and creating a record of employment for him to track you down?"

"As I said, I knew that one day you'd come back for parts or something, so I knew I had to arrange to spend as much time here as it took, awaiting your return. That guy, Tom, I just quit on, was more than eager to hire me and let me spend my time working on the side, for cash. My suggestion, but he eagerly took me up on it. Everybody cheats on the government these days."

Nate nodded, sipping on his drink. "So, here we are."

Frank pushed his empty plate aside and leaned in closer. "Don Belletti knows everything, Nate. He knows you were involved and he's not going to let go until he finds you. You must never let your guard down. Belletti is not a man that gives up easily and his reach is notoriously deep."

Nate examined the restaurant again, a knot forming in his stomach. He'd lowered his guard. Any respite he had with the departure of that couple, vanished. Paranoia flooded back. He'd have to be more diligent.

"I guess I'm not surprised that he found out it was me, but I hoped that the passing of a year might have gotten him to move on. Wishful thinking, I guess."

"I suspect so. I worked for that man for a very long time, and he is not one to let go of much, especially if he takes it personally." Frank went over the details of his last conversation with Belletti that he'd glossed over earlier in their conversation. "And this theft — was personal."

Nate let that sink in for a moment. "What about you, Frank? He's got to be looking for you too. How safe have you been here?"

"I'm off the grid, lad. I have lots of cash squirrelled away and have enough on hand until I leave." He nodded at his knapsack. "Everything I do is with cash. You know I'm capable. I'm not too worried about Belletti. He's mad at me, but I'm not the one who ripped him off. He may understand my involvement in helping you escape but it's you he wants. If I get caught up in his web, all the better, but I am not his primary target."

"So, what's your plan now?"

"Well, I've seen that you're safe and given you what information I could. Now I'm leaving."

"Where?"

"Cayman Islands. You know I have a small place down there, under a different name of course, overlooking Seven Mile beach. I set it up as an escape hatch. A place the family knows nothing about. It's time I officially retired anyway. This really will be the last time we get together, for a long time, Nate. I've spent countless quiet nights arranging my affairs down there. I was lucky to have old friends willing to help."

Nate studied the face of his uncle. He hadn't realized, until this moment, how much he missed him. Especially with the disclosure that he'd lose contact with him again.

"Can we spend some time together before then? Come with me...for a week. Then we will say our goodbyes, Frank. What do you say? For old time's sake."

Frank stared into Nate's eyes. He wrung his weathered hands together and glanced down at the saltshaker on the table. He looked up.

"One week," he said with a single nod of his head at Nate. "Where are we off to?"

"Gibsons." Nate grinned.

Frank nodded again. "Good choice." He turned, waved the waitress over and requested the bill, insisting he'd be the one paying. He left a wad of cash on the table to cover the bill, including a generous tip.

"You got a car, Frank?"

"No, easily traceable."

Nate laughed. "You're going to love my wheels. Wait here," Nate said, nodding to the front door of the restaurant. "I'll be right back."

He walked around the rear of the building and, after paying for the merchandise loaded in the van, he drove up beside Frank, who opened the passenger door and climbed into the cab.

"You a working stiff, Nate?"

"I do favours for some very good people, Frank." He then proceeded to bring his uncle up to date on his set up. "You can stay with me on the boat."

"No, thanks. I'll stay in town, at a motel. Those things are way too cramped for this old body. Besides, I haven't been to Gibsons for a long time. I think I'll enjoy the week doing some exploring and we can get together every night for dinner."

"Perfect," Nate said. "Now where do I go to get your stuff?"

"I'll direct you. Take a left here."

Their journey back to the peninsula was a pleasurable trip, both men enjoying the West Coast beauty, reminiscing and talking over ideas on how to stay safe and out of the reach of don Belletti.

Soon enough they entered the town limits. Nate pulled up in front of a nondescript motel, not far from the marina.

"I know it's not the style you are accustomed to," he said, smiling at him, "but it's clean and close to the marina. It has a small kitchenette so you can keep a few things in a fridge for the week."

Frank assessed the brick building with its green metal roof, stucco exterior, and West Coast gardens. "It'll be fine. Let me settle in and then I'll come find you at the marina."

"Yeah, stop in at the marina store and ask where I am. They'll direct you. I'll let them know you're coming."

Frank grunted and got out of the van, reaching behind the seat for his bag and knapsack.

"You're travelling light."

"All I need. I'll stock up in the Caymans. See you soon."

"Give me a couple of hours to unload the van for Milo."

Nate pulled a U-turn and headed down the road.

A couple of hours passed in a blink of an eye. Frank sauntered into the marina store, where he introduced himself to both Milo and Beka. They had been expecting him and freely gave him the directions to Nate's boat. Their faces reflected their inquisitiveness, which he ignored. He sauntered down to the slip, his knapsack resting easily over his left shoulder.

"You home, Cap'n?" he shouted, aware of how silly he'd sound to anyone other than Nate.

Nate popped his head out from his galley stairs and laughed. "Come aboard, Frank."

It was one of those rare, early season West Coast days, hardly a cloud in the sky and, although the sun was now long on the horizon, it promised to be a beautiful night.

Nate and his uncle settled into the cockpit of his boat. "How were your last couple of hours?" Nate asked.

"Wonderful. After a short trip to the store for some morning provisions, I set out to reacquaint myself with the town. I had forgotten how beautiful it is, especially at this time of year. People everywhere, enjoying the sunshine. Lots of cute little houses covered in vines, hanging baskets with copious amounts of colourful flowers. Boats coming and going in the harbour. I can see why you like it here."

Nate poured two fingers of rum into cocktail glasses, handing one off to Frank. "You should see it when the rain comes." He laughed.

Before long they were giggling like two schoolkids and slurred words became the norm.

"Hungry, Frank?"

"Famished."

Nate fired up the grill attached to the stern railing of his boat. While it was heating up, he showed Frank how to use the head.

He set about getting their dinner ready. Soon they were enjoying a hardy ribeye steak. Nate cooked it to perfection. He opened a bottle of bold red wine for dinner, even though the last thing either man needed, by that point, was another drink.

It was about half gone when Frank said, "You have a nice set up here, Nate. Especially like the portability of it. What kind of a boat is this?"

"Oceanis 41," Nate boasted. "Yeah, I like living on my boat. Nice size and it gives me a sense of security, even though it's probably a false sense."

"Have you seen any unfriendlies?"

"No, a couple of local yahoos come around from time to time, but that's par for the course. Usually tourists. I wish I could turn it all back, Frank. It's hard to get past thinking everybody I meet, for the first time, has an agenda and might try to kill me when I am least expecting it. It's tough."

"I know, I know." Frank slurred his words. "I'd like to tell you it'll get easier, but it won't. The family has a long reach, Nate. You'll have to stay ahead of them for a very long time. You should change towns from time to time."

"Yeah." Nate looked out across the marina, deep in thought. He stared at the store above them.

Frank glanced at him, then said, "You trust these people?"

"Milo?"

"And the girl, what's her name?"

"Beka."

Maybe it was the way he said it. Frank stopped and focused on Nate for a moment.

"Oh my," he said." Yeah...Beka." He laughed and poured himself another glass of wine. "That does complicate things."

Nate ignored the taunt. "I do. Very much. They are a large reason I feel like I belong and have a sense of community. I like that."

"What else do you like very much?" he laughed again.

Nate looked at him. "Nothing." His voice became serious.

"Then you're an idiot. She's beautiful, and I have to say, very charming."

"I don't want to talk about it." Nate rose and cleared the plates from the outdoor table. He returned a couple of minutes later and sat back down, offering Frank a cigar he had bought at the marina store. Frank loved his cigars and, although Nate wasn't as big a fan, he lit one up for himself too.

They smoked in silence for a bit, listening to the sounds of the marina, when Frank turned to him. "Nate, we're both on the run now. We may never see each other again, after this week. You're all I have left in my life that's important to me. So, you need to know what's what..."

Nate was having trouble following Frank. The effects of the cigar and the alcohol made his head spin. The look on Frank's face said he had to focus. He put his cigar down, faced Frank and listened as carefully as he could, as he learned about Cayman and how his uncle had structured his world.

Once Frank had finished, he shot up and, swaying back and forth, proclaimed, "I'm outta here. See ya tomorrow." He moved to disembark, then turned back. "Oh, and one other thing," Frank grabbed his knapsack, opened it and withdrew a dog-eared file folder. He tossed it onto the bench seat near Nate. Nate glanced down at the folder and noticed in large blue letters the word "Beckett."

"I thought you should be the only guy that has that."

Nate looked at his uncle, who was fighting, unsuccessfully, to get his bag zipped back up. Nate stood and reached out for the bag, taking it from his fingers. He adjusted the zipper and closed it up for him, but not before he noticed the butt end of a gun inside it. He looked at his uncle, who swayed as he looked down at him, said nothing, and handed the bag back to him.

"Thanks, lad. A little too much fun, tonight, I think." Frank belly laughed.

He turned to the dock and staggered off the boat, heading for shore. Nate kept his eyes on him, lest he tumble into the harbour. He wondered if his own condition would allow him to jump in to save him, if he fell. He'd sure try. This was a man who had devoted his life to him and one he loved very much.

Nate heard Frank singing an old Italian ballad as he neared the shore. He picked up the file entitled "Beckett," then he heard Frank yell back across the water. "And... get after that girl."

***

Frank Ricci continued singing ballads. He sang *"Volare"* to perfection as he walked out of the marina. He struggled to remember the words of *"Bella Ciao"* as he staggered down Gower Point Road, and completely butchered *"O Sole Mio"* as he stumbled his way into his room. The evenings events had destroyed his singing prowess, he decided as he flopped onto the room's bed. He looked around at the spartan furnishings surrounding him. Life had certainly changed.

He felt it again as it engulfed him. It was the same as it always was. But today it was heightened. Perhaps it had been seeing his nephew. Perhaps it had been meeting Beka. But the loneliness that engulfed him was the worst it had been since he'd left Calgary almost a year ago.

He thought about Nate and the beautiful Beka and what Nate could have if he reached for it. He thought about what level of risk that would add to Nate. He thought about the risk he had and what the future would hold for him.

This was the worst part. He had little fear. But this, this was debilitating. He had learned to overcome it, but tonight...

It's the alcohol, he mused. *Get over it.*

He looked around the room again, gazed down at the phone beside his bed and wondered. He stared at it for a few minutes. His eyes closed. Dreams were banging on his consciousness. His eyes flew open.

He pulled himself up to a sitting position.

What the hell, he thought and lifted the receiver. Even in his drunken state, he was good with numbers and knew just what buttons to press.

"El?" he said into the receiver, trying as hard as he could to sound sober.

***

CHAPTER FIFTEEN

ELENA ROMANO SLOWLY PLACED HER Apple phone on her coffee table. She sat down on her sofa, resting her head in her hands. She had hoped for his phone call every day since he'd left, but she also dreaded hearing from him at the same time. For a moment she stared at the floor and then a tear slid down her cheek. A breach in the dike. She sobbed uncontrollably, making no attempt to stem the flow of her emotions, perhaps hoping the flow of her tears would erase the stain.

Before long, the tears dried, and she went numb. She stood, walked into the kitchen, poured herself a glass of water, and returned to her sofa. She reached for her phone, rejected it like a talisman of death and put it down on the table again. She repeated this process three times. The fourth time, she sighed and stabbed the number she had recorded in her contacts.

It rang once and was answered. There was no hello or any indication that someone was on the line. This was not unexpected, as she had previously been instructed how this call would go.

"He's on the West Coast," she said, her voice devoid of emotion. "Don't know where... north of Vancouver."

Silence on the other end. After a moment she added, "I did as you asked. My obligation to you is over." She hung up, not waiting on a response, her heart pounding against her ribs.

Elena sat rigid, the phone still in her hand, staring at it. She let out a wail. Guilt consumed her, then remorse, then anger. She watched her phone fly across the room, as if it had wings of its own. It slid down the wall, to rest on the floor, but not before scarring the wall.

She thought about the man she betrayed. Frank, tough as he was, was an incredibly caring and special man. She had been unhappy how he left, and wondered if she'd ever see him again, but the next day her email had pinged to let her know he was okay. He asked her to never reply to him, but promised he would keep in touch, from time to time, and he had. Before long, her first task everyday was to see if he had sent her another email. The messages always said little, and came from undisclosed locations, but the affection in them was real and it filled her with hope.

When Frank left, she had not abandoned the store as he had suggested, but rather went to work every day, running it, as she always did. She didn't know what else to do. Perhaps in the back of her mind, she had hoped Frank would come back and everything would go back to the way it had been.

She knew the store was being watched. She had seen the same Mercedes car parked in the parking lot across the street, every day since Frank had left.

A month or two passed when she decided to ravage Franks office, tearing it apart, searching for some evidence of where he might have gone. There was nothing.

Then one day she had a visitor. He came with two additional men, who stayed at the front door. He introduced himself as Antonio Belletti, an associate of Franco's. He asked how she was and wondered if she knew where Franco had gone and when he might be returning. She answered him truthfully, watching his brow furrow, once she explained how well Frank had covered his email tracks. Belletti promised he would keep in touch and that if she needed anything, she should call him. In return, he wanted to know where Franco was if she heard from him personally or learned something in his emails. Feeling uneasy, she lied and promised she would do just that.

Days turned into months and during the first week of every month, Antonio Belletti would come by, asking for an update, in person. He remained personable, seemingly interested in her life. She knew he came from the same world Frank had, so she remained wary of his intentions and began to advise him that Frank had stopped contacting her, despite the occasional emails she received.

Then her daughter, Tiffany, was arrested.

She had been at her wits end, trying to figure out how to help her, when Belletti came by for one of his visits. He sensed her stress and pressed her to tell him what was wrong, hoping, she was sure, that it had something to do with Franco. He pressed her repeatedly, using as much charm as he could. She capitulated and told him all about her daughter and her problems. She exposed Tiffany's troubled life and how she had been arrested for prostitution. She didn't know how to deal with it. Emotion filled her face as she pleaded with him, asking if there was anything he could do to help.

He stared at her, for what seemed an eternity. She could see her confession had taken him by surprise. She watched as he stroked his chin and turned to look out of the front window. He said nothing, a blank look on his face. She began to realize how foolish the request had been and wished she hadn't revealed so much. She voiced his name. She had to extricate herself from this.

He stabbed the air with his hand, silencing her. It was the kind of move a dangerous man would do.

Then he turned with a cold smile and said of course he would help. Her hopes soared until he had made his demands. The charm was gone. A concerned man became a predator. His request for months on end had been replaced with a demand for information in exchange for his help, which he assured her he could give. She was stunned.

When the charges were dropped, a week later, she had felt relief, but no satisfaction. Her daughter thanked her, never understanding how she had helped, or what she had given up. She hadn't called her since. Elena understood what was expected of her and hoped Frank would never contact her again, in any form.

He had, and now her part was done. Payback delivered, if that was ever the case with a man like Belletti. She betrayed the only man that she had felt for, in a very long time, and to make matters worse, it had only emboldened her daughter, as Elena had learned she was back on the streets again.

She evaluated her home. Modest, but she had made a life for herself. Now it felt empty and meaningless. The phone call changed everything, including what she believed was important. She betrayed Frank and now she had to save him. Save him from the same man who made her an informant. Save him from a man she now hated.

Frank had asked her to meet him at the Horseshoe Bay Ferry terminal in two days and that was exactly what she intended to do. She didn't know how to fix what she had done, but she had to try.

She picked her phone up from the floor. The screen was cracked but it still worked. She called her daughter and left a message on her voicemail, informing her that she should not expect to hear from her for a long while. She knew her daughter wouldn't care, but it was what a mother should do. If her problems resurfaced later, it would be up to Tiffany to sort them out. She was finished with her. It was time to look after herself and what was important. Tears welled in her eyes. She shook her head, exercising demons, then headed to her room to pack.

***

Don Belletti called Mario into his office.

"She came through. He's north of Vancouver, which can only mean Whistler or the Sunshine Coast. Whistler is too busy, so get Tony and his crew to take a trip to the Sunshine Coast and scout around. Find me Franco and we'll find our boy."

Mario shuffled his feet and looked at the don with a contrite expression. "Tony's missing, Boss. He didn't call in today with his numbers. I have Angelo tracking him down."

"For Christ's sake," Belletti stormed. "Can anything else go wrong? Get Angelo and Cortez out there then. I want Franco found. Take one of Tony's lieutenants too."

"I can go, Boss," Mario offered.

The don thought about it for a moment. "Send Angelo. He'll be motivated. And tell him I don't want to hear about him being embarrassed again. Find Tony and don't tell me more of my money is gone."

"On it." Mario turned and headed for the door, pulling out his phone as he went. His instructions were clear.

The don returned to his desk and sat down. He began to speculate how he would deal with the boy once he had him. A small smile crossed his face. It had been a long road to find Nate Vickers. Now he would make things right. He reached for his phone and stared at it. It was time to update Montreal. But as always, he would have to be very careful with his words.

***

Angelo was finishing a plate of *putenesca*, at his favourite diner in Little Italy, when his brother called him. He hated travelling, but not as much as he had learned to hate Franco Ricci. Payback time. Pocketing his phone, he drank back the rest of his Amarone, and motioned to his waiter for the bill.

He punched a number into his phone and asked Cortez to get everything ready to head out in the morning. Then he drove to his downtown apartment to pack.

He had just poured himself another glass of his favourite wine, when there was a knock on his door. He walked over, hand on his gun, and peered through the peephole. A delivery guy stood with two boxes of pizza in hand.

Angelo relaxed and opened the door to tell the guy he was at the wrong apartment. As he opened the door partially, it was kicked in, propelling him into the side wall, gun flying from his grasp. Angelo recovered and turned towards his assailant only to be faced with a Glock pistol pointed at his face. He froze.

"What the fuck?" he said, before the pistol slammed into the side of his face. He backed into the room wiping the blood from his face, with the back of his hand.

"Have a seat; I want information about a sum of money that was taken from you."

Angelo studied the man, wondering who he was. He had never seen him before. It made him very nervous. He was considering his options when he noted movement over the man's shoulder. After closing the door softly, his companion stepped around the strewn pizzas and looked in Angelo's direction.

His eyes went wide. He sat down in the chair that had been indicated. This was not going to be a good night.

***

Don Belletti sat quietly and waited. Mario was beside himself, screaming for revenge, demanding to know where to look. There could be no reasonable conversation until Mario tired himself out. It was obvious he wanted a quick fix, but the trail was cold.

Angelo's body had been discovered in the morning, after the building manager had reluctantly agreed to allow a very unsavoury yet compelling man access.

Coincidentally, at about the same time, a distraught farmer made a gruesome discovery of a body – Tony's – when he had gone into his barn to retrieve a tool to fix his tractor.

He didn't believe in coincidences and felt sure all these problems would trace back to the boy. He didn't understand how all the pieces fit together. Yet.

"One problem at a time," the don said, quietly trying to calm Mario down.

Mario whipped his head in the direction of the don. Anger flared again, then subsided just as quickly as he looked at Belletti's calm demeanor.

"He is... was... my brother, Antonio."

"I know Mario, I will look after this. But right now, I need you to head to the West Coast, find Franco and if possible, the boy."

Mario's face softened; rage turned to sorrow.

"I'm sorry this has happened, my friend, but it all comes down to them. I want them brought back to Calgary. Then I can make them pay. *Capisce?*"

Mario nodded, eyes downcast. The don could no longer read his expression.

"I want the boy alive, Mario. If you need to kill Franco, then kill him. Not the boy."

The don watched as Mario's eyes returned to his. He pursed his lips and nodded again. Belletti was satisfied. He'd given Mario purpose and a focus for his anger.

"I will personally attend to the funeral arrangements for Angelo, and I'll have our police contacts get me the information about who did this. We will avenge Angelo's death, once you return."

"Give him to me," Mario implored.

Belletti considered the request. "You have my word. But first I need to understand how everything fits together. It takes time, Mario. This will help you keep busy. I promise I'll keep you informed, as I learn more."

***

Mario de Luca, long-time associate of don Belletti, picked up Cortez, then a member of the *Raiders*. Cortez took the wheel, his sidekick the passenger seat and Mario climbed into the back. As they left Calgary's western edge, he quietly told them what happened to Angelo and then went quiet. Both men glanced at each other but said nothing. They were nearing Banff when Mario broke his hour-long silence.

"I want Franco alive. He will tell me what he knows. Then I'm going to kill him. We clear?"

Cortez nodded. His associate remained silent. This was not the time for discussion.

Mario stared out the rear window, the beautiful Rockies not registering. He slowly closed his eyes and clenched his fists. He allowed boyhood memories of he and his brother to fuel his anger.

CHAPTER SIXTEEN

HE SAW IT BEFORE IT hit him. His boat was keeling beautifully, cutting the waves as she should, but there was no accounting for rogue waves. Not that this part of the world ever had serious rogue waves. They were usually just entertaining. The spray from the wave rolled over the bow and floated towards the cabin. Nate turned away as the mist slammed into his face. He laughed. The wind was blowing NNW at fifteen knots and Nate had reefed in his jib and lowered his main sail, earlier on. The seas were rising, and it appeared he was in for a good blow. He loved it when the whitecaps whipped up and started to roll. It was as if an unseen force synchronized them for his viewing pleasure.

He needed an afternoon on the water to clear the fog from his mind. He knew of no better cure for the hangover that greeted his day. Nate liked rum but the combination of the rum, wine, and cigars together had exacted a toll.

He was on the water for a couple of hours when he noted the sea swells increasing to about five feet. Storm clouds were building on the horizon and appeared to be heading his way. Nate decided it would be a good idea to take shelter. He passed the Northwest tip of Little Popham Island and decided to tack. The sail swung to the opposite side of the boat. He winched in his line and felt the boat keel, as it redirected to Hermit Island. He trimmed his jib sail and his speed increased. He put the auto pilot on and relaxed as he headed for the natural harbour on the south side of the uninhabited island, glancing occasionally at the nearing storm. Twenty minutes later, after dropping his sails and setting his anchor in the soft sands below, Nate went below deck. A torrent of cold rain besieged the boat, as it lay in the secluded bay.

Nate turned on his marine radio and listened for the weather report. He stripped out of his sailing gear and hung it in the forward cabin. Shortly after turning up his electric heater, he was alerted that this weather system was going to be with them for the afternoon, with winds expected to whip up to thirty knots later in the day. He could probably motor back to his marina on the mainland, but it'd be an uncomfortable cruise. Deciding to weather the storm in the cove, he filled a basket with ground coffee and stared out at the rain as it percolated. The aroma filling the cabin was comforting. This was living.

He loved his boat. It was a previous year's model that had never been owned, which allowed him to buy below the asking price. Of course, a cash purchase also helped. The soft warm woods and cream-coloured fabrics, coupled with the gleaming chrome surfaces, served to distract him from his memories of what went on in Calgary. He had christened her *Serendipity* which meant "the occurrence of events by chance, in a happy way." Fitting. There was no doubt he was happiest when he was on her. Nate poured himself a coffee, turning his thoughts to his uncle.

He thought about Frank's arrival and the dire message he brought. Despite Frank's appearance, he felt safe... for now. Frank knew how to take care of himself, and Nate was confident he knew how to disappear without a trace. Don Belletti could look as hard as he liked. Still, he'd have to remain vigilant. The fact Frank had found him was proof of that.

The winds picked up. Nate could hear the lines banging on the mast above. It was going to be some night. He could feel *Serendipity* rolling, just slightly, and knew innately he had found good shelter to ride out the storm. His anchor would hold, he was sure of that. Nonetheless, he knew the night would be long as he would have to set an alarm to check her position every two hours. At least it would interrupt the dreams.

He hated them. They were always the same or of some iteration. Nate reaching for Jess's fingers as she slipped away; sometimes falling from a cliff, sometimes sinking to a watery grave on *Serendipity,* sometimes with her face exploding into a mass of blood and brain matter from an unseen weapon. Then he'd wake with his body covered in sweat. He'd lay still until the mist in his mind lifted. He didn't understand why the dreams kept coming, his affection for Jess was long over, replaced by sadness. He read about survivor's guilt and supposed it had to do with that.

The days were easier though. In the light of day, he could rationalize all that had happened and put it behind him. Being around Milo and Beka, and the routine of their world, helped to provide a sense of normalcy. Then the night would return, and the nightmares would start anew. Was it any wonder he preferred to be awake?

There was plenty in the light of day to give him pleasure, including the kids. Each Tuesday and Thursday, Nate had three of the local boys' board his boat for an afternoon, where he'd teach the art of sailing, albeit at an entry level. They'd be laughing as they ran down the dock, screaming out their joy, until they reached Nate's boat where they'd come up short and formally request permission to come aboard, just as Frank had done the previous night. Nate would nod, with an inviting smile, and the kids would clamour on board, turning at the same time to wave to their parents, standing on shore, as they watched to make sure they arrived safely and did not fall into the clutches of the old seadog named Archie who owned a nearby catamaran, a more comfortable two-hulled version of a traditional sailboat.

Archie dreaded the explosion of sound each day the kids arrived, and made sure Nate was aware of his disapproval. Nate would laugh and wave with a "Good morning, Archie," knowing full well that Archie would huff and turn to enter the salon of his thirty-six-foot Solaris Sunrise. Archie was the quintessential grumpy old man, who had retired twenty-two years ago from the Vancouver police force, and, at the age of seventy-four, was the only other full-time resident to live aboard at the marina. While Nate was always wary of the police, he found Archie to be a good neighbour, and liked having a second pair of eyes watching what went on.

Nate took a sip of his coffee and revelled in these new memories. *Nice to think happy thoughts.* He reached for his laptop and plugged it in. He signed into his satellite internet and downloaded his portfolio. Pity the satellite was so darned expensive, but it's what you had to do to maintain a low profile, living as best you can off the grid. He was a self-taught investor and shortly after establishing his new marine life, he'd voraciously read as much as he could on the so called 'art of investing' and found himself to be a pretty good study. He now had slightly more than two and a half million dollars in the account, and that was after having paid his uncle fifteen percent of his newfound wealth, to help him set up his new life. He was glad he had been successful in leaving his old world behind and with his new identity as Nate Beckett, he was slowly building another life, all ties to family and friends permanently erased. That was, until now.

Frank's arrival was a complication. Sure, he was happy to see him, but having him here brought on a level of additional risk that he had not anticipated. He regretted inviting him to Gibsons and was glad Frank would be leaving for the Caymans in a week, both for his safety and Frank's. In the meantime, he'd make the most of it and enjoy his uncle's company. Perhaps, with a little less libation.

The rain continued and the wind raged. Nate was sliding the curtains closed on the cabin windows when something caught his eye. He peered into the darkening late afternoon gloom. He removed a pair of binoculars from an overhead cabinet and raised them to his face. There, in the growing darkness, was a green light on the horizon with a white light above it. There was another boat in this storm, and it was coming straight at him.

Nate rose from his seat and walked into his berth. He reached below the bed, opened a storage door and pulled out a polished baseball bat. He had bought two of them shortly after acquiring *Serendipity.* You never knew when you might need a defensive weapon. He then walked back to the salon, peered out the window to see the boats progress. He reached over to the control panel and flicked a switch that caused the cabin to go dark. In the grey light, he climbed the few steps to the hatchway leading up to the deck and locked the door from within.

He made his way back to the side window, sat down on the bench seat and waited, his eyes glued on the approaching lights, rolling in equal time to the lines banging on the mast overhead.

CHAPTER SEVENTEEN

NATE AWOKE WITH A START. He checked the hatchway, the door remained latched. How could he have fallen asleep? He'd felt threatened by the approaching boat, but once he'd watched it motor into the cove, and the owner struggle to set his anchor in the gale force winds, he'd breathed a sigh of relief and slouched down on the lounge seat. The darkness had taken hold. He'd slipped into a sleep, this time without his usual bad dreams.

Nate rose from his bench seat and stretched, annoyed with himself for having fallen asleep in a manner that made him so stiff. He assessed the boat anchored across the water from him. Old Bayliner. It was in good shape, the black bimini on the bridge accenting the clean white lines of its hull. Looked to be about fifteen years old.

He could see, in the early morning light, that an inhabitant was stirring inside the cabin. Retreating from the window, he moved into his galley and turned on his stove, to make a morning coffee. While he waited for the water to boil, he unlocked the hatchway and went up on deck to greet the morning air. The storm had passed during the night and the sun was rising above the island hills casting shadows upon the rocky shore. The sea was flat and glistening. A group of cormorants sailed above the water's surface searching for their morning plunder. Gulls called out their mournful call and Nate spotted a large eagle perched upon the top of a tree, at the shores edge.

"Hey, neighbour." Nate spun to face the speaker. "Quite the storm we had last night."

Nate shielded his eyes against the morning sun and yelled back across the water. "Sure was." Hoping to shut down further conversation, he waved and headed below deck to finish making his coffee.

Returning to the deck with his drink in hand, encased in a heavy sweater to fend off the early morning coolness, Nate walked about the boat, inspecting for any damage it may have incurred from the night winds. Finding none, he returned to the cockpit, sat down, searching for the eagle again. He sipped his coffee.

"Where are you headed today?" he heard from across the water.

Nate pivoted in his seat and stared at the other boat. The sun remained in his eyes. He raised his hand to get a better look at the offending conversationalist.

"Heading back home." He said curtly. Nate valued the sounds of the sea life around him in the mornings. The last thing he wanted was to have to deal with others, especially ones intruding on him.

"Whereabouts?"

"...across the water." Nate rose. "You take care now."

He returned to his galley to clean up. It was time to go. His peaceful morning had been shattered. There was something about this guy. After cleaning up and locking the cabin down, he came back on deck and fired up his inboard engine and left it to idle. He walked to the bow of the boat and readied to raise his anchor.

"Looking for a good marina, myself," came another call from across the water.

"Sorry, I can't help you. I'm just visiting." Nate pushed the windlass button, allowing the noise of the rising anchor to block out any further conversation for the moment.

With a clunk, the anchor locked into place and Nate rushed to the cockpit, as the boat drifted. He revved life into the engine. Jumping behind the wheel, Nate steered *Serendipity* to the cove's entrance.

He glanced at the Bayliner and saw its pilot staring at him. He wished he could get a better look at the guy, but the sun restricted his vision. With an uninspired wave, Nate opened the throttle and pushed the boat to its limit. He navigated to open water, glancing back one last time to see the pilot still standing at the stern of his boat, staring.

Normally, Nate would've turned his bow into the wind, raised his mainsail and once the wind took hold, let out his jib to power a wonderful morning sail. The winds were perfect. But today, he decided against it, wanting to power his way home. Uncomfortable with the arrival of the Bayliner, he wanted to put distance between them. He pushed his power to the max and headed for the mainland.

Before long, Nate rounded the corner of Keats Island and headed across Shoal Channel towards Georgia Beach. Early morning dog owners were out walking. He throttled back his engine and cruised between the breakwaters protecting the marina and headed for home, at a crawl. Nate backed *Serendipity* into her slip, feeling the prop wash pulling the boat to one side. He killed the engine at just the right time. Jumping onto the dock, he tied down the bow to the dock cleat, then tied off the stern, making sure his boat was secure. He stood up and looked across the water.

There, at the entrance to the marina, was the Bayliner, dead in the water. On the bridge was a singular man, binoculars to his face, aimed in his direction.

Nate walked along the dock, never taking his eyes off the man. Archie sat out on the back of his catamaran, enjoying a late morning coffee. He stopped.

"Arch, you ever see that boat out there at the harbour entrance?" Nate asked, nodding in its direction.

Archie stood to get a better view, just as the sound of twin V8 engines kicked into gear, echoing across the water. Nate saw the boat turning, heading back to the channel. Only the stern was visible.

"Hard to tell," Archie said with little enthusiasm. "Where have you been?"

"Do you know anybody with an old Bayliner?"

"Nope," Archie slid back into his deck chair. "So where have you been?"

"Had to overnight the storm at Hermit Island - pretty bad one."

"Sure was."

"Had this guy show up in that old Bayliner. He anchored near me, despite the size of the cove. Asked a bunch of questions. Kind of gave me the creeps. Keep an eye out and let me know if you see him trolling around, will you Arch?"

"I can do that. You got a beef with this guy?"

"Nah, nothing like that, just a feeling. Have you seen Milo around this morning?"

"Yeah, he's up at the shack. Happy as always."

"Nice to like your job."

"I suppose you're going to be bringing those noisy little buggers around again this week?"

"Archie, you have to learn to enjoy the fun things of life, like popsicles, Sadie's fresh bread, and the laughter of children."

"Don't you be bringing Sadie into this."

Nate laughed. Sadie was Archie's ex who ran the local bakery. An adorable lady and the antithesis of Archie in demeanour. They'd divorced a few years back, Nate learned, and had managed to have a civil relationship since. That amazed Nate, given how cantankerous Archie could be from time to time.

"Yes, the boys will be around again and every week that the parents allow it, at least as long as the season holds. I love spending time with them, and besides, it's a way for me to give back."

"Give back...you're too young to give back. Try and keep the racket down a bit, will you? I live on this boat so I can listen to the gulls and the crows, not some squabbling snotty nosed kids."

Nate laughed and turned to go.

"I'll do my best," he said, heading up the dock with a wave.

Archie could be a grump, but not much happened on the docks that he didn't know about. Nate was confident Archie would tell him if he saw the Bayliner again.

He headed for shore, waving at familiar faces working on their boats. Up the ramp he went to the office and the marina store. As he pushed through the front door, bells rang out their melodic announcement of a visitor, and both Milo and Beka looked up.

"Where've you been, sailor?" Beka asked with a smile.

Milo waved at Nate, then returned to adjusting the goods on the shelves.

Nate grinned at Beka, feeling a warmth settling over him. "I had to spend the night at Hermit Cove to wait out the blow."

"It was a wild one, that's for sure. No damage, I hope?"

"No, I fared well. But I am getting a little low on provisions and I want to get a new reel for my rod. Hooked a good size Halibut last time I tried fishing for one, but my tuff line seized and then snapped."

Beka smirked. "Stop Nate. I'll let Milo help you with that. I might give you something that will only catch minnows. You know me and fishing gear."

"Not sure any gear will make you a good fisherman, Nate" Milo said with a chuckle. He stood from the lower shelves, rubbing his back. "Come on over here and let me show you the new Penn 330s we just got in."

Nate moved to go over to see Milo, beaming at Beka as he did so.

"Can I put together a basic provision package for you, or do you want to do your own in the village?" Beka asked Nate's back. Nate turned and smiled at her again. She had that effect. "That would be great, Beka. I'll do a bigger shop in town, later in the week."

Nate approached Milo. He was not a big man. He stood at five foot nine inches tall but was solid for his age of fifty-six. Nate had seen him working on some of the boats in the adjoining dry dock and marvelled at his strength. He sported a seventies greying ponytail and had a smile that could be disarming. When Nate had first arrived, Milo had been cool to him, especially when he started talking to his daughter. But as time went by and Milo determined that Nate was not a threat to Beka, they had become friends and their morning coffees had ensued.

Milo coughed a smoker's cough. Nate knew it was from his morning supply of pot and wondered how he worked as well as he did, while imbibed.

"That stuff will kill you, Milo."

He wasn't a fan, probably because he felt he had to keep his wits about him. The last thing he needed was to attract the attention of the local constabulary, who still frowned on pot usage, despite the recent legalization of the substance. He had done a good job of avoiding that complication.

"You tell him, Nate," Beka called out.

"Yeah, yeah. What makes you sure either of you want to be around a Milo that isn't assisted?" He laughed.

Milo went on to show Nate all the advantages of the new reel. In a matter of minutes, Nate had succumbed to the sales pitch and was walking over to the till to pay for it when Beka interrupted,

"You should give Ben a call today, Nate. He has another young guy he thinks would be good fit for your sailing program."

Ben Mills ran the Boys Club in Gibsons. Beka had introduced Nate to Ben when he had told her he was looking for a way to give to his new community, by working with challenging kids. After a vigorous interrogation, Ben agreed to set up a program where Nate could teach sailing to a group of boys, provided they had their parent's approval, which was easily obtained. They were a challenge to their parents and Nate hoped that his effort might result in them finding a passion in sailing, that would ultimately keep them off the streets and away from a bad start in life.

"I have the three amigos for this year, but happy to start working on next year's program," Nate said.

"I still don't get why you don't charge for this, Nate. I'm pretty sure that Ben would pay a stipend."

Nate shook his head. His generosity was one of the traits that he hoped was growing on her. "No, I made a promise to myself, a long time ago, that I would help others if I could. Besides, I get way more out of it than I give."

"Okay," she capitulated, before changing the subject. "Want me to have one of the guys stow the provisions, in the cockpit of your boat, or are you heading back down there now?" she was referencing a couple of the local students Milo hired each summer to assist them.

"I'm going to head over to see Ben, rather than call. Have one of the boys do it, please. Can I pay for this now?"

When she didn't respond, Nate glanced at Beka, unnerved by the intense look on her face. She was no longer looking at him but at something outside the window. Nate shifted to see what had her attention and could see a man standing across the street looking at the store.

Nate asked, "You, okay?"

Beka, turned her gaze back to Nate. "I'm fine; I'll put the reel on your account," she said in a near whisper. Her eyes shifted to the man outside again, then back to Nate. "Say hello to Ben for me." Beka turned back to the papers on her counter, suddenly all business.

"Alright... you sure you're okay?"

"I'm sure. I'll see you later."

Nate headed for the door, opening it. The bells chimed as he exited.

"See you, Milo. Thanks for the new reel." Nate called out, clutching his purchase in his hand.

"Later," Milo replied.

***

Beka watched Nate through the window, as he headed for the man known as Ty O'Reilly. A horrible sense of unease washed over her. She jumped when Milo placed a hand on her shoulder. He kept his eyes on Nate too. She had a clear view of Ty confronting Nate and wished, as she had so many times before, that he would just go away.

"He can handle himself, Beka." Milo said.

"You know Ty."

"Yes, and I know Nate too."

"He's dangerous. You need to stop this."

Milo looked down at his daughter. She didn't look back, her eyes glued on the scene outside.

"Please Dad...why did I ever have to meet that man."

Milo paused. "Have you been encouraging him?"

Beka shot him a piercing glare. "You know better than that."

Milo's face sunk. "You're right, I'm sorry."

Beka turned back to the window. "I wish I could hear what they're saying. You need to go out there. I'd do it but it would make things worse."

Milo sighed. "I'll head out, but let's give it a minute. Nate can handle himself, let's see what he does with this. Okay?"

Beka stared straight ahead, wringing her hands. She was afraid for Nate.

***

Nate addressed Ty O'Reilly, stopping inches in front of him.

"We haven't met," Nate said, eyeing him.

"I know who you are." Ty O'Reilly stared over Nate's shoulder at the side window of the marina store. He had a foreign accent that Nate assumed to be Australian.

"I don't know who you are though."

His gaze turned on Nate. "Ty O'Reilly. You're beginning to annoy me."

Nate stared at O'Reilly. He stood at about six feet and looked to be slightly overweight, but Nate was sure that this man was not someone you should take lightly. He had long curly brown hair and unsettling dark blue eyes. Nate thought that the ladies would probably see him as a good-looking man, if you ignored his personality.

"You make Beka nervous," Nate said, shifting his body sideways to make himself a smaller target. Milo had briefly told him about Ty O'Reilly, over one of their coffees, many weeks back.

"That so?" he said. "And just what business is it of yours, mate? Are you seeing her or something?" Nate could smell booze on his breath, despite it being early morning.

"Just a concerned citizen. Don't like to see people nervous."

"You are the one that should be nervous," O'Reilly hissed. "Where'd you come from anyway? You aren't from around here?"

"Just passing through." Nate said.

"Why don't you keep passing through then? I have some business to attend to."

"Like I said, you're making the lady nervous. So how about you move along."

O'Reilly cocked his head at Nate, taking measure of him. "That lady is mine," he sneered. "You better not be having any designs on her."

Nate took a step back, so he didn't have to smell the booze emanating from O'Reilly's mouth.

"Funny, I've never heard her mention you."

"Who do you think you are, mate? I don't need to answer to you. Now piss right off."

Nate didn't move. He expected to be attacked at any moment, but he had seen the worry on Beka's face and resolved to stand his ground. He wouldn't have done this a year ago.

"Like I said, you're making her nervous, so you need to move along." Nate braced for the attack.

"Well, well, well...if it ain't a shining knight." O'Reilly sneered at Nate again. "I go where I choose to go, Mr. Knight."

O'Reilly's eyes swivelled back to the door of the marina store as it opened. Milo came out and limped over to them. He stopped beside Nate and looked at O'Reilly.

"Everything all right here, Ty?" Milo asked.

"Just getting to know Mr. Knight here, Milo. Other than that, everything is just fine."

Milo let the reference to Nate slide. "Nobody wants any trouble, Ty."

"There's no trouble here, Milo." O'Reilly scowled at Nate. "Any trouble here, Mr. Knight?"

Nate said nothing, his gaze not wavering from O'Reilly's face.

"I was leaving anyway..." he said to Milo. "... you say hi to Beka for me. Tell her I miss her."

"I won't do that, Ty. You know that."

O'Reilly focused on Nate. "Seems I need to learn a little more about you, Mr. Knight. In the meantime, you stay away from my girl. We clear on that?"

Nate stood fast. "I don't think she's owned by anybody. We clear on that?"

O'Reilly smiled a disingenuous smile at him. "Be seeing you Mr. Knight." He turned and swaggered up the hill.

Milo turned to Nate once O'Reilly was out of earshot. "Watch your back around him, Nate. That boy is a mean one."

They stood together and watched O'Reilly until he disappeared over the hill.

"So, I gather," Nate said quietly. He didn't want Milo to see his hands were shaking so he put them in his pockets. "I gotta go see Ben." Milo nodded, turning back to the store.

Nate headed in the same direction O'Reilly had gone. He wondered as he crested the hill, if he would be seeing him far sooner than he wanted.

CHAPTER EIGHTEEN

FRANK RICCI SIPPED A GINGER ale purchased from a vending machine at the Horseshoe Bay Ferry Terminal, waiting for Elena to arrive. He had ridden in the last row of a bus for the short ride from Gibsons to the ferry terminal. He hated bus rides. They always made him feel ill. He hoped the drink would help. The sailing from Gibsons to Horseshoe Bay aggravated the situation, so he decided to sit outside at a lunch table near the reception area for walk-ons, hoping his stomach would settle.

He gazed over the water and marvelled, yet again, at the beauty of the area. As he waited, he perceived animal shapes in the large cumulus clouds billowing on the horizon and had just made out the shape of a greyhound racing dog when Elena's car pulled into the ferry line up and stopped, but not before catching Frank's eye. He scanned to see if anyone watched or followed her. Nothing out of the ordinary.

She exited the car and studied the area. She was wearing a dark blue dress and cream-coloured sandals. Frank noticed her hair was cut a little shorter. It looked good. She spotted him and started walking in his direction.

He rose from his seat and placed the empty can of ginger ale on the table, his nausea abated. He made his way to her, waving as he did so. A smile broke across her face, and she ran for him. She folded into his arms, and he revelled in the comfort of their hug. For a moment, there was no don Belletti, there was no running. There were just two people who missed each other very much. Frank held onto her a moment longer than he intended, then stepped back and took her in. She looked tired.

"How was the drive?"

"Long. It's good to see you, Frank," she said, sounding nervous.

"You too," Frank tilted his head. Something felt amiss.

"We have a bit of a wait ahead of us. Can I buy you a cup of some bad coffee or something?"

"I'd rather a drink, if we can?"

"Sure, let's get a ticket for the ferry first, then we can slide over there." He nodded to a bar across the parking lot that sold sandwiches, drinks, and the like. "I'm pretty sure we can get a beer. We want to make sure we don't miss this ferry. It's a long wait if we do."

They settled into their patio seat with two cans of a local IPA, when Elena asked, "Want to tell me where we are going now?"

Frank laughed. "Sorry about the cloak and dagger stuff." He paused. "Gibsons."

"I thought as much, after you said to meet at this terminal. Have you found Nate?"

Frank nodded with a smile. "I have, and he is doing great, El. He's buried deep and he's making a new life for himself. There might even be a new love interest, but I'm not sure."

"And what have you been doing these past months?"

"I think I told you before that Nate was having a hard time finding himself. That's how he ended up in that dead end job in Calgary. He bounced around a lot, trying to find something, anything, that would give him satisfaction. I thought he'd do something with the degree he earned, but for some reason, he wanted no part of a nine to five job."

Frank could see Elena was perplexed. He laughed at her confusion. "Stay with me," he laid a hand on her arm, leaving it there. "Despite his turmoil, he had one constant in his life. His love for sailing. He'd learned day-sailing on the Glenmore reservoir in Calgary, as a boy. In his teen years, he would save enough money from odd jobs, and head to the coast where he learned to sail yachts. He dreamed that one day, he would get his own yacht."

"I don't understand how this is about you... but go on."

Frank chuckled again. "I figured if he was going to start over, it would be here. I knew he was coming to the coast. So, I came out and started asking questions. A lot of questions. I eventually found a place where I found out he had bought a boat. Then, I waited … a long time. I got lucky; I ran into him at a marina in Vancouver. So that is what I have been doing these past months … waiting."

"Only a man who knew his nephew well, would think to follow him through a dream. I think you might have gotten very lucky finding him that way."

Frank smiled and then went silent.

Elena stared at him, then asked. "What did he do Frank? Why is Mr. Belletti so insistent on finding him?"

"Belletti? What have you to do with him?" Frank ignored the question about Nate.

"He's been asking about you. A lot."

Frank sensed she was holding back. He expected Belletti to be looking for him but why was he approaching her? "Has he hurt you?"

Elena slowly shook her head in denial. "Why didn't you call me before, Frank? I appreciated the one-way emails but... I've been so worried about you."

"I couldn't chance it. Belletti has ears everywhere. I'm not going to go into the why El, but he wants Nate very badly. I didn't want to put you in danger."

Frank saw a darkness come over Elena's face. "What is it?"

She looked deeply into Frank's eyes and opened her mouth, then closed it and stared out over Howe sound and the Coastal Mountains.

"Doesn't get much prettier than this." She said redirecting the subject.

Frank stayed quiet, studying Elena with concern in his eyes.

"What is it?" he pried gently.

She leaned over and gave him a kiss on the cheek. "I'm glad to see you, Frank. So very glad. Thank you for chancing the phone call."

Frank's eyes glistened and a smile lit up his face. Something was off but it could wait.

He turned his view to the water as well. "The beauty of this place has been eclipsed by the beauty of this moment, El," he whispered. He shoved his concern to the back of his mind. It was so good to see her. He'd missed her, but until he saw her getting out of her car, he hadn't realized how much.

He spun and looked out at the line-up of cars readying for the ferry. "El, you didn't notice anyone following you, on the way here, did you?"

She considered the question. "I don't think so. But I'm not sure I would really know, if someone put their mind to it."

Frank nodded. It wasn't the answer he hoped for.

"How long are you planning to stay in Gibsons, Frank?" and then shyly added, "Or can I say...we?"

"We?" said Frank, letting the question tease her.

"I've spent the past year alone Frank, thinking about you almost every day. I've thought over and over that I should have told you how I felt about you. Maybe then you wouldn't have left me behind.

I know you said to come for a visit, in a drunken stupor, but I'm here and now that I am... well... I don't want to go back to Calgary."

Frank's mouth dropped open.

"I don't want to be without you," she added, blushing.

"But what about your daughter?" Frank countered, a mixture of astonishment and hope stirring within.

Elena's face darkened again.

"There is something you're not telling me."

She paused. "There is nothing for me to go back to Frank. She's made a bed that is not one I can accept, and our paths are diverging, I believe, permanently. I would rather focus on a new direction, and I would like it to be with you, if you'll have me."

"I need more, El," Frank said quietly. "That's a big step."

Elena sighed. "She's been arrested for prostitution." She hung her head. "Is that enough Frank? Can I stay?"

So that's what she's been holding back. His face softened. "I'd like that very much, but you'd be putting yourself in a lot of danger. Don Belletti can be a very determined man. If he has been asking about me a lot, as you say, it's because he is looking for me too. That's not good. Really, El, you want to have a life with a man on the run? I certainly can never go back."

"I've thought this through. I know the risks."

"Okay then." Frank beamed. He felt mixed emotions by the decision. His brain argued she should not stay but his heart won out.

"You didn't answer me, Frank. Are you... we, planning to stay here?"

"For a few more days or so. Then we'll be off to the Cayman Islands. I have a small place there. I set it up years ago. I never thought I would need it, but now it seems it was a fortuitous decision."

Elena's eyes went wide, then she smiled. "Let's go tonight, Frank. Let's just get out of here. The longer we stay in Canada, the more risk there is that someone might spot you."

"You have a passport?" he laughed.

"I do," she snapped.

Frank was taken aback by the urgency in her voice but stood firm.

"I just found Nate, El. I'm finding it difficult to go. I know we must, but not just yet. We'll be fine for a few more days. Now drink up, I see the ferry coming. It will be docked shortly."

She picked up her half-finished drink and handed it to Frank. "I've had enough, thank you."

Frank saw her face darken again.

He downed the rest of his drink, then tossed the two cans into a recycling bin. They walked back to her car. She slid her arm through his. He liked the feeling, wishing their circumstances were different. He couldn't shake a sense of foreboding. Something was still amiss. *She's still not telling me everything.*

***

At about the same time Frank was manoeuvring Elena's car onto the ferry, Nate was returning from his visit with Ben. It had been a productive discussion, even though Ben was disappointed that Nate would defer taking any new sailing students on until the following year. Nate had reasoned that he wanted to maintain a high level of training quality with the three boys he was working with now. To add a fourth into the line-up would slow the progress of the others. In time, Ben acquiesced and bade Nate a goodbye after assuring him of how much he appreciated the amount of free time he gave the boys.

His mind, however, was not on the discussion, but rather the one he had earlier with Ty O'Reilly. That had not gone well. Nate was worried that he had allowed it to escalate. That was not how you kept a low profile. He resolved to try and smooth things over later, if possible.

He started down the docks, noticing a man standing in the back of Archie's boat. He wore a grey shirt and midnight blue pants with a very distinctive yellow stripe on each leg. His police issue cap was under his left arm. Seeing a RCMP constable on the docks made Nate uncomfortable. He could see the officer looking in his direction as he approached, making it impossible for him to turn back, without attracting unwanted attention. He kept walking towards him. He passed him with a nod of his head, when Archie called out.

"Nate?"

Nate's heart raced a little faster, but he turned in the direction of the voice.

"Come here a second. Want you to meet our local law enforcement."

Nate strode to the corner of the boat.

"Hey," he said to the officer.

"Nate, I'd like you to meet Constable Steve Quince. Steve, this here is Nate, our newest resident, although not so new anymore."

"Hi, welcome to Gibsons," the officer said, looking closely at Nate.

"Thanks."

"So, you've been here a while?"

"Yeah, a fair while."

"You must like it here." Quince bobbed his head. "I didn't catch your last name."

"Beckett," Nate said. He was feeling uncomfortable with all the questions. He turned to Archie. "Was there a problem on the docks, Arch?"

"Nah, Steve came down to say hello and keep an old cop in the fold of what's happening in the area."

Nate laughed. "Hopefully not much. That's why I came here. I like nice and quiet."

"Where'd you come from?" Quince asked. "We don't get a lot of long-term visitors here, unless they're planning to move here."

"I live on my boat, Steve. Can I call you Steve?" Quince waved a hand in acceptance. "A dream since I was a kid. I came up here from Vancouver, a while back and kind of fell in love with the place. Hope to stay for a bit, but I'm a wanderer."

Quince smiled. "It's funny we haven't met until now. We have such a small town." Nate tilted his head in acknowledgment. "Don't you work, Nate?"

"Sure, but I'm lucky enough to be able to do what I do, from my boat."

"And what is that?"

Nate was about to answer him, wondering how much he should say, when his phone rang. "Excuse me," he said, stepping onto the dock to answer the call.

A few minutes later, he put his phone into his back pocket and turned back to Archie's boat. Constable Steve Quince was just stepping onto the dock, as well.

"On your way?" asked Nate.

"Yeah, duty calls. Nice to meet you, Nate."

"You too," Nate said, glad the direct line of questioning ended. His efforts to avoid meeting the local police had just come to an end.

He watched the officer walk up the gangway, then he turned back to Archie, who was gawking at him quizzically.

"Turns out I might have found out who the guy in the Bayliner was, Nate. Come aboard again, we can have a beer and I will tell you about it."

Nate stepped aboard. This was important. He would think about the call he'd received later.

CHAPTER NINETEEN

FRANK ENJOYED THE BEAUTIFUL LATE afternoon ferry crossing. A perfect coastal day, other than some sea haze; the view across the water unsurpassed. Elena had never been to the Sechelt peninsula, and he enjoyed watching the joy on her face as she looked out over their scenic passage. He grinned at her excitement when five pelicans flew across the water in perfect formation, shortly after they departed Horseshoe Bay. He was glad his stomach had settled down.

Frank asked if she needed some water.

She nodded.

"I'll be right back," he said.

He walked to the stairs leading to the restaurant located one deck below. Entering a queue with two bottles of water in hand, he waited for his turn to pay. There was a partition of glass separating the restaurant buffet from the dining area. Frank saw his reflection in the glass. It acted like a mirror in the light. His image surprised him. He looked happy. He smiled.

There was movement behind him, causing him to look beyond his own image in the glass to those in line. There was a man, two back, staring at his back. Frank studied the image for a moment. He put the water on the counter and dropped to his knee. Tying his shoe, he glanced back. He had a clear view of the man. He stood, this time a chill shot down his spine. He didn't know who he was, but he was sure of the type.

Frank moved forward to the till.

"That be all, sir?" a young attendant asked.

"Darn, I forgot the sandwiches," Frank spun away from the register. He could hear the attendant calling the next person in line forward.

Frank turned in the direction of the man watching him. The man's eyes diverted. He walked back to the sandwich area where he picked up a couple of ham and cheese in pre-wrapped packages. The man followed. Frank spun again, heading back to the till and the bottles he left there. The man had nowhere to turn. He walked past Frank without making eye contact and headed over to the dessert section, feigning interest.

Frank's suspicions were confirmed. He was the kind of man that Frank had seen all his life, one who made a living on the dark side. No doubt this man was following him for no purpose other than to report back to don Belletti. How had they found him so fast? Had they followed Elena?

Frank paid for his purchases and with a bag in hand, he climbed the stairs back to the top deck and crossed over to Elena. She watched the speed in which he crossed the deck floor and seeing the look on his face, she blanched.

"Frank?"

"We have company, El. I don't know if they are following you or they've tracked me down, but we must move... now. Back to the car."

He lightly took her arm. They strode to the stairs and headed for the car deck. On high alert, Elena peered about, allowing Frank to guide her. She looked over her shoulder. Frank felt her arm go tense. She sucked air through her teeth.

"I've seen that man before," she hissed, turning to focus on the next flight of stairs, as they descended. Frank didn't look back. He knew what the man looked like.

"What's he doing?"

"Talking on his cell phone. What are we going to do, Frank?"

"Not sure. I need to think."

Frank thought the decision to go to the car, may in fact have been the wrong one. The car deck was usually deserted. They would be exposed. Then the ship's PA system announced that all guests should head to their cars to get ready for their departure. Frank breathed a sigh of relief.

They arrived at Elena's vehicle; Frank returned to the driver's seat and waited for her to climb in on the opposite side. He hit the button to lock their doors, while adjusting the rear-view mirror in time to see the man walk over to a white SUV and climbed into the passenger seat. Frank aligned the side mirror on the car to improve his view. "There's another one in the driver's seat. Beyond that, I can't tell how many more are in the vehicle."

Elena had adjusted her side mirror to watch them as well. She remained silent.

"I'm pretty sure they won't make a move on a crowded ferry deck, but keep an eye on them, El."

Frank glanced forward and saw the barrier being lifted. They would be moving shortly.

"I thought you didn't think you were followed?" he said, refocusing on his mirror. Without waiting for an answer, he added, "And where have you seen him?"

Elena winced. "Frank, I have something I need to tell you."

Frank's gaze diverted as the cars began to stream off the ferry. "Hold that thought until we get onto the road."

Elena stared out the window at the mountains beyond, as they crested the ferry ramp and started down the highway. Frank shot her a quick look. He briefly closed his eyes and sighed. Something was clearly amiss.

He had to lose these guys. Their safety and that of Nate depended on it. Then he'd get to the bottom of what she wasn't telling him.

***

Nate sat down in a comfortable chair that Archie offered and glanced over the marina. The shadows were lengthening. The waters glistened as the late afternoon sun bounced off small ripples made by boats coming and going. The docks were busy with people readying their boats for the upcoming weekend, and Nate could see a couple of fishing boats returning to their assigned wharf, with their day's catch in their holds.

He made a mental note to pick up some halibut that would soon be hawked at their wharf. A pan seared fish, with capers and cherry tomatoes would be perfect for the upcoming dinner with his uncle. He thought about Frank's call. He'd sounded happy. What was that all about? He talked about having a surprise. Hopefully not another bottle of "special" rum.

"Here you go," Archie said, handing Nate a bottle of Dos Equis beer. Archie loved all things Mexican, and Nate wondered, not for the first time, why he had not retired in Mexico.

"Thanks, Archie."

Archie sat in his chair and looked out over the marina as well. He took a long slug of his beer and sighed. Nate watched him contemplating what to say.

"So?" prodded Nate. "You were going to tell me about Constable Quince and your conversation."

"Steve's a great guy, Nate. A guy you want to get to know, if you are ever in trouble." Nate let the statement float. "He's been posted here for about four years now and some of the fellas tell me he has turned down two postings in Sechelt, at their main detachment, to avoid having to leaving Gibsons. He loves it here. From time to time, he comes by and asks for my thoughts, when he needs some 'old fashioned' wisdom." Archie beamed.

"And are you that wise?" Nate chuckled.

Archie did not laugh. He held Nate's eyes. "Sometimes, but this visit was a first."

"How do you mean?"

"Seems Steve had a visitor this morning, a man from the mainland." The locals always called Vancouver the mainland. "A John Sebastian wanted to let Steve know that he'd be working in the area for a bit."

Nate was having a hard time seeing what this had to do with the Bayliner. "Why would he do that?"

"Cause he's a P.I."

Nate didn't like the feeling twisting in his stomach.

"Seems he's been hired to try and find a certain Nate Vickers, formerly from the city of Calgary. Apparently, he has an insurance payout he's been instructed to pay to him."

"Is that so?" Nate responded, keeping his voice from betraying his spinning head.

"Funny, the two of you having the same names." Archie eyed Nate, seeking a response.

"Lot of people named Nate around, Arch. What's this got to do with the Bayliner?"

"That's the thing of it, Nate. He told Steve he was staying on the boat and if he knew anything that might help his investigation he could be reached there. Seems he is tied up at Freddy's dock. Got me thinking though, why was he watching you? You did say that he made you nervous this morning."

Nate could tell the cop was coming out of retirement. Nate scrambled.

"He did. The way he ended up in the same bay as me last night, coupled with the strange conversation that we had this morning. That's all. I tend to have a suspicious nature, Archie." He tried to smile at Archie, but it came across more like grimace. He turned and looked out over the stern of Archie's boat again.

Archie continued to fix him with a pointed stare. "Why would you tend to have a suspicious nature, Nate?"

Nate glanced back, "Don't know. Always have had. Just the way I'm built." Nate was fighting to control the conversation. He didn't like the direction they were headed.

Archie let him off the hook. "Anyway, Steve didn't like him. Something didn't feel right. That's why he came by. Wanted to know if I ever had this type of an approach when I was active."

"What'd you say?"

"I told him any P.I.'s I ever came across did their level best to stay away from the local police. They found it too constraining."

"Did he say who he was working for?"

Archie considered Nate and took another long slug of his beer, letting out a burp. Archie wiped his mouth on his sleeve, then tacked. "Nate, you are a mysterious fellow. You never like to talk about yourself and work very hard fitting in around here. I like you. But I like our nice sleepy hollow even more. I don't want to see any problems coming this way. So, I hope that the name is just a coincidence and nothing more. I'll also assume that your questions are just out of interest. But I must tell you, my cop's spider sense is tingling."

Nate looked at Archie, drained his beer, and stood up. "Archie, I'm not looking for trouble. I'm just a guy who's off the grid and trying to live a quiet existence. Thanks for the beer." Nate placed his half full beer on the table and stepped onto the dock as Archie huffed, "Uh huh."

He had taken but a few steps when Archie called after him.

"Insurance company."

Nate turned. "Pardon?"

"He's hired by an insurance company, least that's what he told Steve."

"I was curious Archie, nothing more. See you later."

Nate waved and wandered down the dock, certain that Archie was watching him.

He climbed onto his boat, deep in thought. *Insurance...for what?*

He changed out of his boating clothes into a pair of washed denims and a clean buttoned down collar shirt. He grabbed a light jacket and headed for shore, after locking his cabin for the first time since he had arrived in Gibsons. The first step was to understand just who that guy on the Bayliner was.

Walking to the shore ramp, he glanced at the setting sun, the beauty of it lost in the thoughts swirling in his head.

CHAPTER TWENTY

NATE ARRIVED ON SHORE TO see Steve Quince exiting the marina store. He pulled up short, not wanting to have a second conversation with him. He pretended to be interested in something below the dock. Nate waited until the cruiser pulled away and headed to the store. He wanted to know the nature of that visit. He thought he had been circumspect with Quince but had to know if he was asking more questions about Nate Vickers.

He opened the door and saw Milo standing behind the cash register. His face was a mask of pain and rage.

"What's going on Milo?" Nate pushed his problems aside.

"Nothing, Nate. What do you need?" His tone was not friendly.

"What's happened, Milo?"

"It's not your concern, Nate."

"Probably not." Nate stood his ground. His purpose for coming, forgotten. He didn't move or say anything else. He could see Milo was weighing his options. Finally, he capitulated.

"Beka." Milo's eye's shot to Nate's. They began to glisten.

Nate's heart skipped a beat.

"Is she okay?" he said, thinking the worst.

"Ty O'Reilly, that's what's happened. I wish I was twenty freaking years younger."

"Milo, tell me what's happened?" Nate demanded.

Milo stared at Nate, opened his mouth, then closed it again.

"Milo, for God's sake..."

"He hit her," Milo choked.

"What?" Nate clenched his fists at his side. He felt a surge of anger flash behind his eyes. He stepped up to the counter and leaned into Milo. "Tell me everything."

"O'Reilly...got into an argument with her, and it seems he took offence when she made certain comments."

"About what?" Nate asked, his temples pounding from the surge of adrenalin moving through him.

Milo hesitated, "About you."

Nate stared at him. "Why were the police here?" he asked, no longer thinking about his own concerns.

"She's decided to get a restraining order against him. I asked Steve if he could help."

"Where is she, Milo?"

"Nate, she can't take another bad relationship. She has feelings for you. You must see that. Let it go, I'll work through this with her."

"Where is she?" Nate repeated quietly, trying to prevent a rage from taking hold.

Milo sighed and nodded his head to the back of the store.

Nate walked around the counter, squeezed Milo's shoulder, and headed for the rear door. Opening it, he stepped out into the early evening. She sat on an old wooden bench, taking in the twinkling lights of the marina. The rear door light illuminated the side of her face. She was smoking a cigarette. She glanced at him, said nothing, shifted slightly so that her face stayed in the shadows and returned her focus to the mast of a sailboat.

Nate sat beside her. "I didn't know you smoked."

After a brief pause, Beka said, "I don't."

Nate reached over, nobly took the cigarette from her, and squashed it beneath his foot. He sat down and took her hand. She didn't pull it back or acknowledge that this was the first time he had shown any physical form of affection.

"I hope that was okay."

She nodded. Her bottom lip quivered. He reached gently for her chin and turned her face to him. Even in the poor light he saw the purple bruise formed around her eye and committed it to memory.

They sat there, in silence, then she began to shiver. Nate took off his jacket and lightly placed it around her shoulders. That's when she cried, first lightly, then more insistently, until she sobbed. Nate reached around her shoulders and drew her into his body and waited. He could feel her tears saturate the front of his shirt. Soon enough the sobbing stopped, and she pulled away from him, reaching up to pull his jacket tighter around her.

"Wait here," he said, standing. He walked back into the store and returned with a box of tissues. She reached up and took one. Her mouth twitched in appreciation. He sat down again, taking her hand once more in his. She fixed her eyes on him, unapologetic for the way she looked.

"Tell me about it," Nate whispered.

She started slowly. Nate listened without interruption. How she had been raised by Milo after the death of her mother, how he had instilled solid core family values within her. How she had, as a stupid young woman, rebelled against her father and gotten into all kinds of trouble, including making a life for herself with Ty O'Reilly. One day, after a particularly nasty exchange with O'Reilly, she came to accept what her father had been telling her all along. O'Reilly was a dangerous man, prone to violence and she had to get away from his influence. So, she left him and started a new life in Vancouver. A friend of her father was able to get her a job as a health care assistant, where, as a quick study, she learned basic treatments for a variety of problems.

She glanced at Nate to see if he was following. Satisfied, she continued.

She had been in Vancouver for about a year, she told him, when her longing to be back in Gibsons became so strong she abstained from trying to move ahead in the medical field and returned to the marina and her former life. Milo embraced her and they'd run the marina together ever since.

Initially, she stayed hidden from O'Reilly, but that changed when, one day, he spotted her on the dock. She was forced to talk with him, as it became apparent over the following weeks he wasn't leaving. She had made a quasi-peace with him since then, feigning off his constant advances. For the most part she had been able to settle into a semi-normal life.

"So, what happened?" Nate asked gently, not wanting her to pull back.

Beka searched Nate's eyes. "Another man came into my life."

Nate's mouth dropped open.

"Since Ty met you, and you challenged him, he's become very jealous. I didn't understand that until I defended your position. When I wouldn't back down, his anger boiled over, and he punched me."

Nate glowered at the marina, saying nothing for the longest moment. They were still holding hands when Nate suddenly stood up. He asked her for a moment and walked back to the store. The door hit Milo as he entered. It was apparent he had been eavesdropping on the conversation. "Really, Milo?"

Milo blushed but remained silent. Nate told him what he needed and returned to Beka.

"Come on," he said. "I'll walk you to your father's place. You need to stay there tonight."

Beka searched Nate's eyes and rose to her feet. They walked together without holding hands. They said nothing further until they reached Milo's apartment.

He opened the door with Milo's key and let Beka into the suite ahead of him. He waited in the hall as she turned to him.

"Stay with me, Nate," she said, a weary expression coming over her. "Please," she added when he didn't accede.

"For a few minutes," he agreed and closed the door behind him. "I'll make you a cup of tea," he added as she walked over to Milo's old sofa and sat down.

"Thank you."

Nate foraged through Milo's cupboards, and before long had a steaming mug ready for her. He placed the cup on a coaster made from a fir tree, then noticed she had fallen asleep. Rifling through some nearby drawers in the living room, he found an old, but clean blanket which he used to cover her, after helping her stretch out on the sofa.

He stood, scrutinizing her for several minutes, and then reached down to touch her cheek below the purple welt. Silently, he left the apartment making sure the door was firmly locked. He returned to the marina store, told Milo she was sleeping for the night, and headed for the door.

"What did she say, Nate?"

Nate stopped and turned. "Not tonight, Milo. You need to get home to her. We can talk in the morning. Right now, I have to go."

Exiting the store, he strode down to the dock, purposely heading for his boat. He had forgotten about the conversation he wanted to have with the occupant of the Bayliner.

***

Ty O'Reilly finished his dance with a diminutive, but very cute, local high school grad. He returned to his table and boasted to his friends about his future conquest, educating them on how to forgo the urge for a one-night stand, if you wanted a one hundred percent chance of getting the prize.

He quaffed down his sixth and final beer of the evening, bade his friends a good night and walked out to the parking lot, to head home. He reached for the door of his Ford F150 when the bat came at him. He shielded his head from the initial blow, his face registering severe pain from the shattered humerus in his left arm. Grabbing it, he spun towards his assailant, who had readied the bat for another swing. O'Reilly turned away. The bat contacted the side of his stomach. He fell to his knees, in agony.

"You will pay for this," he gasped, glaring up at Nate hovering above him, his face contorted with rage.

Nate raised his foot, put it against O'Reilly's chest and pushed. He collapsed to the ground. Nate dropped the end of the bat near O'Reilly's face. O'Reilly twitched at the sound.

"Perhaps. Touch her again and I won't just hurt you, O'Reilly. I'll kill you." Nate Beckett knelt so that his face was inches from O'Reilly's ear and whispered, "I am her knight, you worthless piece of shit. Remember that."

Nate stood, slung the bat over his left shoulder, and headed back the way he had come. He paused and turned to look at O'Reilly's truck. He walked over to it, swung the bat, this time with a full force, smiling when the spider cracks shot across the front glass from the hole he left in the window.

Pivoting, he returned the bat to his shoulder and disappeared into the darkness, oblivious to the hatred that followed him.

CHAPTER TWENTY-ONE

"WHAT HAVE YOU DONE, EL?" Frank asked quietly, stepping on the gas pedal, pulling Elena's car into the departing ferry traffic. It was getting dark, but he could still see the cars coming up the hill behind him.

"Frank, I messed up...really messed up."

Frank turned to face her. She'd gone pale and she was staring out the front window. She wouldn't look at him.

He was lost in his thoughts when Elena blurted out "I told them you were north of Vancouver."

"What...Why?" he gasped.

Elena's voice cracked, her breathing laboured, tears tumbled down her cheeks silently. Frank glanced over to her but remained silent, allowing her time to regain composure.

His eyes darted to the rear-view mirror. They were in the middle of a long line of cars heading up the Sunshine Coast highway, headlights cutting through the coming night. Frank was pondering if he should start passing cars to get away from the SUV that followed or drive normally, letting his pursuers think that they were still undetected. He decided on the latter. He had to buy time to think through what they'd do next. It was a challenge. Her revelations constantly invaded his thoughts.

He concentrated on the highway, electing to avoid the first exit to Gibsons. He couldn't go there now. These guys were tracking him. He felt sure Nate was their goal. He had to lose them further down the peninsula.

Driving on in silence, Frank constantly checked the rear mirror. They'd passed the second highway exit to Gibsons when Elena admitted to Frank all that happened leading up to her departure from Calgary. This included the sordid details of the arrest and subsequent release of her daughter, along with Belletti's demands. Every now and then her voice faltered, and a fresh torrent of tears ran down her cheeks. Frank remained quiet. When she paused, he would simply add, "Go on." Then she was finished and sat quietly, staring ahead, as if saying nothing allowed her absolution for her betrayal.

Frank was in turmoil. The euphoria he had felt after her arrival was replaced by a concern for her safety and that of Nate's. He thought little of his own risk. He had been in this shadowy world for too long for that to concern him. It was like anything else. A problem that he'd overcome. But this time, he knew his adversaries were capable. He felt sure, it was one of the DeLuca brothers, or both, tracking him down.

He thought he should be angry, but he was not. Nothing good would come of it. He didn't know what to think of her actions. On the one hand, she had led the wolf to the den, on the other, she had taken decisive actions to try and protect him and his business. Why had she done that? Why had she put her life in danger to help him? Did her betrayal change how he felt about her? Could he look past it? Questions he would cogitate upon if they were lucky enough to get away from their friends in the white SUV.

Frank pulled out to pass a car in front of him, allowing space to distance themselves from his adversaries, now just four cars back.

"Aren't you going to say anything, Frank?" Elena asked quietly.

"Can't talk about it right now, El. I need to figure out how to shed our company. You may have noticed; we passed the road into Gibsons." Elena shook her head in dissent. She had been totally preoccupied.

"Where are we going?" she asked.

"I'm not sure. We'll be entering the town of Sechelt shortly, but I don't think we should try to lose them there. Too close to Nate. I need you to set your feelings aside for now. We need to discuss how we get out of this mess, and we need to stay focused. We'll talk about all this later. I promise." He reached over and squeezed her hand.

Frank stepped on the gas and swerved around another, slower car, adding more distance between him and his pursuers. He glanced in the mirror. The SUV was moving too, staying within visual distance of its prey.

Frank saw further movement and saw a third vehicle pull out and pass the slower vehicle behind it. Then another car followed it. He was now travelling at twenty kilometres over the speed limit, a feat that wasn't easy on the curving highway. He understood why the SUV would take a chance to stay with them, but what was with these guys?

"I need you to pull out your phone, El, where does this highway go?"

Elena followed his instructions and in a few minutes she answered. "Looks like to another ferry...place called Earl's Cove."

"How long?"

Elena pounded on her phone. "About an hour"

"Okay, see if we require a reservation to get on that ferry."

She tapped the keys on her phone. "I don't think so. It says it's a non-reservable route."

"Hmm," he said. "Probably would be a pretty quiet ferry." Frank thought for a few minutes, the seed of an idea germinating. Then he spoke. "We're going to have to lose your car, I'm afraid."

"My car...it's all I have left. Other than the money you gave me."

"I know, but we'll be fine if we get out of this..."

Elena shuddered and then peered at Frank quizzically. "Does that mean I'm forgiven?"

"I'm sorry, El, I don't want to talk about this right now."

Elena opened her mouth, then slammed it shut, lips pursed.

Frank handed her his phone. "Let's get rid of these phones. I don't know if they've been tracking you or me, but I'd rather be safe than sorry. I'll get in touch with Nate some other way, once we are away from these guys, to let him know he's been compromised."

Elena took the phone. She looked at Frank for a long moment, then with a nod, she dislodged both sim cards, dropped her side window and flung everything into a passing ditch. She raised the window, turned and watched as Frank concentrated on the road. She closed her eyes.

He spoke. "Here's what I think we have to do, and it won't be easy."

***

"Do you think they've spotted us?" Mario asked Cortez.

"Maybe. They aren't behaving like they have."

"It looks like we're headed for another ferry. Should arrive in about ten minutes," Mario said, referencing the map on his phone. "We'll take them there. I've had enough of this. I'll force him to tell me where the kid is."

"I'm for that." The response came from the back seat of the car.

Mario turned to the biker. "Don't tell me you get car sick."

"It's not a chopper, Mario. I don't like cars and this road is windy."

Mario laughed for the first time since they left Calgary.

"*Marica*," Cortez hissed, laughing at the Spanish word for sissy. The biker scowled at him.

"You'll get over it," Mario said. "Now listen, this is likely to be a much quieter ferry; we need to be subtle."

He explained how he thought they should take down the two of them. "Got it?"

"Got it," Mario heard the men say in unison.

"And remember, I want Franco Ricci for myself. Do not kill him. I want the satisfaction of tossing him over the side personally."

The men knew better than to argue.

***

Frank spotted the terminal in the distance. "You need to stay very close to me, when we get out of the car, El."

"I know."

They pulled their car into a long line up of vehicles waiting for the next ferry. Frank was relieved their arrival coincided with the loading of the ship. There was no need to buy a ticket, tickets onto the Sechelt peninsula were also used to leave. He checked on his trackers. They seemed content to follow. That was good.

Within minutes there were another half dozen cars behind them. Presumably, most wanted to make sure they caught the late afternoon ferry, so that they could get home for dinner. Frank doubted that they would all get on this one.

His eyes scanned the area. He noticed a single taxi parked by the curb, awaiting foot traffic. Passengers that had arrived earlier were scrambling back to their vehicles, from a small dockside cafe. He watched the cars exiting the ferry until there were no more. The number of cars disembarking were nowhere near as many as those getting on.

An attendant motioned and Frank's line started to move. They crossed the ramp and crawled to a designated spot. They had been lucky to get on. The ferry would be full, and several vehicles were going to have to wait.

Frank and Elena sprang from the car, with Elena leaving all but her purse and her knapsack. They headed up the stairs and onto the first deck rather than heading to the top floor for refreshments, as the rest of the passengers did. They waited.

Frank monitored the car deck below and the passengers leaving their cars. He could not see his pursuers. He watched as the last car was loaded on the ferry. They would be departing shortly.

"Come on." He motioned.

He and Elena moved back down the staircase to the car deck. They ran to the loading area at the rear of the ferry. An attendant was closing the barrier for departure.

"Sorry," yelled Frank to the attendant. "We fell asleep. Need to get off." The man looked annoyed, said nothing and stepped back, pulling the barrier to the side, allowing them to exit. They ran down the gangway to shore, heading to the taxi still sitting empty. The driver was talking to a nearby man and noticed them running for him. He was perplexed. They had no luggage, other than a knapsack. Still, a fare was a fare.

Frank heard the ramp retracting. They reached the taxi and turned. He spied three men standing at the railing on the top deck watching them. He could not discern their faces, but he knew that if they belonged with the white SUV, they'd not be happy. The ferry blew its horn and pulled away. Frank smiled. They had outsmarted them, although it had cost them Elena's car. It would take them at least a few hours to return. By then they would be long gone.

He guided Elena to the open door of the taxi and climbed in.

"Where are you off to?" the cabbie asked nonchalantly.

"How much to get us to G…" Frank hesitated. This cabbie could report their destination to anyone who asked about them. "How much to get us to the next harbour?"

"Pender harbour? Not a whole lot." The taxi pulled away from the curb.

Frank reached over and took Elena's hand and said nothing further.

***

Unbeknownst to Frank and Elena, one of the vehicles that did not get on the ferry had watched the entire event play out, then pulled a U-turn out of the line-up and began following the taxi up the hill.

The driver smiled and said to his passenger, "That worked out well. Just like it was meant to be."

The passenger thought about that for a moment. "We got lucky. Now it's like following the pied piper. Don't lose them."

CHAPTER TWENTY-TWO

NATE WAS HAVING HIS MORNING coffee alone. He had decided to forgo his morning meet up with Milo as his thoughts were tempered by worry, having not heard from Frank. He had tried his cell twice only to be told the cell he was calling was not in service. Something didn't add up.

He was sorting out what it all meant, when Constable Steve Quince walked down the dock towards him. He nodded at Archie, who was sitting on the back of his catamaran, enjoying the early morning quiet of the marina, but didn't stop to talk. He kept walking for *Serendipity*. Nate had no doubt as to why he had come.

"Need to talk to you, Nate." He said, stopping at the rear of the boat. "Mind if I come aboard?"

Nate waved him on. "Can I get you a coffee, Steve?" he said.

"No thanks. I'm not here on a social visit."

"Oh?"

"On second thought, sure, Nate. I would like one." He sat on the bench eyeing a trash bag next to him.

"Great, make yourself comfortable." He stepped down the stairs to his galley.

As Nate pulled down a mug from a cabinet and stepped to the counter to pour a cup of coffee, he glanced up the galley stairs at Quince. He saw him fumbling with something. Nate's eyebrows knit a question.

He refilled his own cup and returned with coffees in hand. He handed Quince one and settled into a seat opposite him and took a sip.

"Here, let me move that." Nate placed his coffee on the seat beside him, stood up and moved his morning trash to give Quince more room. He returned to his seat.

"So, what's on your mind?"

"You own a bat, Nate?"

"A bat?"

"Yeah, a baseball bat?"

Nate took another sip of his coffee and eyed him.

"I do, why?"

"I think you know why."

Nate paused. "I don't think so. What's going on?"

"Why do you own a bat, Nate?"

Nate smiled at him, heart beating a little faster. "I could tell you I like baseball, but the truth is I use it for protection. You never know if someone is going to visit you when you least expect it."

"Why do you need protection?"

"I don't know. You hear about how some boats can get highjacked."

Quince looked doubtful. Nate wished he'd fleshed out his story a little better.

"The bat, can you get it please?"

"Sure, why do you want it? "Nate asked.

"As I said, I think you know why. There has been an assault."

"An assault?"

"I want to see the bat, Nate."

Nate nodded and headed down to his quarters. *Be very careful, Nate. This isn't a bumbling cop.* He returned, bat in hand, and extended it to Quince.

Quince studied the bat. It was obvious it had never been used. "Where's the other one?"

"Other one?" Nate echoed.

"The one you used to break Ty O'Reilly's arm."

Nate said nothing. His eyes locked on Quince's.

"The other bat, Nate?" Quince asked more firmly, handing the new bat back to him.

"I don't have another bat, Steve. What is he saying I did?"

"He's not saying anything. His friends said you beat the living crap out of him, with a bat. Not to mention, his truck. At least, that was what Ty apparently told them, as they were taking him to the hospital. In my books, that amounts to aggravated assault, Nate."

"Why would I do that, Steve? I just met him yesterday."

"I don't know Nate. You tell me." Nate remained closed-lipped. "I don't take kindly to new guys in town beating the hell out of our residents. It doesn't matter what the reason."

"Steve, I stay to myself and pretty much hang out in the marina. I don't know much about this guy, but he wasn't real friendly yesterday when I introduced myself. Thinks I have a crush on his girlfriend. That's as much as I can tell you."

"So, you didn't beat him up?"

"You think I would use a bat on someone because they trash-talk me?"

"I don't know what to think of you. I don't really know who you are. But I think it's time I investigated you a bit. In the meantime, if you happen to find that other bat..."

"There is no other bat, Steve, sorry."

Quince leaned forward, eyes drilling in on Nate. "I want you to stay away from O'Reilly. And don't take me for a fool. I get why you'd do this. Beka's complaint was succinct."

Nate tried to look nonchalant. He was sure he was failing.

"It is still assault, and the last thing I need in my town is vigilantism. I'll look after any misdeeds that need to be addressed, if you get my drift."

Nate looked relieved. He understood he was getting a pass, at least for now. "I hope not to see the guy again, Steve"

"I've known him a long time, Nate. He's not one to look the other way. I don't need a turf war starting in my town. I like it sleepy. If he comes by again, I want to hear from you, not about you."

"Like I said, I just met the guy. It didn't go well, and I'd be happy to never see him again."

Quince rose and took a pull on the coffee. "Thanks for the brew." He stepped off the boat, stopped, and turned back. "Why do you think a bat would protect you at all?"

Nate shrugged, "I don't like guns."

Quince didn't rise to the bait, just smiled. He studied Nate. "Don't lie to me again, Nate. It never goes well."

Nate did not respond. He watched as Quince retraced his steps, ignoring Archie's questioning look. He walked up the gangway, where Milo was sitting in his usual morning spot, watching everything with interest.

Quince paused to speak with Milo. Nate couldn't hear what was being said. It was a short conversation. He watched Quince climb into his police cruiser and drive away, at which point he turned his gaze to Archie. He held Nate's eyes for a moment, then nodded. Nate returned the nod, stood up and headed below decks. He was glad he stored bats in both of his state rooms. He hoped the bat he had used the previous night, would never be found in the dense forest undergrowth, where he had hidden it, but one couldn't be sure.

Nate locked up his boat and headed for shore, trash bag in hand. He dumped it into a container and headed for the marina store. He wanted to talk with Milo now. Steve Quince's promise to investigate Nate a little more was not sitting well. He wanted to keep tabs on his enquiries.

Nate wandered over to Milo and sat down in an adjoining chair. Milo turned to Nate as he settled into it. "Did you do it?"

Nate did not look at Milo but replied, "Never could handle guys who hit women."

Milo nodded and said, "She's still at my place."

"What did you and Steve talk about?"

"I told him everything was not always as it seemed," Milo said.

"What did he say?"

"He said 'I couldn't have said it better myself, Milo. Keep him close. None of us really know who Nate Beckett is.'"

Nate felt the rush of fear penetrate his brain. He rose, thought about saying something more. He changed his mind seeing the look on Milo's face. Milo knew.

"Thanks, Nate."

Nate acknowledged his gratitude with a half-smile. He was rounding the corner of the store when he stopped.

"Milo."

Milo turned to face him.

"You see my uncle around last night or this morning?"

"Nope. Should I have?"

"Not so much, he said he was going to call. He's not here for long, and I thought we were going to get together. I have the boys this afternoon, so if he comes by, could you tell him to give me a call? I'd like to see him before we put up sail."

"I'll keep an eye out. Now...off you go. She wants to see you."

***

They had asked the taxi driver where they should stay that was private and out of the way. The driver grinned, as if he knew exactly what type of indiscretion was going on, and said he knew just the place. He drove them to what he said was the most romantic getaway in these parts. When Frank had seen the chalets, he knew it was exactly what they needed. He left the taxi driver with a hundred-dollar tip, asking him to be discreet if someone came looking for them. The driver nodded vigorously, happy to share in their impropriety.

As soon as they had closed the door behind them and surveyed their quaint surroundings, Elena wordlessly melted into Frank's arms as if they had been together all their lives. Despite their prolonged absence and a new understanding of what they meant to each other, they made love with an animalistic urgency, knowing full well that a slower, more endearing approach would follow. And follow it did. Sometime in the middle of the night they had drifted off to sleep, forcing out, for the moment, the world around them.

Frank woke first. He gazed at Elena, who was sleeping soundly. He smiled the smile of a man who was in love. He lay there, warm memories engulfing him. Then the events of the previous day flooded in. He had said they would talk about what she had done. What was the point of that? He had forgiven her already. Last night proved that. She had made a grievous error. One he had to fix. Her tears had shown all the remorse he needed. They'd figure it out.

He reached over and gently shook Elena's shoulder to wake her. She opened her eyes and smiled. He leaned down and kissed her.

"We need to get ready to go. I'll order room service."

Once a plate of bacon, eggs and toast was ordered for each of them, he asked the day manager if there was a public phone on the property. He already determined that the phones in the room didn't connect to the outside world. After arranging to use the office phone in about an hour he headed into the bathroom to clean up before their breakfast arrived. He had to warn Nate that Belletti had found them.

"Breakfast will be here shortly," he declared, glancing into the bathroom to see Elena grabbing a towel after her shower. Marvelling at her nakedness, he allowed his heart to skip a beat. He brushed away the primal thoughts that were tugging at him.

A short time later, a knock on the door forced him to pull his dirty shirt back over his head. He wished he had some clean clothes. Frank walked to the window, pulling the drape back a fraction to see who was at the door. A young man saw the move and waved at him. He heard Elena close the bathroom door as Frank thumbed the latch. A highly energetic server flowed into the room, pushing a cart with their order, through the door. Frank ignored his morning salutations.

His eyes were glued on a truck that was in a parking lot across a wide lawn. Two occupants sat in the cab, staring in his direction.

He retreated into the room and gave the surprised attendant a generous tip, urging him out the door. He then latched the security chain, his thoughts agitated. Who were those guys? That wasn't who was following them. How many had Belletti sent?

"We have company," Frank said, as Elena came back into the main room dressed in her soiled clothes. "Eat as quickly as you can."

He grabbed a piece of toast, stuffing it in his mouth. He walked to the back of the chalet determining if they had an alternate way to escape from their latest pursuers. The very chalet that had made them feel safe the night before now felt like a prison cell, with only one entrance and exit.

"Is it them?" Elena asked as she followed him.

"Eat, El. We may not get food for a while. I don't know who it is, and I don't know if they're a Belletti crew." He was thinking out loud. "They're just watching, so we have a few minutes."

Satisfied that they could escape through the oversized bathroom window at the back of the chalet, Frank tore a blanket from the bed and returned to the bathroom. He studied the large, sealed window, then wrapped his hand in the blanket. He punched the window three times, each successively harder, until it shattered. Cool morning air rushed in. Frank was thankful the noise would be masked by the rushing spring waters in the creek out back. He brushed away remnant glass pieces and tossed the blanket over the sill. He turned to Elena, who had been watching, wolfing down a small plate of food.

They walked into the other room. Frank grabbed a second piece of toast, popping it into his mouth. She placed her plate on a table and grabbed two apples from a bowl of fruit, placing them in her knapsack. Then, as an afterthought, she pulled out three large bills and laid them on the bed. "For the window," she said.

Frank nodded.

She picked up the chair that sat in front of a small desk, carried it to the bathroom, and placed it before the open window. Then she returned to the main room. Frank was peering through a crack in their drapes to make sure their friends had not moved.

"We'd better go, Frank."

He nodded his assent to Elena, who then spun on her heel and walked to the window. Stepping onto the chair, she tossed her knapsack to the ground below, then climbed through the opening. Frank was impressed with her cool demeanour. Being a person with a larger girth, he struggled to get through. He fell to the ground, felt a stab of pain along his left arm where a piece of glass that had not fallen from the frame, cut him. Blood eased to the surface. He would have to see how bad the cut was later.

Rising from the spot he had fallen, he moved to the corner of the building and looked out to see if the truck was visible. It was. The occupants had been very strategic in how they had parked their truck in order to see the chalet. Frank was pretty sure they would need a lot of luck not to be spotted. *Who are those guys?*

"We have to crawl," he uttered, smiling as best he could at Elena.

***

Nate knocked twice on the door to Milo's apartment and waited. It was amazing how these small towns let anybody enter their buildings, he thought.

"Who is it?" he heard from the other side of the door.

"Nate."

The door opened a crack. Beka looked out at him, then unchained the door and let him in. The bruise on her face had worsened through the night and now was a mix of purple, yellow, blue, and some form of green. The sight stirred up Nate's bile. He wondered how hard O'Reilly had hit her to do that to her face. Any nagging guilt he felt about using a bat on the guy evaporated.

"How are you feeling?" Nate asked.

"I'll be fine," she whispered. "Milo thought you had gone after him?"

Nate nodded. "He won't be bothering you again."

"What did you do?" Alarm crossed her face.

Nate told her. She said nothing and showed no emotion. She walked up to him and kissed his cheek. She was pulling back, when Nate reached out and gently took hold of her waist. She turned back to him and slid into his arms as he hugged her in a way that made no mistake about how he felt about her. A few moments later, she pulled back, walking to the kitchen.

"Hungry?" she asked, then added, "and no... you can't help."

"Famished," he admitted, taking a seat at the bar.

After Nate had eaten his last bite of a great ham and cheese omelette, she rose, reached for his mug, and poured him another cup of coffee.

"Enjoy this, while I change, then, maybe you can walk me back to the marina. I have to get back to Milo and I know you need to get ready for the boys today." She was about to enter the bedroom when she turned and looking worriedly at Nate. "He's dangerous, Nate. Please watch your back." She turned and closed the door.

Nate stood. He looked down at his coffee. He'd already had too many today. Glancing at the bedroom door, he poured the coffee down the sink. He began cleaning up the breakfast dishes, allowing her comment to resonate. He wasn't surprised at his lack of fear, he knew how much he had changed since those fateful days in Calgary. Still, he pondered where this would go, wondering what, if anything, he could do about this latest problem and why he was always getting into a mess.

Beka returned, sliding her arm through Nate's. She made no comment when she saw his serious expression and clenched jaw. "Ready?"

Nate walked Beka back to the marina. He squeezed her hand as a goodbye. She entered the store, leaving her sunglasses on. They'd help to hide the bruise around her eye.

Nate figured he had about four hours before the boys arrived. It was enough time to complete a visit to a certain Bayliner, which recent events had forced him to set aside. He wasn't looking for any more trouble, but why was this guy trying to track him down? He had no idea. But he sure as hell didn't buy the insurance nonsense. A simple conversation couldn't bring any more bad news, could it? The P.I. already knew he was here.

He headed up the hill.

CHAPTER TWENTY-THREE

FRANK AND ELENA FELL TO the ground and inched their way to the creek, looking like a pair of large amphibians scampering to a watering hole. As they reached the bank of the waterway, Frank took stock of the truck. It was still there but it appeared empty. He couldn't be certain without giving up his position by standing. Bad idea.

He turned, checking his left, little hope going that way. Too many large rock faces to traverse. At his right, the start of a pathway a little further along the creek. They'd need to crawl another two hundred metres to get to the edge of a tree stand that would provide them some cover to walk. The noise of the creek would, at any other time, be comforting to Frank. In this moment, he wasn't happy about it. He couldn't hear if anyone was behind them.

He motioned Elena towards the trail. She nodded and they crawled again, both feeling foolish, scrambling for cover. They reached the tree stand when Elena looked back and let out a muffled noise. Inspecting the broken window at the back of their chalet was a man, who then spun around searching frantically for them. Frank took it all in. They had moments to hide.

He rolled down the slope, then over a small bank to the edge of the creek. He landed on his arm, the cut reminding him it needed attention. Elena followed suit seconds later, awkwardly rolling on top of the knapsack affixed to her back. She hit a pool of water, splashing water all over her face and hair. They quickly scrambled into a crouch and peered over the bank. They hadn't been seen. Bending low, they ran behind the trees and clambered up to the trail. They cast a look back to the chalets, expecting to see the man running for them but saw nothing. Frank spotted him charging back to the truck. They watched as he jumped in. The engine roared to life but remained where it was parked. Frank turned to view the path before them. Elena did the same. There was no need to voice their fears. They turned back and watched the truck back up, turn, and drive away, tires spinning on the gravel.

Frank scrutinized Elena. Her hair was matted and wet, dirt was smudged across her face, her dress stained with grass and mud.

She watched him laugh quietly and smiled. "You don't look so good yourself." She grabbed his hand to look at the cut on his arm.

"Come here," she said, pulling him back down the bank, to the creek.

She reached down and tore a strip off the bottom of her dress and reached into the cold water to get it wet. "This dress has had it anyway."

She wiped blood from his arm, satisfied that clotting had begun. She washed the blood from the cloth, placing the wet rag over the cut, tying it around his arm. It would do the trick until they could bandage it properly.

Frank silently watched her work. As she finished the knot, he looked down the trail that meandered along the river under large cedar and fir bows again. He wondered if it would take them to safety. "Let's go."

"Who was that guy, Frank?" Elena asked, rising to her feet.

"I have no idea. It's bad enough we have Belletti's goons after us. Now apparently someone else is looking for us too. These two make me even more nervous because I don't know who they are. You didn't recognize them?"

"No, but I only saw the one guy." she said quietly. "This is crazy, Frank. What do we do now?"

"We get back to Gibsons and warn Nate. Then we get the hell out of here."

Frank took her arm and they headed down the mountain trail. Where it was going, he wasn't sure, but they had to get away from the chalets. He had no doubt that when the cleaning crew came by a call to the police would follow and he didn't want to be around to deal with them.

The trail opened to a meadow. Across it, Frank spied a house. He pointed it out to Elena. She nodded, and they headed for it, hoping they wouldn't be spotted.

They reached the edge of the property when an elderly woman with a riot of white hair poking out both sides of her gardening hat gawked in disbelief at the dishevelled pair of intruders.

"My goodness." She stood to get a better look at them.

Frank and Elena stared back. Seconds later, they determined there was no impending threat.

"I know we look a sight," said Elena as they approached her. "We sure could use a phone."

The woman nodded, said something to Elena that Frank missed as he scrutinized the area. She motioned them to follow her into the house.

Elena followed, then turned and called back to motionless Frank.

"You coming?"

"Yeah," he said, trudging after her. Another complication.

***

Nate arrived at Freddy's dock and stood at the top of the embankment scanning the marina. He could see the Bayliner at the end of "B" dock and started down the gangway. He pulled out his phone, putting it on mute, not wanting to be interrupted.

He arrived at the boat slip, a few minutes later, and approached the Bayliner's stern, wondering if its occupant was home. He didn't sense any movement, so he made for the bow, trying to peer in the window. A moment later, a man walked through the salon doors and approached Nate.

"Mr. Vickers? So nice of you to come by."

Nate smirked at him, his heart racing. "My name is Nate Beckett," he said, giving the man the once over.

He stood shortly below six feet, with salt-and-pepper hair combed stylishly to the back of his head. He wore an expensive pair of sunglasses and had a confident demeanour. His clothing matched the era of the boat.

"I see you found a place for moorage." Nate forced his voice to be blasé.

"Come aboard, Mr. Beckett. We have a lot to discuss."

Nate stood his ground, drifting back to the stern of the boat for a closer look at the man.

"Who are you?"

"Can we stop this charade, please? Come aboard. My name is Ross Finlay and I represent some people who would like your assistance." Nate didn't budge. "Come aboard... please. I was just making myself a cup of tea. Would you like one?"

Nate thought for a moment. "Sure, why not." He stepped onto the boat, entering the salon while watching his host pull down two mugs hanging below a cabinet. The kettle had already boiled. The Bayliner was a vintage old boat, well kept. Finlay removed his sunglasses, replacing them with a pair of dark rimmed eyeglasses. It made him look hawkish.

"Black?"

"Pardon?"

"Your tea, would you like it black?

"That's fine, thank you."

"I must say, you are a very perplexing young man, Mr. Vickers." Finlay said, handing Nate his tea.

"How about you call me Nate, since you are having a little trouble with my last name," Nate suggested.

Finlay smiled. "Why Gibsons, Nate?"

"Excuse me?"

"Why run to Gibsons? It isn't very far away."

"I'm not running. Look, I came over here to find out who you are. First, you come find me in the middle of a nasty gale. Then, I see you staring at me through binoculars at the entrance to my marina and finally, I hear that a private investigator, by the name of John Sebastian – that would be you - is asking questions about someone you apparently think is me. And you think I am perplexing."

Ross smiled again and rose. "Excuse me." He went into a stateroom and came back with a small briefcase, unsnapping the locks. He pulled out a sheet of paper and laid it on the table upside down. He then closed his case, placed it at his feet, and studied Nate's eyes. He turned the paper over.

Nate looked down at a photo of himself with his uncle during happier times. He couldn't recall exactly where the photo had been taken and, while it was a picture of the two of them, a few years back, there was no doubt it was him.

Nate looked up and saw Finlay analyzing him. His mouth had gone dry. "Okay. So why is a P.I. tracking me down?" *And how the hell did he do that?*

Finlay smiled. "I'm impressed that you've learned about Sebastian so quickly. You're resourceful. That will be a useful skill in assisting my client."

Nate wondered who the mystery "client" was. "What do you want, Ross, or Sebastian, or whatever your name is? Are you really a private investigator, as you told the police?"

Finlay raised an eyebrow, appraising Nate further.

"What's in a title? Investigator, associate, partner, enforcer... I have many titles, Mr. Vickers. I use whichever one I need at a given point in time."

"And what are you right now?"

"Educator."

Nate watched a smile form on Finlay's face. Kind of a cross between a grin and a sneer.

Nate took a sip of his tea as he focused on Ross Finlay. *Looks like an accountant.* He set his cup on the table.

"I'll ask again. What do you want?"

Finlay looked at Nate for a couple of very long moments, remaining silent.

Nate fought the urge to fill the quiet space, hoping to figure out what kind of a threat this guy was to him. Then he capitulated. "Is your name really Ross Finlay?"

Nate watched Finlay's eyes as they bore into him, as if contemplating a decision. Finally, he spoke. "It's not, but that's unimportant. What is important is that I know you stole a sizeable sum of money from a group of men in Calgary, in what could only be described as a brazen heist." He stopped for effect, taking in Nate's response. Nate blanched and fought the urge to get up and run. He forced himself to be stone-faced, offering no response. Ross continued. "Let's just say that I represent a group of men who are not happy with the fallout that has occurred from your little venture."

"And who would that be?" Nate refused to acknowledge the claim.

"That, too, is unimportant, for now. I will tell you my clients reside in Montreal and are in daily contact with me, which is not how I like to work. Suffice to say, I have been commissioned to clean up the mess and I have determined I'd like your assistance to do that."

Nate sat still, trying to sort out where this was going.

Finlay slurped his tea and went on. "There are a lot of people looking for you, Nate. Some I know, some I don't. But I do believe that if you do not assist me, likely, you will be dead within a week. I might be your only chance to stay alive."

Nate didn't visibly react. The internal conflict he was feeling threatened to overwhelm him. No one had known where he was. Even his uncle didn't know. Now everyone knew.

"How'd you find me?"

Finlay smiled again. Nate resisted the urge to wipe the annoying smile off his face.

"It's rather simple, really. GPS tracking."

"Bullshit. I had a new phone."

Ross said nothing, his eyes never leaving Nate's.

Nate closed his eyes as it dawned on him how he had accomplished it. Frank was the only person who found him. He allowed his phone to be tracked. Rookie mistake. Not like Frank. His eyes popped open, a thought niggling at his consciousness. "Have you done something to him?"

"No."

Nate mulled over his situation. He stared beyond the marina to the strait beyond. His mood was turning ugly. Finlay waited. Nate felt any control he had over the conversation slipping away.

"You must've been tracking him a long time. I just reacquainted with him."

"Patience is a virtue for some, Nate."

Nate needed more. "What sort of assistance are you talking about?"

Finlay leaned in. "The man you stole from - we want you to ask him to join us. Without disclosing our interest, of course."

"What do you mean join us? You mean come here? You are out of your mind." Nate stood to leave. Fear had replaced engagement. He knew what Belletti was capable of.

"Sit down," Finlay demanded, the intensity in his tone stopping Nate in his tracks. "You are under the impression that this is a request. It is nothing of the kind, Mr. Vickers." The intimacy of their talk ended. "It is what you will do... if you wish to stay alive."

Nate glared at Finlay, then reluctantly sat down. This guy was not an accountant. "Stay alive? Just how do I stay alive letting that man know where I am? Do you have any idea what he is capable of?"

Finlay smiled. "But you are so resourceful..."

Nate's eyes blazed. He'd worked so hard to build a new life. "I'm not doing it, Ross! It's a death sentence. Find someone else." He stood again, moving towards the exit.

Finlay slammed his hand on the tabletop. A dish jumped and rattled to a stop.

"You leave without acceding to my wishes, Mr. Vickers, and I assure you that you will be killed. You won't have to worry about Belletti. My clients will find you and they will hurt you. They will make you feel so much pain that you will wish for death. But only after you watch your uncle die before your eyes."

Dread raced through Nate. Dread for himself. Dread for the man who raised him. He turned. "You have my uncle?"

Nate watched that annoying smile light up Ross's face again. He scowled.

"We are more civilized than that. You just need to do your part, Mr. Vickers."

Nate's shoulders slumped. His eyes darted about, as if seeking escape. There was no way to run from this without endangering his uncle. He needed time. "Let me go away and think about how it can be done."

"I'll give you a day or two, no more." Ross stood. The conversation was over. He'd gotten what he wanted.

Nate followed him to the gunwale readying to step ashore. He turned. "So, I suppose this means you aren't going to pay me the insurance proceeds?" Nate spun on his heel and stepped off the boat.

"Very funny, Mr. Vickers. Very funny." Nate turned back to face Finlay. There was no humour in his eyes. "One more thing... my clients will also be wanting to have the money you stole."

He didn't wait for Nate to answer, turning back to the salon. "Have a good day, Mr. Vickers," he called over his shoulder.

CHAPTER TWENTY-FOUR

MARIO WOKE SLOWLY AND LOOKED at his watch. Half past ten in the morning. He heard the cawing of crows which added to the sense of foreboding he felt after opening his eyes. He allowed the morning fog to lift from his brain, assessing the room he was in. It was modestly furnished with the usual nondescript desk and chair. The decor was dark and uninviting, a seemingly apropos back drop for the thoughts swirling around his head.

He was unnerved about the update he was going to provide to Belletti shortly. He could almost hear the increasing octave of his voice as it belittled him, then the obligatory threat if he failed him again. He had seen the don's anger manifest itself many times before, with others. He had no delusions of what would follow if he didn't right this problem quickly. For the first time, Mario DeLuca regretted offering to take on the task of finding Franco Ricci and Nathaniel Vickers.

He remembered the previous day with a groan and swung his legs out of the bed. He padded over to the coffee machine and proceeded to make himself a brew. He couldn't believe how Franco had outsmarted him and abandoned the woman's car.

Begrudgingly, he had to admit, it was a brilliant maneuver, and not one that Mario had anticipated. It certainly answered the question about whether they knew they were being followed.

It also answered the burning question of where they were staying. Somewhere nearby. Mario's guess was that it was Gibsons. It wasn't the largest town on the peninsula – that was Sechelt — but that was where the largest detachment of the police was located, and Vickers would not want to be anywhere near the authorities. No, Gibsons was the likely location, if one wanted to disappear.

It was almost midday when Mario collected his associates from their rooms. He was in a foul mood. They were told they'd be heading back to Gibsons to try and pick up the trail. He wandered off by himself to make the dreaded call to Belletti, who would be waiting for his morning update, no doubt already annoyed by the delay in receiving it.

The thorough undressing was delivered, but Mario was thankful that he didn't receive the anticipated threat, although he had no illusions about what would happen if he failed again. Perhaps the don was feeling compassion as he updated Mario on the investigation of his brother's death. Still nothing resolved, but he was assured progress was being made.

He climbed into the rear seat of their SUV, satisfied that his men were already in place. The grim expression he wore alerted his men to keep their mouths shut. He motioned Cortez to get moving, which he did, his eyes glued on the road ahead.

Mario pondered Franco Ricci again. He had outsmarted his brother, and he had just outsmarted him. Franco was a resourceful man. He respected that, but Mario was equally resourceful and resolved to not make the mistake of underestimating Franco again. The next time they met, Franco would rue the day he crossed the Belletti organization.

Upon their arrival in Gibsons, they found a local diner near the waterfront. They hadn't eaten since the previous day and

Mario needed to appease the whining of his crew. They entered and asked for a table by the window, forgoing a patio seat. They needed anonymity. The bar was decorated in a marine motif with pictures of actors who had visited adorning its walls. Apparently, it had history. Mario had no time for that. He needed to come up with a plan of action to find Franco.

As in all small towns, the people sitting at the bar enjoying their lunch turned to see who entered, lest they were rude in not acknowledging one of their own. That included an RCMP officer, who examined their entrance, then turned back to the all-day breakfast, placed before him by a young man eager to avoid any kind of discussion.

Mario, recognizing the uniform, asked the hostess for the furthest table away. He made sure his back was to the officer as they sat down and advised his crew to ignore him. He looked through the window at the marina below, deep in thought, as he waited for the food. They had ordered from a server that looked as old as the building they were sitting in and Mario wondered if it would take a while to get served. Cortez suddenly tapped the table and nodded.

"That the *chico*, Mario?" he said softly, glancing at the back of the Constable.

Mario focused on a man coming up the gangway of the marina. He was young enough, that was for sure. He pulled out his phone and tapped his photos icon. The man staring back at him from the picture had a different hair colour and no facial hair, but he certainly bore a resemblance to the intense man walking up the hill.

"Could be," Mario said quietly. "That would be a break. Follow him Nick," he said tilting his head at the biker. "I want to know where he goes."

"Should I take him, if I get a chance?"

"No, do as you are told. He'll lead us to Franco, if it's him. I'm sure of it."

The server arrived with their food order. Nick slid around her as she was serving, earning him a disgruntled look. She moved aside, shifting so as not to drop the plates of food. Mario put up his hand for the biker to wait. The server finished putting their plates of food down and left, shaking her head.

"You understand? Do not let him see you," Mario whispered.

The soldier nodded, grabbed a piece of bacon from his plate and strode to the entrance, chewing as he went. He stepped outside, got his bearings and headed after the man.

All of which had not gone unnoticed by the RCMP officer who had turned to inspect them after noticing the server's frustration. Mario had just dug into his food when the officer slid off his stool and wandered over to them.

Cortez coughed to alert Mario.

"Good day," said the officer.

"Afternoon, Officer," Mario said as he turned, addressing the cop respectfully.

"Is that your truck out there?" he pointed in the direction of their SUV parked across the street.

Mario looked. "It is," he said. "Is there a problem?"

"That's a tow-away zone. I would hate to see guests visiting our fair town go through the ordeal of having to get their vehicle back. Our tow-away service is quite effective."

This was not a conversation Mario wanted to have. "Oh, I didn't realize. Thank you, Officer." He nodded at Cortez, who jumped up to go move the truck. How could they have been so damned stupid.

"What brings you to our parts?"

"Going to be doing some fishing. Thought we'd take in the town before then. Pretty place you have here."

"It is. Guess your friend didn't like the food here?"

Mario glanced at Nick's full plate of food, then his empty seat. He feigned laughter. "Saw a friend he hadn't seen in years and darted. His loss."

The RCMP officer smiled at Mario. "Uh huh." He eyed Mario for a bit longer, committing his face to memory. "Enjoy the rest of your breakfast and your stay here."

"Thanks. I'm sure it will be great. And thanks for the heads up on the parking." Mario stared at the cop's back as he walked back to his seat, dropped some cash on the bar, and headed for the exit.

His heartbeat remained steady; his anger surged. The last thing Mario wanted was to have the attention of the local cops.

***

Nate was oblivious to everything around him. His discussion with Ross Finlay had totally unnerved him. He thought he set up a nice quiet life only to learn that his uncle, through an uncharacteristically poor decision, brought a whole new set of problems to him. And where was Frank, anyway?

Nate pulled out his phone and called him again. The line was still not in service. Something was wrong. Finlay had said that they didn't have him. Did he believe him? Nate felt a familiar but unwelcome pit in his stomach.

He kept walking, deep in thought. Could he do what Finlay demanded? He understood what he wanted but he knew the risk would be huge. Although Finlay didn't voice it, Nate was aware that they didn't want him here to shake his hand. There was some form of payback in the works, and he would be the conduit for that to happen. He had no love for Belletti but setting him up was not in his nature. Even after all that had taken place. Besides, if they were unsuccessful, Belletti would be all over him. And he knew how that would play out. And what was with that last demand for the cash? If he met their claim, it would leave him with nothing. Sure, it was better than being dead, but he had expended a lot of effort to build his new life. He'd have to think long and hard. He wasn't going to give up that money easily. He had to find a solution.

Nate turned down Bay Road and soon reached his marina. Beka was coming outside to replenish the pop machine, wearing sunglasses to hide the bruises, despite the clouds that had rolled in.

"Hi, Nate," she said warmly.

"Hey, Beka."

"What's wrong?"

"Nothing." His tone was unconvincing.

"You don't look like the same guy I saw earlier. What's happened?"

Nate looked at Beka for a minute then replied.

"Just got some bad news. I'll tell you about it tonight, after I've had my sail with the boys. Over dinner... okay?"

"I'd like that." Concern furrowed Beka's brow.

"Okay." He brandished more of a grimace than a smile. "I have to go and get ready."

Nate moved down the gangway to the docks below. He glanced back. She was watching him. Even with the glasses on he could see the frown on her face.

Out of the corner of his eye, he noticed a man standing at the railing overlooking the marina. He was rather intense looking and was watching Nate wander down the dock. Nate thought nothing of him until he noticed Steve Quince standing further up the street, watching the man.

Nate let out a long sigh. What now?

He had almost reached his boat when Archie called out his name. "Nate, got a minute?"

Nate moaned inwardly. He turned and walked back to Archie.

"Time for a drink?"

"No, Archie, I can't. I have the boys coming down soon. What's up?" Nate knew something was amiss when Archie said nothing cryptic about the boys.

"Thought you needed to know that a couple of guys came by looking for you this morning, after you left. They didn't look too friendly. Called out your name a couple of times. Caught my attention. I think they may have boarded your boat if they hadn't spotted me watching them. Then they left. I heard what happened last night to O'Reilly and got to thinking. So, I strolled up to the store and saw Beka wearing a large set of sunglasses over what appears to be a substantive bruise on that pretty face of hers. Kind of put two and two together."

Nate watched Archie with a blank face.

"Gotta tell you Nate. Trouble seems to be following you around. But dealing with that son-of-a-bitch O'Reilly the way you did... that took some guts. Don't know for sure, but I have a feeling those guys might have been a couple of his pals and thought you should know about them. Watch your back, son. I'll keep an eye out. Help you anyway I can."

Nate's shoulders sagged and he nodded at Archie. "Thanks for the heads up. Probably nothing Archie."

"Maybe..." Archie continued.

"Got to go, Arch." Nate turned to leave.

"One more thing."

Nate closed his eyes; he turned back.

"You know that guy?"

Nate searched the shoreline for the guy Archie referred to.

"The guy leaning on the rail?"

Archie nodded.

"No, why would I?"

"Don't know, but he's sure interested in you. Hung back while you talked to Beka, then followed your every move down the docks. He has been standing there ever since."

Nate lifted his sunglasses and studied the guy for a minute. His heartbeat was elevated. He needed deflection. What Archie hadn't seen was that Quince was also involved. That would get him more engaged, something he didn't want. "You sure he isn't just enjoying the marina, Arch?"

"Maybe, but I'm a retired cop and something isn't sitting right. I think he may be more than he portrays."

Nate stared at the guy again.

"Thanks, Archie. I think your imagination might be getting the better of you. Got to go."

"Watch your back, young fellow. Like I said earlier, trouble's following you."

Nate headed for his boat. He climbed aboard *Serendipity*. Were those friends of O'Reilly really looking for payback? Great. Nate wished he could go back and deal with O'Reilly differently. But nothing would have changed. The usual guilt of having overreacted flooded his mind. He squashed the emotion, having more pressing issues. He started to replay the conversation with Finlay. His phone rang.

He was about to answer when he saw Steve Quince wandering down onto the docks heading his way again. Nate hit the "do not answer" button and waited. This day was not going well.

"Afternoon, Nate."

"Steve...I'm seeing a lot of you lately."

"I was just thinking the same thing. Why is that?"

Nate gave a Hollywood grin. "Maybe I'm charming."

Quince grimaced. "That might be it or may be that every time something out of the ordinary happens around here, you're connected to it."

"I already told you — "

"I'm not talking about that."

Nate waited for him to continue.

"I was having breakfast this morning at Molly's, when I met some gentlemen. Imagine my surprise when one of them jumped up to follow you as you were leaving Freddy's dock this morning. Seems he wanted to meet up with his old friend." Nate offered no clarity. "Imagine my further surprise, when I followed him, only to learn he didn't really want to meet up with you, just to track you. Why would he want to do that, Nate?"

Nate's mind flashed back to Archie and his thoughts. He wished he had gone back to the store to get a better look at the man. He glanced over Quince's shoulder, but the guy had vanished. "Honestly, Steve, I have no idea who he is. Archie pointed him out too."

"Uh huh." Quince swivelled, a cacophony of shuffling feet and hoots and hollers alerting him. Three boys laughed and cajoled, heading in their direction. Quince eyed Nate inquisitively.

"My class," Nate explained. "I work with Ben Mills at the Boys club teaching the art of sailing."

Quince cocked his head to the side, trying to absorb Nate, as if for the first time.

"You enjoy your day, Nate. We'll have another discussion real soon."

He turned and walked past the boys who were quickly approaching. As soon as they spotted him, they went silent and were on their best behaviour.

"Have a good sail, boys," Nate heard Quince say as he kept walking.

"Thanks," the boys said in unison and then ran to the stern of the boat.

Nate watched Quince saunter away. He had questions about who Quince had talked to. Who else could possibly want to talk to him? Were these Finlay's men? O'Reilly's? Belletti's? Nate let air escape through puffed lips.

"Permission to come aboard Cap'n?" Nate looked down at three grinning faces. He couldn't help himself. He grinned back. "Permission granted." He had an afternoon of adventure ahead and any more negative thoughts could wait. The boys would have his full attention.

Thankfully, they'd provide him a welcome distraction.

CHAPTER TWENTY-FIVE

"THERE'S NO ANSWER" FRANK DECLARED, placing the woman's phone on the kitchen table. "Thank you for letting me use your phone."

The woman nodded. "Can I get you both a coffee? I'll brew a new pot. In the meantime, you can use my bathroom to clean up, as best you can."

"Oh, thank you," Elena gushed. "You're very kind."

Elena beamed at Frank and headed in the direction the woman pointed. Frank pulled out a chair and lowered his frame into the seat, taking a moment to observe the woman's modest home. There were Andy Warhol plates on the wall and two small shelving units displayed a variety of thimbles, presumably collected from all over the world. Her furniture was old but well cared for, including the chrome and Formica table they sat at. Frank felt like he had stepped back into the 50s.

He noticed a copy of the local paper sitting at the other end of the table beside a finished cup of coffee. He could make out the front page which featured a photo of Elena's abandoned car being towed off the ferry. The caption read "Authorities looking for missing woman."

"You two in trouble?" the woman asked, following the direction of Frank's gaze.

Franks brow knitted into a frown, wishing they hadn't come inside. "We'll be out of your hair shortly. I'm sorry...I have been rude and not asked your name."

"Dorothy...Dorothy Higgins."

Frank studied the elderly woman. She had removed her hat and managed to fix the rogue hairs that had come out of her French braid that flowed down her back. She was dressed in a flowing gown and wore open toed sandals. Her face was weathered and reflected what had no doubt been a difficult life.

"Well, Dorothy, it does seem that my friend and I have a wee problem on our hands. Our car broke down and we were seeking help, but got a bit lost in the dark last night and ended up spending the night laying up against a tree. I'm afraid we must look a terrible mess."

Dorothy dropped her eyes to the newspaper again and walked over to it. "I see," she said, quietly. She picked up the paper, brought it to Frank and dropped it in front of him. "I will see to your coffees. How'd you hurt your arm?"

"Tore it on a protruding branch. One shouldn't walk around in the forest on a dark night."

"Ah," Dorothy said as she walked into the kitchen.

Frank scanned the article, determining the police were looking for a certain Elena Romano, owner of a vehicle left stranded on the Earl's Cove ferry. Police were also seeking another passenger accompanying Ms. Romano. The article went on to say that foul play was suspected. This was a good thing. Authorities, no doubt, believed that they had gone missing while on the ferry. It bought them time.

Dorothy returned, carrying a small tray. Two cups of coffee were balanced on it. A creamer and sugar bowl sat beside a plate of homemade cookies.

Elena stepped back into the room, a joyful utterance escaping her lips when she spotted the cookies. Frank smiled. He was reminded of a different Elena, before his world had collided with hers. He hoped he would be able to see her innocence again one day.

Dorothy picked up her empty mug, then retreated to the kitchen to rummage through a cabinet. She reappeared with a First Aid kit and handed in to Elena.

"Thank you."

"Sweetheart, this wonderful lady offering her hospitality is Dorothy," Frank said.

Elena raised her eyes to Dorothy's. "Thank you, Dorothy. Your cookies look wonderful."

"Help yourself, dear," said Dorothy.

Elena reached for one. "Your turn, Frank. We'll dress your wound once you've washed up."

Frank decided it would be a bad time to leave these two alone and declined Elena's offer with a shake of his head. Elena frowned and bit into her cookie.

"This is delicious. You really are too kind."

"Just being neighbourly," Dorothy said, warming to Elena's smile. "Your husband here was just telling..."

"Oh, he isn't my husband," Elena blurted out.

Dorothy smiled again. "...telling me about your car trouble."

Elena's eyes darted to Frank. "Was he?"

"Yes, I'd be happy to call our local tow truck company and arrange to get your car to a garage, if you like?"

Frank jumped in. "Dorothy, you've done too much already. We will finish these wonderful coffees, but if you could call us a taxi, that would be most helpful. We can take it from there."

"I see," Dorothy said for the second time. She walked over to Frank and retrieved her phone sitting in front of him. She punched in a number from memory. "Betty? Dorothy here. Could you send one of the boys by to pick up a couple of folks that need a lift to town? Yes, at the house. Thank you, sweetie." She slid her phone into the pocket of her gown. "The taxi should be here in twenty minutes."

"Thank you again." Elena squeezed Dorothy's arm appreciatively. "Frank, you need to clean up, especially that arm. We don't want you scaring anyone in town." She forced a laugh.

Frank winced. It'd be suspicious if he turned down the request again. He walked down the hallway, deciding to leave the door open and strained to hear their conversation.

"Is he forcing you against your will, dear?" he heard Dorothy say.

"Oh no," Elena replied. "He is the gentlest man you could know. Everything is fine, Dorothy. Really."

"Everything but the cut on his arm. How did he do it, dear?"

"Cut it on a piece of glass, I'm afraid. He'll be all right."

Frank noted the discrepancy, washing up quickly. He returned to the kitchen, wiping his hands on his dirty pants. Returning to his chair, he laid his arm on the table. He needed this done quickly. Too much risk talking with this woman.

Elena removed the rag on his arm, cleaned and dressed his cut. She put a large white bandage over the wound, satisfied it wasn't infected. She stood, closed the First Aid kit, and walked to the kitchen to dump the waste.

Frank caught Elena's eye and shook his head.

Dorothy was having a look-see out the kitchen window. "Cab's here," she declared.

Elena returned to the table, unzipped her pack and slipped the soiled materials from Frank's arm in the bag. She nodded at Frank.

He rose and took the knapsack from her, tossing it over his good arm. They both thanked Dorothy, moved to the door, and strode to the taxi. As they were pulling away, Frank glanced back. He saw Dorothy standing on her porch, phone to her ear. That wasn't good.

Shaking his head, he focused on giving the driver instructions.

***

The taxi stopped at the entrance to the main highway. Frank was contemplating how he'd get this guy to drop them some-where other than the tow company, when the cab driver spoke. He had a dialect that suggested he was from Australia, or maybe New Zealand.

"Have to take you down the road to C-Tow out of Sechelt," he stated. "They're primarily a sea service, but they have a truck that should be able to help."

Frank considered the driver's eyes, peering at him through his rear-view mirror. He wondered what he was thinking. They were a sight.

Elena stepped into the silence. "What's your name?" she asked.

"Noah."

"Well, Noah, that would be appreciated, but the thing is we've had a pretty tough night and while a tow is important, the first thing we need to do is to let our family know we're alright."

Frank jumped in, seeing where she was going.

"Yeah...unfortunately we lost our phones. Do you know a place where we can get one in Sechelt?" Frank reasoned it would be the quickest option.

"Sechelt is no big smoke, mate, but I know just the place. I have all day. I can wait for you, then get you to C-Tow."

Frank looked at Elena and opened the knapsack, pulling out some cash. He handed it over the shoulder to the driver. Noah accepted the cash, his eyes going wide.

"It's a bit much, mate," he said.

"We may need your services further, once we get that phone. Probably need a lift all the way to Gibsons. That work?"

"What about your car?"

"We'll deal with it. It's safe for now."

Noah pulled over to the side of the highway, placing the car in park. He turned in his seat to face Frank and Elena. He was a small man in his early fifties, with a lot of laugh lines around his bright blue, inquiring eyes. He studied Frank for a moment, then turned and looked Elena, who said nothing. She smiled sweetly at him.

"This is a lot of money. I'm no wuss, but you aren't getting me into something illegal here, are you?"

Frank laughed. "No, Noah, we just need to get back to our family. Nothing illegal, I promise."

"What about the tow?"

"We'll come back tomorrow and deal with it."

Noah studied him. Making up his mind, he turned back in his seat, put the car in gear and pulled back onto the highway. "Right then," he said, depressing the accelerator.

Frank leaned back in his seat, zipped up the bag, reached over and squeezed Elena's hand. He turned to glance out the window.

***

"Why have they stopped?" asked the man in the pick-up truck.

"No idea," came his companion's answer. "Just stay back, they could have seen us back there. Pretty sure that old woman did."

"But they didn't."

They'd gotten lucky. The decision to have him follow the trail had paid off. He wasn't sure it would work once they'd doubled back to the chalet but it's all they had. He moved swiftly through the woods trying to catch up. From time-to-time he stopped and saw clear evidence that someone had recently traversed the trail. He thought he might have lost them at one point, when he spotted them. He stayed well back to go unnoticed, then watched from behind a cedar as they entered the old woman's house. Emerging from the forest, he raised his cell phone to his ear and waited for his ride to arrive.

The taxi pulled back onto the highway.

They would not squander their good fortune, he thought, as they pulled into the traffic to follow.

***

The RCMP constable arrived at Dorothy's home. He had known Dorothy Higgins for years. She wasn't one to rattle easily. His name was Constable Jack Forester, and he was a couple of years from retirement. He had been pigeon-holed in the Sechelt detachment for five years now and made up his mind that this was where he would spend the rest of his life, once he hung up his badge. He liked the quiet nature of the place, dealing mostly with petty issues between neighbours, who for the most part were pretty good people. The abandoned car on the ferry had come under his purview, and for Jack, it was pretty much the most interesting thing that had happened for some time. Their theory was a murder/suicide and they had engaged the Coast Guard who were commissioned with the unenviable and difficult task of looking for the bodies.

He had just hung up his phone, where he had learned about the trashing of one of the local chalets in the area, when he received Dorothy's call. Unlikely the strange events happening in his community weren't connected. He decided to see her for a personal interview, but not before stopping at the detachment to retrieve the picture of the missing car owner that had been given to him by the Calgary Police Service.

He walked back to his car deep in thought, after learning of Dorothy's strange morning. She confirmed that the woman was, in fact, the same woman in his picture, and that her companions name was Frank. She had not learned his last name. He was hurt with a nasty cut on his arm, which Jack presumed occurred as a result of the broken window at the chalet. Pieces were falling into place.

But what was with the truck? How did that fit into the picture? Dorothy had explained that as Frank and Elena were getting into the taxi, she had seen two people sitting in a truck, partially hidden in a stand of trees. It had pulled out and followed the taxi.

Jack sat in his car, pondering his next move. First, he had to call off the Coast Guard. He would hear about that. Next, he needed to talk to the Calgary Police Service again to see if he could learn any-thing of Elena Romano's companion. He had already gotten what he could from them concerning the woman and knew his effort would be a long shot. But that was how police work was done. Sometimes the long shots paid off. He also had to find that cabbie.

A few minutes later, after being assured the Calgary Police would do some additional research, he decided he needed to bring the Gibsons detachment into the loop and dialed the number from memory.

"Steve? Jack here. You have a few minutes for a story?"

***

Frank Ricci climbed back into the taxi, burner phone in hand, having left the packaging in the hands of a pimple-faced young man working his first job in Sechelt. The boy had reacted suspi-ciously when Frank said he wanted a burner phone. Frank calmed his concerns by offering him an extra fifty bucks, for his quick assistance in getting it up and running. Frank felt confident the young man would not disclose the transaction, after he watched the boy pocket the extra money.

"Let's head for Gibsons now, Noah, please," Frank said, rubbing his injured arm gingerly.

Noah put the cab in gear and pulled into traffic. He looked up and noticed a pickup truck he was sure he had seen earlier, pulling out behind him as well.

The car's radio squawked. "Noah, you there?"

Frank thought it odd that they still used radios. Most taxis he'd seen recently had converted to cell phones.

Noah picked up the mike. "I'm here."

"Got a call from the RCMP. They want to talk to you about a fare you had. I'm going to send you a contact number to your phone. You need to call right away."

"Roger that." Noah clipped the mike to his dash. He glared into his mirror. "Seems you haven't been entirely truthful, mate."

Frank held Noah's eyes. "It's not what it seems, Noah." Noah stayed silent, eyes flipping from Frank's to the road and back.

Frank clicked his tongue, catching Noah's gaze. "I'll pay you another two thousand dollars, if you ignore that request. We need time, Noah."

"I can't ignore the request. It's the cops."

Elena reached over the seat. In her hand was the money. Noah glanced at it, licking his lips.

"Look, I can buy you some time, nothin' more. I'll get you to Gibsons, then I got to call 'em."

"Half hour after dropping us off."

Noah nodded.

"Fair enough, then." Frank nodded back. He watched Noah take the money from Elena's hands. She sat back.

As they flew down the highway, Frank punched in Nate's number on his new phone. He reached Nate's recording and left a message asking him to call as soon as possible. "It's urgent," he said, and hung up.

Noah searched his mirror again. "Are you expecting anyone to be following you, mate?"

Frank fought the urge to turn and look back. He closed his eyes. "What's it look like?"

"Pickup truck of some sort. Been on us for a while. Saw him pull out behind us in Sechelt."

Elena let out a muffled noise, which Frank silenced by taking her hand in his.

CHAPTER TWENTY-SIX

NATE WAS ENJOYING HIMSELF, AND for the moment had forgotten his troubles. He focused on the eager faces of the boys, as they reviewed the previous weeks lesson. Satisfied they had developed a good grasp of the fundamentals he had taught; he went on to explain the science of why trimming the sails properly created the necessary energy to propel the boat forward efficiently. Sam, Mark, and Elliot listened with rapt attention, their young minds absorbing the details.

"Ready to tack?" Nate called out.

The boys took up their positions. Sam, the oldest, was at the wheel this time, with Mark, the quiet one, attending to the mainsail line, Elliot, the jib line. Nate sat on the bench ready to assist, as needed. The boys were quick studies.

"Tack," he called.

Sam threw the wheel, letting it spin freely in his small hands. At the same time, Mark and Elliot released their lines allowing wind to fill the sails on the opposite side, as the boat changed direction. The boys pulled on their respective lines, allowing the cleats to catch, holding the sails in place as the boat listed to starboard. They reached for their winches and tightened down the lines until the boat accelerated. Tilting their heads back, they noted the tell-tails on the main sail, adjusting their trim until the boat achieved a perfect list. They sat back, beaming at Nate.

"Perfect." A grin lit up Nate's face. He was rewarded with a flurry of commentary from all the boys at once, congratulating themselves on a job well done, as if this was their life's work.

"Take her home, boys," he said to a trio of groans and protestations.

His phone pinged. He glanced down at the unknown number and decided that he had about ten minutes before he'd instruct the boys to drop the sails, allowing him to take *Serendipity* into the harbour under power. He retrieved his message. While he was relieved that his uncle finally contacted him, he didn't like the urgent nature of the call. The events of the last few days flooded back to him in a flash. And, what's with the new number? He pocketed his phone, making a mental note to deal with the call as soon as he landed.

"Prepare to drop sails."

The crew jumped to their respective posts.

Nate reminded the boys of the docking maneuvers. Ensuring they were ready, he backed into his slip and watched as they jumped to the dock with lines in hand, securing the boat as they had been taught. Thanking him profusely, they waved and ran up the dock, passing Archie who greeted them gruffly.

"No running on the docks," he snarled.

The boys ran on. They greeted their waiting parents, their boasts trailing off as they headed for their cars. Nate laughed and turned to cleaning up after the lesson. Boys being boys, he always had a mess after they ate the snack he provided on the water. He finished washing the dishes and went back up to the cockpit, where he retrieved his phone. He was about to phone his uncle at the new number, when he looked up and saw Beka coming towards him.

She had a light blue summer dress on and carried a matching sweater over her arm. A large floppy hat was on her head. She bore a bottle of rose wine in one hand and a picnic basket in the other, and she smiled as she came to a stop at the stern of the boat.

Nate's heart fluttered. She was beautiful. He put the phone on his table and reached down to take the basket, then her hand. "Come aboard, m'lady."

Nate saw Archie give him a thumbs up as he headed back into his salon. Nate smiled.

"You're looking happy with yourself. How was the lesson?" Beka settled into a seat at the back of the boat.

"It was great. They've come so far. By the end of the season, those boys will be able to sail their own daysailer, confidently. I really have grown fond of them. So, to what do I owe the honour? I thought we were going to meet for dinner tonight?"

"We are, but since it is a beautiful day, I told Milo I wanted the afternoon off to visit my favourite sailor. I know you haven't had lunch, you never do on the days of your lessons, so..."

"I did snack on a few things with the boys, but I'm hungry."

"Got time for a sail?"

"You know it."

Serendipity left the mouth of the harbour, and Nate headed out for a second sail of the day on the Shoal Channel. He stood behind the wheel, a breeze blowing his hair back. Once out of the harbour, he turned *Serendipity* into the head wind and raised the mainsail. Beka sat quietly and watched Nate work his lines to perfection and giggled when he maneuvered the sails to a wing-on-wing configuration.

"Show off."

Nate sailed over to a small bay in the Shelter Islands and dropped anchor. He reached out his hand and Beka passed over the bottle of wine. After finding a bottle opener and a pair of glasses, Nate poured them each a drink. They enjoyed a wonderful late day lunch beneath *Serendipity's* bimini. It was a warm spring day and Nate was in his element. He looked at Beka, content in her company.

"You look fabulous, Beka," he said.

She blushed.

"Want me to take off these oversized sunglasses so you can see what I really look like?"

They went quiet for a moment as they both reflected on their O'Reilly experiences. Nate wanted to change the subject.

"Do you know how to sail?"

"A little," she said. "Milo taught me a thing or two." She went silent for a moment, then added, "Nate, I need to ask you a question." Her demeanour shifted.

"Go ahead."

"What is going on? I've noticed a lot of strange people about these days, and something was bothering you this morning. You said you would tell me about it tonight. I'm worried about you. Is there some way I can help?"

Nate gave Beka a fixed look, said nothing, and shifted over to sit beside her. He held her face in his hands, leaned in, kissed her softly.

"That was very nice," she said after he pulled back. "But that was not an answer."

Nate leaned in and kissed her again, this time more passionately. She responded. He stood up and reached out his hand.

"You're going to answer me, sooner or later, Nate." She rose, shook her head at him, reached for his hand, and followed him into the cabin of the boat.

***

Frank and Elena scrutinized each other. They had to improvise and in a hurry.

"What do you want me to do?" Noah asked, studying the truck in his mirror.

Frank smiled at Elena, who nodded. "You need to let us out in the centre of Gibsons, preferably where there are a lot of people. You have done enough for us already, Noah."

"You're in trouble," Noah said, studying Frank in his mirror.

"You might say that."

"Look, mate, I'm not looking for any problems, but I think I can lose this guy and give you a fighting chance. These are my roads. Then you're on your own."

"Noah, that'd be great if you could do that," Frank heard himself saying. He then adjusted in his seat, searching through the rear window. It was the same pickup.

Noah tightened his lips. "You might want to hang on."

He headed down Gower Point Road, slowing to a crawl. The pickup was two cars back and both were forced to reduce speed behind him. He was watching a group of tourists heading for a crosswalk in front of him. He slowed down even more. The car behind him laid on his horn. The group approached the walk. He counted, "One, two, three, four, five." He stomped on the gas as they started to cross the street. The car behind them came to a stop in front of the walkers. Noah could see him throw up his hands in exasperation. He looked back, tracking the pickup. It stayed its course. Noah pulled away from his pursuers. He was coming to a bend in the road when he saw the cars move again. He watched to see if the pickup pulled out to pass until he rounded a corner and lost sight of them. They had a slight advantage now. Noah threw the wheel, turning onto an adjoining street and slammed down the gas pedal again. More horns sounded through his open window. He came to an alleyway and, not seeing the pickup following him, he turned and doubled back to the town centre. He heard a siren yelp and looked down another street as he came to end of the alley. Noah breathed a sigh of relief.

"No worries. Seems your friends have a spot of trouble with the police."

"What do you mean?" Elena asked.

"The RCMP pulled over the truck that was following you. My guess is they were speeding to try and catch up with us. Lucky that wasn't us, but hey, it should give us lots of time to get away. Now, where do you want me to drop you off?"

Frank thought for a moment. "The ferry, please, Noah."

Noah glanced back and laughed.

"Langford?"

"That'd be the one."

"Thought you wanted to be dropped off in downtown Gibsons?"

"That was then." Frank smiled at Noah.

The radio squelched. Noah reached down and turned it off.

"That's going to be a problem," Frank admonished.

Noah shrugged. "Making good money for the bother, mate."

Noah turned in the opposite direction of the police and made his way back to the highway.

Elena touched Frank's arm. He turned his head and smiled at her quizzical look. She said nothing.

***

The cop got out of his car and approached the driver's side window. The window dropped and the driver gawked at him, waiting for him to speak.

"You were going pretty darn fast, sir, almost caused an accident."

The driver did not acknowledge the statement.

"Driver's licence and registration."

The driver pulled out the documents and handed them to the officer.

"Wait here," he said.

The driver watched the cop return to his vehicle to run the plates and registration.

"I guess they spotted us?" the passenger said.

The driver stared straight ahead. "Seems so." He checked to his left, noting the crowds, walking by, on the sidewalk. The beautiful day had brought a lot of the residents out for a stroll. Some turned to glance at him as they walked by. Funny how people always want to see the look on the guy's face who got pulled over. The driver glared back at the people, with a scowl on his face. He shifted in his seat, checking the opposite side of the street.

"What the..."

His passenger faced him. "What is it?"

"Look."

The passenger scanned the crowd.

"At what?"

"That guy coming through the door of that diner.

"I see him." The passenger frowned, then grinned. "That's the first piece of good news we've had today."

The driver glanced at the passenger. "Is it? How can that guy be here? I killed him."

"It's not him obviously. But it is weird."

The driver grunted in response.

"We lost the only lead we had to the money. That guy there just gave us another. So, weird or not, we've got to keep an eye on him." The passenger opened the truck's door, stepped out, and looked back at the driver. "Call me when you're done here. I want to see where he's going. "

***

Quince returned to the truck. He handed the drivers licence and registration back to the driver, along with a ticket. He watched as the passenger walked away but said nothing. After giving the driver instructions on how to pay the fine, the driver hit the switch to raise his window, put his truck in gear, and pulled away. Quince watched after him, then turned his eyes, following the walker receding in the distance. He wished he had gotten a better look at them both. He thought back to the call he had received earlier from Jack Forester. He wondered if this was the same truck that Jack described had followed the persons of interest he was chasing down. If it were, then it was highly likely that Elena Romano and her companion were likely in town too. He made a mental note to update Jack and returned to his car.

Quince didn't like all the activity happening around his quiet town. It all had one frame of reference. Calgary. Something felt very wrong, and he needed to connect the dots.

***

After acknowledging an additional tip that Frank insisted he take, Noah pulled up to the terminal and bid farewell to Frank and Elena. They exited the cab. They took a half dozen steps away when Noah slid the passenger window down and called out, "As promised, half hour, mate, then I have to call the cops."

Frank watched the taxi crest the hill, then took Elena's arm. They walked to the ferry's taxi stand and hailed another car. Frank gave the woman instructions of how to get to his motel. Elena had remained silent until they entered the room. She walked over to the bed, sat down and quietly said. "Now what, Frank?"

Frank put the safety chain on the door, and said, "We get in touch with Nate, then get out of here. But first, we need to clean up. As much as I think you are an incredibly good-looking woman, Elena, you lock a little worse for wear."

Elena laughed. "You go first," she said and closed her eyes. "I need a bit of a rest. It's been quite a day." Frank watched her get comfortable, nodded, and headed for the bathroom.

He returned to find her asleep. Her face looked at peace and a slight smile crossed his lips. He walked over to a desk and wrote a note to her, should she awaken before his return. They needed some new clothes.

***

The sun was lower in the sky, but the day was still beautiful. A warm breeze blew across the stern of the boat when they resurfaced. It could've been pouring rain, and Nate was sure he'd still be smiling. He drank in Beka's dishevelled locks and, grinning, said, "You will need to fix that hair before we get back."

Beka giggled and sat down on a cushion. She reached for his hand. Nate took it and sat beside her. "Now," she said, locking eyes with him. "I want to know, Nate. I want to know everything."

Nate sighed; concern etched on his face. "Beka, sometimes it's best to let sleeping dogs lie. I'm working through some problems, but I'll get through them."

"Serious problems, it would seem."

"Yes...serious problems, but I'm dealing with them."

"Nate, I think you know I'm pretty fond of you." Nate's eyes lit up. "I want to be part of your life, but not if we have secrets. So out with it. I want to know what's going on...all of it."

Nate's mind flashed back to Jessica Reed and her fate. He reached over and touched Beka's bruised cheek. "I can't," he whispered. "It's too dangerous. I can't put you in the middle of this."

"Oh, it's okay for you to put yourself in the way of my danger..." she said, reminding him of Ty O'Reilly, "...but you think I'm too weak to deal with your world?"

"I didn't say that."

They went silent for a bit. "Out with it." Beka implored him with a warm look that melted his heart.

"I don't want to lose you, Beka. You might not like what you hear."

"I'm a lot tougher than I look, Nate. Besides, the best way not to lose me is to be honest with me."

Nate stared at her intensely, searching for a hint of what she might think if he told her everything. After a few minutes, he began. "My name is not Nate Beckett; it's Nate Vickers. I'm from Calgary."

The sun was within an hour of setting when he finished. She now knew as much about him as he did. Well, almost as much. He couldn't bring himself to tell her about Jess' death and had glossed over that detail. It wasn't a necessary piece of information for her to understand his story and he thought it might be too much for her to accept.

He had guarded his secret religiously and now it was out, in all its glory, save the part that had eaten him up for the past year. He would have to tell her later, but not now. There was no expression of shock on her face as she looked at him with soft eyes — just acceptance.

"Say something," Nate implored. "Have I disappointed you?"

"No," she demurred. "We all have a story, Nate. Some are prettier than others. You and I have difficult ones. But now we have a joint story, a story I hope we'll continue to build on together." She leaned in and kissed him.

Nate drew in a long breath and pulled her to him. He looked past her to the lowering sun. "It's getting late," he whispered in her ear.

"Go and raise that anchor, sailor," she said into his neck. "I promised Milo, I would relieve him and close up tonight."

Nate pulled back and mimed a salute. He waltzed up to the bow, marvelling at how well the conversation had gone...at least he hoped so.

He heard the engine fire up as he locked the anchor in place and looked back.

"Are we motoring home?"

"Hell, no," she said with a smile. "Come and sit back down. It's my turn."

She maneuvered *Serendipity* into the wind and raised the mainsail. The wind caught hold, she cut the motor again and the boat headed towards Gibsons. She then pulled out the jib and trimmed the sails to perfection, winching them into place.

"Milo taught you a thing or two, huh?"

She laughed.

The sun disappeared over the horizon as they docked. Nate walked her back up to the marina store and kissed her goodbye before she entered. They decided on a rain check for dinner and made plans for the next day. He turned to head down to his boat again, when Ty O'Reilly stepped out of the shadows. He approached him warily, his arm in a sling.

"You're dead, Mr. Knight," he said. "You won't see it coming, but you are dead. I warned you."

He turned on his heel and walked away. Nate stood and watched him until he crested the hill. O'Reilly didn't turn to look at Nate again. He would be true to his word and at some point, he would come for him.

Great, he thought. *Beka's right, we both have difficult stories.*

Nate wandered back down to his boat. Archie was sitting in his deck chair. He stood as Nate approached, nodding a caution in the direction of Nate's boat. Nate's eyes pivoted. He saw a man sitting quietly in the cockpit of *Serendipity.*

He frowned, walked over to the stern, and stepped aboard. Ross Finlay was sitting with his legs crossed, gazing out over the water.

"I see the appeal of this," he said. "I do hope you'll be able to keep her after you pay us the money."

"What do you want?" Nate's voice was tinged in anger.

"I want to know how you are going to do what I asked."

Nate stood, staring fixedly at him.

"I'll draw him out."

"How?"

"I have some ideas. You just need to know that I will get him here."

"I need more."

"I'll use myself as bait. But I need to know how you're going to deal with him before he kills me."

"Come have a seat, Mr. Vickers. Let's work out some details."

Nate sat down reluctantly. He leaned in and listened as Finlay laid out how he would protect Nate. Nate didn't believe it for a minute but acted as though he did. Hoping to buy more time, Nate added more detail to his plan making sure Finlay knew he was still flushing out certain details.

"Very good, Mr. Vickers. You are resourceful. And when do you think you will put everything in motion?"

Nate pondered that himself. He had to have time to meet with his uncle, time to figure out how to deal with Belletti and with this bastard. "I need a couple of days."

"How about tomorrow, Mr. Vickers? I hate procrastination."

"No, I said I need a couple of days. Consider it prep time."

"Very well, two days. In the meantime, you can start working on amassing the money. I have taken the liberty of providing you with instructions as to where to send the funds. I will expect that you have this done by weeks end. I won't be leaving until I have the transfer confirmed. Please don't disappoint me." He reached into his coat pocket and pulled out a folded sheet of paper, dropped it on the table before him. Finlay paused, then stood up to leave.

"Goodnight, Mr. Vickers. I look forward to hearing from you soon." He stepped back onto the dock.

Nate stopped him. "Mr. Finlay?" he said mocking Finlay's approach. Finlay turned. "You ever step on my boat again, without an invitation, and you'll wish you hadn't."

Finlay smirked at Nate as if he were someone's misbehaving child, said nothing, and walked back along the dock.

CHAPTER TWENTY-SEVEN

NATE POURED A SIZEABLE AMOUNT of Crown Royal into a highball glass and headed up to the cockpit to contemplate his next move. The sun had set, and the cool evening air was settling in. He didn't feel the coolness beneath the light wool sweater he wore, and probably wouldn't have noticed regardless, given his current state of mind. Finlay was a huge problem, but the urgent message from his uncle concerned him even more. Add to that the complication of Ty O'Reilly and it was no wonder Nate fought a degree of anxiety. So many things had gone wrong in such a short period of time. He'd had it all — a new name, a new life, a new lady, and anonymity.

That was until his uncle found him. He wasn't angry at Frank; his heart had been in the right place. He'd come to warn Nate, and Nate had foolishly invited him to his new home. And now, here he was phoning from a number Nate didn't recognize and telling him they had to meet urgently. He needed to meet with Frank and understand what was so pressing.

His mind turned to address Finlay. A year ago, a man like Finlay would've terrified him. But not anymore. Not only was he not afraid of him, but he was now working on how to double-cross the man and make an escape. He had either gotten far more street-wise or he was delusional. Perhaps both.

Nate picked up his phone and tried the number his uncle had called from. He hoped he would answer. He needed to know what was going on, and he needed advice. No answer. He frowned, put the phone back on the table before him, and sipped his drink.

He noticed Beka walking toward him. His face broke into a grin as he stood up to greet her.

"What a pleasant surprise. I thought we weren't getting together again until tomorrow."

"Must have been the kiss." She laughed and stepped aboard. "I was missing you and grumping at Milo, so he sent me to clear my head. He was supposed to go home but I think he knew full well where I wanted to be. How has the rest of your --?"

Nate's phone rang. Beka went silent. He picked it up. "Unknown number," he said. "I have to take this." He hit the receive button and said hello. A weight lifted from his shoulders. "Frank. Where the hell have you been?"

Beka remained silent, listening to the response. She could see his face darken, even in the low cockpit lighting.

"Now would be good, Frank," Nate said quietly. "We have a lot to talk about." Nate listened further. "Who?" He listened again, then, "See you soon." Nate hung up and looked at Beka.

"He's on his way here now. He says he's being followed but will take precautions to make sure he loses them."

"Do you want me to leave?" Beka said.

Nate contemplated the question. "No... I don't." He smiled at her. He hadn't realized how much her coming on board had relieved his anxieties. "While we wait, let me tell you what happened after

I left you at the store." Nate then recounted his run in with Ty O'Reilly and Ross Finlay.

At the name of O'Reilly, Beka paled, but remained quiet. Once Nate had finished speaking, she took his hand in hers. "Maybe you should bring the police in on all this, Nate."

"I can't, Beka. I broke the law, and while I might be able to wriggle out of that with a good lawyer, finding a way around the rest of this would not be as easy." Nate rose. "Forgive me, I've been rude. Can I get you something?"

"How about a tea."

Nate went below to make her drink, leaving Beka to sort out her thoughts. He had just brought it up on deck and sat down when she noticed a burly man heading down the gangway accompanied by a slight woman. They walked hurriedly, checking behind them frequently as they moved.

"Nate..." Beka nodded in their direction.

"Can you take my drink and your tea below deck and close the curtains, please."

Beka stood and did as he asked. A few moments later, Frank reached *Serendipity*. Nate reached out his hand to his uncle who stepped on board and into a bear hug with his nephew. Nate heard a groan and stepped back to appraise the bandage on his arm. He said nothing. He side-stepped his uncle and reached out his hand to the woman.

"Nate...Elena; Elena...Nate."

"Welcome aboard, Elena. Let's go below."

She looked familiar.

***

Milo had seen a man and a woman heading down the gangway at a brisk pace, through the store window. It was late in the evening and unusual for someone to head down to the docks in a hurry.

He walked outside to make sure they were not a threat to Beka and felt much better when he saw Nate and the man embrace each other. *It must be his uncle,* he thought. As he turned to go back into the store, he saw another man standing down the shore, who had also watched as the couple had boarded Nate's boat. The man had reached into his pocket and pulled out a phone, never taking his eyes off *Serendipity.*

Milo stood in front of the store's door and stared at him, willing the man to look at him. He wanted him to know he was being watched. The man briefly glanced at Milo, then turned away, focusing on his call. He recognized the guy from earlier that day. He was the same guy that Steve Quince had been following. Milo's heart skipped a beat when he heard the man declare into his phone, "Birds have come home to roost." He turned on his heel and headed back to the store. He had to call Quince. This was getting out of hand, and Beka was at risk.

***

Quince had just finished updating Jack Forester when his phone rang. After the requisite salutations, he listened and interrupted the speaker with the occasional "I see" and signed off with, "I'll head over now."

He hurriedly signed out of his computer, looking one last time at the name of "Nate Vickers" typed into the search bar, and sighed. He was no closer to understanding who this Nate Vickers was that Sebastian was looking for. But he would get there.

He grabbed his coat from the back of his chair and headed for the door.

***

Nate and Frank faced each other, each willing the other to start. Beka had not removed her sunglasses, despite the lateness of the day. Elena sat beside Beka, looked empty and said little.

Nate introduced Beka and the four of them went through the usual light banter until it became obvious that the two men needed to talk in more depth.

"Perhaps we should go up top?" Frank said. "If you would excuse us, ladies." He rose to make his way to the stairs.

"No, Frank, we need to stay below. Beka is with me and knows everything."

Frank raised an eyebrow at the statement. "Really? Now that is surprising." He pivoted to scrutinize her. "Any chance you might remove those glasses, Beka? It would be helpful to see your whole face."

Beka tilted her head at Nate. He nodded. She removed her glasses. Frank examined Beka, then turned to Nate, an unspoken question in his gaze.

Elena let out a gasp and reached over to put her hand on Beka's arm. She glared at Nate.

"It wasn't Nate," Beka declared, moving closer to him.

"It's a long story," Nate interrupted, looking hard at Elena. He remembered her now from the store in Calgary and had drawn his own conclusions. "And Elena?" he asked quietly, turning back to Frank.

"She's fully in the loop."

Elena remained silent. This was not her discussion to lead. She turned back to Beka, who put her sunglasses back on.

"Really?" Nate said. "Now, that too is very surprising."

Frank smirked.

Nate nodded his assent and added, "We have a lot to cover. Why don't you start Frank?"

Frank told Nate everything that happened since they last met, with Elena adding details when Frank missed an important point.

Nate interrupted sparingly, asking a few questions when clarity was needed. He was already unnerved by the arrival of Belletti's team and Ross Finlay with his demands. Now, he was learning there was another unknown group tracking Frank. He felt the intensity lighten at the description of their interactions with Noah until Frank expounded on their escape from the unknown followers.

Nate went silent, attempting to reconcile all the events. Beka's phone rang. Elena jumped at the sound.

Beka looked at the screen. "Milo," she said.

Nate nodded at her.

"Hi, Dad," she said, answering the call. She listened for a minute or two and hung up after acknowledging a question. "Seems your friend is back, Nate. Same guy as this afternoon. Milo closed the store and is coming to the end of the dock in a dingy to get us all and quietly move us away from the boat. He wanted me to tell you that he also called Quince about him."

Nate closed his eyes. "You have to be kidding me." He focused on Frank and Elena. "We need to finish this conversation, but it can't be now. Belletti has found us, but it gets worse from there. There's a new threat that I am dealing with too. Jesus, what mess." Nate stood.

The others followed suit. "Do you need to call Milo back, Beka?"

"No, he is on his way."

Nate's head spun towards the bow of the boat. He heard glass shattering. He sprinted up the stairs to the cockpit and turned to the bow. Flames shot across the forward deck.

"Shit." Nate used the handrail to pivot back to the lounge area. He ran to the interior console, snapped a fire extinguisher from its bracket, and raced back to the stairs. "Beka, get everybody off this boat."

"Nate?"

"Go. We're on fire."

Nate ran the stairs, stepping up to the guardrail, determining the best way to deal with the flames. He saw a zodiac leaving the harbour at full speed. He pulled the extinguisher's pin, depressed the trigger and aimed the nozzle at the closest part of the fire.

The others headed for the transom and stepped down onto the dock.

"This way!" Beka hollered and ran down the dock with Frank and Elena in tow. They passed Nate; he was gaining on the flames. She ran to the end of the dock where Milo was motoring into view.

"What the hell happened?" Milo yelled as he grabbed hold of a dock rail. Not waiting for an answer, he said, "Get in."

"Dad, you remember Frank, and this is Elena. You need to take them away. Really far away. That guy up there is after them," she said, not telling him that they were after Nate too.

"You get in too, Beka," Frank said.

Beka looked down at Milo. "No, Frank, Nate needs me. Take them please, Dad. You know where."

Nate had heard their exchange. "You all go, Beka."

Milo stared at her. "Please," he pleaded.

Beka shook her head, her eyes locking on Milo's. "I'll be fine. We'll come later." Beka turned and ran back to the boat.

Milo reluctantly shoved off from the dock.

She stepped back on-board *Serendipity* and walked to the bow and stood beside Nate who was surveying the damage. The fire was expunged.

"You were supposed to go," he said, sadness engulfing his face.

"Not without you, I'm not."

***

The man on shore jumped to his feet when the flames lit up the front of Nate's boat. He pulled out his phone and was about to make a further report when out of the corner of his eye, he spotted the RCMP cruiser arrive in the parking lot. The car arrived quietly, lights flashing. The officer sprang from the car and ran down the gangway to *Serendipity*. Flames were obvious from the shore.

Thinking it wouldn't be smart to stand in the open, the biker stepped into the shadows of a tree to watch. As the officer reached the docks, he hit a speed dial.

"You ain't gonna believe this, but somebody lit up the boat." He listened, then spoke. "Far as I know, they are all still there. Now the cops are too. I don't think I should hang around here."

He listened for a few seconds, acknowledged his instructions and stepped further into the shadows. He put his phone on "do not disturb" and waited.

***

Quince arrived at *Serendipity*. Nate had the fire out, and Beka stood by his side. He jumped onto the stern of the boat. Nate and Beka whipped their heads around. "You need permission to come aboard," Nate snarled.

Quince stood his ground. "Actually... I don't. Not when it's an emergency."

Nate glared at him.

"What happened here, Nate?"

"What do you think happened?" Nate snapped back.

"Could you lose the attitude?"

Beka placed a hand on Nate's arm. Nate breathed in and exhaled slowly. He met Quince in the cockpit.

Beka inspected the broken glass and remnants of the burned rag that had ignited the gas. "I'll clean this up," she said.

"No, you won't. This is a crime scene," Quince said.

Nate reacted. "A crime scene? This is my home. You're not welcome here. I'm not planning on pressing charges. The fire is out. Besides, you already know who did it."

"I don't know who is responsible for this."

"He threatened me today...O'Reilly. Told me I was a dead man."

Quince sat down on a bench seat and pulled out his notepad. "Start over...from the beginning, Nate."

Nate glared at Quince. "Get off my boat."

***

After Quince left, Nate and Beka sat on the back of *Serendipity.* They were going over all that had happened, including their discussions with Frank and Elena, when Archie lumbered down the dock to confront them. Nate looked up, a foreboding expression on his face.

"Archie," he said, without inviting him on board.

Archie still held an additional fire extinguisher in hand.

"Nate, Beka," he said with a serious tone. "I saw that Zodiac. Didn't recognize who was in it. I heard you tell Steve it was O'Reilly, but I don't think it was. The guy was too agile. And, as you know, O'Reilly is busted up. Can't say it wasn't someone he sent, though. Thought you should know."

"Thank you, Archie." Beka responded.

"Doesn't mean he wasn't responsible," Nate added quickly.

"No, it doesn't. But lately, you have had a lot of visitors Nate." He left the statement hanging, as if it were a question. Nate didn't respond. "Things will look better in daylight. Let me know if you need anything."

Archie turned to go back to his boat. Nate called after him. "Is there someone nearby who can fix that mess up top?"

Nate heard Beka's phone ring. He glanced at her as she stepped away to answer it.

"I know a guy. I'll call him in the morning. Any structural damage?"

"I don't think so. I got it quickly enough. Just a hell of a mess."

"Get some sleep, Nate. You look like hell. I'll sleep with one eye open tonight." Archie said.

"I saw you coming earlier with that extinguisher, Archie. Had that cocktail been worse, I wouldn't have been able to handle it myself. Thanks."

Archie waved and strolled away.

Nate turned to Beka. "Want me to walk you up?"

"Only if you have a need to be alone, Nate. I'd prefer to stay."

"I'm worried about Frank and Elena."

"They'll be fine. Milo has them tucked away. That was him on the phone. We'll go first thing in the morning and finish our conversation." She stood, walked to the cabin entry, and climbed down the stairs. "You coming?"

"In a few."

Nate scanned the harbour, watching the town's lights twinkle on the water, as if they were fireflies. He put his head in his hands. Things were unravelling fast.

He turned to gaze at Archie's catamaran. He could see him sitting out back looking in Nate's direction. He wondered what the old cop's perspective was. Nate knew he had to make a move. They had found him. Finlay wouldn't wait forever either. He was none too happy this afternoon. Maybe he sent a message tonight? Or Belletti...his team was in town and now knew his location. Was this their work? Nate shook his head free of the debate. He rose and headed below deck.

Usually, he'd leave his door open and enjoy the evening air and cool cabin in the morning. Tonight, though, he slid the door closed and locked it from within. He walked to his stateroom door and peered in. Beka was in bed with a sheet pulled up to her chin, waiting for him. She focused her gaze on him and said nothing. Nate walked over to her and, leaning down, kissed her lightly. He pulled his shirt over his head.

***

On shore, Mario walked up to Nick, observing the marina. "Which one is it?"

"The sailboat at the end of the second dock." The biker pointed out *Serendipity.*

Mario nodded. "Who started the fire? Last thing we need are cops everywhere?"

"I have no idea, Mario. Some guy in a Zodiac. Took off like a bat out of hell. He threw a cocktail, lit rag burning at its neck. It seems Vickers has made some new enemies."

Mario tilted his head in thought. "Take off, but be back at four a.m. We'll take them then, while everyone is asleep. Too many lights burning right now. Don't be late. Understood?"

The soldier nodded.

"Vickers is the prize, but I want them both."

"What about the women?"

"Collateral damage. We need to deal with this fast. I don't know who the competition is, but we need to retrieve that money, before somebody decides to off Vickers."

The biker nodded again, checked his watch. "What are you going to do?"

"I'm staying right here. Now go."

Mario dropped to a nearby bench, watched his man walk away. He pivoted and focused on Nate's boat. The long chase would soon be over.

Because he looked nowhere else, he was unaware of two people walking over to another bench further down the marina pathway. They watched Mario as the soldier headed into town.

***

"Now we know where he is," the man whispered.

"Yes, good thing that guy pointed out the boat."

"Should we take Vickers now?"

"No. I want these guys out of the way first. Call it a personal interest."

"Okay. Want me to take this guy out?" the man said, nodding at Mario.

"Not here, too open. We'll follow them. They're after Vickers too. All will be ours in the end."

They rose and returned to their pickup. They could see Mario's SUV and decided to wait and see what else developed.

***

Ty O'Reilly walked out of the station, furious that he had been a suspect in the firebombing of a boat. A boat, for crying out loud. You don't do that in these parts, even if it was a boat owned by Nate fucking Beckett. He wanted to get Beckett, but he wouldn't be that obvious. He had time. He would devise a far more fitting fate for him. But he'd have to be careful now. Quince was on him. His questions told Ty that he knew everything. Beckett had talked to him. Yes, sir. He'd have to be far more careful, but Beckett had to pay. The debt would be paid in full.

***

Quince stood at the window and watched O'Reilly walk down the street into the darkness. He'd check out O'Reilly's alibi in the morning, but he was pretty sure he hadn't done it. Cop's instinct. So, who did? One of O'Reilly's friends? Doubtful. The guy watching Beckett that he had followed, or one of his associates? Someone else? Who is this Nate Beckett?

Nate Beckett, a man with no known past. Nate Beckett, a man who is being watched by a lot of strangers in town. Nate Beckett, a nice kid, who is very evasive. Nate Beckett, recipient of the only firebomb Steve Quince had ever encountered in his years on the force.

Quince returned to his desk and thought about phoning the lab to create more urgency in getting the results of those fingerprints he'd asked for. They said a couple of days and that's what it would be. He tried to hurry them before, without success. He knew he'd stepped over the line when he removed the brochure from Nate's trash bag the day he questioned him about O'Reilly, but it was all he could think of to move things forward. He'd worry about the lawfulness of it later.

In the meantime, he'd carry on his research of Nate Beckett and Nate Vickers. What was it that P.I. had said? Nate Beckett and Nate Vickers were the same guy? Maybe that was true. The prints would certainly prove that out.

Quince read the bulletin put out by the Calgary Police Service on Nate Vickers, he had previously requested. There had been an incident outside an apartment where one person was dead, and shots had been fired in the direction of Vickers. After that he had disappeared. The CPS wanted to find Vickers, as he was a person of interest. A set of prints, believed to be that of Vickers were attached to the report. Unfortunately, The Calgary Police Service had only a grainy picture of Vickers, picked up from a street cam. He studied the photo acknowledging it could be Beckett, but it just wasn't good enough to be sure.

He needed the prints from his lab. They would confirm if he was the same guy as Nate Beckett. It would explain a lot of what was going on.

One thing was for sure. Nate Beckett was attracting way too much scrutiny to not have a past that had caught up to him. And in his gut, he had a bad feeling that his town was about to see an explosion as a result of all that attention. He had to get to the bottom of it before that happened. Maybe it was time to have another discussion with that P.I.

Quince rubbed his eyes and stood up from his desk. Lots of questions. They would have to wait.

Sleep had become a necessity.

CHAPTER TWENTY-EIGHT

NATE'S CELL BUZZED HIM OUT of a deep sleep. He reached over, snatched it up, and focused on the screen. The bright color advised it was three forty-five a.m. He groaned and pressed the receive button.

"Hello," he grunted.

"You get my message, Mr. Vickers?"

Nate tried to clear his head. "Finlay? Do you know what time it is?"

"I wanted to make sure I could get you. Did you get my message?"

Message? Then it hit him. The late-night fog cleared, anger stirring his mind like a beehive swatted by a bear. "The fire...that was you?"

"Not me, exactly. I didn't think you were taking me seriously enough, Mr. Vickers. I thought it best to remind you how vulnerable you are. I'll ask again, did you get my message?"

"I got it," Nate said in a hushed tone. He heard the menace ring in his voice and hoped his caller could not. He needed time.

"I certainly hope so. There will be no further delays. I trust you have started assembling the money?"

"You honestly think I can make it happen that fast?"

"As a man on the run...yes, I think you can."

Beka was now awake and leaning into Nate who pulled the phone from his ear a bit, allowing her to listen.

"I'm working on it," Nate answered. "I told you I need a couple of days. You could firebomb me every day. It won't change the time needed to put things in motion. If that doesn't work for you, then come and put a bullet in my head. I will be waiting for you." So much for backing down his menacing tone.

Ross Finlay ignored Nate's taunt. "You know the timelines, Mr. Vickers, not a day beyond. And don't disappoint me, for your sake and the sake of the lovely lady lying beside you." Nate's eyes darted to Beka's, who listened, showing no emotion. He was watching.

The line went dead.

"We have to get you out of here, Beka." His eyes darted around his stateroom, searching for alternatives.

"No, Nate," she answered softly.

"Beka..." he pleaded.

"Nate, I know you need to run. I'm coming with you. We will get through this together."

"Beka, these men, all of them, are very dangerous. They want me dead, after they get the money, that is. I couldn't live with myself if something happened to you too."

Beka cocked her head. "...too?" she asked, leaning on her arm, gazing down at Nate.

He had left that part of his story out of their previous conversation. His shoulders sunk.

"It seems you haven't been entirely forthright, Nate. So out with it and if you have left anything else out, I want to hear about that as well."

"Get dressed," he said. "We need to go to Frank and Elena. By the time we get there, you will know the rest."

She raised her eyebrow, studying him.

"Yes, Beka... everything."

He slid out of bed and pulled on his jeans, t-shirt and sweater he'd worn the night before.

Exiting the hatch door, he stepped into the cool air. The black night was beginning to dull. A grey light was emanating on the horizon. Placing his phone on the table, he sat, trying to collect his thoughts. Finlay wasn't making idle threats. He had to do what was demanded of him. His mind went in circles, trying to formulate an escape plan.

He glanced at the marina office, half expecting Milo to be sitting in his usual place despite the early hour. The darkened wall and overhead light proved otherwise. He knew Milo would be with Frank and Elena.

His gaze travelled right and in the shadows of the trees, outlined by an overhead path light, he spotted a man sitting by himself. Was he watching their boat? Nate pretended not to notice him but was sure his presence did not bode well. Rising, he wandered over to the port side of *Serendipity* and uncoiled his dingy line. He knew his activity was invisible to the man on shore. He pulled the dingy to the starboard side of his boat and loosely tied a reef-knot on to the stern railing, making sure he had access to the line from the dock. He wandered back to the cockpit, glancing furtively to shore to ensure the man hadn't moved. The fact the man was there at this time of day did not sit well with Nate. They had to move.

"We gotta go, Beka," he called down to her as he stepped back into the cockpit.

Nate watched her as she opened a cabinet and pulled one of his sweaters over her head. She poked her head out of the hatch as Nate spun to the sound of a vehicle arriving in the marina's parking lot. The noise from two car doors closing travelled across the water. Nate watched as two men wandered over to where the first man sat. They began an animated discussion. He saw one of the men point in their direction.

"Close the hatch and lock it, please." Nate directed Beka. He never took his eyes off the men.

"Forget the lock," he snarled. "Let's go. Their coming." Nate jumped to the dock. The men were now running for the gangway. He turned and saw Beka struggling with the hatch door. "Leave it, Beka. We have to get in the dingy... now."

Beka turned to see the three men running down the dock. One of them shouted something to the others. She fumbled at the lock and heard it catch. She pivoted from the boat and ran to Nate.

"Jump," Nate urged. He was sitting in the rear seat of the dingy, his right hand on the throttle of the engine, his left holding the dingy against the dock.

She dropped in, grabbing the side of the dingy for balance.

Nate pulled on the line, the reef-knot released, and they drifted away from the dock. The men spotted the dingy and ran harder. Nate pulled the cord on his outboard. It sputtered. He pulled again. The men were almost on them.

Archie stepped off the back of his catamaran, clad in a house-coat. "No running on these docks, gentlemen, especially at this hour." He stepped in front of the approaching men, startling them.

Nate's outboard thrummed to life. Archie had bought them valuable time. He opened the throttle up fully and the dingy swiftly pulled away from *Serendipity*. He glanced back to see what he deduced to be Belletti's men. Two of the men had maneuvered past Archie and sprinted to where the dingy had been. The third stood under the glare of a marina light and ignored Archie, who was now berating him. The man stared at Nate, locked eyes with him for a moment, then spun on his heel and made for the gangway, calling out to his men.

Nate's view swung to Archie who now faced him. He wasn't sure, but he thought he saw a tight smile on Archie's face. Crazy old coot.

Focused on escape, he steered the dingy through the breakwater entry, then turned down the shoreline. He checked over his shoulder. He saw the three men sprinting back up the gangway in the pre-dawn light. He lost sight of Archie and hoped he was okay.

Beka watched everything unfold silently. They were lost in thought as they travelled down the shoreline in the dull pre-morning light. It allowed them to see where they were headed. Beka reached out and touched Nate's arm. "We need to double back," she said above the engine noise.

"What? We just got away."

"To where, Nate? They can follow us down the shore and wait for us to land somewhere. We need to get to Milo's truck and make our way to Frank and Elena. There's a spare key in the store."

Nate said nothing, staring straight ahead, searching his mind for an alternate plan. He didn't want to give up their escape.

"They think you're heading up shore," she added. "That buys us some time as they race to find us again."

Nate studied her as he kept the dingy parallel to the shoreline and then, with a thrust of his arm, cut hard right. He headed back towards the harbour. He hoped their adversaries couldn't see their move or it would be for naught.

A few minutes later, he rounded the breakwater, checking the shoreline. No one was watching them, that he could see. He slowed the outboard down and edged the dingy into the heart of the marina. As he did, he saw Archie, now sitting on the back of his catamaran. He was still in his housecoat. He nodded at Nate and gave him a thumbs up to indicate they were in the clear. Nate wondered what the old cop was thinking.

Mouthing the word "thanks" as they passed, he proceeded to the day dock, near shore. He cut the motor and drifted into place. Beka climbed out first and secured the line. The early morning light was illuminating the marina now. It promised to be a beautiful morning, in direct contrast to the stress that Nate was feeling.

He followed Beka up the gangway, watching the road closely for Belletti's men. She reached into a pot of red geraniums beside the store's entrance and recovered a key, allowing them to slip quietly into the marina store.

"Milo's truck key is in the back room," she said.

They headed through the storeroom door. Beka walked over to a desk, retrieved the key, and faced Nate. She appeared clearly agitated.

"What is it, Beka?"

"Nothing, let's go."

Nate didn't move. Trepidation quivered down his back. "Beka?"

She pursed her lips. "I know this isn't the right time, but my thoughts keep bouncing back to 'something happening to me too.' What does that mean?"

Nate sighed. "You're right. We can't do this here; we can't hang around. I'll tell you as we go. I'm sorry Beka. I shouldn't have left anything out. I'll tell you everything. I promise. As soon as we're safe."

Her eyes softened. She nodded acceptance.

Nate felt relief. "If there is anything else you need, grab it now, but we must get away from here."

***

Steve Quince finished his morning ritual of bacon and eggs, dried toast, and a strong cup of Seattle's Best coffee. He strolled over to the front window of his modest bungalow and, for a moment, enjoyed the view of the Salish Sea. His thoughts turned, as they had for the past several days, to Nate Beckett. He hoped that today was the day that he would get the report on his prints. Nate Beckett...what could he have possibly done to warrant so much attention? He returned to his kitchen, cleaned up his dishes, and headed out the door to his car.

He phoned the detachment to advise that he was going to make a stop at Freddy's dock, before coming in, only to learn about the arrest of the local baker's son for drunk driving during the night, and that Mrs. Doherty had wandered off again from her group home. Quince gave directives on how to handle the problems. He had no time for them today. He focused on his upcoming discussion with the P.I.

Quince arrived at the dock minutes later. The sun was shining off the blue waters and the chrome on the boats gleamed in the bright light. Making a mental note to find some time to enjoy the remaining days of Spring, he headed down to the dock and over to the Bayliner. He looked in the side window and noted that John Sebastian was moving about in the cabin. Sebastian spied Quince. He moved to the salon door and stepped onto the deck of the boat.

"Good morning, Constable Quince. To what do I owe the pleasure?"

"Mind if I come aboard, Mr. Sebastian?"

"Yes, yes, of course." He reached down and, grabbing a sweater off the back of the salon's bench seat, motioned for Quinn to take a seat. "Coffee?"

"I'm good, thanks."

Sebastian sat in the pilot's chair, spinning the seat around to peer down at Quince.

Quince ignored the obvious power move. "How are you enjoying our little town?"

"Pretty enough, but it's a work trip for me."

"Have you had a chance to meet up with Nate Vickers then?"

"Not just yet, but I'm working on it."

"That's odd, I have an eyewitness that says you met with him yesterday. Or should I say Nate Beckett, who I believe you think are one and the same person."

Finlay slid off the chair, stepped over to the coffee pot, and poured himself a coffee.

"So I did...so I did, Constable Quince." Finlay smiled. Quince remained silent. Finlay slid back into the pilot chair. "Sometimes I find it easier to deflect a question with a denial. My apologies."

"And why would you find it easier to lie to me, Mr. Sebastian?" Quince decided to stand up to visually reassert himself.

Finlay paused a moment before answering. "I received a telephone call yesterday from my head office telling me to delay paying out the proceeds. Seems there are some extenuating circumstances that have developed that may delay or cause us to never pay out the settlement."

"Really...and what would those be?"

"Seems Mr. Vickers, a.k.a. Beckett, may have been involved in a crime that is related to the payout."

"That so? And what kind of crime would that be?"

Finlay stood up as well. "Murder," he said in a hushed tone.

Quince stood silently, thinking, not allowing surprise to register on his face.

"What were the insurance proceeds for, Mr. Sebastian?"

"I'm afraid I can't divulge that, Constable. I'd be happy to advise you, if in fact, my office finalizes their decision to not pay out, as the policy would then be considered null and void. For now, though, privacy rules prevent me from revealing the policy contents without a warrant. I'm sure you understand."

"I see. I have another question, Mr. Sebastian."

"Yes..." Finlay moved to sit again, then stood again when Quince remained standing. Quince noticed him rubbing his hands together absentmindedly.

"Were you able to ascertain, without a doubt, that Mr. Beckett and Mr. Vickers are in fact one and the same man?"

Finlay nodded. "Without a doubt, yes."

Steve Quince lasered in on Finlay's eyes. "What then, was your purpose in visiting him yesterday?"

Finlay hesitated. "To validate they are one and the same man."

"And he acknowledged that?" Quince asked, finding it difficult not to show his surprise.

"No, he did not. I didn't need his acknowledgment. I just had to get close to him."

"What do you mean?"

Finlay stepped over to his briefcase and pulled out the photo of Nate and his uncle and handed it to Quince. "This is a picture of Nate Vickers, in Calgary, with a family member."

"What's the name of the family member?"

"A guy by the name of Frank Ricci. It's his uncle."

Quince studied the photo. "Did you disclose the policy to Nate?"

"I did, but I told him it was under review and that I would be back to him this week."

Quince thought for a moment. "Who did he supposedly murder, Mr. Sebastian?"

"A man named Angelo de Luca, formerly of Calgary, Alberta." Finlay held his gaze.

Quince nodded. He could think of nothing else to ask. "Thank you for your time. I assume you'll be staying in these parts another day or two then? I may have a couple of additional questions."

"Are you investigating Mr. Vickers for something?" Finlay asked, deflecting the question.

"There are a lot of things going on around here that have caught my attention. So, I ask again, will you be staying in these parts for a bit?"

"Most likely, Constable. I'll let you know if my plans change."

Quince stepped off the boat. Murder? Why had the Calgary Police not mentioned that? Time for another call. He needed to learn more about this Frank Ricci and needed those damn prints.

Quince headed for his car, his mind racing.

Additional questions would have arisen had he been able to see the self-satisfied smirk on Finlay's face.

***

Nate waited for Beka to say something. She knew now how Jess' death fit in with his story, but she was not ready to talk. So, he waited. He would wait all day, if needed, despite the urgency to meet Frank and Elena. They had reached the highway, after leaving the marina and determined they were in the clear. She had turned into a pull-out and placed the car in park, awaiting his confession. It took a good hour to answer all her questions.

Beka's eyes went wide, and she let out a curse. "We have to go back."

Nate snapped a look at Beka. He was bewildered. That wasn't what he expected. She spun the wheel and the truck reversed direction.

"I left my phone on your boat," she said to the obvious question on Nate's face. "If the bad guys get it and find a way to open it, they can find Milo."

"They can't crack your code."

"I'm not taking that chance, Nate. Not with Milo. They don't know where we are now, we'll be all right."

Nate didn't feel as confident but closed his mouth. He had to let her have a win. His revelation about all that had happened in Calgary had rattled her. He knew he had to let her think everything through. He wanted to say something else. Anything. He did not want to lose her but now wasn't the time.

She pulled into the marina parking lot. They exited the truck and headed back into the store. Beka was about to say something when Nate's phone rang. *Frank.*

"Good morning again, Mr. Vickers."

Nate groaned internally. "What do you want now, Finlay?"

"As always, to help you, Mr. Vickers." Nate said nothing. "I just had a visit from the local police." Silence filled the line.

"And..." Nate prompted.

"They wanted to ask me about the involvement of Nate Vickers in a certain murder in Calgary."

Nate's blood ran cold. "Murder?" He registered Beka's eyes flicking to him.

"Seems so."

"What's it got to do with me?"

"You're in big trouble, Mr. Vickers. As I said before, you need me. I can get you out of here, but we need to move the timeline of things ahead. I stalled the cop, but we may only have a day or two at best. Moves everything up a day, Mr. Vickers."

The line went dead. Nate slowly lowered his phone.

"What is it?" Beka asked, reacting to the look on his face.

"They think I murdered someone. I didn't." Nate put his head in his hands. "Everything keeps going from bad to worse."

Beka's face showed nothing but concern. "Who is 'they'?"

"Supposedly the police."

"So says Finlay?"

"Yes."

"And you believe him?"

"I don't know what to believe anymore." Nate dragged his fingers through his hair.

"I think if it were me, I'd be dealing with facts I could confirm, not with comments from a guy that firebombed my boat."

Nate nodded, grabbing onto the logic. He gave her a half smile.

"Let's go get my phone. I need to let Milo know we're okay."

Nate nodded again, pushing Finlay's call from his mind. Beka headed for the front door.

"Nate..." Beka stopped short, pointing at the window. Nate turned; Mario de Luca came into view.

"No," he groaned. "You go out the back, head to Milo's. I will follow when I can. I need to draw this guy away."

"You don't even know where his cabin is."

"Actually... I do. Milo took me there a few weeks back. Go, Beka. Now."

"No, I'm staying with you."

"Beka, you aren't...have you not heard anything I've told you? These guys are nasty. I can't lose you. Please." He walked over to Beka and pressed his phone into her hand. "Use my phone to call Milo. I will come for you as soon as I can. Go now. Please."

Beka grabbed Nate by the neck and kissed him hard. She took his phone and started for the door.

"Beka...we good?" Nate asked before she reached for the door handle.

Beka spun and faced him. She did not smile. "We're good."

Relief flooded his mind.

She opened the door and stepped out, closing the door softly behind her.

Nate walked over to the side window and peered out. He saw Mario down at the dingy poking around. His head whipped up, looking in Beka's direction. He started running up the ramp. Nate knew, without a doubt, Beka was in danger.

He grabbed the door handle and yanked it open.

CHAPTER TWENTY-NINE

FRANK RICCI WOKE TO THE sound of the crows cawing out a mournful song. He looked over at Elena who was sleeping soundly. His mind shot back to the previous night. For the moment they were safe. Deciding to let her get a bit more rest, Frank quietly slipped out of their comfortable bed, slipped on his jeans, tee and sweater, and walked into the outer room of Milo's cabin. It was rustic, but charming in its own way. Frank's eyes were drawn to the large stone fireplace and the two windows flanking it. Milo sat out on the porch, a phone to his ear. Frank ambled into the kitchen, rifling through a couple of cabinets, until he found a mug. He poured himself a cup of coffee from a pot that Milo had recently brewed. He meandered to the door stepping into the brisk morning air.

"Morning," he said, peering over the meadow. An old barn, under restoration, sat directly across from them. Beyond the barn, a forest ascended a small mountain. Milo had a completely private location. The beauty of it was not lost on Frank, despite the angst and the intrusion of thoughts besetting him from the previous day's events.

Milo nodded and hit the call button again.

Frank sat down opposite Milo in one of the four chairs arranged on the patio. "Have you been able to reach them?"

"No. I only have Beka's number. She isn't answering. I'd be lying if I said it didn't worry me. I'm going to go to town and find out what's going on. You and Elena stay here until we all get back. It's probably the safest place you could be right now. I'll try to raise Nate as I walk."

"Where exactly are we?"

"This is my real home. Not many people know about it. I bought it years ago for a song. It had been abandoned and whenever I had a few extra bucks, I improved it."

"It's beautiful, Milo. You've done a good job."

"Barn needs some more effort, but I'll get there. It's livable now and I find myself wanting to be here more and more, instead of the apartment in town. Beka loves it here as well." Milo paused, worry creasing his brow.

"I'm still confused about where we are. That was a long walk through the bush last night."

"Sorry, I guess I didn't answer you. We are about twelve kilometres up the highway towards Sechelt, just outside of a place called Roberts Creek. There is actually a road here, but because we came by boat, we had to take the trail."

Frank gazed over the property. "It's very peaceful here."

"Yeah, it is. Listen, I'm going to go now. I'll take the Zodiac back. My truck is still at the marina. You guys stay here, Frank. I'll get Nate and Beka and then we can all figure out what to do next. How is Elena, by the way? She looked a little worse for wear last night."

"She's strong, but my world has crashed over her like an errant wave. She's amazed me how well she's handled it."

Milo frowned at the analogy. Frank was about to expound on his point when Milo stood.

"If she needs a change of clothes, there are some in the closet. They're Beka's but Elena looks to be about the same size. I know Beka wouldn't mind."

Frank smiled. "I picked up something for her in town yesterday, but since we left her bag, I know she'll be grateful. You're a good man, Milo."

Milo nodded his appreciation and wandered down the porch steps. "By the way...I don't think you'll need it, but there is a shotgun, with shells, in the rear closet."

Frank looked at Milo's stern face. "Okay, thanks." Reality crashed back into his consciousness, his moment of solace evaporating.

"Make yourself at home, Frank. There's food in the pantry. We should all be back in a few hours, at the most."

Milo wandered towards the path they arrived on the previous night. Frank watched until Milo, with his distinctive limp, was hidden in the trees.

***

Beka reached Milo's truck and jumped in behind the wheel. She started the engine and pulled out Nate's phone. She needed to reach Milo. She punched his number into the phone. Three hard raps on the driver window startled her. Ty O'Reilly stood there waiting for her to drop her window. She slammed her hand on the door lock. He tried the handle. The door held. He slapped the window with his good hand.

"Beka, open the door."

Beka heard the phone ringing. She glanced down at it, unsure as to what she should do. She dropped the window a few inches to be heard. "Leave me alone, Ty."

"Open this goddamn door, Beka. For once in your life, can you do as you're told."

Beka felt the bile rising in her throat, as if it were a culmination of the last few days events. "Fuck off, Ty."

Ty O'Reilly froze, shock registering on his face. Rage welled up within him, he swung his casted arm at the window. The window disintegrated into a thousand pieces, showering Beka in the process. She yelled out. O'Reilly's good hand grabbed her shirt. Coming to her senses, she tossed the phone onto the passenger seat, threw the truck into gear and gunned the engine. The effect was instantaneous. O'Reilly released her shirt and jumped back, protecting his good arm. The truck bolted forward, slamming into a cement parking barrier. O'Reilly tripped, stumbled backward and fell to the ground, rolling onto his bad arm in the process. His cry of pain rang out as she was putting the truck in reverse, spinning the tires across the gravel, pointing the vehicle directly at him. He rolled out of the way and climbed to his feet.

"You are mine, Beka. Mine. Do you hear me?"

She heard him. Tears rolled down her cheeks, fear and anger driving her. She threw the gear shift into drive and pulled out of the parking area, tires churning up the gravel. Checking her rear-view mirror, she saw O'Reilly running for a truck he had parked on the other side of the lot.

Beka reached the paved street and gunned her engine. She turned north, away from the marina, tears flowing down her face. She dragged her arm across her face wiping them away. She made numerous turns within the community to make sure O'Reilly couldn't follow. She was driving too fast for this area, but she did not let up. About three kilometres away from the marina, she slowed down and pulled into a nearby seaside parking spot. Her tears were replaced by a dull ache of despair. In the confusion, the phone had gone flying, and she could see it lying beside the passenger door, on the floor. She stared at it. She had to call Milo. She couldn't move, events of the last few days flooding her senses. She felt so weak.

She wanted with all her heart to be there for Nate, but she wondered if she could deal with his world as well as her own. She had said they were good. What did that mean? His world was becoming more violent by the day. Now she had brought Milo into it. Milo, her rock. Milo, her strength. Another tear formed and slid down her cheek, then another and another. Soon she was crying heavily, her lungs gasping for breath with each shoulder heave, as if the very act of breathing would cleanse her of negative thoughts.

Then she heard a voice. "Nate...Nate...are you there?" She stared down at the phone. Milo.

Beka stepped out of the truck and walked around to the passenger door, opening it to retrieve Nate's phone. She put the phone to her ear. A truck pulled to a skid beside her, a door flying open before it stopped. She scrambled to climb into Milo's truck for protection.

The last thing she remembered before all went black was the strength of the arm that pulled her face into a rag filled with a putrid smelling chemical. She didn't feel the man taking the phone from her hand and turning it off. Nor did she feel him pick her up, as if she were weightless, and gently put her into his backseat.

***

Nate heard Beka and a man yelling at each other. Trepidation seized him. He needed to go to her.

The thought evaporated in a flash as his eyes met Mario's. Nate stood at the top of the gangway. Mario stopped short after recognizing him. Then he charged, hatred emanating. Nate braced for the rush, turning his body sideways to reduce the amount exposed to the oncoming assault.

"I want to talk," Nate yelled.

Mario ignored him and kept coming. He swung a fist at Nate's face. Nate reacted, sidestepping the fist, while turning in the direction of Mario, driving his right arm at his stomach. He watched as Mario doubled over, gasping for breath. He followed with an uppercut at Mario's face. Mario deflected it with his arm, stumbling backwards on the gangway. Nate heard a woman scream and out of the corner of his eye he saw Archie step off his boat, a kayak oar in hand.

Mario recovered and with a roar, charged at Nate for a second time. Nate swung a fist at him and missed, and for his poor effort received a perfectly delivered counter thrust to the bridge of his nose. Blood ran. He stepped back, knowing Mario would press his advantage with another punch or worse, if he could get his footing on the gangway.

Using all the core strength he'd developed as a sailor, Nate pivoted, throwing himself at Mario, surprising him when their shoulders collided. They fell onto the gangway together. Pain shot through Nate's arm as the deck cleating tore at his skin. He let out a yelp and watched as Mario staggered to his feet.

"I just want to talk," Nate shrieked.

Mario was up, charging again, aiming a kick at Nate's head as he was rising.

Archie stepped into the fray, swinging the kayak oar as hard as he could at Mario, connecting just above his elbow. Mario stumbled and turned to meet Archie. With a deep cry, he charged at him. Nate regained his footing and stuck his foot out enough to connect with Mario's ankle. Down he went. Archie was on him. All his police training kicked in and within seconds Mario was pinned and could not move. Nate grabbed a loose line from a nearby daysailer and tied Mario's hands behind his back. He then cleated the loose end of the line to the dock. Mario DeLuca was totally immobilized.

He glared at Nate, ignoring Archie who was standing behind him. There were several boaters gathered on the dock, witnessing what was going on. One took out his phone and snapped a picture of the trussed-up man.

"I need to go back to my boat and call Quince," Archie said quietly to Nate. He made a move to head towards his catamaran.

"Archie, I need a few minutes with him first."

Archie turned back to Nate. "Are you kidding? What do you think he was trying to do to you, Nate?"

"I'm aware." Nate wiped blood from his nose.

"I really like you, man, but you've brought a lot of trouble with you."

Nate shared Archie's exasperation, wincing at the declaration. "I wanted none of this. I came here looking for a second chance. But it seems that's not happening. I'm sorting it out, Archie. I need time."

"Talk to Quince. He's a good cop, Nate. Give him a chance. Can you call him on your phone?"

"I don't have it. I gave it to Beka." Nate's mind turned back to Beka and the scream he'd heard.

"You wait here, I'll get my phone to call him. He'll know what to do with this guy."

He turned, hustling down the dock. Nate heard him reassuring an older lady that there was no danger to any of them.

Making a quick decision, he leaned down to Mario. "All I want is to talk to you. What's your name?"

"All we want is our money back and for you to be dead," Mario said flatly.

Nate reached behind Mario and pulled out his cell phone. The screen was cracked in several places.

"What's your code?"

"Yeah, right."

"Hurry up. I want to put a number in your phone. Then I want you to have your boss call me. You got that."

Mario looked at him suspiciously.

"You have very little time here," Nate said, prompting him. "My friend is about to call the cops."

"Six one one eight."

Nate punched in the numbers. The screen lit up. He glanced to see Archie stepping onto his catamaran.

Nate opened the email app on the phone. It took moments to learn his assailants name was Mario De Luca. He saw numerous emails from Belletti. He opened a couple to get the gist of his inquiries, then he opened a new email and typed in his phone number. He'd get his phone back from Beka at Milo's place. He noticed movement and looked up the shore and saw Mario's boys heading his way, at a run.

"I'm going to let you go. You hold those guys at bay. I want to talk to your boss. Agreed?"

Mario nodded as Nate untied him. Within moments, he was on his feet, standing in front of Nate. "This changes nothing. You and your uncle are going to pay for killing my brother."

He held his hand up to his associates and started up the gangway at a brisk walk. Nate stared after him. He wanted to explain that he had nothing to do with the death of his brother, or anyone for that matter, but De Luca was already out of range.

Nate heard Archie yelling, "Hey." He decided there was no time to explain why he had let the guy go. He turned and started up the gangway for the marina store, aware that De Luca could turn on him. Thankfully, he and his goons kept walking.

He heard his name being called out. "Nate...Nate. Hold on."

He waved at Archie to let him know he had heard him, then continued into the store. No time to explain anything to Archie. He had to find out what happened to Beka. Her scream resonated.

And... he needed to get to his uncle. De Luca's declaration put Frank in as much danger as him.

He squinted out the store window. Archie had stopped and was talking animatedly into his phone. Nate locked the store's door and headed out into the rear parking lot, hoping that Beka might be there. Seeing it empty, he turned to leave, then noticed heavy tire tracks in the gravel. He inspected them, as the sun flashed off numerous pieces of something in the gravel. Stooping down, he picked up a piece of safety glass; a window had been smashed. Nate felt queasy. The tire tracks led into the concrete parking barrier. He wandered over and touched the light brown paint mark on it.

He'd hail a taxi in town. Beka was destined for Milo's, and he had to make sure she arrived safely. Apprehension gripped him. Heading up the hill he heard an engine in the marina and turned. A Zodiac pulled into the day dock. Milo. He scanned the dock. Archie had retreated to his catamaran, allowing him to get to Milo without explaining anything further.

Skirting around the back of the store, striding for the gangway, he ran into Ben Mills.

"Ben?"

"Ah, Nate. I was looking for you," Ben said awkwardly, staring at the blood on Nate's face.

"What's up?" Nate's eyes darted between Ben and Milo.

Ben shuffled his feet, averting his eyes to the marina. He drew in a long breath, "Heard about the fire on your boat, Nate."

"Yeah, still don't know who did it," Nate said, feeling the guilt as he lied.

"It creates a problem, Nate."

"Not really. It was more a mess than anything structural. Archie is helping me get it fixed up. We won't even know it was there once the boys come for their lesson, in a couple of days."

"About that...it's a small town, Nate. Lots of discussion going on and I had a call from one of the parents."

Nate knew what was coming; his legs felt like lead.

"I need to pull it, Nate. I'm afraid the kids won't be coming anymore."

"C'mon Ben. It was random."

"Maybe...but I can't take the chance. I'm sorry. I know you're disappointed, and the boys will be too. Maybe next year, once this all settles down. Okay?"

Nate inclined his head slowly.

"I'll see you, Nate." Ben spun on his heels, walking back into town.

Nate stared after him. A sadness engulfed him. He loved those outings. He loved teaching the boys. He loved their energy and their innocence. His new world was crumbling.

His eyes darted to the marina. Milo was on the dock, securing the Zodiac. Archie was still inside his boat.

He didn't move, his mind awhirl, trying to reconcile what was happening to him.

Today's events were sure to be reported to Steve Quince, no doubt adding more fuel to suspicions about him.

Beka had some form of altercation when she left. Was it with O'Reilly? He was frustrated he wasn't there for her, and he didn't know if she had gotten away unharmed.

His head was spinning. He had to line up the pieces. Finlay had put a full court press on him. He had to deal with that, but nothing further could happen until he had talked to Belletti. He knew he had to show some evidence shortly, that he was amassing the money for him and wasn't sure what to do about that.

He had yet to finish his conversation with his uncle who was in as precarious a position as he was.

And now, he had lost his boys.

And Beka...

What a mess.

He stood rigidly, watched as Milo marched to him.

"Nate," Milo had reached the top of the gangway. Concern was etched on his face. "Nate, where's Beka?"

***

Steve Quince confirmed that Nate Vickers and Nate Beckett were in fact, one and the same guy. The fingerprint match was unequivocal. Okay, but murder? Beckett didn't seem the type. Quince replayed the discussion he'd had with John Sebastian. Something was not right with that guy.

He typed into his database the name of Angelo De Luca, when his phone rang.

"Quince," he announced.

"Steve, it's Archie."

"Hi Archie, what's up?" He wanted to get back to his research. Archie filled him in with what had happened at the marina. All thoughts of De Luca vanished.

"Where is Beckett now?"

"Talking with Milo, who just showed up. I tried to persuade him to tell me why he let the guy go. He wanted no part of it."

"Did you see where the guy went?"

"No, he joined up with his friends and they headed up the hill. I didn't follow, hoping to talk with Nate."

The word "murder" flashed across Quince's mind. "Let me handle it, Archie. I'm on my way." Quince logged out of his computer, grabbed his hat, and headed for the door. He spotted Andrea Maitland working studiously at her computer. She was a seasoned veteran of the force and, while she was usually desk bound, Quince decided he better have some back up and asked if she could assist him.

"What's up?" she queried.

"I'll explain on the way to the marina," he said. Maitland smiled. Quince knew she had a crush on him, and he should get someone else. That would take too much time. The incident at the marina was pressing and he needed backup.

CHAPTER THIRTY

"AS FAR AS I KNOW, she took your truck and headed for your place, Milo." Nate's face tensed with worry.

"Something has happened, Nate. Listen to this."

Nate put Milo's phone to his ear. He heard the glass breakage and the undeniable voice of Ty O'Reilly. He could feel the rage welling up within him.

"Where does he live?"

"I'll deal with him, Nate. She got away, but something happened after that." Milo explained what he heard until the phone went dead. "You need to get to my place. If she got away, she'd go there. I left your uncle and Elena there as well. We'll be safe when we're all together. In the meantime, I'll deal with Ty O'Reilly on the off chance he got to her. I've put up with his crap for far too long."

Nate heard the menace in Milo's voice. "You can't take him on by yourself, Milo. He is too strong and has too many friends. Let me help."

"No. I'll do this my way. You have enough to worry about. Besides, you've crippled him already. Take the Zodiac and get out of here."

Nate was perplexed. He had never searched for Milo's cabin by water. "To where, Milo?"

Nate could see Archie approaching them. Milo explained where to land along the coast and which trail would take Nate to his property.

"It's a fair hike, Nate. Get going. She needs you and I need to know she's safe." Milo turned and limped towards the gangway. He noticed Archie, heading their way, but didn't acknowledge him.

Archie strode to Nate as he was releasing the lines for the Zodiac.

"What the fuck, Nate?" he said to Nate's back.

Nate had never heard Archie cuss with such force. He let out a long breath and turned. "Look, Archie...I'm in big trouble. I can't bring Quince into it. I did some things. Some things I'm not proud of and now they're coming home to roost. If I could undo it, I would, but I can't. People I love are paying for my mistake. I need to right this."

"That's why we have police, Nate."

"Arch, I don't have time to explain, and I don't have the time to make Quince understand. Please trust me."

"Quince is coming now, Nate. Stay... please. He can help. I've known him a long time."

"I can't. I'm sorry, Archie. I will do this on my own." Nate stepped into the Zodiac and tossed the line across the seat. He fired the engine to life and faced Archie. "Thank you for everything, Archie. You are a good friend. I'm sorry I've brought chaos to your world."

***

The Zodiac pulled away from the dock. Archie remained where he stood, watching Nate head for the marina entrance. He watched with a growing sense he might never see Nate again. A sadness engulfed him. Once Nate cleared the corner of the harbour, Archie headed back to his catamaran. He stopped as Quince's RCMP cruiser pulled into the parking lot. He saw Quince and another officer exit the vehicle and head his way. Nate had not been exaggerating. He was in serious trouble. The only time a squad car, in these parts, carried two officers was when they felt they needed backup.

Archie continued back to his boat, his mind mulling over possibilities. He sat down on his deck chair. Quince and Andrea Maitland neared his boat. Archie waved them aboard.

"Hey Steve," Archie said to Quince, then cast his eyes on Maitland. "Andrea, nice to see you again."

"Archie." She gave a brief smile.

Archie pulled up a third deck chair and motioned for them to sit.

"Is he on board?" Quince nodded to Nate's boat.

Archie looked at the sailboat and shook his head.

The repair crew hired to fix Nate's boat were coming down the dock. They stalled, unsure of whether they should approach, noticing the police. Archie held his hand up, indicating they should hold back.

Archie locked eyes with Quince. "He's gone. Took a Zodiac and headed out of the harbour."

"Which way?"

"Couldn't really say, Steve."

"Couldn't say...or won't say?"

"Little of both...I need to know what's going on."

"I can't talk about that," Quince said. "You know that."

Archie let that hang. "How serious?"

"Reportedly...quite serious."

"Says who?"

"I'll take a water if you have one, Archie, if you please," said Andrea Maitland.

"Give me a moment, Andrea. I need to talk with this repair crew." He nodded towards the men standing out of earshot. Archie stepped off the boat and walked towards the crew leader.

As he stepped off the boat, he heard Maitland say to Quince, "You can't tell him anything."

Archie held back, motioning the crew leader to come to him.

"He's one of us, Andrea," he heard Quince say.

"No, he's not. He's a retired local cop. You are playing with fire, Steve."

"He's a good resource; I need to keep him engaged."

The crew leader approached, and Archie focused on giving instructions. He could no longer hear Quince's conversation.

The crew headed for Nate's boat. Archie stepped back on board. Quince and Maitland sat silently, watching the repair crew board.

"How much damage to the boat, Archie?" Quince asked.

"It's mostly cosmetic. Nate got the fire out fast." Archie's eyes bore into Quince's. "You were saying, Steve?"

Quince glanced at Andrea. "Remember the guy on the Bayliner...the P.I? It is his allegation."

"I don't like that guy. He's an 'in your face' type and I'd bet he has his own agenda. I've met a few P.I.'s in my time, most of them stay in the shadows. Not this one."

"You've met him?"

"Watched him," Archie clarified. "A man who walks onto another man's boat, makes himself comfortable without an invite, is pretty bold."

Quince's expression said he wanted the details, but Archie held back. He hoped Quince wouldn't press the conversation further. He wouldn't enjoy lying to him.

"Let me know if he comes back to the boat, Archie...and stand down on this one, okay? At this point in time, Nate Beckett is considered very dangerous, and I don't want you in the middle of it."

"You know, I've met a lot of kinds during my career. I'm telling you, that kid may have problems, but he's a good kid. He isn't the violent type. He may defend himself, but he doesn't go looking for trouble. I suggest you spend a little more time probing the P.I. Something isn't right there, Steve."

"Noted. Which way did he go?"

"North...I don't know his destination. He didn't say. He could have gone around an island and then turned south."

Steve signalled Andrea and stood. Archie rose as well.

"Where are my manners? I completely forgot that water, Andrea. Have you the time? I can grab it now."

"I'm good Archie, thanks anyway." Andrea stepped to the rear of the boat.

"Call me when you see him, please." Quince moved to join her on the dock. Andrea turned back to Archie.

"Does he ever get any visitors, Archie?" she asked.

Archie gazed at Nate's boat. "Not many. He keeps to himself mostly, other than the boys from the boys' club he teaches."

"Uh huh." Archie could see she had doubts but decided not to elaborate further. A small sense of guilt enveloped him. He was siding with Nate. This went against everything he developed, as a cop, over a lifetime of service. He pushed it from his mind, as he watched her jog to a departing Quince.

***

Maitland called out Quince's name. He was lost in thought. She caught up with him as they reached the shore. "Want me to look into John Sebastian?"

"Sounded like good advice, didn't it? Please do. I'm focusing on learning a lot more about Nate Vickers. There's a storm brewing, Andrea. We need to get ahead of it."

"Should we get a car to head upland and see if they can spot him?"

"No, we have no idea where he was headed. He'll surface soon enough. Then we'll pull him in. If Archie's right and this kid isn't as he has been painted, we need to get him to trust us."

***

In Elena's dream, she and Frank were running through the woods. Frank was pulling away from her. She couldn't see what chased them, but it was evil. She ran until her lungs felt like they would burst, constantly checking behind. Frank disappeared ahead of her. She focused her efforts, running where he vanished, ignoring the threat from behind. She burst through a hedge. A large chasm opened before her and before she could get her footing, she plunged over its edge. She could see Frank lying broken on the rocks below. As she fell, she glanced back; the evil was upon her, smiling down.

She woke with a start. The room, unfamiliar. She searched for Frank to no avail. Her breathing was laboured, panic born of a nightmare. She gazed about the room where she lay. Rustic, but clean. The events of the previous night flooded her memory. She let out a groan and covered her eyes with her arm.

A few minutes later, she pulled the covers off and got out of bed to dress. No clothes, save a clean dress and accompaniments, laying across a chair. Strange. She picked them up and headed for the bathroom outside the bedroom door.

The dress fit a bit snug but worked. Elena headed into the kitchen and spotted Frank as he sat. Wandering onto the porch, she settled beside him, morning coffee in hand. Her eyes twinkled;

her shower having washed away the bad dream. Frank smiled at her but said nothing.

"You want to tell me how you pulled this off?" She fanned the dress she was wearing with her hand.

"Like to claim credit, but it was Milo. It seems you and Beka are a similar size. Your other clothes are in a waste bin."

"You just bought those."

Frank laughed. "And you ruined them."

Elena recalled the fall she had taken in the dark the previous night, as they wound their way through the woods to Milo's place.

"It is nice to feel clean again," she said, and tossed her damp hair to help dry it.

Elena's eyes were drawn over the meadow, bathed in mid-morning sunshine. "Where's Milo?"

"He's gone to get Nate and Beka."

"And what do you need that for?" Elena pointed at the shotgun resting against the cushion of a chair.

Frank glanced at the gun. "Milo told me he had it, and, given last night's events, I decided it would give me comfort."

"About that, Frank..." She hesitated. "I'm so sorry I brought all this to your doorstep, and Nate's."

Frank thought about that for a minute. "Elena..."

"Let me finish. I had the worst dream last night." She proceeded to recall it. "I've never been one to believe in dreams but - "

"It was just a dream, El."

"Frank, we narrowly escaped from the guys tracking us at the ferry. Then Nate's boat is firebombed. Maybe it wasn't Nate they were after, but us."

Frank considered that. "I don't think so, El. No one really knew where we were going. When Nate gets here with Beka, we'll get his thoughts and figure it out between us; what we all know and what we need to do."

"Then we need to go, Frank. Or we need to bring in the police. This has become too dangerous. I can't bear the thought of losing you." She grimaced as her mind relived the vivid nightmare.

"No police, El. I'm sorry. It wouldn't work out well for Nate. Let me talk to him. Once I know his plan, and I'm satisfied he'll be okay, we're gone. I promise."

Elena's skepticism showed on her face.

"I promise," Frank reassured.

Elena stared over the meadow, finding solace in the sway of the grasses as they danced in the breeze. For the moment, she was at peace. "God, it is beautiful here." She stood and walked over to the rail. She felt Frank following her movements.

"Matches the company," he said.

She turned her head, gazing back at him. Her eyes radiated her feelings.

"I will protect you," he vowed.

She hoped he could.

***

Nate arrived at the location Milo directed him to. He motored into the mouth of a creek and found the sheltered bay where Milo said he could tie up. He beached the Zodiac, securing it to an arbutus trunk, and searched for the path leading him to the cabin.

Thirty minutes later, Nate came to a clearing. He recognized the cabin and the barn in the distance, eliminating doubts he carried with him. He stood quietly in the trees and surveyed for activity. Seeing none, he crouched low and ran across the meadow to the back of the cabin. He moved cautiously along the rear. He stood, peeking into a window as he went. No movement. He searched around the side of the building and then across the meadow. Seeing nothing, he edged to the side of the cabin, inching his way to the front. He stopped. Voices. He recognized Frank's voice and heard a female voice that he guessed was Elena's. He waited to hear if there were more. There were none. He stood at full height and walked around the corner.

The movement registered out of the corner of Frank's eye. He reached for the shotgun, levelling the barrel in Nate's direction.

"Frank!" Nate yelled.

"Jesus, Nate, you want to get yourself killed?"

Nate laughed and stepped onto the porch, looking into the cabin as he went. "Where's Beka?"

Frank could see the worry on Nate's face. "I thought she was with you?"

Nate's shoulders drooped and Elena covered her mouth with her hand. "Something has happened Frank. She was on her way. It has to be that freaking Ty O'Reilly." Nate darted down the steps.

"Nate, please wait. We'll come with you."

"No, you stay here where it's safe. I'll double back as soon as I have her."

"Nate." Frank jumped to his feet, hoping to stop him.

Nate was gone, running full tilt across the meadow, retracing his steps back to the Zodiac.

CHAPTER THIRTY-ONE

BEKA EMERGED FROM HER FOG, head pounding. She reached for her face, and then realized in horror that she was bound. Hands to the arms of the chair, legs to the feet. There was a gag in her mouth. She screamed but her muffled attempt only brought her captor into her field of vision. She went silent, glaring at him, willing him to speak. He didn't. He stood there, staring at her for a minute, his head tilted to one side, then the other, as if he was assessing what to do with her. She was paralyzed with fear.

Turning, he wandered to a nearby table and picked up Nate's phone.

"The code?" he snapped at Beka, removing the gag from her mouth.

"I don't know it."

He raised his hand to slap her. Reconsidering, she turned her head sideways before providing the number Nate had previously given her. It bought her time to understand what was happening.

He roughly replaced the gag. Ambling back, he snapped a picture of her. He inspected the image, seemingly pleased, no doubt because of the fear she knew her eyes portrayed. He disappeared from her field of vision, and she heard another voice behind her.

"Good. Take it to the boat with this note."

Beka felt her anxiety grow as she realized there were two people in the room. She strained to hear if anything else was said but only registered a door closing and the sound of footsteps receding down a hallway.

She pressed at the ropes that tied her to the chair, fighting for a weakness. Then the second captor came into view. Beka ceased struggling. The person in front of her was hideously disfigured. A hand reached for her hair. She recoiled. The ropes held her firmly in place.

"My, you are a pretty one." The detainer's eyes roamed across her body, settling on her face. "Did he do that?" A finger traced the bruise around her eye. "Don't worry, we'll hold him accountable as soon as we're all together."

Beka fought against her restraints, muffled words drowning in her gag.

"Shhhh... You need to be quiet now. I can't allow you to speak. But I do need to know where your boyfriend is. I can't rely on him returning to his boat."

A small table was moved over beside Beka's arm. On it were a pad and a pen. "I'm going to release the ropes on this hand. I want you to write down on the pad where he is. Understand, I have little compassion for your predicament, so don't make me mad by doing something foolish."

Beka stared at the pad. She did not acknowledge her jailer. Suddenly, Beka's head was whipped back, her hair pulled by a strong pair of hands.

"Understand?" came a hiss, inches from her ear. She grunted, which her captor accepted as an acknowledgement.

Beka flexed her fingers as the bonds were released on her right hand and picked up the pen. She clicked on the knob to bring the nib into view. She attempted to write on the pad but only succeeded in knocking it to the floor. The pad was retrieved. As it was being placed on the table, Beka suddenly thrust the pen at her captor's hand, who snatched it away before impact. The pen shattered.

It seemed almost surreal to Beka, as the hand twisted, turned, and in one single motion came around in an arc to deliver a striking blow to her face.

She shrieked into her gag, falling sideways to the floor, still trussed to the chair. The bruise on her face tingled afresh from the new assault.

Her captor clasped her free arm and with a grunt brought her back to a sitting position.

"Aren't you the feisty one. I can see what he likes in you. Now, where were we?"

***

Milo made three calls from his store. All to lifelong friends he made as a fisherman in his early years. All knew Beka and watched her grow up under the tutelage of her father. And all readily agreed to help once they had heard Milo's story. Theirs was a small community and most knew how nasty a man Ty O'Reilly could be. Together, they would force O'Reilly to tell them where he had taken her.

It was midday and rain clouds were forming offshore. One of the men noted that the dry sunny weather Gibsons enjoyed was coming to an end. As they sat in a van belonging to Milo's oldest friend, Chad Nystrom, the sea breeze kicked up and the men heard it rustling through fir boughs of the old growth forest. Milo gazed through the van window, wondering if they were in for a storm. That would be problematic.

They settled in for a long quiet wait when Chad spotted O'Reilly walking towards town, which surprised him. O'Reilly seldom walked anywhere. This would make things much easier.

O'Reilly appeared agitated, screaming into a phone that was held awkwardly by his casted arm.

"We're on," Nystrom said.

Milo nodded.

The van had a large sign on its side that pronounced 'Village Seafood - Fresh is best.' Chad was renowned in Gibsons for his daily catch. It cruised up behind O'Reilly and slowed to a crawl. The passenger window eased down, and Chad leaned towards the opening.

"Hey, Ty," said Nystrom, casually resting a thick arm out the window.

O'Reilly turned his gaze to the familiar van. "I'll call you back," he said into his phone and hung up.

"How are you doing, Chad?" he grumped.

"Not bad, where's your truck?"

"In for a new window." He sneered as if everyone knew what had happened to his window.

"Need a lift?"

O'Reilly thought about it for a minute. "Yeah, thanks." He wandered over to the passenger door. It was locked.

Chad dropped the passenger window a few more inches. "Sorry, new insurance rules, Ty; no riders. You'll need to hop in back, where no one will see you. What they don't know won't hurt them, right?" Chad said, forcing a laugh.

O'Reilly grunted and reached for the panel door, sliding it open. His eyes widened as Milo and two dock fishermen greeted him. He was about to take a step back when two sets of hands grabbed him roughly by the shirt, hauling him into the van. The panel door slid closed.

"What the hell," O'Reilly bellowed. He scrambled to procure a defensive position.

Milo swung the van's tire iron into his stomach. O'Reilly doubled over, gasping for air. In seconds, his hands and legs were bound together with zip ties. He'd barely found his breath when

Milo dropped the tire iron to the floor with a clang, reached for a harness he had brought and slid it over O'Reilly's head. He reached behind him to lock it in place. O'Reilly spat at him.

"Nice," Milo sneered, reaching for a rag to wipe the spit from his shirt. Bill Thomson and Buck Skinner held O'Reilly's arms. They were old sea dogs, but powerfully built, more than capable to thwart O'Reilly's attempts at escape.

Milo pulled a piece of duct tape, previously placed on a rib of the van. Thomson put O'Reilly's head into a headlock, allowing Milo to place the duct tape over his mouth.

"That will keep the spit where it is supposed to be." He said to an angry set of eyes.

He reached beneath O'Reilly and snapped the harness buckle into place between his legs. O'Reilly renewed his struggle against the arms of the fishermen. Milo slammed a fist into O'Reilly's midsection. He went limp. Thomson and Skinner looked at each other.

Milo nodded, and Skinner tossed him a bag which he slipped over O'Reilly's head. The last thing O'Reilly saw was Milo glaring at him.

***

Steve Quince rubbed his eyes. Maybe it was time to get the glasses his optometrist said he needed. He was pouring over the computerized files he had requested from the Calgary Police Service.

There was little in them specific to Nate Vickers, other than the usual drivers abstract and health records, except for the police report saying he was a person of interest in a homicide. What was interesting was that the name of the deceased was not Angelo De Luca, not even close. Was Beckett involved with two homicides? The report outlined the circumstances of the death and the subsequent chase by a local biker gang when Vickers made his escape.

But it was the final detail in the police report that piqued his interest the most. The investigating officers suggested that Vickers had last been tracked on street cams, heading east out of the city. Why go to the east, and how had he ended up in Gibsons?

Quince opened a second file pertinent to the death of Angelo De Luca. He read the grizzly details of his death and then checked them back against the timelines of the Vickers Report. De Luca's death happened days after Vickers' departure. The timeline didn't make sense, unless he'd doubled back to do the deed. And if so, why? Hardly fit the profile of a guy running for his life. He read the remainder of the report and frowned.

He reopened the De Luca report and looked to the profile section of the deceased. Then back to the profile section of the deceased in the Vickers report. Both were known associates of one Don Antonio Belletti, renown crime boss for the Castelli family out of Montreal.

He knew he should apprise the Calgary service of Vickers' whereabouts, but reckoned he had lots of time to do that. This mystery needed resolution. Besides, it would be better if he had Vickers, a.k.a. Beckett, in lockdown first.

He sat back, rubbing his eyes again.

He was scribbling his thoughts in his notebook when Andrea Maitland arrived at his desk.

Quince looked up at her. "Let me guess?"

"Go for it."

"The insurance company has never heard of him."

"Worse than that, the company doesn't exist, nor is there any John Sebastian registered as a P.I. anywhere in Canada."

Quince jumped to his feet, grabbing his hat. "Let's go. Time for some answers. I'll fill you in on what I've learned about Nate Vickers, also known as Nate Beckett, on the way to the marina."

***

The man reached the marina parking lot. He sat for a moment, scanning for danger. Nate's phone rang in his hand. He stared at it; it rang twice, then a third time. Finally, he pushed the answer button and waited. He heard breathing on the other end.

"This is Nate," he lied.

"Antonio Belletti," came a snarl.

Silence passed between them.

"Mario said you wanted me to call you."

The man quietly listened.

"Are you there, Vickers?"

"I am," he lied again.

"You know you're a dead man?" Silence. "I want my money back. Is that why you are calling, Vickers? You want to make a deal?"

"You know where I am. You want your money? Get on a plane and get out here. I may be a dead man walking, but the idiots you sent can't execute your order. You really should get better help."

Belletti ignored the barb. "You will give me my money back?"

"Depends, what do I get in return?"

"You're in no position to bargain. You wire the money to me, and I might consider letting you live. You don't, well, you know what happens." Silence. "You there?"

"I'm here. I can't wire it to you. It's all in cash. You want it, you will have to come. I want to look you in the eye and know you are telling me the truth. If I like what I hear, I'll give it to you."

"No... you'll give it to Mario. He'll give it to me."

"You know, Belletti, you may be used to pushing everyone around, but you don't control me. I made a mistake. I'd like to right that mistake. It has made my life a living hell. But if you want the money, we're doing it my way. You come in person, or I disappear... with the money... again."

He knew the don was determining his next move. He held the phone to his ear, listening to Belletti breathe.

"Where are we to meet?"

He breathed a sigh of relief. "I'll let you know."

"You better."

The line went dead.

The man smiled. His impersonation worked out far better than he hoped. He copied the phone number into his own phone and climbed out of his truck, heading for the gangway, eyes casting about in search of threats.

He stopped at the stern of the boat, surveying the area. Sensing he was alone he jumped into the cockpit and noted the locked entry. He reached into his pocket, pulled out Nate's phone and the note he had been instructed to leave and set them at the base of the cabin door. He then stepped off the boat, and scurried for shore, unaware his every move, since walking onto the docks, had been observed from a pair of eyes peering out of the window of a catamaran.

***

The eyes watched the man retreat to the shore and disappear. Archie then strode off his boat and walked purposely to *Serendipity,* stepping aboard. Archie spotted the phone and note and walked over to them. Making a quick decision, he reached down, retrieved them and put them in the pocket of his windbreaker. He'd give them to Nate next time he saw him, if he saw him. While he was there, he decided to check on *Serendipity's* repair, nodding in a satisfied manner. At least that had gone well for Nate.

Returning to his own boat, he pulled the phone and note out of his pocket and studied them. Curiosity getting the better of him, he opened the note, read it, and inspected the phone. He pushed the "on" button hoping there was no code required to operate it and cussed when he learned there was one. Placing the phone on the table in front of him, he picked up the note again and reread the script.

Staring at the note, Archie contemplated what to do next. Then he reached for his own phone.

CHAPTER THIRTY-TWO

BEKA FELT CRUSHED. ALL IT had taken was a broken baby finger. She looked at her left hand. The bottom half of the finger veered to the left. It throbbed, but she ignored the pain; the disgust she felt for herself was more pronounced. She recalled the shock that followed as the captor snapped her finger as easily as a dead twig. Then the promise the others would follow. When she, in no uncertain terms, told them where they could go, her index finger was grabbed. As the pressure mounted, she screamed in pain and then folded.

She told her captor about her relationship with Milo and where his cabin was. She advised she didn't know where Nate was, but that they were all to meet at Milo's cabin in the afternoon. She pleaded for Nate and Milo's safety but could see her pleas fell on deaf ears. She didn't share anything about Nate's uncle as she was not asked. She hoped it might turn the scales, at some point.

Then she was alone, her captor having left the room, abandoning her to absorb the pain from her broken finger and her self-loathing, in silence. For the second time that day, she cried, further infuriating her. She cried, not for her predicament, but out of anger that she was trapped and had betrayed the man she had fallen in love with. She strained to free her hands from her bonds but the jolt of pain she felt in her finger, stopped her effort. She was sick of people hurting her.

She pushed with her legs to see if the leg restraint might come loose. There was a little give. She pumped her legs into her chest, as best she could, and thrust down. She felt some additional movement. She repeated the move once, twice, each time gaining a little more give in the ropes that bound her. When she was able to draw her legs up for a more powerful thrust, she pushed against the ropes again. Harder.

The chair tipped, as if in slow motion, until the momentum thrust her to the floor, sending her pain receptors into overdrive, as she landed on her bad hand. She let out a long moan.

Beka lay on her side, staring at a bug as it crept across the tiled floor of the room, she was in.

The door opened and her jailer returned. "Been a little busy, have we?"

Beka grimaced, willing herself into a painful silence as she was hauled back to a sitting position. She watched as the bonds around her legs were untied.

"All you had to do was ask."

Beka ignored the sarcasm.

"I'm leaving your arms tied to the chair for now. Pretty soon we're all going on a road trip. I want you to be able to walk to the truck, so flex those legs." Her captor walked over and sat down on a heavily stained sofa and stared at her. "I'll sit here to make sure you behave yourself."

Beka stretched her legs, castigating herself for feeling grateful for the freedom. She let her gaze wander, determining if there was a form of escape, now that her legs were free.

Her darting eyes caused her captor to rise and walk over to her. Fingers grabbed her hair and yanked her head back. "Just give me a reason..."

***

Steve Quince arrived at the Bayliner, Andrea Maitland at his side. They cautiously approached the stern of the boat. Andrea freed the lock on her holster, then rested her hand on the handle of her pistol. Quince stepped aboard and approached the salon door. No movement inside. He tried the door. It was unlocked.

He motioned to Maitland. She drew her revolver, released the safety, and stepped onto the transom of the boat. Another boat owner jumped onto the dock, cell phone in hand, pointing it at her.

Quince cursed inwardly, wishing this new world of police monitoring by the public would stop. He focused on the task at hand. With one last glance at Maitland to make sure she was ready, he opened the door and called out. "RCMP, Mr. Sebastian. Please acknowledge your presence."

Hearing nothing but the creaking of the old boat, Quince entered the craft. He was alone, the boat was deserted. It was as if no one had ever been there. He scanned the salon looking for something that would help them in finding Sebastian.

His phone rang. He brought it to his ear, as he walked into the main stateroom.

"Quince."

"Archie here, Steve. I think you had better get over here. Something is very wrong. It has to do with the kid."

"Everything has to do with that kid, these days," Quince sighed. The stateroom was equally sanitized. There was nothing more he could do here. "On my way, Archie." He hung up.

Maitland holstered her pistol and locked it down. Her eyes shot up as Quince re-entered the salon.

"Andrea, let's treat this as a crime scene. Have it dusted, after you search for anything that may have been left behind. It looks pretty worked over, but maybe we'll get lucky, and you'll find something that will tell us who this guy actually is."

"There hasn't really been a crime, Steve."

"I think there has been or is about to be. This guy is up to something. Humour me...please. I'll authorize it and take the heat if we have a problem."

"Okay. You know we're on camera." She nodded through the salon window at the bystanders watching from a distance. "The guy in the red shirt was filming us."

Quince took a deep breath. "Yeah, I saw him. Play it by the book, but I want you to go over this boat with a fine-tooth comb."

"Where will you be?"

"That call was from Archie. He says I need to get over there. Something about Beckett, as usual. I feel like I am chasing this guy all over hell's half acre. Are you good here?"

She nodded. "Be careful," she said as she spun around, surveying the salon. Quince heard her calling for assistance as he stepped onto the dock.

***

Ty O'Reilly lay on his side on the bottom of the boat. The hood remained over his head. Blackness added to his apprehension. He tested the strength of his bonds. Secure.

He heard the steady thrum of twin Yamaha engines as the boat headed out of the harbour. He had been roughly shoved onto a pile of nets laying on the deck of what, from the smell, had to be a fishing trawler. He heard the engines winding up, as the boat moved into the open sea, and wondered how they had gotten him on board without someone seeing them.

He seethed with anger. He would make Chad and Milo suffer and they would tell him who the other goons were. Nobody did this to Ty O'Reilly and got away with it. Nobody.

He attempted to stand, only to find his feet being kicked out from under him, landing him back onto the pile of netting. Not one word had been said since they had hauled him out of the van. O'Reilly decided he had no choice but to see where this would go, but a nagging angst was forming. Try as he could, he could not eliminate it.

The engines slowing down only added to his unease. Two pairs of hands reached down and grabbed him by the arms, lifting him to his feet. One set of the hands let go. He felt something latch onto his ankles. He squirmed. Was he hobbled? He twisted his body at his assailant, earning him a blow to the stomach which left him wheezing for air through the duct tape. He felt the zip tie on his legs being cut loose. He tried to kick out, but his legs were now bound by something heavier. He heard the snap of a buckle attach to the harness he was wearing. He yelped into the tape on his mouth.

The hood was yanked off his head, the duct tape torn from his mouth. His eyes fought the intrusion of light. He hadn't seen it for several hours. The wind whipped up and he felt the swell beneath the trawler as it drifted. The engines had been cut. He opened his eyes to see storm clouds racing overhead, threatening to dump their load imminently. Four men stood before him. He felt humiliated that he had been taken down by geriatrics.

His eyes sought out Milo's. He shot him a hard look. Milo remained silent, rocking with the waves as the boat bobbed on the rough seas.

O'Reilly assessed the harness he wore, then the tackle above him. Glancing down, he could see the weights added to his ankles. He blanched, then went wild. "Milo, you cut me loose... now," he hissed, fighting the binding on his hands.

"Where's Beka?" Milo uttered, ignoring his demand.

O'Reilly glared at Milo. "You can't do this, Milo. This is fucking kidnapping." O'Reilly squirmed to release himself from his harness. He pulled hard at his hands. The zip ties held.

Milo disregarded his commentary and nodded to Chad. He stepped forward and grabbed O'Reilly's arms to hold him still.

"I'll make you pay for this, old man." O'Reilly spit at Milo for a second time.

This time, Milo sidestepped the spit and nodded to one of the men behind him. O'Reilly heard the small electric motor before he felt the harness go taunt and lift him from the ground. He now understood. "For Christ's sake, Milo, stop what you are doing... please."

He was pulled above the gunwale, before the hoist turned, carrying him above the open water.

"Wait, wait ..." O'Reilly screamed into the wind. Waves smashed into the side of the boat spraying him with salty water.

Milo limped over to the gunwale and asked again. "Where's Beka?"

"I don't know. Bring me back in."

"Bullshit. Once last chance." Milo's voice rose in intensity. O'Reilly saw the loathing in his face.

Milo turned and nodded again. The pulley released for a second, causing O'Reilly to drop a few inches. Waves lapped at his feet. He screamed out.

"I really don't know, Milo. Please pull me in. What are you doing?" Fear replaced anger. For the first time in his life, he felt helpless. He felt something warm on his legs and realized he had pissed himself.

Milo stood at the gunwale and hollered at O'Reilly as he dangled above the sea. "I was on the phone with her when you smashed the window, asshole. I heard it all. I heard everything you said to her. Now, I'm going to ask you again... where is she?"

"She got away. I didn't get to her. I'm telling you."

Milo reached out and took control of the winch. He stepped back and tilted his head at O'Reilly. Milo hit the "descend" button and watched as O'Reilly dropped over the side of the boat, plunging beneath the waves.

The cold Salish Sea enveloped him. The shock was instant. He struggled to free himself again, but knew it was impossible. His only thought was of death.

The chain above went taunt. O'Reilly was pulled above the waves, water pouring from him. It had started to rain but O'Reilly was oblivious to it. He started to shake, fear and cold water exacting a toll.

He watched Milo drop the controller, as he limped to where O'Reilly swayed in the wind. His shivering intensified.

"P-Please, Milo," he stuttered.

"Where is she, O'Reilly?"

"M-Milo, listen to me. I smashed the window to get into that truck. I did. But she got away."

Milo shook his head. He stepped back and picked up the controller. He punched the "descend" button again, halting it as O'Reilly fell to the top of the waves. A terrifying sound escaped his lips.

"Sh-She slammed into the barricade and reversed right at me, before she took off. My arm prevented me from getting to the truck key. I swear. She got away."

O'Reilly struggled against his restraints. "For God's sake. Please don't kill me," he screamed.

Milo stared at him with unwavering eyes. "If she got away, then where is she?"

Milo hit the button again. O'Reilly slowly dropping back into the sea.

"No," he wailed.

Water covered O'Reilly's ankles, then his waist. His vision swivelled to the other men.

Chad stared at him and looked over to his friends. They shuffled from foot to foot, watching as O'Reilly dropped further into the water.

The chain was lowered, water surrounded his neck. O'Reilly screamed for mercy.

"Milo, we didn't sign on to kill him," he heard Chad cry out.

O'Reilly sunk beneath the waves.

He could see the men standing there, peering down at him. His eyes stung from the salt water. It all seemed so surreal. He saw Milo hit the control button repeatedly and the men yelling franticly at each other. He watched Milo drop the control and scurry to the side of the trawler, grabbing the chain above him.

His lungs were bursting. He felt death coming.

He watched the others join in, pulling on the chain. He had to hold on. The need to draw a breath became a command. He opened his mouth. Water flowed in.

O'Reilly's head broke the surface. Water flowed into his lungs. He choked. Then gagged. Water spewed from his mouth across the gunwale. He retched again. More water escaped his blue lips. He felt his leg smash into the side of the boat as he was unceremoniously dumped to the floor.

His coughing subsided. Milo hovered over him as he shivered anew. He left for the pilot house, returning with a blanket to throw over him. He kneeled next to his ear.

"You'll live, O'Reilly. You're lucky. I chose not to kill you. You have attacked my little girl twice and I should see you dead, but you aren't worth the price. But make no mistake, three strikes and you will be out. You will never see me coming. Don't ever go near her again. We clear?"

O'Reilly stared at him, his body shaking violently. He nodded his head once. He was too cold to give much thought to the request, but he knew if he didn't agree, things would go from bad to worse.

Milo limped to the pilot house but didn't enter. He focused on the mainland. The rain had worsened, and O'Reilly watched the water drip from his nose.

"I have to get to my place," he said to no one in particular. "As quick as possible."

Chad nodded. "Just got the winch working again." He wandered into the pilot house and started the engines.

Milo spun and locked eyes with O'Reilly. His prone body shivered in waves, the blanket covering him, now soaked through. O'Reilly had seen hate before in other men's eyes, but he had never seen hate fuelled by determination. He shivered again. A different kind of shiver. One born of fear.

CHAPTER THIRTY-THREE

NATE TIED UP MARIO'S ZODIAC; a light rain was falling. He swiped the drizzle from his face and made a mental note to grab a cap from his boat.

He needed to find Beka. Something had obviously happened to her. Past visions of Jess popped into his head. Angst clutched at his heart. Was he destined to live a life that hurt those who were closest to him? Why had he allowed his world to consume her? Would she be able to forgive him? He had to find her.

He strode purposely down the dock only to find Archie standing between him and his boat.

"You need to come aboard, Nate."

"Archie, I'm in a hurry. Can't this wait?"

"No Nate...it can't."

Nate heard a car door slam. He turned his head towards shore. Steve Quince was heading for the dock. He had his eyes squarely on Nate.

"What have you done, Archie?" Nates shoulders slumped.

"A very unsavory man was on your boat this morning, Nate. He left a phone and a note. Obviously, I couldn't open the phone, but the note made me realize how deeply you are in trouble. I called Steve to come and help."

Nate's face went dark. "Archie, why can't you mind your own business?"

Archie appeared shocked by Nate's tone. "I don't know what you have done. I don't care to know. But you are in trouble and the Nate Beckett I know is a caring and kind man. I have no intention of seeing you dead, if I can help it. Steve Quince is a good cop. He can help you. You may need to answer for some things, but you will stay alive."

"You have no idea what you've done. Give me the letter and phone."

Archie reached for both from the seat behind him. He was about to hand them over when Steve Quince arrived and stepped onto the catamaran. "Perhaps we should look at that together." He walked into the salon.

"Archie...Good morning, Nate," he said with a nod to both, a false smile encasing his lips.

"Good morning, Steve," answered Archie.

Nate remained silent, glaring at Quince.

"Let's have a look then, shall we?" Quince sized up the mood that preceded him.

Archie handed the note to Quince, who read it out loud. "You have twenty-four hours to give us the money or all hell breaks loose. Will be in touch."

Quince read it once more and handed it to Nate, watching for his reaction, which remained stoic. He nodded at Archie, reaching his hand out. Archie handed Quince the phone. He hit the power button. "Do we know whose phone this is?"

"Mine," Nate admitted.

He handed it to Nate. "Punch in the code, please."

Nate accepted the phone. He considered telling Quince he needed a warrant, but he needed what was on it and fast. He punched in his code. A picture of Beka tied to a chair stared back at him. She was in obvious pain. He collapsed onto a seat.

"May I?" Quince asked.

Nate stared up at Quince but didn't hand it over.

Quince stared back, waiting. He broke the silence. "I know you're Nate Vickers. You are a person of interest in a homicide in Calgary and a man named John Sebastian, which appears to be an alias, has been in contact with you. John Sebastian is now missing. Did you have something to do with that?" Quince paused, allowing his comments to be absorbed.

Nate showed no emotion, no acceptance or rejection.

Quince continued. "I also know very unsavoury people are following you and an even more unsavoury group is following them. You've been garnering a lot of negative attention, Nate. The only reason I'm not marching you up to that car in handcuffs is that this man" – he nodded to Archie — "thinks that you are a good guy who has stepped into a bad situation, and that I should give you the benefit of doubt. To do that, I need you to give me a reason to believe him. So, what's it going to be Nate? The phone."

Nate relinquished. He handed the phone to Quince.

"Jesus." Quince wasn't expecting the image on the screen.

"I need to deal with this, Steve," Nate said. "My way. Please?"

"Not a chance. This is a kidnapping. Who has done this, Nate?"

"Honestly, I don't know."

"Bullshit."

"I have no idea who wrote that note, Steve, but it is all tied to the mob out of Calgary." Nate decided to give up something to buy time.

Acceptance washed across Quince's eyes. Archie's mouth dropped open. Nate heard the intake of his breath.

"Did you do something with Sebastian?" Quince resumed.

Nate's fatigue was showing, and he snarled at Quince. "Who the hell is Sebastian?"

"He's the guy on the Bayliner."

Nate answered slowly. "That's not his real name. I don't know his real name. I know him as Ross - "

The phone pinged an incoming text.

Nate glanced at Quince, who nodded his agreement, handing the phone to him.

Nate opened the text.

We have your girl, Vickers. You have something we want. You have 24 hours to get a million dollars to us in unmarked bills or she dies. Come alone or she dies. No cops. We will meet you at the cabin, at this time, tomorrow. Be there or she dies.

Nate set the phone on the salon table.

***

Her captor sneered at her, holding a phone up to indicate a text had been sent. "Now we'll see if he thinks your life is worth a million dollars."

The door opened and in walked her other abductor. He had been gone a long while. The front door had been left open and Beka could see a truck parked outside. He walked directly over to her, a rag in hand.

"No... please." She struggled at the bonds holding her, pain shooting through her finger. The man walked behind her, grabbed her head by her hair, held the rag over her nose and face. She fought as best she could. Not again.

***

Nate leaned forward, placing his head in his hands.

"What does it say?" Quince queried.

Nate took the phone from the table and made to hand it to Quince. He let it slip from his grasp. It clattered to the wood floor. He had no intention of letting Quince know the details of what was happening. His phone was useless. He had deleted the text message after reading it.

As Quince knelt to retrieve the phone, Nate bolted for the dock.

He rounded the corner of the catamaran and headed up the dock at a sprint, when he heard Archie yell out, "Nate, don't do this." He ran. Quince jumped from the boat and was in chase. Nate had a good lead on him. Up the ramp he went, glancing back. He figured he had about a thirty second head start, at best. Quince was obviously in shape. He heard him talking into his shoulder microphone, requesting backup. If he was caught now, it was over.

He crested the ramp, approaching the marina store. He bolted down the front of the store and turned the corner heading for the parking lot. There was a bank of trees on the other side. He had to get to them. He was halfway across the parking lot when Quince rounded the corner and spotted him. Understanding there was no danger to himself, he resumed the chase. Nate gained extra time. He was about to enter a trail in the woods beside the main road when a pickup slid to a stop, its window rolling down.

"Nate, get in."

Nate eyed the unknown truck, not slowing down his pace. Milo sat behind the wheel, beckoning. He changed direction, slipping on wet gravel as he did and ran for the truck. Quince had made up ground. Nate reached for the door handle and pulled the door open; the truck had started moving again. He reached in, grabbed the handle above the door, and pivoted into the seat. Milo stepped on the gas.

Quince reached the rear panel of the truck, but Nate was gone. He was sure Quince would have spotted Milo in the driver's seat.

Nate reached out for the door, slamming it shut as the truck accelerated.

Nate spun in his seat to see Quince. He was doubled over, catching his breath. He rose and pressed the microphone on his shoulder as the truck disappeared around a corner.

Nate swivelled back to Milo who was checking the rear-view mirror as he sped down the street, well beyond the posted speed limit. A concerned homeowner waved at him to slow down. He kept his foot firmly pressed to the floor.

"She's been kidnapped, Milo," Nate screamed above the engine noise.

Milo stared, anger reddening his face. "Who?"

"I don't know. I thought it had to be O'Reilly, but none of this makes sense. We need to get rid of this truck. Where'd you get it, anyway?"

"A friend." Nate waited for more, but no further explanation was proffered.

"I saw Quince radio us in. I'll explain everything I know, but we need to get out of Gibsons or we're both in trouble." Guilt washed over Nate. Milo didn't deserve any of this. What had he brought upon these good people? He gazed out the window, searching for solace.

Milo snorted and turned onto another road. Nate could see the highway directly ahead. Milo made another quick turn, the tires chirping as he did. He turned to Nate. "It wasn't O'Reilly." He focused back on the road ahead.

Nate glanced at Milo, reading his expression. What he said was true. Milo had gone after O'Reilly. He could tell by the look on Milo's face he had found him. He wanted the details, but instead said, "Where are we going?"

"Down Lower Road. I know a place we can dump the truck, but we will have a good hike from there to get to the cabin. Why were you running?"

"I'll answer that, but how did you find me?"

"I didn't... just ran in to you. I spotted you tearing across the lot as I was about to enter it," Milo said. "I was going to the store, to get my other rifle. Guess I'll do without it now." Milo glanced at Nate. "Your turn?"

Nate watched the windshield wipers beating back the light rain. "They are piecing my life together. Quince was looking for more information, but I was pretty sure I was destined for the station with him. I couldn't let that happen. I need to find Beka."

"This doesn't look like it will end well, Nate."

"I need to try. Let me tell you what I know."

Milo turned left and stepped on the gas. Nate explained everything that happened to him after he left Milo that morning.

Milo's face darkened; eventually his grimace was replaced by determination. There was nothing more to say.

Nate closed his eyes. A darkness engulfed him. Where was Beka? How could he save her from these people? How could he get the money they demanded together so quickly? And Milo. He was now involved. Beka would never forgive him. He groaned.

Milo glanced at the sound. He turned back to the road. He reached for the radio and turned the knob. Nate listened to Martina McBride crooning a ballad about life on the road, as the trees flew by.

Milo pulled the borrowed truck into some brush, camouflaging it a bit, hoping it would slow down their pursuers and then pointed to a path. "That's where we start. Let's go. And Nate...I want to know everything about you now. You hear me... everything."

Nate's face flushed with shame as their situation bore down on him. He knew he had no choice but to tell this man his whole story.

CHAPTER THIRTY-FOUR

DON ANTONIO BELLETTI WAS IN an ugly mood. He stared at the tops of the cumulous clouds and wished the one-hour flight would go faster. He wanted this over with as soon as possible. He did not take kindly to being ordered about. Looking at the image in the window staring back at him, he realized his anger would have to be brought under control before he landed. He allowed his mind to switch gears. There was an awards ceremony being conducted tonight for his years of philanthropy. He wanted to be there, but reluctantly he had needed to call the event coordinator to advise them his wife would be accepting on his behalf due to an unforeseen business requirement. This too made him angry.

Vickers would pay for the problems he created and for the extreme disrespect on the phone. There was no point in running a crime syndicate if you couldn't mete out justice from time to time.

And what to do about Mario? Belletti could hardly believe that his battle tested sidekick had been out maneuvered by a kid. Maybe his brother's death was impacting his ability. He would have to deal with that too. Allowing failure was not an option when you ran the mob.

Belletti had barely closed his eyes in an ill-fated effort to calm down, when the jet slammed to the Vancouver tarmac. His eyes snapped open at the irregular landing. Everything fed his bad temper.

He'd instructed Mario the night before to meet him at the airport, and after the long walk through the terminal he slid into the passenger seat of the SUV. He glared at Mario, and nodded to his boys, in the back seat. Mario was noticeably nervous. Belletti watched silently as he stepped on the gas, pulling away from the curb. Then he spoke.

"Bring me up to speed...all of it." His voice left little doubt, in his listener's minds, that the don wielded full control of their situation.

Belletti listened, asking clarifying questions to ensure what was being said fit with what he previously understood. Once he was sure he comprehended their situation, he pulled his phone from his pocket, and opened his recent calls. He pressed the number used to summon him to the coast. His face went dark as he listened to the ring.

***

Steve Quince returned to his detachment after he recovered Nate's phone from Archie. On the way, he put out an all-points bulletin, on the truck that Nate and Milo had escaped in. He was furious with himself for listening to Archie and not arresting Beckett the moment he stepped on the boat. And now the kid had brought Milo into his mess.

Milo didn't deserve this. He dealt with enough earlier in his life. Quince hadn't been there for that, but small towns being what they are, he'd heard the stories of Milo's losses on more than one occasion. He felt for him. The last thing he wanted was to see Milo throw away everything he had worked so hard for. An inherent sadness welled within him, which he fought by stoking his irritation at himself.

He telephoned Andrea Maitland to see if anything further turned up on the Bayliner. Her initial observation found John Sebastian to be a careful man. She ordered a dusting of the boat for fingerprints to identify who their man really was but based on how thoroughly the boat had been cleaned, she wasn't hopeful they would get much.

She wanted to know what had happened on his end. She'd heard the recent APB announcement, so Quince brought her up to date on how he was outmaneuvered by Beckett. Quince became annoyed when she laughed. She quickly became serious, recognizing the solemnity in his voice. Quince asked her to expedite the prints, if she found any, as soon as she could. He signed off and contemplated his next move.

Milo had a place somewhere further down the coast. He learned that valuable piece of information from the owner of the diner many months ago, during a mid-morning coffee. He was waiting for the detachment administrator to get back to him once she completed a property search with the B.C. Registry. As soon as he had it, he would pick up Andrea and they would head out there, this time with the firm intention of arresting Beckett, if he was there, and to take Milo into custody, for aiding and abetting a fugitive. He wasn't sure if that would stick, but he was damned sure he wanted to send Milo a message.

He had gone over the fingerprint report on Beckett, earlier in the morning, before Archie called. He wasn't surprised, given all the recent events and discussions, to see a confirmation that Vickers and Beckett were one and the same person. It was difficult to reconcile the Nate Beckett that he met with the Calgary Police report on Vickers as a person of interest in their homicide case. He was internally debating this when Beckett's phone rang.

Quince gaped at it for a moment, then reached over and pressed the answer button. He put the phone to his ear. For a moment it seemed there was no one there.

"Hello."

Quince thought about how to handle this and tentatively answered, "Yes."

There was a brief pause. "This is Antonio Belletti. I'm here. Give me directions."

Quince's eyebrows thrust upwards in surprise. He thought quickly. "Change of plan, I'll come to you. Where are you?"

"What are you talking about? Don't play games with me, Vickers."

"I'm not. It would be easier if I came to you."

"Who is this?"

Quince wanted to get to this man. "Nate Beck- Vickers."

Click.

Quince stared at the phone, listening to the dial tone. Damn.

Things are coming to a head if the Calgary crime syndicate boss was here in person. Quince called Andrea Maitland.

"Andrea, leave the boat with our analytical team. I need you back here... now. Things are going from bad to worse. We need to get Beckett in lockdown before we fill the morgue with bodies."

***

Nate trudged beneath the bows of the large cedar trees, a few steps back of Milo. The trail had been cut long ago and the forest was working hard to take it back, making it difficult to navigate at times. Nate knew that if Milo wasn't with him, he'd be totally lost. As they rounded the first bend of the trail, he begrudgingly told Milo the story of his Calgary escape, who all the key players were here, at least as far as he understood them to be, and their efforts to reacquire the money he stole.

"Go on..." was all Milo managed through clenched teeth.

Nate could feel Milo's contempt for him grow. He understood it. He had put his daughter at risk. Nate didn't hold back, despite the overwhelming shame it caused. This man and his daughter had trusted him.

He told Milo everything as they trudged forward. He held nothing back. Deep creases furrowed Milo's brow when Nate drifted into the more violent aspects of the story, including what had happened to his partner, Jess.

He stopped and spun on Nate, fury creasing his face.

"What have you gotten us into?" he snarled. "She's my baby."

"Milo..."

"Did you really think they wouldn't come for you?"

"I thought I was buried. I didn't plan this. I tried to stay to myself. I really wanted to change and be part of..."

"Shut up, Nate."

Nate slammed his mouth closed.

"If anything happens to her—"

Nate cast his eyes to the ground. "I love her, Milo."

"How much does she know?"

"Everything."

"Goddamn you." Milo closed his eyes, then turned and started to limp forward again. He said nothing more. Nate saw the strain across his shoulders, as he swatted at the boughs of the trees, that encroached.

He had hoped when he told Milo everything that a weight would be lifted. But the opposite happened. He felt the full gravity of his guilt resting on him. He wondered if he had the ability to see this through. He had to. It was Beka. He would give his life if required. It was time to make this right.

They were halfway through the trek when Nate cussed quietly under his breath and stopped. Milo walked on for another couple of minutes, lost in his thoughts, before noticing that he was alone.

"Now what?" he asked, retracing his steps back to Nate. He wiped light rain from his face.

"They said to meet at your cabin, Milo. Whoever has Beka will be there, and they'll be expecting me and the money. I cannot ask you to walk into any more danger. Hell, I don't even have the money. I can't show up there with nothing."

Milo sighed and collapsed on a fallen tree. He buried his face in his hands.

Nate closed the distance. "We can't just charge in there, Milo. We need a plan."

Milo removed his hands from his face and stared at Nate.

Nate shuffled, then placidly added, "And, I'm not letting you go in there. It's not your risk to take. It's too dangerous."

"That's my little girl, Nate. And it's my property. Don't even think you can keep me out of this."

"Milo, listen to me—"

"I need to understand one thing," Milo interrupted. "What did she say when you told her 'Everything'?"

"She said we would get through it together." Nate looked at the ground, humiliation filling his face.

"And you let her get in harm's way." It was more of a statement than a question. Nate answered anyway.

"I tried to convince her to step back, Milo. She wouldn't have any part of it. She's a strong-willed woman. You know her." Pain registered on Milo's face. "I am so sorry."

"She is my only family, Nate. I made a pact with myself to always protect her. For the life of me, I didn't see you as the threat you've become. Now look at the mess we're in. You and I are due a very serious talk, if we get out of this."

Nate agreed, his eyes welling up. "I love her, Milo."

Milo stared into the forest, letting Nate's declaration hang. "You better hope we are enough to save her, Nate. Otherwise, I'll never forgive you."

"We'll get her back. And my uncle and Elena, if they're cap-
tives now too. It would be nice to know if they were able to see the
danger coming. Do you have your phone with you? Will it work in
these mountains?"

"No, not until we round the corner of that mountain there,"
Milo pointed ahead to a mountain shrouded in low hanging
clouds. "That's about three quarters of the way to the cabin. We
can call then."

Nate nodded. Milo stared down the trail.

"You're right about one thing," Milo turned back to Nate. "We
need to devise a plan."

Despite both men's anxieties, they slowly formulated a scheme
as they walked. Not one without risk, but it had a chance of
success. A short time later, they set out in different directions. Nate
headed east, following the path to the clearing beside the cabin.
He had Milo's instructions on how to get there firmly committed
to memory. Milo headed in the opposite direction.

Nate rotated and looked back, just as Milo neared a corner. He
watched his quickened pace, his limp more exaggerated. Then the
forest swallowed him.

He spun on his heel and marched forward, doubts assaulting
him. He had put Beka and Milo in so much danger. He hadn't
planned to. He wished he could undo everything. He pocketed
Milo's phone and pushed on; a firm resolve slowly edging the guilt
to the back of his mind.

One outcome was driving him. No matter what fate had in
store, he would save the woman he loved.

CHAPTER THIRTY-FIVE

ELENA CAME THROUGH THE PORCH door, second coffee in hand, and walked over to Frank, who was still sitting quietly, taking in the meadow. She leaned down and kissed him softly. Frank could smell lavender in her hair, it made him stir. She'd added a light-weight collared sweater to fight off the morning coolness. Her hair was still damp, she looked lovely in Beka's dress.

She sat down on a chair beside him. "Your turn to clean up, mister."

"I have a better idea," he grinned her way, with an expect-ant expression.

Elena was about to respond when she caught movement over Frank's shoulder. A truck approached slowly up the lane to the property.

"Frank..."

Frank turned in its direction. He hesitated momentarily, "Go..." he ordered, "... into the house."

They scurried back inside, hoping they hadn't been spotted. Frank swore, returning to the porch door. He crawled back onto the deck and grabbed the shotgun from the back of the chair and slithered back. He looked out the window. The truck was creeping forward slowly.

"Let's go El, out the back."

"They'll see us. You sure it isn't Milo?"

"No, I think it's that same truck we spotted at the ferry, then in town."

"How could they find us?"

"I don't know. But I don't want to take any chances. That truck is coming here for one reason and one reason only. It's surveying the property now, looking for someone. I suspect it's us. The cabin isn't safe...we need to get to the woods. C'mon, we'll keep out of view of the truck."

Frank estimated that it would take them about three minutes to make it to safety. It would take the truck longer than that to reach them at its current speed. They headed for the rear door and stopped. Elena jumped as Frank primed the shotgun, readying it for use. Frank snuck a look at Elena, noting the determined look crossing her face. Nodding, he pushed opened the rear door and they stepped out.

The truck wasn't spotted again until they were safely tucked into the underbrush behind the house. Frank squatted down where he couldn't be detected. Elena pulled up short, peering over his shoulder.

"Why are we stopping?" she whispered.

"We need to know what's going on."

"We need to get out of here."

"I want to know who these guys are. I'm tired of running from this phantom. Let's hunker down and watch for a minute. I promise, if it looks like we're in danger, we're out of here."

Elena gave him a questioning look, then peered out at the truck.

Frank shifted in the brush until he had a clear view. The vehicle inched up the driveway to the cabin, where it stopped and idled.

Frank could see the occupants scanning the property. He ducked his head to avoid detection. Elena copied the move.

A moment or two later, it was in gear again, this time destined for the barn. As it neared the entrance, the passenger door opened and the occupant stepped out of the truck, drew what appeared to be a pistol, and headed back to the house. From this distance, Frank couldn't make out who it was.

The driver pulled closer to the barn and parked. He got out and cautiously inspected the barn. He too had a gun drawn. Frank glanced at Elena, whose eyes were wide from terror. Whoever these two were, they were not to be taken lightly.

"Let's go," Elena muttered urgently.

"Hang on, El. Sink down lower. We can't be seen."

The rear door of the house opened. Frank dropped flat; thankful Elena had listened to him. He peered through a fern; his view compromised. He gripped the shotgun tightly, hoping he wouldn't have to use it. He laid perfectly still, losing sight of his adversary.

The door slammed shut. He pulled a fern leaf aside for a better view. No one there.

His field of vision shifted to the barn and saw one of the accosters reaching inside the truck. The other came into view, hustling over to assist. Frank maneuvered himself to get a better angle.

A woman was pulled from the rear of the cab. She was struggling to keep on her feet. Her mouth was covered by duct tape, and she stumbled into the arms of the man who roughly dragged her to the barn entrance. His accomplice added assistance, grabbing the woman's other arm after shouldering a knapsack she retrieved from the truck. Her head turned. Frank crouched higher to get a better look and groaned.

"Jesus," he gasped.

Elena, staying low, looked at Frank, worry written all over her face.

"What?"

Frank kneeled beside her. "They have Beka."

Elena clasped her mouth. Too dangerous to scream.

***

Beka stumbled. Arms held her upright. They half-walked, half dragged her towards the back of the barn.

"We'll tie her here."

She was roughly forced to the ground, back to a post that held an upper floor in the barn. She was tied to it with a rope brought in from the truck.

"Someone's been here."

"How do you know?"

"Empty coffee cups and an unmade bed in the cabin. Looks like two people. They left in a hurry."

"Is there any sign of them?"

"No. We'll have to be very careful. Get her ready. I will go move the truck and come back. Make the call as soon as she's secure."

The man nodded and turned towards Beka. He tested his knots, then reached into his knapsack, withdrew a bottle of water and tossed the cap to the ground. He pulled the duct tape from her mouth and put the bottle to her lips. Beka struggled to regain her wits.

"Drink this, it'll help."

She hesitated, then accepted the water, allowing it to rehydrate her parched mouth. He then pulled the bottle away.

She drew in her breath, readying for a scream.

"No," the man said harshly slapping the duct tape back on her mouth. He slammed his foot on the ground before her, as if to kick her. She recoiled. He smirked. "You are becoming a pain in the ass." He shook his head at her.

He walked a few paces away and pulled his phone from his rear jean pocket. He looked at the number he had added to his contacts and punched the send button.

***

"What is it, boss?" Mario asked, after the don slammed his phone on the dashboard.

"The cops have that little shit's phone." He paused. "Gotta be the cops, smelled like 'em. Did I come out here for nothing? Why the hell are they involved, Mario? I sent you out here to get things done. To get my money back. Now we are in the middle of a cluster, and you've given me nothing."

The don was enraged. He could see Mario's men trying to be invisible in the back seat, especially Cortez who looked out the window, attempting to be anonymous. Mario cowered, unsure of what was coming next.

The phone rang again. Belletti looked at the screen and stared at the unknown number. After a pause he answered it and said nothing.

"Belletti." The don paused.

"Are you here?" came the voice on the other end.

"Who is this?" Belletti assumed the cops were behind the latest call.

"You think I brought you all the way here from Calgary to play games?"

"Vickers?" Belletti hissed through his teeth.

"You were expecting someone else?"

"Actually yes, since the cops were on the line recently." Belletti noted the pause. He had unnerved Vickers. Good.

"Never mind, I have a different phone now. By the time the cop's figure anything out, we'll all be long gone."

Belletti was thoughtful. He didn't know, for sure, who he was talking to, but he decided to take a chance. He hadn't broken any laws — yet. They couldn't touch him. "Do you have my money?"

"I do. Now listen carefully. I'll give you directions on how to get it. Oh...and Belletti? Leave the stooges behind. If I see them again, you get nothing...*Capisce?*"

"*Capisce.*" Colouring in the don's face caused Mario's brow to furrow as he watched in silence. The don's anger was palpable. Belletti reached into the glove box of the SUV, withdrew the car insurance document, flipped it over on the dash, and made notes with his gold-plated pen.

With his call ended he turned on Mario. "I need a rental car."

Mario put the car in gear and headed for Gibsons. He looked confused.

"Cortez, find me the closest rental company," Mario said to Cortez in the rear seat, who jumped at his name.

"*Si.*" He pulled out his phone and started a search.

Belletti glanced over at Mario, who was facing dead ahead. He turned in his seat and looked at him directly. "This is what we are going to do. And Mario, this time you better not screw it up."

Mario grimaced and listened intently as he drove for Gibsons.

***

Ty O'Reilly was no longer capable of rational thought. He wanted revenge. He knew how to do that. The cabin was no secret to him.

He heard Milo saying that he was going to his place. He felt sure that meant the cabin. Well, that was just fine with him. The old man would pay for the humiliation he put him through. His earlier fear rapidly morphed into anger. Milo had made a mistake, letting him live, and now he would get a taste of his own medicine.

Milo didn't know he knew the cabin's location. Beka had told him about it, long before things turned soured between them.

Maybe with a bit of luck the two of them would be there together, and he could exact revenge on both. He knew now he would never get her back so he would hurt Milo and make her watch. He'd put the fear of God in them both when he torched Milo's beloved cabin. They'd soon learn not to mess with Ty O'Reilly.

He put the gas can in the back of his borrowed truck and jumped into the cab. He gunned the engine, glared into the mirror, and put the vehicle in gear.

**

Ross Finlay was incensed. He couldn't reach Nate Vickers. All calls to his cell rerouted to his voice mail. Had he been picked up by the police? Perhaps he had overplayed his hand with the bumbling cop? He didn't appear too bright, but you never knew. He had watched the RCMP swarm the boat he had chartered; grateful he had the insight to abandon it and have it sanitized. Maybe he had underestimated Quince. If he had Vickers, it created a problem.

Out of frustration, Finlay made his way back to the marina to see what he could learn. Surprisingly, the store was locked up, as if abandoned. After querying some of the local boaters, he learned none knew what caused the proprietor of their local marina to close shop. No doubt, Vickers was somehow involved. That boy was becoming a major problem. *Serendipity* also appeared to be abandoned. Something had gone wrong.

Finlay watched the annoying old guy from the catamaran leave his boat, heading for shore. He felt it best to make himself scarce from his inquisitive eyes. He made his way back to his rental car and climbed in. He grabbed his coat from the back seat and pulled it over his head, feigning sleep. He left his window cracked open. If there was a commotion, he didn't want to be left without the option of escape.

As the old man reached the top of the gangway, Finlay heard him being called.

"Archie...Archie?"

Finlay peeked above the dash. He watched the old man look around before settling on a man in the shadows.

"Milo, where the hell have you been?"

"Shhhh... come here..."

Finlay cocked his head as the old man entered the marina store behind the proprietor.

That's interesting, thought Finlay. He saw an opportunity. He threw the coat behind him and got out of the car, locking it with his key to avoid the beeping sound of a fob lock.

He retraced his steps, walking like he belonged. He sauntered past the marina store and headed down to the docks. Time to see what Mr. Vickers had been up to. He approached *Serendipity,* never looking back. Onboard, he walked over to the hatch, pulled out a lock set and kneeling, so as not to be seen, unlocked the door with a few deftly managed hand movements. He slid the hatch open, entered the cabin and nudged the door closed behind him. No point in letting the locals think Vickers had returned. With the window curtains closed, he turned to the task at hand.

CHAPTER THIRTY-SIX

MILO CLOSED THE DOOR BEHIND Archie as he entered. He limped over to the main window and glanced over the marina, his eyes darting about. Satisfied that he arrived undetected, he turned to Archie, who stood rigidly at the entrance.

"Milo, what are you doing? You have a heap of trouble in front of you. And for what? Beckett? Was he worth it?"

"Archie, you need to listen to me. Nate Beckett is the least of my troubles. Beka has been kidnapped."

"By Beckett?"

"No. I don't know who has her. I thought it was O'Reilly, but it wasn't him."

"Why did you think it was him?"

"Cause he's crazy enough." Milo addressed the quizzical expression on Archie's face. "You don't want to know."

It was clear Archie did want to know but changed course. "How do you know that Beckett isn't involved? God knows, he's involved in everything else these days."

Milo shook his head.

"You need to call Quince now, Milo. This has gotten way out of hand."

"They'll kill her. I'm doing this my way. Don't you dare call Quince." The threat was implied, but Archie had been a cop for too long to not see the signs of a viable threat.

"Why'd you call me in here?"

Milo hesitated. "I want you to do something for me. And I need you to trust me." The statement was said as a question. Milo then explained what was needed.

"Why would I do that?"

"For Beka. You've known her all her life. She loves that kid and right now, he's headed into the lion's den to take these characters on. He may have a past, Archie, but we all do. I'm helping him. I need to know if you'll help too?" Milo let the question hang. "I'll be right back."

He wandered into the back office and spun the dial on a small wall safe. He retrieved what he came for. Archie wandered to the open door and watched as he placed a Springfield XD pistol on his desk. He opened his desk and withdrew a small box of ammunition.

"C'mon, Milo. This is crazy."

Milo started to load the gun. "Yes, or no?"

Archie stared at the weapon in Milo's hand. "I like the boy, Milo, but Steve has been telling me a little of his past. It's bad. You can't seriously want Beka near that past or that man."

"That may be the case, but I have gotten to know him quite well over the last while, he has a big heart. You know that. Besides, I have a little girl who will not abandon him. And I will not abandon her, so I'm all in."

"Yeah, how's that working? She's been abducted."

Milo was pulled back into the moment with the question. His face darkened. He slid the pistol into his waistband.

"Archie?" Milo said, finality in his voice. Archie stood ramrod straight, his eyes fixed on Milo's. A full ten seconds passed without a word being said. Milo wheeled and opened a cabinet, pulling out a large silver travel case.

"I don't have time for this." Milo headed for the door. "Lock up after me." His hand was reaching for the doorknob when Archie responded.

"I'll move the boat," he said. "But that's all I'm doing."

***

Nate watched the sky expanding through the canopy of the trees, glad the rain had stopped. The clearing had to be in front of him; he'd followed Milo's instructions to a tee. Turning a corner, he spotted the backside of the cabin. Now he would get some answers.

Worry rested on him like a heavy blanket. He had been unable to reach his uncle by phone. He approached the meadow cautiously and was about to step from the trees, when a voice spoke from behind.

"I wouldn't do that if I were you."

Nate jumped at the unexpected voice and spun around. Frank and Elena were standing beside a large Douglas fir tree. They were hard to discern in the late afternoon light. Frank had the shotgun hanging loosely at his side.

"You scared me half to death, Frank," he hissed, wandering over to them. He gave a half smile to Elena. Elena nodded in return. She looked like hell.

"You ever heard of stealth, Nate? You need to walk quieter if you expect to sneak up on anyone." He spoke in a hushed tone.

"I wasn't making that much noise. What are you two doing out here?" Nate glanced at the shotgun in Frank's hand.

"Keep your voice down. We have company." Frank nodded towards the barn. Nate looked across the meadow.

"The barn?"

Frank nodded. "Where's Milo, by the way?"

Nate explained what had transpired with Milo. "I had to get back here. Beka's been kidnapped. They instructed me to come here with a million bucks if I wanted to see her alive."

Frank gave Nate the once over. "And you have that in your pocket?"

"No. I have a plan. Well, sort of a plan. Milo's securing a gun and a suitcase."

"Where's the money?"

Nate paused. "Where it has always been...invested."

"That's your plan?"

"What do you want from me, Frank? I need to try something. I'm not having another dead girlfriend on my hands."

Frank glanced at Elena; there was disquiet deeply etched on her face.

"And why didn't you answer your phone?" Nate stared at the barn entrance.

"Yeah, that's what I'd need. A phone ringing while we're hiding in the forest."

Nate ignored the sarcasm. "Any sign of Beka?"

Frank nodded, then tilted his head towards the barn.

Nate closed his eyes. "I have to get in there."

"Well, you obviously need some help. There are two of them. They both have guns."

"You recognize them?"

"No. It's too hard to see this far away. Bad enough we have Belletti's crew to deal with. Now we have new players with an axe to grind. They have been on us since I picked up Elena at the ferry. Any idea who they might be?"

Nate thought for a minute. "I wish I knew. I've been racking my brain since I got their call. I thought I knew all the players I was up against. It was bad enough that I had to deal with the added problem of Ross. Now this." He paused, shaking his head. "But they're informed. They know about the money and what Beka means to me."

Frank studied the grim look on Nate's face.

"Did you see Beka? Is she all right?" Nate didn't voice the real question he wanted answered.

"Yeah, though I think they roughed her up. She also seemed to be drugged. They half dragged her into the barn. Her legs were moving but she struggled to stand."

Nate exhaled slowly. His jaw ached as he finally unclenched his teeth. His attention swung back to the entry. It looked like a gaping maw in the afternoon shadows. Nate's jaw locked down again.

"What do you want to do, Nate?"

"I'm going in there."

"That's suicide."

"They won't shoot me. Not when I don't have the money on me. Remember, they kidnapped her to get the money."

"And when they don't get the money?"

"Milo's bringing it, and a gun."

"You're risking Milo's life? C'mon, Nate." Frank's voice rose.

Elena reached out and placed her hand on his arm.

He clamped his mouth shut.

Nate's tone hardened. "It's his daughter, Frank. I tried my damnedest to talk him out of it. He wouldn't hear of it. You got a better plan? Let's hear it."

"Well...two guns." He glanced at the one in his hands. "That's a fairer fight."

"No," hissed Elena. "You promised." Frank's eyes spun to hers. "you said if it became too dangerous, we were out of here. Listen to yourself...guns, suicide..." She stabbed an animated finger at Frank. "You promised Frank. You said we would go."

"She's right, Frank. You guys need to get out of here. Follow the path I came in on. It will take you a good half hour, but you'll find the main road."

Frank took Elena's hand. "All of this has happened because we brought them here." Frank smiled at Elena. A tear escaped, and slowly rolled down her cheek. "I can't let him do this alone." He glanced at Nate, then back to Elena. "I am so sorry, El."

Nate countered. "You didn't bring this to me. I brought this on all of us and it's time for it to end. You have a new lease on life." Nate nodded at Elena.

Frank reached over and gingerly wiped the tear from her face. "I know, and I'll be picking up on that, when this is over. Now, what's our plan of attack?"

"Frank..." Elena grabbed his sleeve.

"Enough," Frank snapped. Regretting his tone, he placed a hand on her cheek.

Nate gazed apologetically at Elena, who slowly slumped to the forest floor, her back leaning against the base of a fir tree; her collapse announcing defeat.

Nate turned and motioned at Frank; he was all in.

***

Quince had studied the land deed provided him. He was glad a blueprint of the layout had been attached as well. Best to know what they were walking into.

He was in his car, Andrea beside him. As they reached the highway, Andrea switched the lights on, deciding to forgo the siren. Two shotguns were locked in place in the front rack. Little was said on the drive. They knew their directive. No more discussions, until Beckett and Milo were in cuffs.

Quince stepped harder on the gas and watched power poles slide by them like forest trees.

CHAPTER THIRTY-SEVEN

NATE DECIDED TRANSPARENCY WAS THE best approach. He rounded the south side of the cabin heading for the barn's entrance. Rain fell from heavily ladened clouds. He barely registered it. His heart yearned to free Beka, but his head envisioned a bullet ripping through his body. He supposed that was a fitting end given the long difficult journey since the day of the heist. He could accept that, but he knew if it happened, Beka would have the same outcome, which he couldn't bear. He advanced on the barn, a bead of sweat on his brow, despite the lateness of the day.

As he walked, Nate saw her smiling at him, the wind whipping though her hair as they sailed the Salish Sea. He saw her lying naked in his cabin and heard her telling him her deepest desires. Laughter always near the surface. He saw her determination when she demanded he tell her everything. 'No' was not an option for her. She was his joy, his need, his everything. And she was in trouble. She didn't deserve to be in the middle of this. She was too good of a person. He had been a fool to let her into his life, no matter how much he had grown to love her. It was selfish. He had too much baggage. The situation they were in proved it. He vowed he'd save her; she had to come through this. Even if it meant giving his life. Worry spread over him, like a heavy sea fog. He kept his legs moving.

He arrived at the open door and stopped. He peered into the gloom. A flash crossed his eyes when he spied Beka tied to a post. A man stood beside her, watching him closely. A lone light bulb showered them with shards of light, leaving the back part of the barn in shadows. He wondered where the other abductor was. An imaginary bullet tore a path through his chest again; he fought the urge to run. His breathing laboured. The rain no longer fell on him as he inched into the barn.

"Come closer," the man called out.

Nate studied the man, then scanned from side to side, but couldn't see the second gunman. He had never been inside Milo's barn. It was run down and laden with debris, yet to be restored. Old bales of hay were strewn haphazardly about. They had been there a long time. He moved forward.

Beka, in clear view, stared at him, her face pasty white with pain. Anger flared. He suppressed it. She rolled her eyes to the side of her head. The second gunman was in the shadows to her right.

"Close enough," the man ordered. "Where's the money?"

Nate stopped. He paused before speaking. "You think I'm stupid enough to walk in here and hand it to you without assurances?"

The man raised his hand, pistol pointed at Nate. "Take a seat." He motioned towards a hay bale.

Nate frowned and stayed on his feet. No advantage to sitting. "Remove the tape from her mouth."

"Sit down." The gunman snarled, raising the pistol higher.

Nate's heart echoed, a drum in his chest. "Take the tape off."

The man stared at him, rage colouring his face, then he shrugged, walked over to Beka, reached down, and ripped the duct tape from her mouth. She let out a whimper but didn't take her eyes from Nate's.

"Now...sit down."

Light illuminated his face. Nate's eyes went wide. "I know you." His mind fought for understanding.

Out of the shadows and into the light, the second gunman approached.

"Hello, Nate."

***

Ty O'Reilly left his truck on the road and crept towards the barn, the weight of the gas can strained his arm. Light emitted from the barn entrance, underscored by the late afternoon gloom. There were no lights on in the cabin. They had to be in the barn.

He slunk to the back of the building, a plan forming. He would force them out, then attack Milo as she watched.

The barn had a small door in back, a window beside it. Likely the door was unlocked. He tried the handle, validating his expectations. Peeking through the small window, he got his bearings. He stepped through the door quietly.

***

Nate stared at the person walking out from the shadows. A woman. She was hideously disfigured; red scars ran from her forehead to her chin. Her lips were deformed, unable to seal with a proper fit. Other scars ran perpendicularly across her cheeks, intersecting with the horizontal cuts. The shock of her appearance was surpassed only by the shock of her identity. She was dead, but her chest rose and fell with each breath.

"You look good, Nate. Money suits you well."

His eyes riveted on the woman.

"Jess...How is this possible?" Nate glanced at Beka, whose gaze switched from Nate to Jess and back again. Her eyes wide with shock. "I don't understand. They told me you were dead."

"Did they now? Who said that? No, I was never dead, but the guy who did this to me most certainly is." She reached up to her face, rubbing her fingertips across her scars with her left hand. A gun hung loosely in her right. "Do you still think I'm pretty, Nate?

Nate's eye's flicked to Beka. Jess stepped towards her.

"You remember Digger?"

Nate's eyes shifted over to Jess's brother, who inched closer to Beka.

"Digger has graciously helped me find you. In fact, I've seen another side to my little brother. He has thoroughly enjoyed our journey, even though you have been very difficult to find. Imagine my surprise when I met little Miss Sunshine here. I have to say, I thought you would mourn for me a bit longer. I was shocked and, of course, disappointed to learn that wasn't the case."

Jess neared Beka and reached for a strand of hair, gently running it through her fingers. "I'm going to have to thank the Calgary cops for keeping the press ignorant about that body bag. Took me a while to understand they'd done that. I never did understand why they didn't declare who was in it. Maybe it was fate. I doubt we'd be able to have this little reunion, had they declared it wasn't me. Little Miss Sunshine here wouldn't even be in the picture, would she, Nate? I'm sure you would have searched for me. Wouldn't you? What do you think, Digger, would he have searched for me?"

Digger ignored the game his sister was playing. "Where's the money, Vickers?"

Nate ignored him; eyes locked on Beka. His head was spinning. "Are you okay?" he asked. She nodded ever so slightly.

"She's fine, Nate," Jess sneered. "Just a broken finger. Imagine... that's all it took for her to sell you out."

Nate watched Beka's eyes fall to the ground.

"I would've expected you to find someone with a little more fortitude."

"Enough," Digger barked.

He put the barrel of his pistol to the side of Beka's head. "The money, Vickers?"

Nate tensed; his eyes bore into Diggers. This wasn't the guy he met. He knew he worshipped his sister, but he would never have expected him to be this ruthless. He had changed. Had Jess molded him to her now twisted world or had Digger snapped when he saw what happened to his sister and veered into her life seeking restitution? If he had only saved her. If only he had stopped her crazy plan. Everything would have turned out differently. All this craziness was his to own.

"Yes, Nate, where is the money...my money?" Jess strode a few steps towards Nate.

"I have a guy ready to bring it to me when I call him. Like I said, do you really think I would be so stupid as to walk in here with the money and get killed for my efforts?" Nate heard the words of bravado escaping his lips, even as his mind was frantically searching for a way out of his predicament.

"What do you mean a guy? Jess hissed, spit escaping through her twisted mouth. "We told you to come alone with the money."

Nate watched as both Jess and Digger scanned the horizon for a threat.

"Now there have to be consequences." Jess spun around, stepping back to Beka. She stuffed her gun in her waistband and pulled a knife from a sheath attached to her belt. "Perhaps you would like all your women to look alike." Jess expected Beka to recoil in horror. Instead, she sat perfectly still and glared at Jess, saying nothing.

"Touch one hair on her head and you'll never see a cent," Nate snarled at her.

Jess stood beside Beka, reached out and took a lock of hair in her hand again.

"Do you mean this one?" She sliced out and severed the hair, holding the lock in her hand.

She turned back to Nate again, slipping the knife back into its sheath. Nate exhaled the trapped air in his lungs.

Jess studied him, her feet slightly apart, hand on her hip. "I always knew you weren't stupid. I would never have expected you capable of this vanishing act. Who helped you, Nate?"

Nate eyed her back. "Money buys friends," he said. "Perhaps I should seek a refund. Apparently, I didn't vanish well enough."

Jess grinned a cold, ghoulish smile.

Nate supposed she knew the effect the scars had on her once pretty face and used it for effect.

"Hard to buy the kind of friends you need in that town, especially under the nose of Antonio Belletti. Oh...forgive me, I forgot to tell you, he'll be joining us shortly. He can't wait to make your acquaintance."

Nate let that sink in, then looked over his shoulder, surveying the entrance, as if he expected Belletti to march through the door.

"You're doing all this for Belletti?" he asked, bewildered.

"Yeah, right." Jess laughed. It was no less hideous than the smile. "Now...about the money. The million is a down payment. I know you've got more than that. I want it all. My operation. You were never supposed to end up with any of it."

Nate's brow furrowed as he listened.

"Oh, you're shocked. Did you really believe in me, Nate? You're such a softy. So, as I said, consider it a down payment. In the meantime, Darling stays with us and if you are quick about it, Digger won't have his way with her."

Nate's fingers balled into a fist.

He needed to buy time. "I don't believe you. It was always going to be fifty-fifty."

"That was before these." She rubbed her scars. "And how much effort Digger and I expended in finding you." She drew near Nate and reached out to caress his face. He pulled back from her touch. "How soon I've been forgotten." She slithered back to Beka. "Perhaps you really should look like me, Darling. Then he won't be able to tell the two of us apart." She pulled her knife from its sheath again.

"I will kill you if you touch her," Nate hissed. Digger moved in and levelled his gun, readying to shoot.

"My, my...haven't you grown a pair? Then you better tell me right now where my fucking money is."

Nate was thinking fast on his feet. He hoped Milo was close.

The rumble of an engine silenced them all. They turned to the door, a beam of headlights, cut through the grey light.

Jess nodded and Digger checked the entrance to confirm who it was, then returned to Jess' side. They heard the engine turn off. A car door opened, then closed with a thud. Don Antonio Belletti stepped through the entrance of the barn, into the dim light. He let his eyes adjust and absorbed the room. Belletti was accustomed to controlling his environment, he didn't rattle easily.

"This isn't quite what I expected," he said, closing the gap between himself and Nate.

"I assume you are Nate Vickers?" He locked eyes with Nate. Nate nodded.

"And you, madam, who might you be?"

"That would make me his partner...past partner."

Belletti studied Jess. He wasn't shocked by her appearance; he had ordered his crew to exact the damage and retrieve his money. "I wondered what happened to you. You really did make a mess of my man."

"Is it you I should thank for keeping my name out of the papers?" Jess asked with an undertone of disgust in her voice.

"That's been added to your bill. It took a lot of political capital to assure that. I knew it would be more difficult to get my money back or exact my revenge on you if you were behind bars." Belletti took in Digger and then Beka. "And who are the other two?" Jess took control. "Doesn't really matter, does it? What does matter is that I have two of my least favourite men here before me." Nate watched as she pointed with her gun in their direction. "The one that stole my money and the one that did this." She stroked the scars on her face again.

"As a point of order," said the don, "it's actually my money."

"Well, that aside..." replied Jess. "We're missing it." Jess and don Belletti simultaneously turned to Nate.

"Or should I say that most of us are missing it." Jess stepped to Beka and placed her pistol at the side of Beka's head. Digger pointed his gun at the don.

"Time's up, Nate," Jess snarled.

CHAPTER THIRTY-EIGHT

TY O'REILLY WASN'T PREPARED FOR the scene playing out in the barn before him. Who were all these people? Normally this would've caused a hasty retreat but seeing Beka tied to a post on the floor caused something inside him to crack. She was still his girl.

He quietly placed the gas can on the floor. The shadows gave him cover. He closed the door, but did not latch it, lest the noise give him away. He was enraged to see his Beka being treated this way. His anger was redirected. Someone was hurting her, and he would save her.

He inched closer, surveying the environment, taking shelter behind a small half wall. He saw Beckett standing there, conversing with the people who had kidnapped Beka. A man was pointing a gun at him. *Good, maybe he'll kill him.* He dropped to the ground and moved forward. No one was paying attention to him.

He now understood Milo's protective anger. He was one with it. Milo would still have to pay for what he did, but that would wait. Right now, he had to rescue Beka. Then she would forgive him, and everything would go back to the way it was, before Nate Beckett. He crept forward, pausing behind a stack of hay bales. He was very aware of the guns in the kidnappers' hands.

Another truck drove down the driveway, moving fast. It came to rest at the opening of the barn, beside Belletti's car. He watched as everyone stood transfixed by this development. The driver's door opened, and Milo stepped out, limping over to the tail gate. He assessed the situation and, opening the tail gate, declared to the group. "I believe you've been waiting for this?" He raised the silver suitcase above the box of the truck.

"Throw it in," the man demanded.

"There are two more of these. Let the girl go," Milo replied calmly. "If not, I am driving out of here."

He watched as a disfigured woman pressed a gun hard into Beka's temple. She let out a shriek.

O'Reilly's world shattered. The kidnapper aimed to kill Beka. He threw caution to the wind and with a roar, rose, charging the woman. All eyes turned to him.

The man swung his pistol towards O'Reilly. The woman stepped back away from Beka, shifting to confront him as well. Milo lurched around the back of the truck, pulling his pistol from his back. He walked three strides into the barn, calmly levelled his pistol at Jess and pulled off a round. The bullet picked her off her feet and slammed her to the ground. The impact dislodged her knife from its sheath. Beka squirmed, fighting at her restraints to no avail.

"Jess," the man screamed and spun on Milo, his face contorted with rage. He levelled his pistol at Milo.

"No," bellowed Nate. He charged at Milo to knock him away. The pistol went off. Nate collapsed to the barn floor, groaning in agony. Beka let out a wail of horror. To O'Reilly, it sounded like a primal scream, drawn deep from within her.

Seeing an opportunity, he scrambled for the knife, and slid behind Beka. "I've got you Beka, he whispered. He began sawing at the rope that bound her to the post. It was a dense line and difficult to cut. He heard the retort of another weapon but didn't look up. He was trying to understand why his fingers were no longer working the knife. Numbly, he looked down. A red stain was forming on his shirt. His eyes flitted to the top of Beka's head. He tried to stroke her hair, but his arm would not lift. Then he fell over, landing hard on his side with a dull thud, his eyes empty and unblinking.

***

Jess rose onto one knee, her left arm useless. Her pain receptors pushed into overdrive; she pushed back. She looked down at O'Reilly's lifeless form, wondering who he was. She glanced at Nate sprawled on the barn floor and made a move towards him. She hoped he wasn't dead. He was the key to the money if it wasn't here. She would kill him later.

Where was the guy with the limp? She searched the barn. He had to be stopped. He was the last one between her and the money, if in fact it was in that truck.

A movement out of the corner of her eye forced her to reassess her situation. The guy with the limp would have to wait. She watched as the don approached the truck, bending down to retrieve the suitcase. Glancing about the barn again, she saw no immediate threats. Determining that Belletti was now her biggest challenge to retrieving the money, he could not be allowed to flee. Jess called Digger's name. Holding her bleeding arm in place, she nodded at him, as he turned in her direction. With a quick nod back at her, he rose from the safety of the hay bale he had chosen for protection. They advanced, bullets flying at the truck.

The don took one in his leg and fell to the ground. He let out a cry of pain and cursed. The case slid from his hands. Jess and her brother slowed, paces matched, and walked towards him, guns levelled. Blood dripped from Jess's left hand.

They heard a crash behind them. The rear door of the barn burst open, Belletti's men scrambled in, weapons drawn, and opened fire at Digger and Jess as they approached the don. As their heads spun around at the noise, bullets whizzed by them, sounding like a hive of bees. A couple thudded into the ground by their feet. Jess dove to the ground, scrabbling to get behind another hay bale, pain in her arm causing her to scream out. Digger finished his roll to safety and whipped his head around at her cry. He clambered to his feet, firing his pistol blindly at the back of the barn. None found their mark. He started running towards her.

"Stay!" she screamed.

More bullets flew, this time fully concentrated on Digger. Jess watched in what appeared to be slow motion as Digger's head exploded in the latest volley, blood splattering her face and arms. His body fell to the ground at her feet, with a loud thud. She roared out in anguish and rose, arm forgotten, her disfigured face contorted by her fury. She fired at the three approaching men. The biker fell, clutching his chest. He was dead before he silently hit the ground. She pointed her gun at Mario, who threw himself to the ground, but not before three more shots missed their target, slamming into the barn walls. Cortez took full advantage. He extended his pistol in two hands and unloaded his clip at Jess. Six shots were fired; three rounds found their mark. She dropped to her knees, clasping her chest with her good arm. Oddly, she felt no pain. She tried to rise, then fell sideways to the floor, her head smacking into the hard dirt, near where Nate lay groaning.

She could feel her life force ebbing away as she stared at Nate. It had all started with him. She thought she saw him move. Blood trickled from the sides of her mouth. She coughed. She watched as his eyes found hers. She smiled at him, this time warmly. He did not smile back. She was trying to understand why when she closed her eyes for the last time.

***

Mario walked to where Jess lay. He placed the gun at her temple and squeezed the trigger. The weapon recoiled, the scent of gunpowder in the air. He knew she was already dead, but it gave him satisfaction. She had been a real problem.

He turned his gun on Nate but paused when he saw don Belletti struggling to his feet. The boy wasn't going anywhere fast. He watched the don hobble over to the silver case, the bullet in his leg slowing him. Mario moved towards him. Grunting from the effort, the don reached down and picked it up. He placed it on the hood of his car and opened it. He closed his eyes. Reaching in, he withdrew a rock and stared at it. He let it drop to his feet. Closing the case, he tossed it into the grass. Then he turned to Mario.

"Clean up this mess. There is nothing for us here. We'll head for the ferry, but first I'd like you to kill that son of a bitch." He pointed at Nate, who was struggling to rise. Mario, and then Cortez, turned back to Nate, who was now on his feet. His face wore the pain he was in. Mario's gun arm began to lift. A cry caused him to shift his gaze.

***

From hay bale to hay bale, he slowly made progress, gun extended in his hand. Milo saw Nate go down, assumed he was dead. Sadness engulfed him.

He slithered to Beka's side. She looked beat up, both mentally and physically. He briefly glanced at O'Reilly and silently thanked him for trying to save his baby girl. He spotted the knife and picked it up, laying his pistol beside Beka. He rose to his knees and began sawing at the rope, trying to finish what O'Reilly had begun. He used all his strength and had a moment of relief when the rope finally broke. He quickly uncoiled the line, releasing Beka, who immediately cried out for Nate.

That's when he saw the men pivot, raising their pistols at them. Pushing Beka to the floor, he fell on top of her. He heard the bullets hit the post where he stood a moment before. Milo rolled over, reached out for his pistol and readied himself to rise and shoot back. He knew he was at a huge disadvantage and that he would probably die. But Beka had to be protected. He made a move to stand. He watched as Frank stepped through the door at the same time and levelled the shotgun at Mario. The retort sounded like a cannon in the barn. Mario fell face first into the dirt.

Cortez spun on Frank, but Milo's pistol placed a well-aimed bullet through his temple. Cortez's body arched sideways and crumpled to the ground.

***

Don Belletti headed for his car, grimacing from the bullet in his leg. His head spun around when he heard the shotgun blast. He saw Mario fall. He pulled his gun from a shoulder holster and levelled his arm to fire at Frank. A violent force slammed into his body, launching his pistol from his hand. His body crumpled, as his injured leg gave out. He struggled to roll over to assess the hit. Elena stood over him, her fists bunched into a ball

"You," he hissed.

Frank ran to her side and levelled the shotgun at Belletti. He had one shell left.

"We had history, you and I, Antonio. You were foolish to come after us. Now all your men are dead, and you will follow them. You should have known I'd protect my blood."

The don stared cold. Frank cocked the shotgun's hammer.

"No..." Frank heard the anguished cry and turned to Nate. Beka was holding him against her right side. They slowly advanced. His shoulder was covered in blood, his left arm hung loosely at his side. His other arm clutched Beka's shoulders.

"Enough, Frank," Nate said quietly, closing the gap.

Milo followed a short distance behind.

***

Nate motioned with his head that he wanted to go to the don. No one moved, least of all Belletti. Beka helped Nate cross the distance to where the don lay, wincing at the effort. Belletti stared only at Nate. Nate let go of Beka's shoulders and Beka stepped back. She grabbed her elbow, steadying her pulsating finger. Milo stepped to her side; a protective hand placed on her back. Frank and Elena also retreated to give him space.

Nate tried to stand straight. "We're done, Belletti. Your money is gone. Make some more. In exchange, I have a gift for you."

The don looked at him, awaiting clarity. "What could you possibly give me that is worth millions?"

Nate walked a few paces to the don and knelt, the effort causing him to flinch from pain. When he was within a few inches of the don's face, he started whispering in his ear. No one could make out what was said. In a couple of minutes, Nate stood and wobbled. Beka strode back to him, steadying him with her body once more. He reached around her shoulders and drew her close.

Don Belletti smirked at Nate. He said nothing further. He rose, not allowing anyone to see the effort it took. He limped to the side of his car and climbed behind the wheel. He locked eyes with Nate for another long moment; Nate stared back at him silently, then Belletti started the engine and drove down the lane.

Nate turned to Frank and nodded his appreciation.

Milo came and stood beside them.

One after the other, they each turned to face the carnage. Nate's shoulder throbbed. He was glad to have Beka's arm around him. He felt lightheaded and wondered how much blood he had lost. He looked down at her face, recognizing the toll she paid from the ordeal. It was harrowing, but they had all survived.

Milo limped a few steps into the barn. His usually well-tied grey ponytail in disarray. Elena stood a few steps away, taking it in. Frank walked to her side and reached for her hand.

"You're amazing," he spoke without looking at her. She squeezed his hand.

Milo gestured to Frank. "Give me a hand getting these two moved," he nodded to the don's men.

Frank frowned but did as he was asked. Soon the two joined the other corpses, inside the barn.

Nate dislodged himself from Beka's arm and stumbled over to the bodies. He stared at Jess' lifeless eyes and disfigured face. Beka watched from a distance. He wondered if he should give her an apology, but the words would not form. Too much damage. He stood for a moment more, then laboured to a knee and closed her eyes.

He looked over at Digger and slowly moved to him. He saw the bulge in his rear pocket and bending down, retrieved a phone. It was his own.

He rose and slowly made his way to Beka and handed it to her. She put her arm around his waist to steady him. This time Nate noticed her flinch.

"You're hurt?"

"Just the broken finger," she whispered. "What did you say to him?"

"Belletti?"

She nodded.

"I told him I was forced to lure him here so his friends in Montreal could take care of him. I told him about Ross Finlay and that he had very little time to escape."

A thin smile crossed her lips.

Nate went silent and watched as Milo walked to the back of the barn and picked up a gas can. Where did that come from? He watched Milo limp about, pouring gasoline on the hay and across the floor splashing ribbons of gas onto the barn posts, as he went. Beka, seeing what he was doing, cried out.

"No, Milo, you can't."

Milo threw the can onto the hay and walked back to her.

"I know what I'm doing, Beka. Move everyone out." He smiled at her and waited. She made a motion and Frank and Elena stepped out of the barn. She assisted Nate to do the same. Milo reached into his pants, pulled out his zippo lighter, struck it, and watched the flame ignite and hold. He walked over to the nearest hay bale, leaned down and ignited the gas. He retreated. Within minutes, the barn was engulfed in flames.

They all stood and watched, saying nothing, lost in their individual thoughts. Then Milo saw blue and red lights flashing in the treetops.

"You need to go. Now. We have but a few minutes."

"Come with us, Milo," Nate said weakly.

"I just got home, and my barn was on fire. I will rebuild. Beka, go to Tillicum. Don't go to our marina. Go." He handed Beka his pistol. "Get rid of this as soon as you can." He gently pushed her forward.

They set off. Nate groaned from the effort, but Beka urged him on, silent as to her own pain. Frank gently pushed on his back as well, encouraging him forward.

Nate glanced over his shoulder and saw a stationary Milo, watching his barn being consumed by the flames. He didn't look back to see his daughter leaving.

Nate, Beka, Frank, and Elena reached the safety of the woods, then stopped to view the blazing barn. Beka had tears rolling down her cheeks. She watched as Steve Quince approached her father. Andrea Maitland was on the phone, presumably calling for the fire brigade out of Sechelt. Nate saw Milo turn and glance over Quince's shoulder in their direction. Beka raised her hand to say goodbye, then with one final sob, turned and led them down the trail. She maintained a slow pace so Nate could keep up. Every footfall was an effort for him.

Nate watched Beka walking in front, her shoulders set in grim determination. He hadn't lost her, but he'd paid for that with blood.

PART THREE

CHAPTER THIRTY-NINE

THEY WEREN'T BEING FOLLOWED. BEKA pressed the group through the forest with light provided by a half moon that shone from time to time through broken clouds. She was glad the rain had passed. They reached a secluded area and decided to rest as Nate was struggling with his injury. Beka assisted Nate to sit on a fallen log. She found a spot beside him and turned to see how he was doing. Even in the poor light, it was obvious he was doing poorly. She pursed her lips and shook her head.

Frank wandered over. "Mind if I have a look at the injury?" he asked.

Beka searched Frank's face, then turned to Nate. "You okay if we have a look?"

"Yeah," he heaved and closed his eyes. When he opened them again, he saw Frank's face before him, a frown creasing his brow. Beka took Nate's phone from her pocket and turned it on. Not much battery left. She turned on the light, directing it at Nate's shirt.

Nate attempted a smile, as Frank pulled the blood-soaked shirt away gently. His smile morphed into a long groan.

Frank studied the wound, then pulled Nate forward, lifting the shirt off his back. "It looks like the bullet went right through. That's good, but you're still losing blood. No wonder you're so weak."

Nate nodded. There was nothing to say.

Beka rose and with phone in hand, walked over to Elena. "I need your help." She lifted her hand and adjusted the light for Elena to see. Her baby finger protruded from the rest of her fingers. "Can you set my finger?" With raised eyebrows, Elena slowly nodded her acceptance.

"Do it quickly."

Elena flinched as Beka cried out in pain when the tiny broken bones shifted into place.

Nate heard her cry and struggled to stand. Frank held him down.

"It's okay, Nate," Beka assured him through gritted teeth. Nate's body relaxed back into its own agony.

Beka motioned to Elena, and they rose in tandem, wandering over to a small bog. An intense throbbing replaced the painful shock of having her finger set. She pushed the feeling to the back of her mind.

After receiving instructions, Elena got onto her knees and with bare hands started to sweep away leaves. Beka stood above with Nate's cell phone emitting light, so Elena could see. Beneath them, wet sphagnum moss lay on top of a rotting log. She delicately tore at pieces that would be of a suitable size and laid them by Beka's feet.

Frank walked over to see what was going on. "What are you two doing?"

Elena stood up, ignoring the question. "Frank, we need to find a couple of small willowy branches or vines nearby and a couple of firm sticks. I need to make a splint for her finger. Will you come with me?"

Frank nodded, reached for the phone offered by Beka and they wandered to the edge of the path, foraging for what they needed.

Beka picked up the moss pieces with her good hand and wandered back to Nate in the moonlight. "Sphagnum moss," she said, laying the moss beside him. He looked dumbfounded but asked nothing. "It will act as a bandage and has some healing properties. We can't clean the wound here, but it should help you in the short term."

Frank and Elena returned. "Will this work?"

Beka took some small aspen branches from Frank along with two twigs wide enough to act as the splint. She studied them in the phone's light. "I think they will."

Elena began stripping the leaves from the branch, snapping them to the size she needed. Holding out her hand Beka watched as Elena used the willowy branches to tie the splint in place. Beka winced with every movement needed.

"Hopefully, this will hold." Elena nodded at Beka.

"It will have to do. Can you help me with Nate now?"

Frank directed the light onto Nate. Elena pulled the shirt from Nate's body as thoughtfully as she could. He moaned loudly when dried blood tore at the wound. His body began to shake. Beka leaned in and packed the wet moss onto the wound with her good hand, grimacing as Nate whimpered. She asked Elena to hold the moss in place and then asked Frank to soak Nate's shirt in water from the bog. He handed the phone to Elena and wandered away.

Searching Nate's face, Beka said, "It'll be cold, but it will keep the moss moist."

He nodded. She wasn't thrilled to be using his blood-soaked shirt again, but she had no choice. She then pulled her shirt over her head, gasping when she bumped her finger. She asked Elena to tear the bottom of it apart, and then instructed her how to tie the fabric around Nate's shoulder to hold the moss in place.

Frank returned with Nate's shirt and looked away. "Phone's dead". He handed it back to her, his eyes diverted.

Beka nodded, slipping the phone into her rear pocket. She put what was left of her shirt back on. "It's just a bra, Frank. I think we're well past subtleties."

Frank turned back again, embarrassed.

Satisfied that she could do nothing more for Nate for the moment, she sat down beside him again. Her finger pulsated. She held her arm steady willing the ache to subside.

Frank coughed to get her attention. Beka glanced up at him as he stood before her. "That cop will have everyone out looking for us. I've been thinking about it, and I think Elena and I should leave you at the road and head in an opposite direction. As couples it may be easier to avoid them."

"It'll be very hard for you to get off this peninsula," said Beka after a moment's thought. "With just one road in and out, you can be sure they'll lock it down."

"I don't want to separate, but the four of us will attract way too much attention. We need to break up. We're resourceful. We'll find our way out of here. But I'm worried about Nate."

"I can clean the wound when we get to the First Aid kit on the boat. Then he will need rest. Unless the wound gets infected, he should be okay."

"You're a very resourceful woman." Elena commented.

"Learned a few things during my time in Vancouver. I received some medical training there and you don't live in a small place like Gibsons without learning some things about surviving in the woods. Long story, best left for later."

Frank nodded. "Even if we did stay together, we can't go to the boat. They'll be all over it."

"They'd have to find it."

"What?"

"I'm not sure, but when my dad said to go to Tillicum, I'm pretty sure he meant the marina. Somehow, I think he got Nate's boat there."

"What if you're wrong?"

Nate raised a hand, then let it flop to his side. Three sets of eyes turned to him. "Milo asked Archie to move it," he gasped." I think he'll come through."

They all stared at him.

"What?" said Frank.

Nate bobbed his head.

"My dad isn't sending us there for nothing." Beka smiled at Nate, then pivoted back to Frank and Elena. "Come with us. We'll have a better chance to escape together, on the boat."

Frank hesitated, even as Elena beseeched him with her eyes.

"There are a lot of islands out there, Frank. It's very hard to patrol. You know I'm right."

Elena stood, walked over to Frank, and took his hand. "Her thinking is sound, Frank, we need to stick together."

Frank was about to argue the point further, when Nate lost his strength and fell sideways to the ground.

"We can't stay here. He's getting weaker." Beka jumped to his side. "We need to keep him moving. We have nearly nine more kilometres to cover to get to that marina. I don't know about you guys, but I want to keep the cover of darkness. Frank? You on board? I'm going to need your muscle to help with Nate."

Frank's argument vanished over his concern for Nate. "We'll stay."

"Right then, let's go." Beka helped Nate to sit up, whispering into his ear. He raised his head and smiled a weak smile. With assistance, he slowly stood, and they started down the path. "Promise?" he uttered through gritted teeth.

Beka grinned in the dark. The moon disappeared behind another cloud.

Soon they left the forest in favour of the highway. They were getting closer.

"Almost there." Beka encouraged Nate.

Each time they saw lights coming down the highway, they would retreat to the woods until the car passed, aware of the effort it took from Nate. Frank and Elena would assist him back to the highway.

"Come on, baby, just a little further," Beka whispered into his ear when she saw him stumble on one occasion. Concern smothered her, yet she kept urging him on. They were not yet safe.

At one point, she noticed they were near the shore and, excusing herself, walked over to a cliff to toss Milo's pistol as far into the sea as she could. She returned to the rest of the group and motioned for them to continue. She helped Nate back to his feet as he sat on a rock, waiting for her. Her worry for him grew when she spotted beads of perspiration covering his brow, despite the coolness of the morning. She pulled his arm around her shoulders, and they hobbled on.

They crested what she believed was the last hill when leaning in, she kissed his cheek." Not much more Nate. You're amazing." She felt his arm flex against her neck in response.

They arrived at the entrance to the marina as dawn was sending its first glimpse of what the day would hold. Cumulous clouds floated in the sky; rays of morning sunshine were colouring them in seams of peach. A heavy layer of sea fog covered the peninsula.

It had taken them far longer than she hoped to get to the marina. They were exhausted. Elena was limping slightly, each step seemingly very tentative. Beka suspected she'd developed blisters on the long trek through the forest.

Beka scanned the docks and smiled. There she sat. *Serendipity* was moored beside the marina's only boat house. It was early morning. No one was about. That suited her, just fine.

She put her finger to her lips and motioned for them to follow her. She slid her arm through Nates' good one, led him down the dock, and stepped aboard. Frank and Elena waited. She helped Nate to a seat along the cabin wall. He nodded his gratefulness for being back on his boat, then closed his eyes. Beka motioned for Elena to take the opposite seat, which she gratefully did. She looked dead on her feet. They couldn't rest yet. They were still at risk.

Beka moved to the hatch door and pushed it open, descending the stairs to the cabin below. She came back a moment later, key in hand, and fired up the inboard engine. The noise was magnified by the quietness of the morning.

Frank, meanwhile, stored his shotgun under the seat of the dingy, resting at the stern of *Serendipity*. He then climbed aboard and joined Elena.

"Not sure why you brought that," Beka said to Frank. "I hope no one saw it."

"I don't think so. I was keeping an eye out. You're right though, I should have discarded it at the same time you got rid of yours. I'll get rid of it once we're at sea."

Beka nodded. She examined the sky and frowned at the low ceiling of cloud that was now forming. So beautiful a short time ago. It signalled a wet day. She jumped from the stern onto the dock and quickly freed the bow and spring lines with her good hand, then jumped back on board, releasing the stern line at the same time. Her hand ached, reminding her that she too needed rest. They drifted from the dock as the current took hold. Settling in behind the wheel, she engaged the inboard engine and pulled away from the dock. She glanced at Nate, who had slumped against the bulkhead and appeared to be asleep. She would like nothing more than to be curled up against him, but she knew she had to get them into the safety of the islands. As they were exiting the marina, she let the dingy out. She glanced again at Nate and asked Elena to feel his forehead. She confirmed the worst; he was developing a fever.

They came around a point of land. "Frank, come and take the wheel please. We're in the Sechelt inlet and we want to take a straight line until we reach Earl's Cove." She pointed out the direction she wanted him to go. "Keep us in the center of the channel."

Frank rose and stepped to the helm, too tired to question her.

Beka went below, grabbed up a blanket for Nate, and wandered to the galley desk. She pulled out a chart and studied their course. Then consulted the tidal charts. Satisfied, she reached into an overhead locker and pulled out the First Aid kit. She opened it to make sure it had what she needed and turned back to the galley stairs, when she startled at the sound of an unknown voice.

"And where might we be going, miss?"

Beka spun around, the First Aid kit and blanket slipping from her hands, as she stared into the barrel of a Glock 9mm handgun. Holding onto the gun was an older man. Though he was dressed impeccably, his hair was unkempt, as if he had just woken up.

"You?" Beka snarled.

He smiled a false smile at her. "Yes, me. Shall we go up top?"

Beka said nothing and reached for the kit.

"Uh...leave it." Beka turned towards the man, who took a step back. "I don't want to hurt you," he said.

"What's going on, Beka?" Elena called down.

"Be right there."

Ross Finlay frowned. "Who's up there?"

Beka hesitated. She looked at the pistol in his hand. "There are four of us. Nate's hurt. I need to tend to him; I'm taking this kit up to do just that."

"What do you mean, he's hurt?"

"He's been shot."

Finlay smirked. "I'll see for myself. Now leave it there and let's go."

Beka glared at him, her eyes flicking between his face and the gun. "No, I'm going to tend to him...now. If you don't like that, shoot me. I have had a really bad day, and that might be a fitting end."

Finlay studied her as she reached for the kit. "Do you have any weapons on board?"

Beka wished she hadn't thrown Milo's pistol away. She thought about Frank's shotgun and inwardly cursed that it was now in the dingy. "No."

Finlay sought the truth in her eyes. She spun on her heel and stepped up the stairs. "We have company."

Frank was still behind the wheel when Beka stepped aside, and Ross Finlay came into view. Finlay pointed the gun at Frank and stayed on the top stair at the entrance. Beka ignored him and walked over to Nate. She motioned to Elena who joined her. They removed Nate's tourniquet, then removed the sphagnum dressing.

Finlay observed the scene. "What happened?"

"He was shot," Beka said, "by some of your friends."

"And my friends?"

Beka turned her head and stared him down. It'd be all over the news soon anyway. "They're dead."

Finlay absorbed the news. His eyes turned to Frank. "I take it, then, that they did not get the money?"

Beka ignored him, focusing on Nate. A light misty rain began to fall.

"You," Finlay said, gesturing to Elena.

Elena flashed him a look of contempt, her brows furrowed and her soft lips tightening in what almost looked like the beginnings of a snarl. "My name is Elena. Who are you, and what's with the gun?"

Finlay ignored the question. "Pull that dingy in, Elena, won't you please?"

Beka stopped her bandaging to address Finlay. "What are you doing?"

"There are too many people on this boat. These two are getting off."

"No, they're not." Beka barked.

Finlay moved with lightning speed onto the deck, grabbed Elena by the hair, and pulled her to him. She let out a squeal. Frank roared, then charged. The gun swivelled, levelled directly at him. Frank came up short.

"Pull that fucking dingy in," Finlay demanded, "or she dies."

"Cut the engine." Beka ordered.

Frank glared at Finlay and his gun, then walked back to the helm and did as Beka commanded. They had gone but a couple of kilometres down the inlet.

"Pull it in," Finlay directed again.

Frank reached for the line and pulled the dingy in. He quickly tied it off on a stern cleat, all the while glaring at Finlay.

"Consider yourselves lucky. I'm not usually so generous. Now get in." Frank and Elena hesitated. His gun swung to Beka. "Now."

Frank and Elena slowly climbed into the dingy.

Beka peered at Nate; he was still asleep. It told her everything she needed to know about how badly he was faring. Treating him should be the priority, but now they had yet another set of problems to deal with. She feared they were done. No one aboard had energy left to deal with this.

Finlay walked to the helm; his gun still pointed at Beka. He reached down and released the dingy line from its cleat. He threw the line overboard. Once the dingy was free of the boat, he put the engine in gear and *Serendipity* moved down the channel. The rain intensified. Beka stared at Frank and Elena as they pulled away, drizzle blurring her view.

Frank pulled his shotgun to his shoulder. Seeing his move, Beka ducked, shielding Nate.

Finlay turned; saw the shotgun. He dropped to a knee and aimed at Frank, pulling the trigger on his Glock. Frank discharged the last shell in his shotgun at the same time. Beka heard Elena scream and watched as Frank's body stumbled back and tumbled out of the dingy, shotgun still in his grip. Elena screamed again as Frank's body rose to the surface. She grabbed a dingy oar and started paddling to Frank for all she was worth.

Finlay checked his body to make sure he hadn't been shot. Frank hadn't had time to aim properly. His shell had fallen harmlessly into the water. He reached for the controls and gunned the motor, increasing the speed to pull away from the dingy and Elena's frantic effort.

"You have to go back for him," Beka hissed.

"No, I don't," said Finlay. "He brought it on himself."

"So, you're just going to let him die?"

"Yes, I am... now, where were we? Oh yes...you tend to Mr. Vickers while I get us further along. Then I want you to wake him. He will need to make a small e-transfer for me. Well, maybe not that small. Do you think you can make that happen?"

"We have to go back for them!" Beka screamed at him.

"No, we don't. He shouldn't have shot at me. And you... you're lucky I don't shoot you for lying to me. You knew there was a gun in that dingy. His death is on you. Now, tend to Mr. Vickers — or do I need to send your body to the depths as well?"

Beka scowled at him, then gazed at Nate. Guilt overwhelmed her. After taking another desperate look at the dingy fading in the distance, a flood of hatred coursed through her. She would feed on it.

"You'd best work on him a little harder, dear. You are quite useless to me if he dies." Finlay waved his gun at Nate.

With one last look at the dingy, she clenched her teeth, and turned to Nate. She was grateful the bimini was keeping the rain off him. She cleaned the wound and applied a suitable dressing and bandage to both the entry and exit wound. At one point Nate groaned, opened his eyes and managed a faint smile. His body shivered.

"I need to get him a blanket from below."

"No."

"He lost too much blood. He has a fever, and he needs to rest. If you want him to do anything, he needs to sleep. He can't do that like this." She stood and started for the stairs.

Finlay reached down and hit the cruise button and moved away from the wheelhouse and followed her. "If I see you reach for anything other than a blanket, I'll shoot you."

Beka stopped, glancing over her shoulder at him. "I get it." Stepping into the galley, she retrieved the throw blanket from the floor. She followed Finlay, who backstepped up the ladder, his pistol never wavering from her.

"Could you go back to the helm please. I need to look after Nate."

"I agree." Finlay backed up until he was behind the wheel and manually engaged the motor again. "You have about a half hour by my calculation," he said referencing the chart plotter beside the helm. "We should be near, what is this...Egmont. I assume we'll have coverage there. You will wake him then."

"There's no service there, and just so you know, we can't get through the narrows until there is a slack tide, or we'll capsize. That is in about an hour. The first service we'll find after that is in Saltery Bay."

Finlay frowned. "If you are stalling — "

"You may have the gun, but if you want to live and get what you want, you'll listen to me."

Finlay looked at the chart again. He lifted his eyes, locking on hers. He throttled down *Serendipity*.

CHAPTER FORTY

MILO WATCHED AS THE FLAMES engulfed his barn. By the time the volunteer firefighters arrived from Sechelt, the decision was made to let the building burn. They concentrated efforts on preventing rogue embers from igniting the cabin. They deemed the forest too wet to be a risk, but posted a man to observe, nonetheless.

Milo said little, except to answer Quince's initial questions about what had happened. "I have no idea...I arrived to see my barn burning." When pressed for more answers, Milo went silent, feigning shock.

Quince made the decision to take him downtown. Andrea Maitland stayed behind, declaring it a crime scene. Milo remained silent on the drive to the police station, going over his story again and again. He would have to be sharp to steer them all clear of criminal charges. He hoped the others had escaped without issue.

Quince placed Milo in a holding room and left him with a cup of coffee. Milo wondered what Quince's game was as the hours passed. He was just standing up to stretch when Quince opened the door and entered with another constable Milo had never seen before.

"You go have a nap, Steve?" Milo fabricated annoyance in his voice.

Quince gave him a rueful smile.

Introductions were made, and Quince motioned Milo back to the seat taking his on the other side of the table. He dropped a pad of paper, followed by a pen on the table. The unknown constable stood by the door, reflecting no emotion.

Milo sat down on the indicated chair. Quince pressed a button on an attached recording device, announced who was in the room and the date and time. Milo felt the gravity of his situation set in.

"Where is Nate, Milo?" Quince started.

Milo addressed him casually. "I haven't seen him since yesterday."

"All right, where did you take him?"

"I dropped him at the Gibsons Garden Hotel. He said he was meeting someone there."

Quince rubbed the back of his neck. "Who?"

"He didn't say. I didn't ask. He wasn't in the mood to talk."

"You saw me after him, Milo. Yet, you swept in, threw open a door, and sped away. That makes you an accomplice to whatever is going on with Nate. Are you aware of that?"

Milo huffed. "Actually Steve, I didn't see you. I saw Nate running like a maniac and a figure, apparently you, chasing him down. I like Nate. I thought I was helping him."

Quince's expression said he wasn't buying it. "You've got to be kidding. You're telling me you couldn't see my uniform?"

Milo locked eyes. "No, I'm not kidding. My eyes are about as good for distance as my leg is for running. Did I break a law picking him up?"

Quince's mobile buzzed indicating an incoming call. He snatched up the phone, verified the caller, then barked into the line. "Talk to me." He listened for a few minutes, then said sternly.

"Thank you. Keep digging. Did you get the APB's out for Sebastian and Beckett?"

Milo couldn't hear the answer but assumed they had been issued.

Quince dropped the phone back to the table and said nothing for a few minutes. Then he addressed Milo squarely. "Seems we have a dead body in that fire, Milo."

Milo acted as shocked as he could. "What?"

"I said, there is a dead body in the rubble of your barn."

"Who?" Milo demanded. "Why would somebody be dead in my barn? Is that why it was on fire? Good God." Milo placed his head in his hands.

"That still has to be determined." Quince rubbed his face, then changed his tactic. "Where's Beka, Milo?"

Milo hesitated. "Beka?" His eyes went wide. "Do you think Beka is the body? Oh, Lord. I need to get out of here, Steve."

"You're not going anywhere right now. We have no evidence to suggest it's Beka. Forensics will tell that story. And that takes time." Quince hesitated watching Milo shake his head from side to side. "The problem we have here is that we now have a dead body in a fire at your place and a whole lot of missing people, including Beka. You need to tell me what's going on. It's the only way I can soften what's coming at you. You need to cooperate, and you need to do it now."

"I told you, I arrived shortly before you. I know nothing about this. God, Steve...Beka? You need to let me go. I need to find her. It's the only way I'll know it's not her."

Quince's phone buzzed again. His brow furrowed in annoyance. He answered it, listening for a few minutes, then said. "Get the Coast Guard on it." He hung up again.

"Seems Nate and his boat are both missing. You know anything about that?"

"No. Maybe he's out sailing with the boys?"

"Milo, what are you doing? Nate Beckett set you up. There are a lot of very serious people here, all wanting a piece of Nate Vickers, a.k.a. Beckett." Quince was studying Milo's face, searching for signs of deception. "You're sitting in an interrogation room, Beckett and Beka are missing, and you really don't know anything about that? Why is that? We discover a dead body in your burned-out barn, and you know nothing about that either. Come on."

Quince's phone rang again. He snapped at the caller; his frustration evident. "What?" He listened, then laid the phone on the table slowly.

"Correction...dead bodies in your burned-out barn. We've also come across a couple of vehicles nearby that we've seen before."

Milo watched Quince's mind churn. He stared at Milo, letting silence pass, before continuing. "But you knew that, didn't you, Milo? I think you may have been there for the whole thing. If that is so, you didn't do this on your own."

Quince stood and made for the door. "I'll find them, then I'll get to the bottom of all this and if you are involved, Milo, it won't go well for you. If you have something you need to tell me, do it now."

Milo slumped in the chair. "All I'm hearing are assumptions and accusations, Steve." Milo started to wring his hands. "I am tired, I am pissed that someone burned my barn to the ground, and I want to find my daughter. Will you let me find Beka?"

Quince shook his head. "Not right now, Milo."

Milo allowed his shoulders to sag, "I guess I need a lawyer, then. I am not staying here if she's in danger."

Quince nodded, then turned to the Constable, standing by the interrogation room door. "Make him comfortable. It's going to be a long night."

"Now, Steve."

"I heard you, Milo. You'll get your lawyer."

He looked at his watch, opened the door and turned to analyze Milo. "Funny, most people would've reacted differently, when learning multiple people died in a fire on their property."

Milo hesitated before answering. "I'm only worried about one person, Steve. You should know that about me by now. I don't know what happened on my property or who all those dead people are. That's your job to figure out. Milo closed his eyes.

Quince remained at the door, observing Milo a few minutes longer, then, sighing, closed the door behind him.

CHAPTER FORTY-ONE

SERENDIPITY APPROACHED SKOOKUMCHUK NARROWS. The current was lessening, but still too strong for Beka to navigate safely. She could see the whirlpools forming as the outgoing tide met the incoming. This was one of the most dangerous narrows in the world to navigate, especially in a sailboat. Beka knew this firsthand.

Finlay had moved to the bench and was eyeing Nate. A groan escaped his lips, followed by an incoherent murmur.

"He doesn't look so good. I hope for your sake you patched him up well enough."

Beka was now behind the wheel of *Serendipity,* her eyes cast between Nate and the narrows. Every time he made a noise, she worried more.

Finlay's gun remained levelled at her, and she could tell the constant effort of pointing was straining his forearm. "You're going too slow," he said.

"It's too dangerous to run the narrows. We need to wait for the slack tide."

"We're not going to wait here for the authorities to catch up with us. Now get going." Finlay directed with his gun.

Beka bore her eyes into Finlay's. "I told you, it's too dangerous. What good is Nate's money if you're dead?"

Finlay shifted position, pressing the barrel of his Glock to Nate's temple. Nate groaned in response, his eyes flicking open momentarily. "It's not his money. Now go."

Beka, shook her head. "You're out of your mind. Do you know anything about these narrows?"

Finlay glared. "Last chance."

Beka shook her head, in frustration. "I can't do this alone. You have no idea what these narrows can do to a boat, especially a sailboat with an engine that's not strong enough to power through it. Slack tide is in a half hour. We have a chance then and it will still be crazy. Look at those rapids ahead of us."

Finlay's eyes followed where she was pointing.

"Those cross the entire narrows. I get you think the police finding us is a problem, but that pales in comparison. We'll capsize and likely drown if we go now."

He looked at his watch and slammed his hand on the seat in anger. "You have fifteen minutes. Not a minute longer."

Nate's eyes fluttered open, his gaze holding on Beka.

She reversed *Serendipity* to adjust for the current pulling them into the narrows. She checked the plotter, analyzing the best method to traverse the rapids. If they went now, they'd lose control. They might have a chance in fifteen minutes. It'd be close and one hell of a ride. Beka adjusted the reverse throttle again holding their position. From time to time, she throttled up, to avoid the boat turning to a starboard beam.

Finlay studied her as she maneuvered the boat in the current, then glanced at Nate. "I don't know what it is you see in this loser."

She saw Nate had closed his eyes again. Then she looked at Finlay. She felt her lips curl in disgust. He waited, expecting a response. A sneer warped his features.

"Goodness," She quietly said.

"What goodness? He's a crook." He laughed, glancing at his watch. "Six minutes."

Beka glanced to the shore. Several people lined the route. They came down to see the rapids at their finest, largely thought to be some of the ocean's biggest in the world. Some of the waves crested at about two metres, although the waters were settling down with the rise of the reverse tide. Rare to see a sailboat coming through these narrows. The locals knew they were in for a show.

"Time's up. Let's go. No more waiting."

She shot Finlay a look. "Since you aren't being reasonable, I'm adding some power to this motor. I'm putting up our main sail to allow the wind to push us from the rear."

"No, you're not."

"You think you know how to get us through here? You come here and sail this boat. I would rather die in the arms of the man beside you. Otherwise, we can wait for the slack tide which is still fifteen to twenty minutes away."

Finlay weighed his options and relented. "What do you have to do?"

"I need to bring her into the wind, then bring the main sail up. We'll turn into the rapids, and I will hit full power on the engine. You will have to use that boat hook to push any large logs away from us as we move through the narrows." She pointed to a hook attached to the port side of the cabin wall.

Finlay noted various pieces of wood going by them on the fast, moving current. He then looked at the pole she was referencing.

"You sail it. I'm sitting right here."

"I told you, I can't do this alone. You want a deadhead to puncture our hull as we clear these eddies? Sure, let's go through all this, so we can sink to the bottom. I don't know if you remember, but we don't even have a dingy to escape in."

Finlay considered the facts. "I will kill you if you try anything stupid. Now get on with it. We're going now."

Beka drew in a full steadying breath. She felt her gut tighten. She had never tried to push against an intense tide and didn't know what to expect. She hoped the sail strategy would give them enough power to get through the rapids in one piece. She threw the wheel and turned *Serendipity* into a head wind. She released the mainsail cleat, hauled the sail up, and winched it into place. She felt her splint release from the exertion but ignored it and the jolt of pain she suffered. She pushed the throttle into gear turning in the direction of the current. The sail luffed for a moment, increasing the noise around her.

She yelled at Finlay, "Grab the pole, get up to the bow, and push away the deadfall. Hurry, there is a deadhead straight ahead." She was vaguely aware that several of the locals on shore were pointing in her direction, as they jumped to their feet.

Finlay stood, studying her for a long moment. The log slammed into the side of the boat, rocking it. Finlay staggered.

"Come on Finlay," she screamed. "We got lucky with that one."

He watched as she throttled the inboard engine up and pointed the bow of *Serendipity* in the direction, she determined offered their best chance. Finlay saw another log heading their way and pointed.

"Go," she hollered.

He put his gun into his waistband, reached for the boat hook, extending it out as far as it would go. He made his way up to the bow, his legs buckling beneath him from the pitching of the boat. He grabbed hold of the railing. Glancing back, he nodded at her, as if they were old friends and out for a friendly sail.

Beka gunned the engine to its maximum RPM and winched the main sail to an eighty-degree angle. Her finger screamed at the strain. She could feel the power as the sail added necessary thrust. The current had them, propelling them forward. She threw the wheel to her starboard side, hoping to angle *Serendipity* to a quieter eddy, but the sea would have no part of it. The water pushed them into the middle of the narrows, *Serendipity* bouncing over the rapids like a rocking horse. The pain from her finger coursed through Beka with every jolt. Finlay was having difficulty keeping his feet. He was hanging onto the bow rail with all his strength.

A sudden pitch of the boat brought her back to full attention, Finlay, and even Nate forgotten for the moment. Her sole concentration focused on the strong riptide and eddies ahead, that could force them onto the rocks. *Serendipity* shuddered. Beka could see a couple of yachts, on the other side of the waterway, waiting for the tide to go slack. She wondered what they must be thinking, watching her hit the force of the current. Her eyes swivelled to Nate, who was now fully awake, watching her intently through exhausted eyes. She could feel his torment.

She shifted her view to Finlay. He was clutching the bow rail as if it were a lifeline. The boat hook was lodged between his fingers and the rail. She saw a partially submerged tree coming at them and was about to shout at him, when he used the extended pole to push the tree away. The pole caught in the tree's limbs, and as the tree bumped the side of the boat harmlessly, he lost control of the hook. She heard him curse as he grabbed hold of the bow rail again, lowering his centre of gravity to gain stability as they hurled forward.

Beka spotted a large eddy, directly in front of them. She released the mainsail a fraction and watched the sail open further. She was already at full power and the sail trimming was all she had left to allow her control. Her arm screamed as she pulled on the winch. No use. She didn't have the strength. She let go. Her head jerked up as Nate stumbled to her side. The violence assaulting his boat had provided a rush of adrenaline. Using his good arm, he pulled on the winch with all his might. She felt it move a couple of teeth forward. Glancing at him, she saw the anguish the effort caused.

Beka used both hands to master the wheel, holding the rudder where she wanted it. It was enough. *Serendipity* slid to the edge of the eddy and catapulted by, towards a smaller eddy beyond it. They repeated the maneuver, this time with Nate managing the winch and mainsail line. Beka glanced again at Nate. He was white as a ghost, but she recognized the determination in his face.

There were several more eddies ahead of them, but they would make it. The boat oscillated violently, but they were nearing the end of the narrows. The waiting yachts were near shore, their crews standing at their rails, watching. Some clapped, to show their appreciation for an amazing display of sailing ability, some shook their heads in dismay. She ignored them as they slipped by.

Within minutes, the rocking subsided and Nate, trusting her, slipped back onto a bench seat. *Serendipity* was hers to captain. She released the winch, allowing the mainsail to swing back into its optimal position, the rear wind keeping it full. She eased back the throttle. It would be enough to pull them through the last of the rapids.

She glanced to the bow; Finlay's arms released their tension. He turned, pulled the gun from his waistband, and headed for the cockpit. She had no doubt that her time to come up with a plan, to save them, was waning. If she didn't come up with something soon, a bullet in the head awaited them.

He was halfway back and looking at where his feet were going when she threw the wheel hard to port. The boat heaved, he stumbled to the gunnel cable, reaching for it to prevent a fall. Gaining partial control, he swivelled his body to aim his gun at her. She released the mainsail winch and heard the whiz of the line as the wind took hold. The boom swung hard. Finlay let out a cry, raising his arms to protect himself. The boom hit him squarely across his forearms, catapulting the gun from his hand before it carried him over the gunwale and into the frothy sea below.

Beka watched his body float past the stern, arms flailing to try and stay afloat. He would have little time to survive in the cold waters of the Salish Sea, but she made no attempt to save him. Besides, she no longer could, she rationalized, as *Serendipity* didn't have a dingy or a boat hook.

She watched him struggling until they were well down the waterway. She pitied the boat owner who was now headed his way to save him. They had no idea what they were getting into, but that was not her concern. She was sure they'd radio in a distress call that would attract the attention of the Coast Guard. They needed to be long gone before it arrived.

Beka regained control of the mainsail. She let the jib out and trimmed it perfectly, maximizing her speed. She left the engine at full throttle to increase their power as well. She had to reach the islands as quickly as they could. She put *Serendipity* on auto pilot after setting her course and walked over and sat down beside Nate, who was huddled under his blanket again watching her. She felt his forehead. Still warm, but no worse at least. She was hopeful that he would recover.

"That was a hell of a way to treat our guest," he said.

"Maybe so, but I am really tired of men telling me what to do."

"I'll remember that."

She laughed and took his hand. The image of Frank catapulting out of the dingy formulated in her mind. She would have to tell Nate. But not right now. He wouldn't be able to take it. She closed her eyes.

Nate squeezed her hand. After a moment, she opened her eyes and squeezed his hand back gently.

"Let's talk about where we're going."

CHAPTER FORTY-TWO

IT HAD BEEN TWO WEEKS since the fire and, despite Steve Quince's doubts, Milo was being released. The arson team and the investigative team that the Sechelt detachment sent in determined it a crime syndicate fight and believed Milo was an unwitting bystander. At least that was the official report. Quince had his doubts, but decided he had no appetite to fight his superior's decision. Nor did he really want to bring down a good man over what was obviously a crime syndicate problem. Perhaps it was time to give up police work? Nate, Beka, Frank, and Elena were now wanted as "persons of interest" in the case, but Quince thought that finding them was a long shot. Mr. Beckett was skilled at avoiding the law.

He decided to drive Milo home, hoping he could get their relationship back on track. But Milo rode in silence, ignoring Quince's attempts at conversation. Quince pulled up in front of the marina store.

"Going to be tough to run this store without her, Milo?"

Milo nodded. "It will. I wish I knew where she was. Maybe she'll come back soon."

Quince wasn't convinced by Milo's assertion. "That would probably be a bad idea."

Milo nodded again.

"There's nothing says you can't go away for a visit, though. I promise not to ask where." He smiled at Milo. "What are you going to do with yourself?"

"Gotta work on rebuilding the barn now that the site is released. Care to help?"

Steve Quince laughed. "No, I don't think so. You and I know it will take you years to get it done. Besides, I think it's time for me to move on. I'm thinking of leaving Gibsons, maybe the Force, in fact."

Quince frowned at Milo's lack of response. He changed direction. "I hope your insurance claim comes through."

"Not looking good, I'm afraid. Something about insurance companies not liking arson claims."

"Sorry to hear that."

Their conversation ended. Quince felt a sadness engulf him, as he understood there would always be a chasm between them now. He watched Milo leave the car and head for the store's door.

Quince opened his door and got out. "You take care, Milo."

Milo stopped and turned back to Quince. He thought for a moment. "Things aren't always as they seem, Steve."

"So it would appear. So it would appear." He paused. "That might be the most honest thing you've said since the night of the fire." He laughed.

Quince watched Milo smile and walk into his store.

***

Milo closed the door, turned to the window, and watched Quince's cruiser head down the road. He gazed around the store. It had lost some of its appeal without Beka being there. He hoped that would change. He walked back outside and raised his face to the sun. After spending two weeks in custody, he appreciated the warmth of the sun's rays.

He heard laughter coming from the docks. He glanced to his right and saw a group of three boys clambering onto a catamaran. Milo stepped forward to watch. A smiling Archie looked up, with a grin on his face and waved to Milo. Milo laughed and waved back. He was glad that Ben's boys would still be on the docks. It gave life to the marina. He rotated and started for the store. He noticed the mail truck pulling into the parking lot and waited.

"Good morning, Milo. Glad to see you back. Sorry to hear about your place."

Milo shrugged. "Good morning, Mike. Thanks. I appreciate that. Got some mail for me?"

"Always."

Milo accepted the package and entered the store. The post office had been holding his mail. He rifled through bills and miscellaneous advertising flyers and came to an envelope written in familiar handwriting. He checked the stamp; his heart skipped a beat. He tore open the envelope and pulled out a bank draft. A note fell to the floor. The draft was for five hundred thousand dollars, drawn on a Canadian Bank, payable in his name. He stooped to the floor and retrieved the note. It had four words on it: *Will be in touch.*

Milo studied the draft again, shook his head and ambled to the window overlooking the marina. It was going to be a beautiful day. Milo smiled and his heart swelled. She was safe.

And now that darned barn was going to get built.

***

Ross Finlay returned to his townhome in downtown Montreal. Having just finished a lunch consisting of mussels and frites at the highly regarded Brasserie 701, he allowed himself a satisfied moment. It was his first outing since his slow, painful, ninety-day recovery. He'd have no feeling in a couple of his toes, certainly not his left index finger, but he felt lucky to be alive. Just a few more weeks, his doctor told him, and he would be good as new. Well, sort of.

He was beginning to feel like his old self when his employer came to visit. Upon his departure, Finlay had no illusions. The family was not happy with the outcome of his West Coast task, but he'd asked for a second chance to make things right and that was exactly what he intended to do. He hoped they saw the merits of his argument.

He resolved to finish dealing with don Belletti, but he'd also focus on finding Nate Vickers so he could conclude their business, post Belletti. He'd underestimated Vickers and his companions, and it had cost him. It was not a mistake he'd repeat.

Mr. Vickers' email account was still active, so he'd toss a grenade and see what happened. Perhaps it would give him the lead he needed. If he got the money back, it would go a long way in getting his standing back with the family.

He stared at his computer screen, then began to type. Satisfied the message would have its intended effect on Vickers, he hit "send."

He pulled on a light coat and headed out. The day was cool but bright. A walk along Mount Royal Park would be perfect to help him organize his thoughts further. He was feeling great. Things were looking up.

He descended the steps from his upscale home. Hopefully his damaged foot wouldn't act up again. He reached the parks edge and chose the pathway toward the Sir George-Etienne Cartier Monument. He spotted an empty bench seat and decided on a moments rest in the sunshine. He gazed at the monument. The West Coast was beautiful, but Montreal? He was glad to be home.

A homeless man pushed his cart past him. He wondered why the city couldn't figure out how to help these people.

A shadow crossed his face. He glanced up, shielding his eyes from the sun. Shock gripped him. What was he doing here? Don Belletti stared down at him. His face was passive, his eyes searching him.

Finlay's mind spun. He remained seated, unable to move, unable to understand how the don had identified him. Belletti stood solidly in front of Finlay, legs slightly apart. Finlay checked his hands. No weapon.

Belletti spoke first. "It seems you were hired, by a group we have a mutual interest in, to have me terminated."

Finlay rose to his feet. "That's not true."

"Isn't it? A mutual friend of ours allowed me to live in exchange for letting him keep a sizeable sum. He told me a story, one in which you played a lead role."

Belletti waited until realization crossed Finlay's face. "Vickers? He's a liar. You know that. I was hired as a backup plan to retrieve the money. A substantial portion of that was the family's, as you know."

"I see. Well, I wanted you to know that I have come to Montreal to fix this myself with our employer. So, I am asking you to stand down."

Finlay nodded, melting into the bench. He would have to seek further instructions. He watched as Belletti retreated down the pathway. He had underestimated Vickers yet again.

Finlay twisted in his seat. He saw that the homeless person had not gone far and was looking into a garbage can. A frown crossed his face. The homeless man turned his cart and headed back towards Finlay, who was now focused on him. He looked familiar. His body went rigid, his eyes widened in disbelief. He knew this man. He'd met him at a family dinner, what was it, a couple of years ago. Finlay wished he'd brought a weapon. He watched as the man reached into his cart, withdrawing a pistol, silencer attached. He aimed it at the back of don Belletti's head as he walked. Two quick pops brought him to the ground.

Finlay saw a pool of blood emanate from Belletti's lifeless form. His head swivelled to the homeless man, who was now upon him. He nodded at the enforcer, staring into his unemotional eyes. The gun's silencer was cold as it pressed into his temple.

He had not expected the family to do this, another miscalculation. The image of Nate Vickers popped into his mind. Then all went dark.

EPILOGUE

CHAPTER FORTY-THREE

THUNDERHEAD CLOUDS WERE FORMING ON the starboard side. Nate stood behind the wheel of *Serendipity*, admiring them. They had always held a fascination for him. Perhaps it was the dark beauty of them, perhaps the absolute power within them.

The day was warm with a relative humidity rating of 75 percent. It'd feel hotter on land, but the twenty-five degrees was perfect on the water. He closed his eyes and allowed the fifteen-knot breeze to flow over him like a cascading waterfall. The crossing through the Panama Canal had been unbearably hot.

Beka popped her head through the hatch and placed a plate of sandwiches on the floor. She added to that a pair of wine spritzers and climbed into the cockpit, placing their lunch on the table.

"How's the shoulder?"

"Stiff, but functional."

They had been on *Serendipity* for three months. Each day that passed had improved their chances to remain undetected. Beka's suggestion to head north in late fall had been a stroke of genius. She'd reasoned the Canadian Coast Guard would focus their search on the waters between the Sunshine Coast and the U.S border. So, they'd sailed north, away from the border, hugging the mainland, past Powell River and Harwood Island before crossing over to the eastern shores of Vancouver Island. They'd found secluded bays, where Beka would expertly anchor for the night. And still they'd headed north, through late fall rains, wind gusts that challenged her marine skills, extreme tidal conditions created by a near full moon. They'd found their way into the Discovery Islands, an archipelago off the north-central part of Vancouver Island, where they sought out an isolated cove and set up camp.

Nate hadn't been able to do much, but day by day he'd grown stronger, thanks to Beka's nightly redress of his wound and the rehab she forced him to do. Beka's finger had healed, the pain withdrawn, but it would never be quite the same.

They'd spent their days watching bald eagles soar overhead and laughing at seals that relished the feedings they tossed them. Then, as the afternoon sun laid on the horizon, they'd head inland for provisions, in a dingy they acquired at a nearby island. Nate's beard had grown longer, and he constantly wore a ball cap. Beka wore floppy hats to shield her face. If local authorities had been notified to watch for them, they did their best to lessen the chance of being discovered.

After forty-five days of seclusion, they'd figured that was enough, so with the boat full of provisions, they'd headed north again, until they'd reached the northern waters of Vancouver Island, before turning south on the open ocean of its west side. They'd battled winds and rain together, never complaining as they fought their way south. It was a dangerous ploy to sail these waters, but they felt it was the only way to cross the U.S. border undetected.

Days had turned to weeks and weeks into months as they sailed further and further south. They'd bypassed border control when they sailed into U.S waters, necessitating a continuous sail, each of them sleeping and taking the helm according to a shift schedule.

Stress had finally abated when they'd sailed into Mexican waters, where they hoped their passports wouldn't be flagged, and they could go ashore for much needed provisions. All went well.

They'd marvelled at their tanned bodies, covered in sweat, as they'd cruised through the Panama Canal. Beka had squealed in delight as they'd headed into the Caribbean Sea. A short week later, their journey was coming to an end. Nate had arranged moorage at the Grand Cayman Yacht Club, which they reached by nightfall.

Finally, after securing *Serendipity*, Nate and Beka climbed into the back of a Legacy taxi. Nate gave the driver the address they wanted. A mere twenty minutes later, they reached the location. They stepped out of the taxi and stood in front of a Georgian-style home, with its beautiful columns and black shutters. It was as Frank described, so many months ago.

The door flew open, and Elena ran for them. She lunged into Nate's arms and then gave Beka a bear hug. Nate stared into the empty door. Frank stepped onto the porch, cane in hand. He was smiling, tears running down his cheeks. Nate left Beka to answer Elena's rapid-fire questions.

Frank descended the steps, one at a time. Nate absorbed the fact that his uncle would never walk easily again. He fell into Frank's arms, and Frank held him for what would've been too long a year earlier, but now wasn't enough. He felt the embrace tighten as his shoulders shook with sobs.

They dined on local fish that evening. Frank and Elena had prepared it expertly, together. Nate and Beka learned about how Elena had managed to save Frank, somehow yanking him back into the dingy with very little help from the wounded man, and how the two had managed to elude police, benefitting greatly from Frank's experience on the wrong side of the law. They eventually found their way to his Cayman home, with the help of some of Frank's contacts. Nate and Beka beamed when they learned that both had applied for permanent residency under assumed identities.

BRUCE F.B. HALL

"You know, Frank, I could use new I.D.'s for Beka and myself."

"I recall the last time you asked for that it was a huge mistake," Frank replied, a twinkle in his eye.

They both laughed heartily.

Before long, the night came to an end. They climbed back into a taxi, over the protestations of his uncle, and promised to return the next day with overnight bags in hand.

They were reflecting on the beauty of his uncle's home; it's incredible view of the turquoise waters, as they stepped aboard *Serendipity* for a nightcap in celebration of a wonderful day. Beka headed below to get the drinks. Nate did the same and returned with his laptop in hand. He sat down and fired up his computer, opening a page on local real estate, when it pinged, advising he had an email. Nate stared at it. He glanced below at Beka, who was putting the finishing touches on their evening drink. He opened the email.

You disappointed me, Mr. Vickers. Very much. I look forward to our next get together. It was signed R.F.

Beka reached the top stair and stepped into the cockpit. She stared at Nate's face.

"What is it?"

Nate hesitated, then slowly closed his laptop. "Nothing... Nothing at all."

He stood, taking the peach bellini from her. "I propose a toast."

"And what would that be?" Beka said.

"To new beginnings."

They sipped their drinks and stared over the twinkling lights of the harbour. Nate placed his glass on the table and reached for hers, setting it beside his. He reached for her waist and spun her to him. Their lips came together.

She pulled back. "To new beginnings," she said and folded into his arms. "But let's try to do it a little differently this time."

-END-

Printed in Canada